AND THEN THEY ASKED GOD

Novels by Helen Gumienny Glowacki

When God Broke Grandma's Heart
When God Took Grandma Home
When Grandma Chased the Spirits
The Granddaughter and the Monkey Swing
Grandma's Little Book of Poetry: The Story of God's Plan of Salvation
Abiding Faith, Hidden Treasure
And Then They Asked God

Why God Why Series by Helen Glowacki

To What Purpose?
Why God Why?
Why Trust Scripture?
What Should I Know About Life after Death And The
Coming Tribulation?
What Does God Want Me To Do *RIGHT NOW*?
Do The Little Sins REALLY Count?
What Do Angels Do?

Other non-fiction Books by Helen Glowacki

Politically Incorrect: The Get Some Gumption Handbook
When Enough is Enough
What No One Is Telling You about Addictions
Overcoming Depression: How to be Happy

****

Authors Website: www.Helenglowacki.com

Face book: http://www.facebook.com/pages/The-
Grandmother-Series/155300907853909?ref=ts

AND THEN THEY ASKED GOD

A Story about the Power and Defeat of Evil

HELEN GUMIENNY GLOWACKI

Library of Congress Control Number: 2010915498
ISBN: Soft cover   978-1-9847-2116-0

This book was printed in the United States of America.

To order additional copies of this book:

Visit the author's website at:
www.helenglowacki.com

For wholesale or multiple copy information:

Send inquiry to helen@helenglowacki.com

Contents

Dedication

This book is dedicated to a wonderful young man who gives so much of himself to others. He knows the meaning of service, honor, and integrity and understands how this combination, along with a return to God and biblical principles, can heal our people and our country.

For

Danny Landolphi

Book Reviews

From Dallas, Texas:

I have just read one of the most inspiring books I have read in a long time! The story and characters reveal real-life situations in a remarkable and inviting form. I am certain that such a riveting story can also serve as an effective supportive tool for pastoral and mental health counselors. Ms. Glowacki described the stages of grief and God's comforting plan in an extraordinary way and through characters that really grab the heart. She is an author I expect to see on the best seller lists very soon and for many years to come. I look forward to the next books in her wonderful, inspiring series. A pleasure to read, a masterful idea, *When God Took Grandma Home* by Helen Gumienny Glowacki is filled with the most beautiful insight into God's plan for us! (Reverend Fred Krueger, retired Lutheran minister of twelve years and clinical social worker for twenty-six years)

From Sea Cliff, New York:

Helen Gumienny Glowacki is a magnificent writer who is truly able to weave a story that will make the reader become emotionally involved in the character's lives. It was a joy to read this book, and the reader will appreciate the strong Christian values portrayed therein. This book will certainly whet the appetite for the other books in the series. *When God Broke Grandma's Heart* by Helen Gumienny Glowacki is a certain bet to be a best seller. (Reverend Richard C. Freund, president, New Apostolic Church USA)

Once again, Helen Gumienny Glowacki enthusiastically presents a scenario which will delight readers and bring comfort to anyone who is grieving. This book *When God Took Grandma Home* will inspire all readers and give them a deeper insight into the afterlife. This book is a masterful portrayal of young people searching for the truth. It is sure to be a great success. (Rev. Richard C. Freund, president, New Apostolic Church USA)

From Odenton, Maryland:

As a counselor to many who struggle with challenging circumstances in their lives, I found *When God Broke Grandma's Heart* an inspirational story of hope. Despite cruelty and betrayal from those she trusted, and the multiple adversities Grandma endured, she was able to find strength and understanding through her faith in and love of God. Helen Gumienny Glowacki beautifully portrays the phases that individuals move through and the transformation that can occur when one is able to let go of negative events in their past and strive toward the understanding that regardless of how unjust, none of the pain was for naught. (Tammera L. Shelton, M.S. Psychology)

From Port St. Lucie, Florida:

When Grandma Chased the Spirits: one star—Star of Bethlehem—rating! Helen Glowacki's novels serve the reader in a similar manner as the Star of Bethlehem served earlier seekers . . . it leads the reader to a beautiful spiritual experience. It shows us the gifts God offers that leads us to inner peace and understanding. Helen's work is so special that I believe it will become a shining navigational tool for many who search for understanding, just as the Star of Bethlehem once served as a navigational tool for those who searched for the Christ child. Helen Gumienny Glowacki has, with extraordinary skill, created characters who express their love for others in a beautiful way and have the desire to go the extra mile to help those struggling with doubt and those who have been misguided. Through the manuscripts and journals created by "Grandma" and discovered by the various characters in Helen's stories, one can actually see into the caring nature and loving heart of the author. Her stories eloquently reveal her love for God and her diligent search for truth. Five-star rating? This work is worthy of more . . . the one-star rating mentioned above . . . the single Star of Bethlehem rating. God Bless you "GiGi," and thank you for sharing your magnificent gift with us. (Frank Geores)

From Clifton, New Jersey:

I am the wife of a retired minister. Many times during my husband's ministry, I was aware that a parishioner was living through a difficult circumstance, but because of my husband's responsibilities to provide assistance and counseling, I was not always able to help in the matter. Helen Gumienny Glowacki's series of novels are a wonderful way to provide help and support to someone in need when other avenues of communication are closed. These books are inspiring, uplifting, educational, and heartwarming. The characters are loving and believable, and every story ends with a beautiful example of how God explains our pain, renews our hope, shows us the way out of our situation, and creates a miracle for our lives. I love this series. (Edith Stier, forty-two years as the wife of a minister)

From Jupiter, Florida:

I have just finished reading *Abiding Faith, Hidden Treasure,* and it was so interesting that I hated to put it down and couldn't wait to pick it up again. I have read all of Helen's books and am amazed how she can prove every point the characters make, support every adventure they undertake, and show what they should do in every circumstance through God's words. I am ninety years of age and have been very depressed from losing loved ones and from life-changing events, and Helen's books have really helped me to use God's help through scripture, prayer, and belief. (Susan Day)

From Palm City, Florida:

Abiding Faith, Hidden Treasure—what do these four words have in common? To begin with, the title of this book piques one's curiosity, and a sense of searching begins with the hope that the answer will unfold within each page. As we meet the many characters, we develop a close empathy with them, and as one's situation is resolved a new issue arises. Some of the situations are troublesome, filled with raw emotion, others a battle between scientific knowledge and the awakening of spiritual knowledge. Still others are easily resolved by rulings of the heart. Ms. Glowacki has a skill for the details and for providing vivid descriptions of events. They are so brilliant that the reader feels that they are a part of the moment. Throughout the novel it becomes clear that each difficulty leads to the discovery that God's hand is working and providing the characters with the understanding that nothing happens that is not planned by Him. Does one find the "hidden treasure"? Each reader will answer that for themselves. *Abiding Faith, Hidden Treasure* is a mosaic of God's plan of Salvation. (R. Schaal)

From West Palm Beach, Florida:

I am a retired minister. I spent forty-eight years serving the children of God. Before and after serving as a minister, I spent another thirty years as a member of the congregation. This series of books are the first stories I found to contain a perfectly accurate account of what God wants of us and for the future, and why we suffer. Ms. Glowacki's grasp and application of scripture is really spirit driven, and the people in her stories stand for the principles God wants in all of us. (Frederick Rothe, retired minister)

From Brookfield, Wisconsin:

Wow! I've just finished reading the third book in this series of wonderful novels and can't find words great enough to describe them. At a time when there are so many troubles in the world and so many people who suffer, these books are a real eye opener about God's plan of salvation and why bad things happen to good people. They remind me of Jim LaHaye and Jerry B. Jenkins's Left Behind series. These books are a *must read*! (Ben Lodwick, avid reader)

From North Palm Beach, Florida:

Grandma's Little Book of Poetry: The Story of God's Plan of Salvation is a wonderful book about the successes and failures of real life and the story of the Good News of God's love for us. All of Helen's novels are wonderful to read, but more importantly, they are a balm for the soul and an education to the seeker. (Dr. Walter Forman)

From Boca Raton, Florida:

To Ms. Glowacki, author of a wonderful series of novels, so grateful to have found your books. I think it is refreshing to find a Christian author who sees the *difference* between religion and spirituality, *and* that the two can be, and should be, used in the same sentence. (Luke Jansen, senior vice president, Medical Connections)

Reader Reviews from online bookstore Web sites

Five-star rating—*When God Broke Grandma's Heart*: (A) well-written, heartwarming story of Grandma's struggle to overcome heartbreak and tragedy through her belief in God. This story will touch your heart. A worthwhile read for all generations. I look forward to reading more from this author. (A reviewer, a reader in Kentucky)

Five-star rating—*When God Took Grandma Home*: Remarkable for someone looking for answers! Found it extremely inspirational and deeply moving. A fascinating storyteller with a real message. (Fred D'Alauro, Florida)

Five-star rating—*When God Broke Grandma's Heart*: This book is written from the heart with such thoughtfulness and grace.

The author provides the reader with a meaningful experience. The messages are gentle yet powerful to the soul even though experiencing grandma's struggles and grief throughout the novel. The author shares the ideas of strong beliefs in ourselves, carries our faith, and shelters us in times of need and guides us home. Transformation and courage are profound themes of this novel to find truth and faith within all of us. The reader will be captivated at the books end and will want to read what comes next. Thank you "Grandma." (Debra Forman, New York)

Five-star rating—*When God Took Grandma Home*: Heartwarming! This book touched my heart. It is both heartwarming and very spiritual. (Debbie Espeland, Connecticut)

Five-star rating—*When God Broke Grandma's Heart*: What an outstanding writer! I chose this book because throughout my life, (my) grandma was always there for me making things become rosy. This book kept me riveted—there are many valuable lessons. Helen is an angel sent to help us through our trying days. I am now reading her second book. Thank you for helping me find some peace in this world. (Robert W. Rothe, USMC 1970-1976, a reviewer, Tennessee)

Five-star rating—*When God Took Grandma Home*: Wonderful, inspirational novel! I enjoyed reading this book. It is well written with stories of disappointments and pleasant experiences too. Guidance is given through a loving "grandma" who shows through her example the kind of positive attitudes we could have in our lives. The Bible references through the book are helpful. The list of ways to achieve peace of mind and soul written by "grandma" are very good for facing what happens in our lives. (Patricia Robinson, Indiana)

Five-star rating—*When God Broke Grandma's Heart*: Fantastic! A must-read for all generations. (A reader)

Five-star rating—*When God Took Grandma Home*: Must read! Touching story of life's tragedies and heartaches and how lessons learned from these heartbreaking events can turn into blessings. (A reviewer, a Kentucky reader)

Five-star rating—*When God Took Grandma Home*: A very captivating book, keeps you moved from the beginning. (A reviewer)

Note to the Reader

The King James Version (KJV) of the Bible, which is public domain in the United States, is used throughout the books of this series. However, for further study, the author recommends the New King James Version (NKJV) of the Bible for easier reading and less usage of the old-world language while remaining true to the original text.

This book contains a Scriptural Index. Instead of assembling this index according to the Chicago Manual of Style, it is assembled in a format that might be more useful to the reader. Key words that may highlight the reader's specific concern or interest are listed in the index and under those words are listed the scriptures that address those concerns. This index style will better support a teaching program based on this novel.

Acknowledgments

To my husband Wally who has always been an incredible support, a champion for my work, and though losing me to computer, Bible, and concordance for long periods, cajoles my computer into behaving and painstakingly reads my manuscripts; to my children and grandchildren for their love and encouragement; to BRB who read my first work and encouraged me to publish, and T. Davis Bunn for his kindness, advice, and encouragement. To Richard Levinson whose help in my life can never be repaid; to the ministers and deacons of the New Apostolic Church; to new friends and old friends who pray for me, never doubt, and in so many wonderful ways grant me the greatest friendships I could ever ask for; to the readers who have asked that I keep writing; to all those who contributed to this effort and to the many others who helped make my novels a success. To those who diligently look after my spiritual life and keep me in their hearts and in their prayers; and most importantly, to my Heavenly Father who guides my life, gives so much, loves so much, and made all this possible! My heartfelt and humble thanks.

Message from the Author

An author writes in the hope of developing a reading experience that will inform, comfort, or entertain the reader. My desire is to meet all those goals and address the heartache we so often encounter in life. I hope to explain why we must have these often difficult experiences and have chosen a venue that many use to relax or to be entertained, namely a novel. The characters in my stories struggle to understand why they are plagued by a constant series of varying circumstances that bring heartache to them or to those they love. They, like us, sometimes ask God why He allows so much pain to exist and why He does not appear to provide His help in what we think is a timely fashion.

Those who are familiar with the treasures of scripture are aware that there is an answer to the age-old question of why only the good seem to suffer and evil appears to prosper. My challenge is to create a thorough understanding of this complex question and explain why and by whom God's children are harmed. This is a daunting challenge when coupled with the goal of placing this information into an interesting story that the reader will enjoy.

While writing requires a simple succession of words, to be effective those words must also move the heart, offer respite from pain, and provide comfort for the spirit. Most importantly, those words must provide an understanding of a spiritual warfare so malevolent and desperate that we acknowledge that we are all in jeopardy, even our children. My job is also to demonstrate through my stories the magnificence of a loving God despite the pain we endure, why we must be tried in the fire of life, what God seeks to accomplish, and what He does to help bring us through our difficult situations.

The characters I have created for my novels face the situations and the emotions that many of us face, and their quest for answers, the path they choose to follow, and the understanding they gain as they endure their heartache may be similar to our own experiences. But for those who struggle in their difficulties and do not understand why it is necessary, I hope that how my characters find their answers will open the door for many to learn about the powerful enemy that fights God to prevent its own demise. I hope to explain, in every novel, why that enemy fights so hard and uses us as a pawn to prevent God from completing His plan of salvation. I hope to explain that we can thwart this enemy if we tap into the power of love, the power of prayer, and the power of the perfect plan God placed into the physics of our world to help us.

While my stories are fiction, they do portray real-life struggles and tragedies, real emotion, and the hopes, dreams, and wishes we all have. I hope that those who feel alone will learn from these stories that they are not alone, that others have felt heartache and despair, that everyone has experienced disappointment and at one time or another has questioned why God allows so much suffering. Our Heavenly Father knows that we can become exhausted from the constant battles we face, or when there seems no end to our problem and no reason for it. He also knows that as we learn, we gain an understanding of why we are attacked, and that it is through that understanding that we can endure and be transformed.

What I hope to impart through my novels is a greater understanding about the enemy we have, why he does what he does, and how to thwart his efforts. When we engage in a battle that we understand, recognize as necessary, believe we will win, and know will bring a great reward, we are filled with courage and are willing to fight harder. We will also fight wiser. But when we do not understand, when we wonder why we must live through such difficulty or when we blame God for our heartache, we lose our hope and our strength. When we learn of God, His enemy, His plan, we begin to trust that He is always with us to uplift us, protect us, and provide us with the energy and determination to see the battle through to the end. As we learn of our enemy we understand why He is desperate, why he must attack, and how God's plan will bring us through all difficulties to the final triumph. As we learn, we also build the hope and trust we need to strengthen us and allow us to open our hearts to God.

Sadly, our struggles increase as we move closer to the ultimate goal of our faith, the First Resurrection, because Satan works harder than ever to prevent us from believing and trusting Our Heavenly Father. He knows that his end will come when the number God longs for is fulfilled, and therefore He works to prevent God from fulfilling that number. If we are to be a part of that number, Satan will actively work to harm us and destroy our faith. Our children and grandchildren may also be those who make up this final number that God longs for, and sadly, they too may become a target of utmost importance to our enemy.

We can't fight an enemy we don't know exists. We can't fight an enemy if we don't know that he wants to harm us. We can't effectively fight an enemy when we don't know how to identify him and don't know how or why he attacks. Sadly, few people do know this, and if we do not understand, we cannot teach our children. Thus, fewer and fewer children are taught about their powerful and selective enemy and they become adults who cannot teach their own children what they need to know.

This is why, through all my novels, my characters learn about this enemy, why he needs to prevent God from reaching His goal, why he attacks, and how they can gain protection. God wants us to win this battle and will help us. We are never alone. He hears our cry for help and offers us everything we need to be successful. Our circumstances will not change however if we don't seek God's help, if we are complacent, if we do not enter into a relationship with Him that is important to us, and if we are not willing to love God, and because we love Him, learn and follow His words. It is through God's words that we come to know Him and then to finally understand why we go through such heartache. It is through His words that we develop the trust that allows God to step in and thwart our enemy and help us endure and then overcome.

In recent years, we have seen an incredible rally of political interest and awareness. More and more individuals recognize what path they want their country to follow and what our country is on the brink of losing. Along with this awareness is a new appreciation for the values we have taken for granted and the gift that God gave this country because of its Christian principles. Many have rallied together in a refusal to accept the loss of these values and the loss of freedom that would accompany such a loss. Their newfound appreciation of God's gifts has led to a populous that is eager to learn and determined to not only teach their children but to encourage other venues such as school systems and text books, politicians, government, and all who teach or act as role models for their children to espouse and articulate godly values.

Sadly, it is the loss or the potential loss of what we believed would always be ours that causes us to recognize its importance. Loss can jolt us out of our complacency and inspire action. It can cause us to acknowledge that many in today's world do not have an understanding of the principles and values taught in scripture. Honesty, integrity, morality, faith, and loyalty are those virtues which once determined how we interact with others both privately and publically. But, as biblical principles are lost or devalued, so is mankind's ability to cope with the same lies in effect today which Satan used to trap Eve. "Is it *really* not okay if you . . . Are you *sure* God meant . . . Surely it's *okay* if you . . . Is there *really* a God who cares about you?" Doubt begets confusion, indecision, and then complacency.

In recent years, political corruption and terrorists have plotted the death of our faith, our way of life, and our country. Political agendas and the corruption used to attain those goals are not much different than the murder of innocent people by terrorists who profess to love God. Both consciously act in ways that bring harm to others for their own personal reward. Matthew 22:37-39 describes the conversation between Christ and a Pharisee who asked him which was the greatest commandment: "Jesus said unto him, Thou shalt love the Lord thy God with all thy heart, and with all thy soul, and with all thy mind. This is the first and great commandment. And the second is like unto it, Thou shalt love thy neighbor as thyself."

This scripture demonstrates that an act to specifically harm another is *not* God's will. Thus, in my stories I have endeavored to explain the activities of the *real* instigator of the heartache and confusion we see active in so many people today. Satan wants to convince as many people as he can that they should harm others and worship a god whose values are contrary to those found in scripture. I hope I can show you why our world will get worse, why the children of God will continue to suffer, and why this confirms that we are closer than ever to the most beautiful moment we will ever experience. Most importantly, why we need to cherish our faith, cherish the original values and principles upon which our country was founded and cling to them even if they are lost to the world.

There is much tumult today, much done in the name of God that does not adhere to what we know God tells us in scripture. Many stand back, afraid to become involved, afraid of the few who want to turn aside our biblical principles in the name of social justice. It is shocking to know that the few who want to take these principles from our schools, our government, our churches, our press, and even indoctrinate our children are far outnumbered. But their power comes from Satan, and it goes forth so easily because we have been complacent.

Those who desiccate our freedoms and our faith have been given a dire warning from God. Revelation 3:15, 16 says, "I know thy works . . ." *and* "because thou art lukewarm . . . I will spue thee out of my mouth." And Psalm 73:19, "How are they brought into desolation, as in a moment they are utterly consumed with terrors," and Malachi 2:8, warns, "But ye are departed out of the way; ye have caused many to stumble at the law; ye have corrupted the covenant of Levi, saith the Lord of Hosts."

A child of God must remain true to the values God teaches us in order to be a role model who can capture hearts. We can accomplish this noble goal if we know what God says, if we live our faith every day, not just on Sundays . . . and live our faith as Christ asked us to live it. But we also need the courage to *fight* for our faith and our values and the beauty of our God-given Constitution or we too will be considered lukewarm by our complacency.

Amazingly, scripture makes reference after reference to what we should believe, who we should allow to be our role models, what actions God deems evil, and what actions please Him. God speaks to us through scripture about the pitfalls we will encounter in this world and teaches us about the enemy who wants us to harm one another and wants to destroy our faith. He tells us how Satan can blind men to God's words and cause them to act as they do when they do not cling to God. He also tells us how we can be assured of His protection from these enemies by learning what He asks of us and following those directions. This creates in us the "overcomer" God loves.

In Proverbs 3:29, God says, "Devise not evil against thy neighbor . . ." And in Proverbs 11:12, "He that is void of wisdom despiseth his neighbor . . ." And even more clearly in Zechariah 8:17, God says, "And let none of you imagine evil in your hearts against his neighbor; and love no false oath; for all these are things that I hate, saith the Lord. "

God not only shows us what dangers we should watch for, but He also shows us how to live together, how to set the right example, how to instruct our children, and clearly and unequivocally promises wonderful rewards for doing so. He promises us His protection. He gives us the most wonderful guarantees about our life and our home. This doesn't say we won't have problems, but it does say we will be brought through those problems, will be refined in the process, and that we need not fear the outcome when we do go through these difficulties.

Each of us will have to answer for our actions, but we will also have to answer for any stumbling we cause a child of God. The punishment for this is stated in Mark 9:42, "And whosoever shall offend one of these little ones that believe in me, it is better for him that a millstone were hanged about his neck, and he were cast into the sea."

To follow God's instructions, we must learn of the dangers that exist from the spirits that serve our enemy, the ease with which they can lead us astray, and how envy and fear, money and power can be used to make us complacent about our faith. This is the incredible subtlety of our enemy. Our enemy is not only clever and seemingly unobtrusive, but also seductive, tempting, and as dangerous as He was when he presented the innocent apple in the Garden of Eden that brought sin to everyone who ever lived or died. It is easy for us to forget that this powerful enemy still lurks today, more potent than ever, still the sly and enticing stalker who revels in the chaos of our daily lives. We should remember that Satan rarely takes the obvious path and that he uses people to harm people.

My novels highlight the fact that there *is* evil in this world and that some who profess a faith in God act not by God's words but by the influence of evil. I try to write stories that will explain how God will help us and explain in detail why we must endure the days of evil, how we can cope, what the incredible reward will be, and why we must be a constant role model to others. My stories are about the power evil has over us when we do not adhere to God's word and the power that can thwart that evil.

If we are complacent in the face of the destruction of our right to pray, our right to an unbiased education, to a free and honest press, and to a corruption-free government, we are giving Satan a huge platform from which to work. We give him carte blanche to bring us harm. While my characters learn the harm that a loss of faith can bring and the fall that can result, they also embrace their struggle to climb from that fall to triumph over evil. They learn that evil has plotted and waited and watched for the opportunity to bring about their pain and want their fall from grace.

God doesn't let those who love Him remain in the dark recesses of evil. He fights for them and wins! God is willing to overlook our shortcomings when He sees that our hearts are pure and willing to strive to overcome the evil that attacks us. God has provided grace for us, and thus my stories and my characters also explore the gift of grace and how to obtain it. My hope is to highlight the dangers that God wants us to avoid and the gifts and protections He gives us to offset these circumstances.

Almost everything good can be perverted into something that our enemy can use to harm us if we do not know what God wants to tell us. God's word is our most potent protection and the most potent protection our country can have against its current onslaught. Instituting God's words into our minds and hearts, and thus our lives, can help us immensely not only because we now live in a world of uncertainty but also because we long to attain the goal of our faith . . . an eternity with God. If you, the reader, will share what you know and what you learn about God's plan with others so they too can understand, you will touch the heart of God.

May God bless you and keep you always, and may He grant you the wisdom to understand His ways, His words, and the future He so freely offers us all. And may He open your understanding to the wonder of His word and to His all-encompassing love for us.

Helen Gumienny Glowacki

> *Blessed is the man that walketh not in the counsel of the ungodly,*
> *nor standeth in the way of sinners, nor sitteth in the seat of the scornful.*
> *But his delight is in the law of the Lord; and in his law doth he meditate day and night.*
> *And he shall be like a tree planted by the rivers of water,*
> *that bringeth forth his fruit in his season; his leaf also shall not wither,*
> *and whatsoever he doeth shall prosper.*
>
> *Psalm 1:1-3*

Synopsis of Novels

by Helen Gumienny Glowacki

When God Broke Grandma's Heart is a story about a woman who rose from the ashes of sorrow to become a beacon of faith for others. She struggles to maintain her marriage despite a truly evil husband until she learns that God supports our leaving situations where we are unequally yoked. From the suffering she endured because of her husband's cruelty and her sister's betrayal, she learns the incredible power of forgiveness and how it can heal her broken heart. She then becomes a legacy of love and faith to her granddaughter who shares that legacy with her friends and family.

When God Took Grandma Home describes God's incredible plan for those who were unjustly treated, and for those who die too young or under unfair circumstances. It is a story about drug addiction, about an enemy who uses drugs to destroy an innocent child, and why righteous anger must sometimes be implemented. It is a story that explains why we need to forgive, why we should retain the memory of injustice, and why we should pray for those who have entered into eternity.

When Grandma Chased the Spirits addresses the subtle magnetism of idolatry and its dangerous, invisible power. It is a story of a young couple decorating their home through the ancient art of feng shui, and the granddaughter Sarah and her fiancé Matt's budding friendship with them. It is about a childhood trauma that caused debilitating panic attacks, about the dangerous power of feng shui, and how God brings forth a miracle for a situation thought impossible to resolve.

The Granddaughter and the Monkey Swing is a story about a wedding, about renovating and decorating a home through divine proportion, and about friendship and being a role model. It introduces many new characters into this series of novels and describes how hidden concerns can live in our hearts, remain unexpressed, and bring worry and sadness. It is a story of friends helping one another through a broken engagement, worries about a serious illness, a frightening discovery about Halloween, and a large wedding that culminates in the unveiling of a long-held secret.

Grandma's Little Book of Poetry: The Story of the Plan of Salvation is a whimsical story of the angels in the verdant land of heaven watching the inhabitants of the cold bleak planet below them struggle to learn of God and it is a story that is appropriate for all ages. Sarah finds a manuscript in the back of Grandma's old desk, and as she reads the manuscript she realizes that it is the story that Grandma read to her and Josh and Caleb when they were children. But when she wants to share the story with others and decides to publish, she also knows that because the story speaks of God, Satan will attack.

Abiding Faith, Hidden Treasure is about a young man named Jim who has served in Iraq and has lost his faith in God because he cannot understand how a truly loving God would allow so much heartache in the world. His views are challenged by a young woman who invites him home to debate with her family, and when they show him how creation and evolution can co-exist and describe the enemy that causes the injustices he blames on God, he is amazed and wants to learn more. His pithy comments almost alienate him from his friends, but then letters from the grave bring him a profound experience of faith and begin to melt his hardened heart.

And Then They Asked God addresses the dangerous situations that young people can encounter at college. Rebecca, too trusting and overwhelmed by the betrayal of others, falls to the spirits of the world who wish her harm. Turning from the values she once cherished fills her with guilt so monumental that she cannot forgive herself. But through the love and prayers of friends and family and the recognition of the powerful evil that doesn't want to let her go, she learns so much more about grace and how to forgive herself.

Coming Soon: *What Every Christian Needs to Know* is a hard-hitting, no-nonsense nonfiction book that addresses fifty tough and timely issues that face Christians today. It clearly defines what position scripture suggests that Christians take on many controversial subjects such as politics, drug addiction, creation and evolution, divorce, racism, homosexuality, and self-esteem. Each is addressed in a short three-page biblically supported directive that will surprise the reader with its hard hitting facts while providing an excellent way to unite and defend Christians who are attacked for their godly values.

Description of Characters

Grandma

Grandma's early life was filled with the debilitating pain of sibling betrayal and marital abuse and is told in the first book of The Grandma Series, *When God Broke Grandma's Heart.* Her legacy of faith, her interest in alternative medicine and interior design, her love of chiming clocks, her empathy and ability to love come to rest in her granddaughter's heart, and she in turn shares these treasures with friends and family. Grandma's prolific love and godly wisdom carries throughout the saga of her family's walk of faith and reminds them to create their own memories and protect the gifts God has given them. From poetry to recipes, from home remedies to her famous boxing stance, Grandma lives on in the heart of those she loves and reaches into the soul of strangers who come to know her through her family.

Sarah

Sarah helped her grandmother write her journal and thus learns about the power of God, His unwavering love, and His desire to help mankind. She also learns about a powerful, subtle enemy who wants to harm her and also learns how to fight against him. She struggles through a period of grief when Grandma dies and she discovers the suppressed anger she must acknowledge. She and Matt marry, purchase and renovate a house, meet new friends, and experience a number of challenges as they carry on Grandma's legacy of faith. Matt and Sarah eventually have a son named Jason.

Matt

Matt, Sarah's husband, has a rocklike faith in God and the ability to see problems with the glass half full rather than half empty. He suffers through the loss of a loved one and overcomes his anger at God for the injustice he witnesses. It is through this process that Matt learns about God's incredible plan of salvation and the role God wants him to take in that plan. Matt loves their new home and enjoys the renovation process through which he makes new friends and proves his worth as a role model willingly seeking God's word.

Paul

Paul is Matt's older brother who earned a captain's license to operate a seagoing tugboat. He married, had two children, Becky and Christina, and lost them when his wife took the children and ran off with another man while Paul was out to sea. Paul's extraordinary faith in God and how God sustains him through terrible circumstances is a testimony to his family, but his pain causes Matt to question God's decisions, until Gods provides Matt with an incredible experience of faith.

Mary

Mary and Kevin become Matt and Sarah's neighbors, and soon the two couples become close friends. After struggling through a dangerous need to seek good luck by any method, Mary and Kevin tell their new friends that Mary still suffers from a traumatic incident which occurred when she was fourteen years old which continues to cause her to suffer panic attacks. When hearing of the tragedy, Matt and Sarah assure them that God can bring about a miracle. As they learn of Matt and Sarah's faith in God and learn the dangers of feng shui, they change course, cease their ventures into the world of feng shui, and witness a miracle they never thought possible.

Kevin

Kevin, Mary's husband, is delighted to have Matt as a friend and neighbor and wants to learn from him how to be the kind of husband who can lead by example. Matt has shown him what God asks of him and teaches him about an unscrupulous enemy longing to harm his family and how to thwart those efforts. He is happy with Mary's plans to renovate the carriage house and delighted by the changes that have come into their life as a result of their friendship with Matt and Sarah and their family.

Elizabeth

When in her mid-forties, Elizabeth adopts Rebecca and twelve years later she loses her husband to cancer. Shortly thereafter, Elizabeth is confronted with a potentially deadly illness and decides to search for Rebecca's birth mother. She is delighted when she also meets John and pleased when John's grandson becomes a role model to Rebecca. Because of her unselfish, loving, and down-to-earth nature, those who meet Elizabeth come to admire her, but her faith is once again tested as she learns of Rebecca's plight.

Rebecca

Rebecca is the child Elizabeth adopted and fashions into a fine young woman. The loss of her father, the illness her mother faces, and the role Mary plays in her life requires a struggle to understand God's plan for them. Her friend Jayden strengthens her faith and helps her acknowledge her anger at God for all they have endured. Rebecca and Jayden form a friendship that blossoms under the teaching of those around them, but when Rebecca enters college, she faces a series of challenges that almost destroy her.

John

Years earlier, John lost his wife to a debilitating illness and has worked to help others through similar ordeals. He has become Elizabeth's friend, and his faith in God, developed by his service as a deacon in his church, sustains her in a time of need. He also uses his faith to help his daughter Ruth and grandson Jayden cross the rock-strewn bridge from the devastation of divorce to the joy of God's love, and to place a deep faith into his grandson's heart.

Jayden

Jayden is John's grandson and becomes a friend to Rebecca. Jayden has grown up in the church and knows a great deal about approaching God with personal problems. His faith increases as he listens to his elders speak of their difficulties and solve them through prayer. He is active in the youth group at church and invites Rebecca to join him. Their friendship blossoms as they share their heartaches and the many ways that God has helped them. But Jayden is devastated when he cannot reach Rebecca as she flirts with danger and encounters evil.

Ruth

Ruth is Jayden's mother and John's daughter. She has experienced a difficult divorce and struggled under a financial burden when her ex-husband did not meet his obligations. She is shy and sweet, but her past experiences leave her traumatized, and her loneliness affects both her father and her son. She harbors a secret anger at God for allowing her to go through what she has, but finally learns to let go of the past when love once again comes into her life. She is delighted to be included in Matt and Sarah's family circle.

Joshua

Joshua is Sarah's younger brother. Joshua's expects too much of others, which made him demanding and judgmental and affects his relationship with Debbie. They face many serious issues that need to be resolved and break their engagement when Josh decides it's unmanly to show his pain, or to give in to Debbie. Only Caleb can finally reach him. But as he recognizes what it means to be a husband, he begins to grow into the man Debbie can love.

Debbie

Debbie is delighted when she is asked to be a part of Matt and Sarah's wedding. She grew up without a good role model and looks happily to Joshua's family to fill that void. She learns quickly, but needs to learn how to curb her impulsiveness. The insecurities she developed during her childhood and her inability to communicate well under pressure bring her into a situation that may ruin her relationships. She learns that with God's help she will grow into the person she wants to be. Debbie and Josh eventually have a son named Johnny.

Caleb and Ann

Caleb is Sarah and Josh's older brother and has been a source of strength and protection for them since their mother died when Sarah was eighteen years old. They'd turned to Grandma for help and guidance, and through her love and faith, learned to accept God's will and to continue the education their mother wanted for them. Caleb has grown so much in spirit over the years that the family now looks to him as they once did to Grandma. Ann, Caleb's wife, always lends a helping hand. Often unacknowledged except by God and Caleb, Ann quietly prays for the entire family and provides strength and support to those she loves. But, there is a secret sadness in her heart that needs to be addressed. Ann and Caleb have two children, Andrew and Lorraine.

Barbara and Jim

Barbara is Matt's sister and a close friend of Sarah's. She has excellent communication skills in addition to being talented, down to earth, creative and willing to take charge of family gatherings. Her husband Jim had never been willing to join her church but listens carefully to the family's discussions of faith. He is family oriented, hardworking, smart, and up-to-date on political issues. He loves to play devil's advocate when the family gets into the debates they love to have and has fun playing matchmaker for his best friend Wade. Together, Barbara and Jim venture from exhilarating debates about politics to the awesome evidence of how God works in their lives. Barbara and Jim eventually have a son named Paul.

Wade

Wade is Jim's boss and best friend. They worked together in Iraq for four years in an atmosphere of extreme difficulty and danger. Wade is a great big bear of a man with a huge and loving heart who suffered greatly from the loss of his wife to breast cancer after being married only a few years. While in Iraq, he and Jim rescue a pregnant woman and her small son after a terrorist attack; sadly, a child is born as the mother dies. Concerned for the well-being of these children, Wade adopts them and brings them to the United States. He impresses Ruth with his loving nature and eventually makes her his wife.

AND THEN THEY ASKED GOD

Heza and Bara

Heza and Bara are children that Jim and Wade met in Iraq. They endure an attack by a suicide bomber when Bara was just one and one half years old and Heza as she was born. Bara lost his foot in the attack and now walks with a prosthetic but their mother was killed in that attack. After seeing the children in the orphanage, Wade decides to adopt them and brings them to the United States. They too become children of God and enjoy a special relationship with their new "cousins," and Bara now runs and plays with the best of them.

Chaldeth

Chaldeth is one of the fallen angels sent to destroy the faith of Grandma's family. He plots to initiate the problems Rebecca and Jayden face when they enter college. The properties of an angel give him the power to understand God's plan of salvation, to know scripture well, and to influence mankind. He works furiously to break the faith of all children of God so he can prolong his life. His countenance grows in ugliness as he becomes more malevolent.

Durk

Durk is a sophomore attending the university that Rebecca and Jayden attend. He grew up under a brutal and demanding father and has begun to emulate his father's ways to achieve his goals. When he meets Rebecca, he sees qualities in her that remind him of his mother and grandmother but is too entrenched in his ways to change. When Jim enters his life, he takes a new look at his future.

Professor T. Nagorra

Professor T, a tenured professor, befriends Durk and uses him nefariously. He is intrigued by Rebecca and encourages Durk's relationship with her for his own underhanded motives. But when Rebecca demands that Durk relinquish the activities that could bring him and others harm, the professor needs to intervene. He has deposited large sums of money in an offshore account in case he has to run.

Professor Emils

Professor Emils, also a tenured professor, teaches only his personal and biased view of politics to his students. Rebecca calls him on his approach, and he becomes so furious with her that he decides to give her a failing grade. Wade later uncovers the nefarious activities in which this professor is engaged.

Dean Peerca

Dean Peerca is a friend and supporter of both Professor Nagorra and Professor Emils. He covers for them in all conflicts, and to line his pockets with gold, he brings harm to the entire campus.

Professors Doog and Sendnik and President Legna

Both professors and President Legna want to help Jayden and Rebecca and do not believe that they are guilty of any wrongdoing. Initially, they are not aware that they share a similar faith in God, a similar love for their country, and the desire to be a role model to their students; but when they finally meet Rebecca and Jayden's family, and learn that they share these common values, they are delighted and know that God will help them uncover the truth and save the university.

Chapter 1

Chaldeth, the Evil

He stood in the corner of the room, wings falling from shoulder to floor and folded against his back. His arms were also folded but across his chest as he stood silently, gleefully aware of his victory, watchful over that victory.

Chaldeth had worked long and hard to win this battle, thinking so many times that he had broken one of those belonging to the family he'd hated for so long, yet he had failed to break them. For years, just when he would think that he was about to win, they would resist, call upon God for help, and then suddenly and unexpectedly turn from that last step, that final trap he'd laid to engulf them. It angered him to remember each time they had escaped, and to remember that every time he thought he was on the verge of victory, he'd failed.

Now, however, he felt a rush of pleasure. As he stood, finally so close to winning, he savored watching the family squirm, watching them suffer because there was nothing they could do about Rebecca's plight. Chaldeth *relished* his victory. His ego soared to know that they fully understood that it was *he* who had made it happen. The family knew he was here; they knew his extraordinary power, and they were afraid! It was his power and their fear of it that gave him the exhilarating sense that his long-awaited victory was so close. He was filled with such arrogance that it caused him to lift his chin and hold his head high and haughty, as evil often unconsciously does in its show of contempt.

Chaldeth understood that built into the physics of their world and his, he was far stronger than they were . . . any of them. And now he'd finally forced them to acknowledge his superior strength and the power that this gave him over them . . . over Rebecca. He loved the power, the control . . . and delighted each time one of them glanced toward the corner of the room as if aware that he was watching. Adrenaline flowed through his body as he anticipated the harm he would do to the others as they were forced to acknowledge their inability to help Rebecca. All he had to do now was get them to blame God. Then he could *really* harm them, and destroy the sick devotion and trust each of them portrayed.

But though Chaldeth gloated over his show of strength, he was aware that he had to remain diligent and vigilant in order not to lose his advantage. His ugly body stiffened in anger as he thought of how they would fight against him . . . but he would watch carefully this time and not let them gain the upper hand. As far as he was concerned, Rebecca was his, and he would make sure that she belonged to him forever.

Chaldeth was only one of many assigned to destroy this family. He and his cohorts had been working at this for years. Yet he was the one who'd broken through . . . he was the one who'd won! He gloated for a moment then cackled under his breath as another wave of exhilaration ran through his body. He would not allow anything to interfere with his plans; he would make sure that he could nip anything in the bud that would offer even a glimmer of help or hope to them. He wasn't about to let this win be compromised!

He watched Rebecca for a moment as she lay on the stiff white sheets of the hospital bed, her mind lost in an abyss of gray clouds that stopped the pain of her regret by blocking her memory, her consciousness. He knew that she was protected by those clouds that carried her deeper into sleep each time she began to remember. He knew that she could hear the sounds around her, but that she was too tired to understand all that was said. He knew that her mind could not assemble the meaning of the jumble of words being uttered. She wanted to stay asleep; her subconscious mind knew that she needed to escape the pain of awareness. But Chaldeth wanted her to remember, and to suffer. Her suffering would bring suffering to the others.

As Chaldeth thought of the sense of hopelessness and unrelenting guilt he wanted to inflict on Rebecca, Jayden walked into the room and toward the bed. Jayden was one of Rebecca's entourage of friends and relatives who Chaldeth hated. He watched Jayden carefully and also watched for any response from Rebecca. He concentrated on Jayden's thoughts so he could intercept any threat to his power over Rebecca. He knew that Jayden sensed Rebecca's withdrawal and that somehow he too understood that it was a protection for her.

Jayden had been praying when he walked into Rebecca's room and continued in his prayer as he reached for Rebecca's hand. He was reminding God of how much Rebecca loved Him and how much love she had always shown others. He reminded God of how faithful she had been, and how much they all loved her. He asked God to help her, to comfort her, and to assure her that all would be okay again. Jayden reminded Rebecca of the power of God's unconditional love for her and the power of His grace. But she never moved, never acknowledged his presence.

Chaldeth did not want Jayden to connect with Rebecca. He especially did not want Rebecca to sense any of the understanding, empathy, or forgiveness that was being offered. His strength depended upon Rebecca's sense of guilt, her belief that she could *never* be forgiven. Chaldeth wanted to fill her mind with an unrelenting, never-ending memory of what had happened and of what she might have done but did not, of how she had disappointed everyone, including God. He wanted her to feel shame and be overwhelmed by it. He'd learned long ago that personal guilt through memory wore people down, exhausted them in mind and body and spirit. God's grace had forgiven them and forgotten their sin, but their own lack of forgiveness, their own egos, worked to Chaldeth's benefit.

His strength would also be in keeping Jayden angry about what had happened. In fact, Chaldeth wanted the whole family to be angry, to focus on blame and injustice, not on love and compassion and grace. He wanted to batter their minds with negative thoughts, fill their hearts with anger, destroy their ability to sleep, wear them down, and encourage them to hate those who'd harmed Rebecca. He could not let them blame the evil and thus *not* blame the individuals through whom Chaldeth had worked. Keeping hate alive and misdirected was good for Chaldeth and would help him reach his goal. He wanted them to hate; hate was what he wanted to bring into their lives abundantly. In most cases, keeping hate alive and misdirected was easy to accomplish; and Chaldeth knew that once he did that, he could cause their hate to spawn disillusionment with God.

When Chaldeth was first assigned to this family, it was just before his cohorts had gained control of Grandma's first husband. As they began to succeed with their invasion of his soul, it had appeared that they would be able to destroy Grandma's faith through his relentless abuse. But despite their ownership of Grandma's husband, they could never get to Grandma. She was too stubborn, and although they'd often pushed her into the depths of despair, she picked herself up before they could cause her to succumb to them. Therefore they hated her. Breaking Grandma became a challenge that had continued in their evil hearts and over her lifetime. They'd never won. They'd taken *everything* from her . . . like they had with Job. Chaldeth and his cohorts had broken her spirit but not her faith, and that had been a devastating blow to them, especially when Grandma was later to touch Sarah's heart and bring that same strength of faith into Sarah's life. They'd all felt defeated when that happened and vowed that someday they would break this family.

They'd retreated for a while, but then they regrouped and gave one another pep talks to assure one another that evil was stronger than any mere human and that they could win if they'd just continue their attack in a more subtle manner. "We have to take our time, not rush . . . just move slowly . . . little by little into the heart we want to control," Chaldeth told them. And so they began working on every family member and even on their friends . . . this time, slowly, insidiously.

Years later Chaldeth had gotten close to breaking Sarah's faith, but there too at the last minute, despite her miscarriage and her confusion about God's plan, they'd failed. He'd also had a few years of success with Jim by causing him to question God and to feel angry about the cruelty God allowed to be inflicted on so many good people and angry about the heartache God seemed to allow in Iraq. But then Barbara and Sarah and the others had finally gotten to Jim, and Chaldeth had lost again. By this time, furious from these defeats, Chaldeth changed course and set his evil eyes on the young ones. They weren't as wise, and they weren't as watchful. They'd surely be easier to crack. If Chaldeth could get to the children, that would also diminish the number of souls God wanted for His plan of salvation. It would prolong Chaldeth's life because God would need to replenish that number.

Chaldeth remembered when he'd first had the idea to attack Rebecca and Jayden. He'd seen that Elizabeth had begun to worry about them leaving home to attend college. She'd been voicing her concerns about the liberal views and lifestyles so prevalent on college campuses. Elizabeth spoke of professors who were safe in their tenure, thus free from worry or sanction about their progressive agenda and free to indoctrinate the trusting and innocent minds of their students. She also spoke of mothers currently fighting to force elementary and high schools to correct the newer history books that negated the Constitution, the Christian values of the forefathers, and the kindnesses our country provided to other nations through generous gifts of food and medicine, economic support and advanced technology.

Elizabeth wondered if she had taught Rebecca enough about God and evil and the potential of evil influences on others. Elizabeth knew that most children were denied, throughout their studies in middle and high school, the correct information about creation, honor, ethics, patriotism and the Christian values upon which this country was founded . . . so Elizabeth had tried to teach Rebecca these truths at home. But now she wondered if she'd taught Rebecca enough and if she'd taught her the importance of the armor of God that she would need to fight the forces behind what she might encounter in college. Elizabeth worried about what Rebecca might experience and who she would meet in college. Her worst fear was that Rebecca might not recognize the spirits that sought to pervert the truth or sought to harm her—they knew how to be subtle.

Chaldeth remembered the day that he'd listened to Elizabeth speak of her concerns about Jayden and Rebecca. It was eighteen months ago. He remembered the exact day and time when Elizabeth had been reading the Bible and had laid it on the table next to her chair as a sudden rush of fear entered her heart. She'd been reading from Matthew 12:45, "Then goeth he and taketh with himself seven other spirits more wicked than himself, and they enter in and dwell there . . ." With those words came the thought of Rebecca going off to college and having to face the spirits that might seek to break her faith, bring her harm. Rebecca and Jayden had been spending hours together perusing the college campus brochures they had either received in the mail or been given by their guidance counselor at school. They talked endlessly about college as their upcoming and exciting new venture.

Watching them, heads together, bent over the table in concentration and listening to their conversations of the pros and cons of each curriculum, finally convinced Elizabeth that they might really be leaving after all. She didn't want Rebecca to go. She wondered how she would react to waking up every morning to an empty house and not hearing Becca's happy chatter and have her loving companionship which gave so much purpose to her days. While she understood that time marched on, that Becca eventually would leave her nest, Elizabeth was not yet at the point where she could accept it gracefully. She was wise enough to understand that while emotionally she couldn't bear the thought of being separated from her daughter, nor of her daughter out in a world filled with so much danger, intellectually she *wanted* Becca to become independent, to obtain a good education, and to prepare for her future. She also knew that as Rebecca became more self-sufficient, and Elizabeth saw that Rebecca could recognize a bad or evil situation and would run from it, she wouldn't worry so much. But then she would wonder: *Would Rebecca run from danger? Have I given her what she needs? Have I taught her well enough for her to be prepared, have I taught her how to recognize the subtleties of evil and how to remain safe?*

Elizabeth had been in her forties when she and her husband adopted month-old Rebecca, and even then she'd worried about being almost seventy when Rebecca graduated from college and could step out on her own. At that time, neither she nor her husband had seriously considered the consequences to Rebecca should either of them become ill. She shared these thoughts with her friend John, knowing that he too was experiencing the pangs of preparing for his grandson's departure to college.

John had practically raised Jayden, so Elizabeth understood that for John it was more like letting a son go rather than a grandson. Always pragmatic, John assured Elizabeth . . . and himself . . . that Rebecca and Jayden's foray into college life was important to their future and that he and Elizabeth *had* to support and encourage it. But Elizabeth knew that secretly, despite his words of comfort, John also suffered. Jayden had been the focus of John's life for so many years that when Jayden left it would be John who felt the impact the most. John too knew the dangers that would lurk at the college, any college.

John's daughter had recently remarried, and though John was delighted by her marriage and grateful for the good man her husband was, he missed the constant companionship they'd shared before his daughter had met her husband. Ruth's happiness was well worth whatever loss John felt. Before she remarried, Ruth had been despondent, worn down by the responsibilities of maintaining a home for Jayden, raising him alone and having to struggle financially on her single salary. She'd been thankful that John had stepped in, had retired from his job so he could help by being there when Jayden came home from school.

John had invested much of his time in Jayden's scholastic and spiritual life by checking his homework and tutoring him when needed. He brought him to Sunday school, then confirmation classes; and as Jayden got older, John brought him to the youth events that the church sponsored and encouraged. John had become Jayden's role model and Ruth's strength, and he'd also helped financially because Jayden's father hadn't been making the child support payments ordered by the court. But now, in the space of only a few years, everything had changed. Ruth no longer needed him as she once had. Ruth finally had a wonderful husband who John liked immensely, and best of all, Jayden also liked him. John had enjoyed feeling needed but knew the importance of his loved ones being able to do without him. Soon Jayden wouldn't need him. And John was glad. That's how it should be.

John also knew that with Jayden going away to college he could engage in a new activity . . . something that would benefit others. With the economy such a mess, and the job-loss rate about 10 percent, John reasoned that while he could go back to work, he would not want to take a job from someone more in need. Thus he determined to increase the numbers of hours he worked as a volunteer at the hospital and look for other areas where he could be of use to others. "After all," John told Elizabeth, "Christ himself said in Matthew 25:45, 'Verily I say unto you, Inasmuch as ye did it not to one of the least of these, ye did it not to me.' This means that if we do not help others, we do not help Christ."

Because John understood that Elizabeth was going to miss having Rebecca close at hand, he wanted Elizabeth to join him in his volunteer work at the hospital. Rebecca had been Elizabeth's only focus since her husband had died . . . and with no relatives, no family other than Rebecca's birth mother, she would be hard hit by Rebecca's departure. He hoped that joining him in a visit to the hospital and by accompanying him on his "rounds," Elizabeth's interest would be piqued. Though he planned that they would only volunteer a few hours at present, once the children left, he and Elizabeth would be ready to take on additional responsibilities immediately.

So John made a proposition to Elizabeth requesting that she accompany him to the hospital where he volunteered his time a few days each week. He wanted to show her what duties he performed as a volunteer and the rewards it brought. She hadn't wanted to go . . . hospitals held bad memories for her. But since she knew her thoughts to be irrational, when John was persistent in his request, assuring her that *his* hospital would bring her *good* memories, she had agreed to go. He'd told her that she could make a difference in the lives of others, and this statement had finally catapulted her into agreeing to accompany him.

Elizabeth appreciated John's efforts to help her find a way to be productive once Rebecca spread her wings and began her flight into adulthood. But she wasn't sure that she would go along with John's plan. The smells of a hospital still conjured up the pain and fear she'd had to fight for so long to overcome. Antiseptics, anesthesia, the distinct odor emanating from the radiology department, even the general odor of sickness and death assaulted Elizabeth's sensibilities whenever she entered a hospital and each brought back unpleasant memories. A hospital was where her husband had been diagnosed, where he had undergone many surgeries to stop the progression of his cancer, where he'd later received his radiation and his chemotherapy, and from where he'd finally been sent home to die. They'd simply said that there was nothing more they could do for him.

John had been so persistent in his quest that Elizabeth "give volunteering a try" that finally she had given in, but only after extracting a promise from John that if she still felt the same way about hospitals after one week of helping him he would no longer expect her to accompany him. He'd agreed to her terms. He knew that hard work, serving others, and feeling needed were all a balm for the soul and that Elizabeth's natural desire to help others would be aroused.

When John's wife had died so many years ago, he'd gone through many of the same experiences that Elizabeth had experienced when her husband had died. Every day that his wife had been ill, John had fought the anger he felt from the injustices that life had brought them. He could deal with injustice for those who were unjust, but it was especially hard to bear when injustice kept coming at those who were so innocent, those who *deserved* goodness and kindness.

John's wife had contracted Lou Gehrig's disease. Watching her lose her ability to function, become totally debilitated, find it such a struggle even to breathe, wrought a tremendous anger in John. His wife had had her full mental acuity right up until the end, and because of this, she knew *exactly* what was happening and knew what *would* happen to her, yet she had remained cheerful and loving. Her incredible attitude toward what she had to bear made John's anger even stronger because he felt that what his wife had to go through was so unfair. His anger was directed toward the disease and the cruelty that this particular disease imposed upon its victims. He knew that this direction for his anger was okay, especially if he could channel that anger toward his determination to help others or to help raise funds for research. But his anger was *also* directed toward God, and he felt guilty about this. John wondered why God allowed evil to live happily and unfettered, prosperous and fulfilled, while good was beset by so much hardship. This anger had filled John's heart with bitterness and had taken him a *very* long time to resolve.

Elizabeth had had a similar experience. She had watched her husband die, slowly, in pain, yet faithful and loving and accepting God's will to the very end; and it had broken her heart. She and her husband had known one another since they were teenagers, and she had always loved him, even before he ever noticed her. He had been her role model, and their life together had been perfect. They never had children of their own but had adopted Rebecca when they were in their forties. Rebecca was a perfect child and brought them much happiness. For years it seemed as if their life was idyllic. But then her husband had gotten sick, and then he had died when Rebecca was just twelve years old.

Two years later, as if the loss of her husband wasn't enough, Elizabeth began suffering some vague but frightening symptoms. The symptoms prompted her physicians to tell her that it might be the onset of a serious and debilitating disease. "It might not be," they'd said, "but it's best to be watchful and to continue to test for anything that could help pinpoint what is happening to your body."

After long discussions with Rebecca about what would happen if she did become seriously ill, and finally agreeing on what they should do, they had set out to find Rebecca's birth mother. Elizabeth felt that if she should die, Rebecca would still have a family. They weren't sure that they would find her birth mother since Rebecca was not yet eighteen and the birth mother may have asked to keep the records closed. But Elizabeth prayed fervently that they would find Rebecca's birth mother, and that if they found her, she would be worthy of a daughter like Rebecca.

Their search brought spectacular results. The birth mother had wanted the records open and available to her child whenever she might search for them, and she had placed a loving note in those records so Rebecca would know that she would welcome a meeting with her. Thus Elizabeth and Rebecca did locate Rebecca's birth mother, and when they met, she had been overjoyed to find Rebecca. Their prayers were answered. Mary was lovely, loving, and to Elizabeth's relief, very appreciative of Elizabeth's role in Rebecca's life. That had allayed a fear that Elizabeth had in her heart and had never shared with Rebecca.

Along with finding Rebecca's mom Mary, who'd given birth to Rebecca when she was only fourteen years old, they'd met Mary's husband, Kevin, who was also a loving and wonderful person. It was through them that Rebecca and Elizabeth met Matt and Sarah and their family—Ann and Caleb, Josh and Debbie, and Jim and Barbara—who also welcomed them with open arms. Later they were to meet John, Jayden, Ruth, and Wade, along with Hildegard and all the children. These special people soon became Elizabeth and Rebecca's extended family.

Elizabeth knew that God had heard their prayers; He had arranged everything perfectly. Mary too had been praying that someday she would be reunited with Rebecca. Thus Elizabeth and Rebecca gained a close-knit new family, and best of all, learned that they were people who loved God and practiced what they preached! It was such a blessing to each of them, and as they exchanged their stories, they recognized the incredible miracle God had wrought for them. Their meeting was an engineering feat; one of God's incredible miracles put into place years before it came to fruition!

Looking back, Elizabeth could pinpoint the many little things that had to occur for them to finally meet Mary, and she was filled with wonder by the amazing number of things that had to come together to bring this miracle to them. So life was good . . . it was just this transition period that seemed so difficult. It was this . . . letting go . . . this empty nest thing that both she and John would have to cope with in the coming years. It was also just . . . well . . . just this sense of apprehension that she was feeling that was so difficult to bear.

The children still had another year of high school to finish before they left for college, so the worries that John and Elizabeth shared were even a bit premature. *Is it a natural phenomenon to experience these concerns? Is it that as parents we begin recognizing that our children's lives will become filled with outside interests and we must acknowledge that our position in our child's life will be changed forever? Do all mothers experience these emotions?* Elizabeth wondered. *Is it that there must be a gradual moving apart of a child and parent in order to come together again as friends . . . still bonded, but somehow differently?*

Elizabeth thought of a saying she'd once heard that spoke about holding a bird in your hand and allowing it to fly away from you, thus giving it the freedom to choose to come back to you. And that if it came back it would be yours forever as opposed to imprisoning a bird and then never truly have it be yours. *Maybe it is in the letting go of a child that the decision to hold on can be formed in a child's heart. Maybe an adult relationship can only be formed when* both *parties work toward nurturing it, when* both *parties consciously decide to undertake the responsibilities that come with sustaining a trusting and eternal relationship. Maybe it's to take all the work of sustaining the relationship off the parent and begin to allow the child to become an adult by doing their part in sustaining that relationship, and thereby making it stronger. But that would not be a conscious decision on the part of the child . . . or would it? But then again, if it were, wouldn't that cause the commitment to one another to be even stronger?*

Elizabeth had been an only child too, so she tried to remember what she'd felt about her relationship with her mother. She'd always been close to her mother and had always loved her and respected her . . . and had always enjoyed being with her mother . . . but then again, it was a different time, a different generation, a time when it was expected that parents and children remained connected throughout life. There were fewer options then. It was just . . . well . . . *understood* that a mother and child would remain bonded for life and *want* it that way. *But,* she thought, *it's also different in each mother and daughter relationship, isn't it? After all, look at Debbie and her mom. They are as far apart as can be.*

Elizabeth knew that maintaining a close relationship between any two people is a two-way street . . . one can't demand that a close relationship develop, especially without the other wanting it to happen as well. She knew that whether that relationship existed between friends or relatives, between husband and wife, or parent and child, it needs nurturing from *both* parties, and it needs trust between them as well. *I hope and pray that Rebecca and I will never lose the desire to remain close. I would be devastated if our love could not be sustained, let alone flourish, during our separation from one another.*

There are so many unknowns in life, so many different personalities, differing opinions, so many times when we are sure we are right only to find that we were wrong. There are so many circumstances that wield an influence on the way we think and act, Elizabeth thought. *What can we do? What should we do to keep safe, to keep our relationships as we want them—as God wants them?*

Elizabeth realized that no one can just order up such a relationship. She knew that one needed to lay a foundation of love, honor, integrity, and respect in a child, and do this spiritually as well. Then when rough times came, or a separation occurred, prayer and love would eventually mend any parts that occasionally became broken. *With God, all things are possible,* Elizabeth thought. But she also knew that *without* God good things broke down and might never be repaired. That thought sent a shiver up her spine, and she suddenly wanted to ask Rebecca if she felt that her faith in God was strong, unshakable, firmly rooted. *Why don't I know this for sure?* Elizabeth wondered, horrified by such a thought. *I do know that answer . . . I don't have to worry about that. I know she is firmly rooted in her faith and that's that! Stop making a mountain out of a molehill!*

Elizabeth, like John, felt that faith in God was paramount to life and would bring them through all difficulties. *Their* faith led to their children's faith, and it brought them a source of strength and a beacon of light they could all share. She'd read in scripture that God wanted parents to teach their children of Him and wanted children to honor their parents. Proverbs 4:1-2 said, "Hear ye children, the instruction of a father, and attend to know understanding, For I give you good doctrine; forsake not my law."

It was interesting that scripture demanded that children honor their parents and yet warned that in the end times they could turn one upon the other. John and Elizabeth realized that what God was explaining was that, as the First Resurrection neared and the morality of the world broke down, not everyone would remain faithful, thus one would be a child of God and the other would not. The ungodly would turn against the godly even within families. This saddened Elizabeth. She remembered the words in Matthew 10:21 that said, "And the brother shall deliver up the brother to death, and the father the child: and the children shall rise up against their parents, and cause them to be put to death."

Elizabeth always had her concordance at hand so she could look up those verses for which she had only a phrase committed to memory. The concordance allowed her to find the exact verse in the Bible that she sought, so she could reread it. She looked up the verse she had recalled in Matthew and read further to see what else scripture would tell her about this sad event. She found the scripture she wanted at Matthew 10:33 and read, "But whosoever shall deny me before men, him will I also deny before my Father which is in heaven." Then in Matthew 10:35, she read that Christ explained, "For I am come to set a man at variance against his father, and the daughter against her mother . . ." Then in Matthew 10:37, Christ said, "He that loveth father or mother more than me is not worthy of me: and he that loveth son or daughter more than me is not worthy of me."

She understood these words, understood that God asked children to honor their parents and parents to teach their children of God, and that doing this demonstrated that they followed God's statutes and placed God first in their lives. But when either of these two parties didn't do this, Satan gained an opening through which he could destroy that relationship. If this occurred, sometimes the one who loved God and determined to follow God's statutes must choose God over the relationship. *That would be such a heartache*, Elizabeth thought.

As Elizabeth thought back over the past few years, she could identify the times when God's blessing was evident in their lives and she and Rebecca had blossomed in joy and appreciation. But she could also identify the times when Satan struck, when pain and heartache filled them, and when they struggled to accept their circumstances. Then they searched God's words for answers, for the comfort they needed, for the assurance that God was still in control. Elizabeth realized that she could identify those hard times . . . and mostly, identify the time *after* the heartache. For it was indeed *after* the attack when God blessed them for their faith, gave them the comfort they needed. It was *during* the attack that God gave them the strength to endure. Although at the time they had not recognized that gift Elizabeth did realize now that these hard times were the times when their faith had grown. Elizabeth felt that if they learned from what had occurred in those difficult days, they would have less to go through in the future.

Thus Elizabeth knew she would endure as long as she remained faithful, as long as she trusted God in all things, as long as she kept God first in her life and her prayer life strong. She was sure that Rebecca knew this too. *Did she?* Elizabeth pondered. *Certainly she does; I taught her myself. But did it stick? Does she remember it today?* She needed to talk to Rebecca, see if she remembered, see if she still understood how to fight evil and to watch for it and follow what God told her to do during these attacks.

Elizabeth thanked God for her new friends, her newly extended family, for the faith they had in God, and the example they were to her . . . and to Rebecca. She thanked God for giving her the joy of raising Rebecca and watching her grow up, and then for Jayden coming into Rebecca's life. Jayden was a good friend and wonderful role model for Rebecca. His faith in God was remarkable for such a young man; it was strong, fearless, trusting, and giving.

So instead of thinking about the troubles that might appear in the future, Elizabeth determined to think only of the good things they had right now. Difficulties would come, Satan would attack, but they had God on their side . . . they had their faith to sustain them . . . they had a future with God to fight for. Elizabeth decided that she would tell these truths to Rebecca, again warn her to stay faithful, to do as God asked even when it hurt, so she would always have His blessing. She would make sure that before Rebecca left for college, they would have many talks about the dangers she might encounter. *But will my warnings take root in Rebecca? Children always feel invulnerable . . . they believe that they could never be attacked against their will. But the reality is that they don't really fathom the power of evil or why it* must *attack.*

With these thoughts, Elizabeth recalled a Bible verse that she'd always loved and decided to write it down and keep it with her. When she was worried, she could read it again and be reminded of God's presence. She found her Bible and with pen and paper wrote the words she found in John 14:1-2, "Let not your heart be troubled: ye believe in God, believe also in me. In my Father's house are many mansions; if it were not so, I would have told you. I go to prepare a place for you." And in John 14:27, "Let not your heart be troubled, neither let it be afraid."

Chaldeth knew what Elizabeth was thinking. That was one of his special powers. He was gleeful because it was in listening to Elizabeth's fears that he began to formulate his plan. Elizabeth had been correct to believe that children and young people easily forget how vulnerable they are to the forces of evil. To them, evil and its power over them sounds ridiculous, and the trend toward supernatural movies and TV shows add to their belief that spiritual warfare is not real and certainly not a threat to them.

The world to which Chaldeth belonged had masterminded the myth that spiritual warfare is only something found in movies and science fiction. Planting that belief made the evil they inspired so much easier to accomplish in young souls. They had succeeded in causing young people to scoff at the thought of a spirit who could stalk and attack them. *That is the stuff of a storyteller, a movie, a book, a television show . . . it is surely not reality,* they thought. The belief that the spirit world was harmless or didn't exist came from the entertainment world but took effect because of the neglect of most parents to teach their children about Chaldeth's leader, Satan, and the goal he was pursuing. It was helpful to Chaldeth and his cohorts that so few people took them seriously . . . or understood their purpose at all!

It wasn't that these people had never heard of Satan, it was that they didn't understand that evil had power and consequences. They were not aware of how it pertained to them or of the reality of the war being waged . . . for their souls. They were in the midst of a matter of life and death, and so many of them were unaware of it! They didn't know God's plan, they didn't know about why evil existed and their lack of knowledge and complacency helped Chaldeth's cause immensely. Thus, as he plotted against Rebecca and Jayden instead of the adults, he felt that this time he would succeed. He'd trap the adults by first getting to their children, and he'd do so because the children would be away from home and free of their parents' influence. It was a great plan, a marvel of his scheming, evil mind, and he cackled with the pleasure of anticipating its success.

Neither John nor Elizabeth understood the depth of vulnerability in their children, nor did they understand the power and the determination of the forces that *had* to win the war against God, *had* to stop Him from obtaining the number of souls He wanted. Few parents could conceive of the seemingly innocent and yet powerfully dangerous and carefully engineered circumstances that their children could encounter. Neither John or Elizabeth remembered the words in Psalm 120 that warned, "Deliver my soul, O Lord, from lying lips, and from a deceitful tongue." Neither did they understand how *subtle* the temptation would be as their children faced challenges and made choices at college. From friends to fellowships, from which groups to join to what classes to take, from honorable professors to those with hidden agendas . . . their children were to be bombarded, and courted . . . and sorely deceived.

Chaldeth knew that Elizabeth was right to be afraid, and he recognized the opportunities he would have with Rebecca and Jayden once they were away from the influence of their family. His entire plan was based on the kindhearted and trusting nature of both Jayden and Rebecca. Chaldeth planned to be subtle at first, but then he'd sink his claws into their hearts at just that last moment before they would realize what was happening. *And they will never get free*, he cackled.

Thus, when Jayden and Rebecca arrived at the college campus, Chaldeth began bringing into play all the people and the circumstances for the events through which he would work. In preparation of what was to come, Chaldeth had already engineered many situations developed specifically to draw certain people to the college Jayden and Rebecca would be attending. He created social and political groups, preventing the more conservative groups from forming; he courted those whom he would use. He worked on them to remove any vestige of right and wrong so that they would not think of good and would accept evil when the time came for Chaldeth to strike through them. Chaldeth would need full control of those who would actually do the deeds that would bring Jayden and Rebecca down. Chaldeth needed to cause his handpicked pawns to do his will at just the right moment.

Two of the many who Chaldeth began to influence were a young man named Durk and a college professor named T. Nagorra. Durk had an abusive father who loved sports and forced Durk to join every sport his school offered. He taught Durk that winning was everything and that sportsmanship was only for wimps—not for Durk. He beat Durk when he didn't win and told Durk over and over again that he must win at any cost. Durk's dad was a bully and taught Durk well . . . of course Chaldeth used his power to contribute to those actions and that way of thinking.

Chaldeth chuckled to know that so few of his targets knew he was involved in their lives, and certainly had no clue about the power he wielded. Even those who'd read parts of the Bible and had once been told of the power of evil were not able to digest how dangerous evil was for them personally and why Chaldeth had been able to lead them. They'd been taught that God protected them, but they didn't know that they had to put certain things into place to obtain that protection. Chaldeth laughed aloud. *This is so simple.* Exhilarated, he danced around the room, unseen and unheard as he chanted a short list of his powers into the air around him, glad of the stupidity of humans. *They have no idea that all of us from the spirit world can produce signs and wonders, hinder people, blind the mind, move men to our bidding, cause illness, create lies, enter men, steal God's words from their hearts. And these are but a few of the things we can do,* Chaldeth thought gleefully. *How can I lose?*

Chaldeth had worked hard to get Professor T. Nagorra into a position where he would be able to use him to influence and harm others. Nagorra wasn't bright, but Chaldeth drew him through the good-old-boy network system through which he eventually obtained a number of degrees which rendered him suitable to become a professor. Chaldeth had chosen him to help bring Rebecca down because it was easy to work in a heart that was filled with bitterness and jealousy. Nagorra fostered an anger toward those who were smarter or more talented than he. It was through his jealousy that Chaldeth could push Nagorra into wanting to bring anyone more successful than he down to the same level playing field. Nagorra always wanted to even the odds he'd always felt he had to fight. *Ah, that is what social justice means . . . it's what I deserve.* In the end, Chaldeth had him in the place he'd wanted him to be.

Chaldeth arranged for Nagorra to become a counselor to freshman students the year that Jayden and Rebecca would be arriving at the college. He also arranged that Nagorra would be on the committee that arranged some of the social activities and provided some of the gathering places for the students. Later he arranged for Rebecca and Jayden to be placed into Nagorra's student counseling group and to cause Nagorra to take a special interest in Rebecca. Chaldeth planned to inspire a love/hate relationship in Nagorra that would cause him to first admire Rebecca's virtues, but then feel inferior by them. This would create Nagorra's desire to bring Rebecca's standards down to the equal playing field of his own most liberal standards. To Chaldeth, the best part of his plan would be when he could influence the fall of Rebecca and the destruction of Jayden and then just sit back and watch it happen.

Chaldeth's only fear for his plan was that God would step in. He was fully aware that God knew of his plans and would act to help Jayden and Rebecca if faith and grace were brought into play. This is why he had to thoroughly break Rebecca, pull her so deeply into sin that she would forget how to call upon God, and would then give up to Chaldeth's influence.

What so many humans didn't seem to understand was that Chaldeth and all his minions knew the Bible well. They knew God's words and knew the verse in Isaiah 27:20, 21 that said "Come, my people, enter thou into thy chambers, and shut thy doors about thee: hide thyself as it were for a little moment, until the indignation be overpast. For behold, the Lord cometh out of His place to punish the inhabitants of the earth for their iniquity; the earth also shall disclose her blood, and shall no more cover her slain." And immediately following in Isaiah 27:1, "In that day the Lord with his sore and great and strong sword shall punish leviathan the piercing serpent, even leviathan that crooked serpent; and he shall slay the dragon that is in the sea." As one of the helpers of the leviathan, of the serpent and of the dragons, Chaldeth would also be punished.

In Revelation 12:6-10 were the words that frightened Chaldeth the most and caused him to fight as hard as he could against God. He did not want God to obtain the number of souls He wanted for if He did the era would begin when the words in Revelation would be fulfilled. "There was a war in heaven . . . against the dragon and the dragon fought and his angels and prevailed not . . ." and in Revelation 20:2, 3 the scripture said: "Laid hold on the dragon, Satan . . . cast him into the bottomless pit and shut him up . . ."

Chaldeth hated those words and feared them. He was torn between the fear of being slain for going against God and the need to work as hard as he could against God to prevent God from killing him. Their only hope was that God would only enact this punishment when He obtained the number of souls He sought. It was to prevent this that those in the lower spiritual world fought to stop God from attaining His goal. They all knew that they could *not* stop it . . . only *prolong* the time it would take for God to gather the souls He wanted. They would *all* die, but not until that number was found. They *had* to stop that from happening. Chaldeth *had* to stop Rebecca, and by stopping Rebecca, stop Jayden and open the door to stopping the others from becoming a part of that number.

And so Chaldeth went to work and caused both Durk and Nagorra to become powerful and cruel and to desire personal gain above all things. Chaldeth wanted them to enjoy the pain of others. Chaldeth caused them to prosper and made them believe that their power came from their own superiority, never allowing them to know that when Chaldeth was finished using them, they would return to nothing and be worse off than they had been before Chaldeth intervened in their lives.

Chaldeth brought Professor T. Nagorra and Durk together when Durk entered the college as a freshman, one year before Jayden and Rebecca would arrive. It was immediately after he heard Elizabeth worrying about Rebecca going off to college. Chaldeth caused Durk and Nagorra to become friends and help one another make a good impression wherever they went so their status could rise. Nagorra tutored Durk when he needed to bring his grades up and during those tutoring sessions, often supplied him with the answers he'd need for his exams. Durk reciprocated by building Nagorra's reputation with the other students and the coaches and by feeding Nagorra's ego with his fawning. Durk needed Nagorra and would do anything to keep in Nagorra's good graces.

As their relationship grew, they shared stories about their forays into petty theft when they were young, about the women they'd known, the people they hated, and even the movies they viewed. They recognized within one another a kindred soul and a similar attitude toward fulfilling their needs in any way that would provide them with what they wanted. Chaldeth's plan was working.

Chaldeth had also provided Nagorra with a way to make a great deal of money and had planted the idea of an early retirement in one of the Caribbean islands in his mind. He also caused him to enlist Durk's help and to provide a larger income to Durk through this scheme. This was an important part of Chaldeth's plan.

The remaining parts of Chaldeth's incredible and far-reaching plan included developing a romance between Durk and Rebecca. Chaldeth would arrange for Durk to fall in love with Rebecca and court her. He planned to wreak havoc with Durk's emotions and push him to gain further intimacy with Rebecca. If Rebecca thwarted his efforts, he'd cause Durk's anger to rise and his natural desire to get what he wanted to reach such a height that he would willingly bring harm to Rebecca.

Chaldeth also planned to instigate a deep-seated jealousy in Nagorra. This would be easy to accomplish since Nagorra's envy of Durk's relationship with someone so far above their level of integrity would cause him to want it for himself. Chaldeth knew that Nagorra felt that there was prestige to be had when with someone who was admired and respected. Chaldeth would have to balance these two carefully since he wanted both Durk and Nagorra to vie for Rebecca. His plan would create a competition between Durk and Nagorra, and Chaldeth would use this to entangle Jayden as well. A perfect way to thoroughly destroy Rebecca and to compromise Jayden!

His plan would end with Rebecca's fall and the blame laid on Jayden. Durk and Nagorra's hatred and jealousy of Jayden and their desire to capture Rebecca would help Chaldeth as he nudged them into bringing harm to Rebecca and arranging for Jayden to be blamed for it. Perfect! Chaldeth would get two for the price of one.

Everything was moving along just as Chaldeth had arranged. He had instilled in everyone's heart and mind what they needed to do and where they needed to be to prepare them for the ensuing drama. His planning was complete. Jayden and Rebecca had chosen the college they would attend, and were awaiting their letters of acceptance. The only problem Chaldeth now faced was that the entire family had begun to pray for God's protection for Jayden and Rebecca. They told Rebecca and Jayden to pray too. They suggested that Jayden and Rebecca ask God to help them make the right choices, provide them with His angel protection, help them discern the spirits that might seek to harm them, and to always wear the armor that God provided for His children. This could mean trouble for Chaldeth. So much was at stake, so he needed to get Rebecca and Jayden to the school and away from their family as quickly as possible.

Chaldeth could see that both Jayden and Rebecca were excited about leaving, about being on their own, about having the freedom to make their own choices . . . and he knew that he could use this to his benefit. He had to separate Jayden and Rebecca from the family and begin to place a wedge in their hearts, cause them to forget to pray, to think all was okay, to believe that they didn't need all the precautions their elders had asked them to take, and to believe that everything on campus was beneficent.

Both Jayden and Rebecca thought that they might be in the same dormitory but on separate floors. Rebecca chose a decorating theme that employed various shades of lavender, and Jayden, hating to make these choices, chose green. They'd received their acceptance letters and the list of items they would need to bring with them. They'd shopped . . . not only for clothing but for the special accoutrements they might need for their dorm rooms. They also purchased new tennis rackets and balls and a trunk that could store all their extras.

They were pleased with the attention they were receiving, and soon the day that they were to leave was almost upon them. Every friend and relative wanted to have a dinner for them to wish them well, but finally it was decided that one big family and friends get-together would be the better choice. Wade, Jayden's step-dad, offered their home for the large gathering, and his offer was immediately accepted because of their wonderful yard and their huge outdoor barbeque. The gathering was planned for the first week of August since Jayden and Rebecca were to be on the campus by August 15.

The guest list was huge: It included Jayden's mom Ruth and her new husband Wade; Elizabeth and Mary, Rebecca's adoptive and birth mothers; Mary's husband Kevin; and Jayden's grandfather John. Then of course there was Matt and Sarah, Jim and Barbara, and Ann and Caleb along with Josh and Deb . . . that made fourteen adults. With Bara and Heza and the wonderful Hildegard who looked after them, and the other children, Andrew and Lorraine, Teddie, Little Paul, Johnny, and Jason, another nine people were added to their list. Thus, with Jayden and Rebecca there would be a total of twenty-five hungry mouths to feed.

They all looked forward to playing a wonderful game that Sarah would create for them. Surely it would be something that would feature . . . and embarrass . . . both Jayden and Rebecca. But since they knew that everyone would play, they didn't mind and were pleased by all the attention. Josh and Deb, the most recent college graduates in the group—about four years ago—teased them about the list of dos and don'ts they had created for them. Sarah said that everyone would have to read an item from their list and then act it out in a pantomime. It would probably be hilarious to watch. The list of dos and don'ts made for Rebecca and Jayden was sure to include some very unique situations!

Chaldeth knew that he had to get over this last hurdle of family togetherness, and when he did, he'd be set to move once again with his plan. He hoped that they'd keep the party light and festive and not get into any of this "be careful . . . be aware . . . pray . . . go to church" stuff. So far everything had been right on track toward the full implementation of his plan. He hoped that within five months, just before Christmas, he would be able to claim his victory.

However, when the family began to speak of the all the precautions they wanted Rebecca and Jayden to take, Chaldeth began to worry and called in a few more of the minions to help him. He was so close, his plan so perfect that he was not about to let anything interfere with his plan. He *must* not fail. He *must* pull this off. He would lose face if he didn't make this work. He would also have wasted years of effort. He didn't want Jayden and Rebecca reminded of what could harm them . . . nor of what could protect them. He wanted them complacent, thinking only of all the things they needed to do to get to college and then all they needed to do to remain there.

When these conversations about taking precautions, about praying, and about watching for evil began, Chaldeth distracted them. Once he distracted them from their conversation by having one of the children fall and scrape their knee, another time by having the barbeque fire flare up, and once by drawing a policeman to the yard looking for donations for one of their funds. His strategy worked, and they never got around to the conversations they'd planned about Rebecca and Jayden's safety on campus.

In just another few days, Chaldeth would have them to himself . . . on campus . . . so distracted by their busy schedules that they might even forget to pray. He was ready for the next step in his plan. All they had to do was follow the lead of what he'd put into place. First, both Rebecca and Jayden would join in the culture of the campus, want to fit in and not be different than their classmates—peer pressure always worked well—then they would enter Nagorra's counseling session and then they'd meet Durk. It was a simple plan. The only difficult part would be when he went after Jayden. It could get a bit more difficult because timing would be of the essence. But Chaldeth was determined to make it work, and now, finally both Jayden and Rebecca were ready to leave for college where Chaldeth would be able to bring his plan into fruition. He'd worked so hard and for so long, but he could see nothing on the horizon that he could not handle. Soon, very soon, he would claim the victory he'd waited so long to obtain.

But what Chaldeth had forgotten was that in the end, he could never win. God's children would be saved.

And at that time shall Michael stand up,
the great prince which standeth for the children of thy people:
and there shall be a time of trouble such as never was
since there was a nation even to that same time:
and at that time thy people shall be delivered
every one that shall be found written in the book.

Daniel 12:1

Chapter 2

The Campus

Everyone was excited by their plans for a two-day outing to the little town where Rebecca and Jayden would be attending college. Though they promised that they wouldn't "interfere," Jayden and Rebecca felt somewhat overwhelmed—embarrassed actually—when they learned that everyone would be coming with them. The family, on the other hand, felt that it would be the perfect opportunity to visit the campus, walk around the historical areas, and visit the quaint little shops on the side of the hill that they'd heard so much about.

The college was a four-hour drive from their homes. Their travel plans were formulated by the women when they sat around Sarah's large dining room table where they gathered on a Saturday afternoon for this very purpose. Sarah made ginger tea and two huge apple pies that were timed to come out of the oven shortly before they would indulge in their sweet/tart aromatic splendor. Over dessert, they made plans to arrive at the campus shortly after lunch so Jayden and Rebecca would have time to register, to learn to which rooms they were assigned, and for the family to unload the vehicles and carry everything to their respective rooms for unpacking and placing. After these chores were completed, they would all go to dinner together and then return to the dorms for their final good-byes.

When the women were gathered at Sarah's to discuss their plans, Mary was the first to comment on the wonderful aroma that accosted them when they entered Sarah's house. "Oh, Sarah, those pies smell so good . . . cinnamon and sugar and warm Granny Smith apples, mmmm good!"

"Mary, that's not all that Sarah puts in those wonderful pies of hers. She also adds pecans and dried cranberries! And correct me if I'm wrong, Sarah, but I think I also taste a sort of crumble. Perhaps you've made it from flour, butter, cinnamon, vanilla, and maybe some minced pecans? Am I right?"

"You're right, Barbara," Sarah replied. "And amazingly, this recipe came about from a mistake I made! I had been making regular apple pies one day and decided that instead of the lattice-work crust I usually put on top, I would make a cinnamon crumble topping. After mixing the crumble topping, I was distracted by a phone call, and when I came back to the pies, I inadvertently added the crumble mix to the apples and had no choice but to leave it in the apple mixture. So I added a lattice crust to the top instead of the crumble mix, which was now inadvertently in with the apples, and voila, a new recipe. Matt loved the pies with the crumble mixed in with the apples, so now I always make them like that!"

"It's wonderful, Sarah, because the crumble, as you call it, offsets the tartness of the Granny Smith apples . . . and of course, because I like it sweet!" Deb added.

All eight of the women who made up the close-knit group of family and friends planning to accompany Jayden and Rebecca to college had gathered at Sarah's; Mary and Elizabeth, Rebecca's "moms"; Barbara, Ann, and Deb, Sarah's sister-in-laws; Ruth, Jayden's mom; and Hildegard, who cared for Heza and Bara and often the other six babies and toddlers in the family.

"It's hard to believe that a year has gone by since the newest baby came into this family," Deb said. "Sarah, your little Jason was born almost one year ago, and my baby Johnny eighteen months ago, and little Paul to Barb a month before that! Ruth, we're gonna blame your hubby Wade for all this . . . he started this wonderful trend when he brought Heza and Bara from Iraq. Ann and Caleb, not to be outdone, quickly gave us Andrew and Lorraine, and Mary followed with Teddie! Now there are eight . . . that's not counting our grown-up kids, Jayden and Rebecca!"

"Okay, blame Wade . . . he'd be overjoyed to be thought of as being responsible for bringing all this joy into our lives! In fact, he loves kids so much that he's always asking me to get them all together for a picnic in our yard just so he can toss the ball, run around, and feel as if he's a kid again himself. Gosh, I'm lucky—blessed, really—to have met him! Sarah, do you remember the game you had all of us play at one of your fellowships where we all had to wear a rubber nose or ear or some weird eyeglasses if we missed a question? Well, it was that night that we fell in love, and both of us were too shy to do anything about it for so long!"

"Ruth, I also remember when Hildegard and I plotted endlessly to bring you and Wade together by inviting the kids over for dinner and asking you to pick up Heza and Bara and ask Wade to join us!" Elizabeth chirped. "It was a riot . . . we all saw how moonstruck you both were, so we just had to give you two a nudge!"

"I'm so glad you did!"

"Aw, shucks, gals . . . we were all moonstruck by our guys, weren't we? And we are all so very blessed to have husbands who like each other so much, who love being a family, who are such great role models, and most of all who love God, and through that, bring a blessing on our homes!"

"You're right, Sarah, each of us has been blessed in our husbands, our children, and in one another. And we need to cherish and nurture these blessings," said Barbara. "And you know, because we also recognize and appreciate the power of prayer and pray for one another, I would like to ask that we all begin praying a little bit harder and more often for our children. I for one am appalled by what I see out there in the world. We live in a protected environment because we have tried to learn God's words and help one another stay on the straight and narrow, but our kids are going to have to go to schools where many teachers are extremely liberal, where they may encounter people with little moral substance, and certainly many kids who have never been given the proper parental guidance . . . it's frightening! And television . . . boy, it's hard to find programs, even for kids, which don't glorify some pretty terrible examples of behavior."

"That's why I am so worried about Rebecca going off to college," Elizabeth added, "and I would really appreciate your prayers for her, and of course for Jayden. This trip to the campus will give us all a little better perspective about their surroundings, and we can pray for the kids with a little better picture of where they are and where they go."

"Ya, Elizabet, I don't like dat dey go avay. I vorry too . . . undt I vill pray much. I know from where I come from dat children get brainvashed . . . and den dey forget about God undt about doing goot. Dis country is soooo goot, but it ist in trouble now unless things change back. Vee haff to pray for dees children . . . and for dis country too."

"Wow, Hildegard, you sure do clearly understand what's going on nowadays, don't you? And you're right," Ann added, "let's all make a pact that we will pray every morning and every night for all the children. Let's ask that God will protect Rebecca and Jayden as they go through every class, socialize with every friend, and as they walk to and fro. And let's also pray that they never forget their faith and what that entails. In fact, let's pray for them now." They joined hands and each prayed aloud one at a time, for Jayden and Rebecca especially, and for all the children and agreed to intercede for them every day.

The women made their plans and were excited to have a special day to look forward to. Their "college day excursion" would consist of fifteen adults and eight children in addition to Jayden and Rebecca. Sarah had reserved an entire floor of rooms—eight in all—in the largest hotel just outside the town. They expected to drive from home to the campus in just four hours and buzzed with excitement as they made their plans. Neither Jayden nor Rebecca had the heart to tell them that they would rather have been on their own. Though the family assured them that only Ruth, Wade and John would accompany Jayden, and Elizabeth, Mary and Kevin would accompany

Rebecca to the buildings where they had to sign in and complete the paperwork for their identification badges, their cafeteria passes, and their room keys, they were still embarrassed by the entourage looking after them *as if they were still children.*

They came in two SUVs and two trucks filled with family and friends and with Rebecca and Jayden's clothing and bedding, computers, TVs and other needs. They sang in the car because they were so happy with the sunny day, the exciting occasion, and the beautiful countryside. After an hour's drive they began to see rolling hills, green and lush foliage, and cows and horses dotting the landscape. There were fields filled with corn or hay or apple trees, farmhouses and barns with windows sparkling in the sun, and tractors moving through or between fields, and they excitedly pointed these out to the smaller children.

Their route brought them from the main highway to a smaller highway and then onto a country road that flattened out to pass through a long valley. This road was dotted with small businesses from landscape nurseries to mechanic shops, from mini-marts to antique shops, and from plumbing stores to kitchen showrooms. The women wrestled a promise from the men that on their return trip, once the vehicles were emptied of Jayden and Rebecca's belongings, they would take the time to stop at some of the antique shops.

Most of the buildings they passed were old and somewhat rundown, most made of large planked barn wood from which any vestiges of paint had long disappeared. But they were quaint and complemented the distant hills and supported the sense of antiquity and heritage that the barns and the farmhouses represented. They noticed that many barns and larger buildings had faded geometrical paintings on their broader sides. They could discern that these paintings had originally been created with bright reds and vibrant primary blues and yellows, some with black outlining the shapes within its frame.

As they admired the landscape, Kevin used his Blackberry to obtain some information about the unique paintings and learned that the paintings were commonly called hex signs and had reached their height of popularity during the twentieth century. Hex signs had originated with the Pennsylvania Dutch and derived their name from the German word *hexe* or the Dutch word *heks*, both meaning witch. "Some, however, believe that the word originated from the Greek root word *hex*, which means six," Kevin told them.

"There are also two opposing beliefs about these signs. One belief is that they act as a talisman to ward off bad spirits, and the other, that they are nothing other than an expression of ethnic identification. But because of its association with the occult when viewed as a talisman, neither the Amish nor the Mennonites allow their use. Many superstitions are associated with certain hex-sign themes, but despite this, many see them as purely decorative, or 'chust for nice,' as they would say in the local dialect," Kevin told them.

"The art depicts stars, birds, tulips, the tree of life, or compass roses painted inside an octagonal or hexagonal pattern. These geometric patterns are also found in quilts and on uniquely painted wood furniture as well as on birth, baptismal, and marriage certificates, and used this way are known as *fraktur*."

John, Elizabeth, and Hildegard were traveling with Mary, Kevin, and Teddie in their SUV and enjoyed Kevin's short history lesson. John suggested that Kevin text the information to the other three vehicles so they would all understand what they were seeing. Kevin thought that John had a good idea but said, "I can do better than that, John . . . Caleb, Matt, Josh, and I each bought a powerful walkie-talkie for our vehicles just so we could communicate with one another during this trip!"

"What a great idea, Kevin . . . good thinking!"

"Caleb, Matt, Josh . . . pick up," Kevin said into his handheld communication device.

"Hey, Kevin, Caleb here, what's up?"

"Okay, Kevin, I'm here," said Josh.

"Me too, Kevin," said Matt. "Whassup?"

Caleb's truck carried the accoutrements Jayden was transporting to his dorm room along with Ann, Lorraine, Andrew, Jayden, and Rebecca. Deb, Josh, and Johnny were traveling with Jim, Barbara, and Paul in Josh's truck, which was laden with Rebecca's belongings. Sarah, Matt, and Jason, in Sarah's SUV, were traveling with Ruth, Wade, Heza, and Bara.

They were all very pleased to hear what Kevin had learned about the artwork they saw on the barns they were passing. When Kevin completed his lesson, Sarah asked if any of them wanted to hear one of the songs that Grandma had been taught by her father. "It's just a silly song and just something I remember hearing as a child."

"Sure, Sarah, go ahead and belt it out!"

And Sarah began to sing.

> *"Oh Dundenbeck, Oh Dundenbeck, How could you be so mean,*
> *to ever have invented the spanking spoon machine?*
> *Now all the kids and parents will nevermore be seen,*
> *for they've all been hiding to get away from Dundenbeck's machine!*
> *One day a boy came walking, a walking in the store.*
> *He bought a little ice cream cone and dropped it on the floor.*

He started in a-whistlin, a-whistlin up a tune,
and when Dundenbeck saw what he did he chased him round the room.
But the boy was very wily and could easily run away
And Dundenbeck was flustered and didn't have much to say.
But the village people plotted to steal the horrid old machine
for they loved the children dearly and would never be so mean.
One day the darn thing busted, the darn thing wouldn't go,
and Dundenbeck climbed into it the reason for to know.
His wife was having a nightmare and walking in her sleep,
and gave the thing one very strong crank, and Dundenbeck was beat!
Ohhhhhh Dundenbeck, Oh Dundenbeck, How could you be so mean,
to ever have invented the spanking spoon machine?
But now you had a sampling and now you're never seen,
For Dundenbeck disassembled his spanking spoon machine!"

Ruth and Wade burst into laughter, and Wade said that he had once heard that song with different words meant to spoof the food rationing necessary after the Second World War. "It was probably meant to spoof the hardships of rationing and make the people laugh and forget for a moment the struggle they had," Wade said, "but this version is much better." Ruth interjected, "It's amazing that this song lasted so long, and amazing that you should remember it, Sarah."

Sarah smiled with the memory of her family singing this song as they drove through the countryside on their way to the lakeside cabin that Grandma's aunt had offered them to use for a short vacation. She and her brothers had changed the words from those that Wade must have remembered because they'd felt that those words weren't really, well, nice. "Let's all sing it now," said Sarah.

It only took them three or four rounds before they all, including the children, knew the words and melody to the song. They sang at the top of their lungs, exhilarated by the camaraderie they shared and the fun and anticipation of a wonderful weekend together.

"Aunt Sarah," ventured Heza, "I love you and love all the fun and games you always teach us. Thank you, Aunt Sarah." And Sarah was so pleased. Ruth and Wade were pleased by Heza's words as well because they remembered how shy Heza had been when Wade first brought her from Iraq.

"You are quite welcome, Heza, and I thank you for the wonderful compliment!"

"Well . . . I don't want you to be mad at me, but I feel bad for the kids that got spanked."

"I would be too, Heza . . . but the machine was destroyed after spanking only the man who created it!"

"Yeah, that's right. You know, Aunt Sarah, that I'm going to marry Teddie when I grow up, and I would like Bara to marry Lorraine, so let's get them to sing too!"

Bara screamed vehemently, denying that he would ever marry *anyone*! "No, I won't, and you shouldn't say stuff like that, Heza. I don't like girls, and I am not going to get married . . . ever!"

"Oh, Bara, yes you will . . . *everybody* gets married and has kids and buys a house . . . you're really dumb not to know that!"

"I am not. Mama Ruth, tell her not to be mean. Tell her that I don't have to get married if I don't want to."

"Bara is right, Heza," Ruth said, "no one has to get married . . . but most people *want* to marry when they get older so that they have someone to love and to share their life with."

Heza, quite indignant, replied, "Well, I heard Uncle John read from the Bible, and it said a man should rejoice with the wife of his youth, and then I heard Aunt Mary laugh and say that behind every good man was a great wife. So how can Bara ever be a good man without a wife?"

"I can too, Heza!" Bara interjected. "I will be a good man, *and* I will never get married! Girls are dumb!" Luckily, Bara hadn't seen the giggling of the adults who had been amazed by Heza's statement, and amazed that she would put those two statements together the way that she had.

"Now wait a minute, Bara, both you *and* Heza are right. It is good for all of us to have a helpmate in life. What you mean, however, Bara, is that you are not ready to think about those things right now. You are both only six and seven years old! So let's agree that you are *both* right and that neither of you are wrong. It's just the timing that makes your statements vary. Okay?"

"Yeah . . . okay, Mama Ruth. Oh look! Look . . . stores! Can we stop for lunch now, huh? Huh? I think that I have to go to the bathroom too. Can I talk to Uncle Matt on the walkie-talkie and ask him to find a place to stop?"

Sarah and Matt were in the lead car and gladly told Bara that they would look for a place right away. When they saw a sign advertising a nice-looking diner two miles ahead, they signaled to the other vehicles that they would pull into the parking lot of the diner to check it out and discuss everyone's thoughts about eating lunch at that location.

A few minutes later, they pulled off the road and were glad to see a lovely diner sitting on a small hill just a few hundred yards away. There was also a gas station on the lower level in front of the hill, and the men decided to fill the gas tanks before eating. The women and children climbed from the vehicles and chose to walk up the hill to the diner and let the men follow when the gas tanks had been filled.

It was still early, just past 11:30 a.m., and the diner was almost empty. Seeing so many people enter at once, the waitresses quickly suggested that they could push the center tables together to form one large table that would accommodate all of them. They were delighted since they had assumed that they might have to split into smaller groups. With five tables pushed together, ten sat on one side, eleven on the other, and two at each end. They could talk with one another easily with this arrangement of tables and chairs.

The diner was immaculate and adorable, and a step back in time—a time when jukeboxes, lots of chrome, and bright Formica counters were popular. The counters were green, and the booths and stools were lipstick red. The tables in the center where the family sat were covered in red and white checked vinyl, and the chair cushions were green to complement the color scheme. Lots of chrome on the counter fronts, the backdrop of the food prep area, the chair legs and the stools completed the art deco décor. The booths even sported tiny chrome tabletop jukeboxes! They all loved it.

The food was wonderful and the service excellent. They talked about their own college days and the many ups and downs that had taught them about the realities of life. "College, even outside of the academics, is a good experience because you meet people from many walks of life. You can learn from what others experience, as well as from what you experience as you venture into the realm of independence. Hopefully you make the right choices," Jim said.

"With the right background . . . I mean one where you have been taught right and wrong, where you understand why God wants you to follow a certain path, and you watch for those situations that will bring you spiritual, physical, or mental harm, you will be okay," Caleb added.

Jayden tried to change the direction of this conversation because he knew the deep concerns that John and Elizabeth had about he and Rebecca being away at college and said, "Rebecca and I have a strong faith in God and believe that He will help us and protect us. We know that we are to watch and always pray, so please don't worry. We'll be okay! Hey, what we're gonna have to do is develop the muscles needed to carry our laptops and other classroom needs up and down all those hills every day!"

Deb responded just as Jayden had hoped. "Ah, within two weeks you'll be acclimated to the walking, and the stairs and the hills, and feel as if you've been there forever, and your bodies will be primed for all that exercise and you won't even notice the hills anymore."

Rebecca, quick to understand the diversion that Jayden wanted to create, added, "I've been walking on Aunt Mary's treadmill and putting it in the uphill position so I can train my leg muscles so that it won't be too difficult to deal with. Hope it has worked for me."

"Okay, okay, we see that you kids are trying to divert us from our worries—we didn't fall off a turnip truck you know—but seriously, I'll say just one more word about this. I want *both* of you to promise us that you will pray in the morning and at night for protection, and for the ability to discern the spirits and to promise that you will phone us if there is *anything*, I mean *anything*, wrong. Deal?"

"Okay, Uncle Caleb, we promise, and please stop worrying . . . all of you," Jayden replied.

"Boy, what a bunch of worrywarts . . . it's only college, and how can anything go wrong if we pray and you do too? So stop worrying!" Rebecca added.

The restaurant staff began clearing the dishes from the table and asked if anyone wanted dessert. Of course all the children did, and a few of the adults. Before they brought the desserts, the children, giggling, burst into the spanking spoon song again, carefully watching the surprised faces of the adults. Andrew said over the singing voices, "We just want to 'make a memory,' like Aunt Sarah always says Grandma would want us to do." And then he too joined in the song.

The entire staff at the diner gathered round, along with the few customers who'd come in for lunch. Everyone applauded when the children finished their song. Two older gentlemen said that they'd heard that song in their childhood but with different words which spoofed a time when people did not have enough to eat.

Hildegard huffed and puffed. She was upset. "I dint vant to say nothink ven you sang it . . . but you hef to understand dat . . . vell . . . you shouldn't make fun."

"Oh, Hildegard, we are so sorry," Sarah replied, "I didn't know that it would upset you. What is it about the song that upsets you?"

"Vell, Sarah, you didn't mean notting. But you don't know . . . another ting . . . it's not a goot example to children to talk about someone climbing into a machine, and ist not goot to scare the children about da spanking."

"I'm sorry, Hildegard, you are right. I didn't think about that."

But then Hildegard began laughing saying, "But golly gee whiz, efferybody liked you to sing it! Und dem vords maybe iss funny, yah? Maybe dat makes it goot, is okay, huh?"

Everyone was relieved that Hildegard was okay again. They spoke for a little while about how easy it was to say things that were funny instead of taking a good look at the words to see if they required change, if they might frighten a more sensitive child, or offend someone unintentionally.

With tummies well satisfied, with a few laughs under their belt, with a sense of having shared some great conversation and fellowship, they were off to complete their trip to the campus. When they left the diner, they walked back down the hill to where the men had left the vehicles after deciding to follow the women's example and walk rather than drive up the hill. Each person climbed into their respective truck or SUV in anticipation of Matt and Sarah again leading the way.

In a little more than an hour later, they entered the single-lane road at the bottom of the hill that would lead them to the main college campus on the plateau above the hill. They found themselves on Main Street, which was lined with a myriad of tiny boutiques advertising their clothing, shoes, jewelry, restaurant, vintage clothing, handmade items, gifts, books, skin-care products, and little souvenirs.

The town was old yet quaint, and the streets and sidewalks were filled to overflowing with the young adults attending, beginning, or interested in the college, and also many of the parents who were bringing their children to the campus for the first time.

They drove to the top of the hill to find the administration building where Jayden and Rebecca were to check in and obtain their room keys. There were a group of buildings built of dark red brick, and both the solid appearance of the brick and the age and architecture of the buildings provided the area with a marvelous sense of antiquity and stability. The main and largest building sported a large double-door entry with white trim and lighting fixtures in keeping with the age and design of the building. It had been built on the plateau at the very top of the hill.

Beyond the older buildings was a complex of more modern buildings flanked by a huge expanse of parking spaces that seemed out of place in the marvelous atmosphere that the town and shops and older campus buildings had imparted. They thought that these modern buildings would probably be where Rebecca and Jayden would be living. At the end of this complex, a huge water tower stood as if guarding the parking lot and keeping watch over the entire campus.

Elizabeth began to cry quietly when she saw the cold modern buildings. She knew that they represented Rebecca's new life and their separation. Her sense of loss and secret fear for Rebecca's well-being overwhelmed her. Comforted by Rebecca, who'd seen the tears slip down her mother's cheek, she quickly placed a smile on her face, and once they had parked and disembarked from the vehicle, she wiped away all vestiges of her sorrow. Elizabeth hugged Rebecca and then walked over to Jayden and said to him, "Look after her, Jayden, promise?" Jayden was surprised by

Elizabeth's words and turned to look into her eyes. He saw her concern and felt a pang of fear move through his heart as well. With strong emotion and feeling in his words, he replied, "Don't worry, Aunt Liz, I will . . . and remember . . . we will be relying on your prayers for us too."

"You will always have that, Jayden . . . . and, thanks," Elizabeth replied.

Mary too took a special moment with Rebecca, telling her that they loved her and would miss her and assured her that she and Kevin would look after Elizabeth. "I'm so blessed to have two moms," Rebecca said as she hugged Mary and then Kevin. Then Matt, always an organizer, gathered everyone together.

"Okay, everyone, we're here, but we can't *all* descend on the administration building. Why don't we split up and meet back here at a specific time so we can all help unload the trucks, and cars, and then we can separate again to set up the rooms and when we are finished, we can meet for dinner at that pub down on Main Street where that huge beer vat and wagon are placed in the window. It is 2:00 p.m. now, so why don't we meet back here at the vehicles at 3:30 p.m. to unload and set up the rooms, and then whoever wants to go to dinner can do so. Jayden and Rebecca can decide at that time what they want to do . . . stay and meet friends, go to the school cafeteria, or come with us. Deal?"

"Deal," they all responded.

And off they went. Jayden with Wade, John and Ruth, and Rebecca with Elizabeth, Mary, and Kevin went to the administration building. They were already somewhat familiar with the campus since they'd visited the campus when Rebecca and Jayden were making the decision about which college they would attend. They carried their completed paperwork as instructed. The others walked in the opposite direction to explore the campus until three thirty. They had locked the vehicles after unloading strollers and diaper bags and backpacks carrying what they might need and then began walking across the plateau of the hill before descending to the shops along Main Street.

The first group walked toward the administration building which proved to be crowded and noisy. However, they found that the registration process was orderly and well-marked lines directed everyone along quickly. While they had to move from table to table to complete the registration and sign-in requirements, they were relieved to see that their route was clearly indicated and that there were monitors ready to answer questions and direct everyone to their proper place. They were finished in less than an hour and one half. They were issued their room assignments and the student identification tags and plastic cards that they could swipe to use to purchase food, take books out of the library, or to enter the outer doors to the buildings. They also received a huge list of regulations, a schedule for their college orientation, and a map of the campus. Each student was required to enter additional data into a computer, many of which were lined up along one long wall for the students to use throughout the registration process. When they had received their final okay regarding their financial support and their paperwork, they were finally allowed to leave.

The other group, unfamiliar with the campus, had opened a map of the campus that John obtained for them before leaving home and began to walk around the campus. They found a large football, baseball, and soccer field on the back side of the hill, down and behind the brick buildings and the dorms. The number of bleachers and lights and two huge scoreboards attested to the popularity of the sports program. But to the women, the stark and empty expanse of field looked barren and unwelcoming, and Sarah said that for some reason it gave her a sense of foreboding. Matt told her that when the field was full of players and spectators it looked quite different and not at all barren. They didn't see a gym but decided that it might be enclosed in one of the larger buildings scattered across the top of the hill.

There were many buildings that belonged to the college, mostly of the old red brick, most touting signs telling them that certain buildings were used for a specific area of study. As they walked further down the hill to the right of the Main Street, they found hundreds of quaint, tiny, zero-lot-line houses that had wonderful architectural detail, were built mainly of wood, and appeared to house the upperclassmen. Some For Rent signs in their tiny front yards indicated that these might be personal rental units. Lots of young people congregated on the porches and stoops and walked along the streets.

Halfway down the long hill, they turned left toward Main Street to visit some of the little shops they had passed as they drove through the town. They passed young people with backpacks and observed every variance of dress style and hair color and length imaginable. Some had purple hair, some had mixed colors of purple, red, and yellow, some wore braids, some wore their hair long and straight and others short and curly, and it seemed that every color and style was worn equally by males and females. Many wore jeans that either had holes in them or were faded or sported large or small areas that had been bleached almost white. But they also saw some students dressed in vintage clothing: long bohemian-style dresses, waist sashes, large sunglasses, and fabric flowers on their lapel or in their hair. They were surprised that those who wore their trousers so large and low on their hips that they were close to falling off and required constant help to stay up were few in number. They commented on their hope that this may have become an outdated style.

But all the students they saw looked happy and waved to one another, and many called out a greeting to them, and all seemed content and unafraid to walk everywhere. There was so much to see and so many shops and restaurants that looking around and seeing so many different decors and colors and items was a feast for their eyes. The hill was steep, and they found themselves huffing and puffing as they crossed the street and turned to walk back up the hill. "This will be great exercise for Rebecca and Jayden, won't it?" Josh said. "All this walking . . . and uphill to boot."

"Yeah, but I wonder what they do when it's raining," asked Deb.

"Tough it out and walk in the rain . . . it can be fun when you are young and have someplace you want to go to meet your friends!"

"I guess you're right . . . I enjoyed that stuff when I was younger too, I guess. In fact, I can remember that once Josh and I did a jitterbug in a parking lot in the rain because the music on the car radio had such a perfect dance beat. We simply climbed out of the car and into the rain, not caring at all that we'd get wet, in fact, we laughed *because* of the rain! But now, as old as I am and feel, I'm glad to stay dry, and in fact, glad that we thought to bring the strollers. If we hadn't we'd be exhausted carrying the kids as we walked uphill. They have been so good and seem to enjoy looking at all the sights. But now I think we'd better get back so we can begin bringing all of Rebecca and Jayden's belongings into the dorms."

"You're right, Deb, it's almost three already so we'd better start walking . . . uphill . . . back to the vehicles."

Within fifteen minutes they reached the parking lot and found the others waiting for them and ready to begin carrying the items from the vehicles to the dorm rooms. Rebecca and Jayden had their room assignments and their key passes and decided to roll some suitcases up to the rooms first so that Elizabeth and John could unpack them and then sit in the rooms to "direct the distribution of stuff" while the younger, stronger ones brought the heavier and larger items from the vehicles to the rooms.

Jayden and Rebecca were delighted to be housed in the same building. Jayden's room was on the fourth floor and Rebecca's on the second. When Jayden opened the door to his two-room suite, he found his roommate had already unpacked and was relaxing on his bed reading. His roommate's half of their shared bedroom had posters on the wall depicting some of his favorite sports figures.

As soon as Jayden walked into the room, his roommate jumped up and walked toward Jayden with his hand extended for a handshake and said, "Hey, I'm Ken. I'm glad you're here. How are you?"

"Hi, Ken, glad to meet you. I'm Jayden. Sorry for all these people, but we figured that many hands would make it happen more quickly. We'll be out of your way in no time."

"No problem, Jayden, I'll just keep reading if you don't mind . . . unless I can help you or anything."

"No, no, but thanks . . . we have so much help already . . . but yeah . . . go ahead and read . . . we'll try to be quiet so you can concentrate. Uncle Matt, this is my roommate Ken . . . Ken, my Uncle Matt . . . oh, here are the others . . . these are . . . well . . . really friends, mostly, but I call them 'uncle,' ya know . . . a respect thing . . . Uncle Josh, Uncle Kevin, Uncle Caleb, Uncle Jim, and my grandfather John and stepdad, Wade."

How do you do, sirs! Glad to meet you."

"This is my mom Ruth, my aunts Mary, Sarah, Elizabeth, Barbara, Ann, and Deb."

"Geez, man, you sure have a large family. That's really great!"

"Thanks, Ken. They're not all exactly family, many are friends, but we are sort of like a family. Well, we better get to work so we'll be out of your way and less noisy. Maybe we can talk later when everyone has gone, okay? Uhh, a question . . . this half of the room is mine I know, but are there any restrictions? I mean . . . I noticed your posters, so is it okay if I hang some of mine? And . . . . uhh . . . . do you mind that these two baby strollers stay here while everyone runs back and forth to the vehicles . . . the kids are asleep . . . and if they wake up they'll be good until someone comes for them."

"Sure . . . cool. Just do your thing! And if you have stuff left over, you can hang them in our sitting room . . . though as you saw it's really small."

As Jayden turned back to his unpacking, Barbara, teased by the family as being the greatest organizer ever created, began telling everyone where to put or hang or store each item that they were carrying in, and the move was soon completed. As the last of them filtered out of Jayden's rooms and back to Rebecca's room to let them know that they had finished, Jayden turned to Ken.

"Ken, would you like to come to dinner with us? We'll be going down to some large 'pub' one of my aunts spotted in town . . . it has a huge vat and a wagon in the window? I'd really like you to come if you would like to."

"Cool . . . yeah, sounds good. I know just the place you are talking about. What time? Should I just meet you there?"

"We're going now . . . we are having an early dinner because my family doesn't want to get back to their hotel too late because the little ones will start getting cranky if they aren't fed and then put to bed. They will drop us off back here after we eat."

"Okay, let me just wash up and I'm ready. Thanks for the invite. I never turn down a chance to eat . . . especially in a restaurant!"

Rebecca's roommate was not in their suite. In fact, it looked as if she hadn't been there at all, because there were no clothes or other belongings in the room when Rebecca first arrived. Rebecca's suite was larger than Jayden's because it had two smaller but separate bedrooms, while Jayden and Ken shared a bedroom. Rebecca had been assigned the *A* bedroom and her roommate the *B* bedroom, so Rebecca knew where she should place her belongings and not infringe on her suite mate's space. They would be sharing, like Jayden and his roommate, a tiny sitting room outside their bedrooms, and also like Jayden and his roommate, a tiny kitchenette, and one bathroom with two sinks and two showers.

Aunt Barbara, running up and down the stairs between Jayden's room and Rebecca's room, assigned a particular task to everyone so they would be sure to put everything in its proper place. As boxes were unpacked and carried empty, back to the vehicles, and as clothes were placed in the closet and dresser drawers, and office supplies in and on the desk, both Rebecca and Jayden's rooms began to take on their personality and to look well organized.

Those in Rebecca's room finished their tasks in a little over one hour and found that the group who'd been assigned to help Jayden had also finished and were trickling into Rebecca's room. After washing up and taking a final and satisfied look at each one's quarters, they went down the stairs to their vehicles where the men had removed the tape that held the boxes together and flattened them so they stacked neatly and compactly in the storage compartments of each vehicle. They were finally ready to travel the short distance to the restaurant. They were happy that Ken would be joining them and told him that he could ride in Caleb's truck with Jayden.

Ken hadn't realized that there were so many people, and children, traveling together, and he hadn't realized that Jayden had a friend who was attending their college. When Ken met Rebecca, he immediately thought that she was incredibly sweet and hoped that he, Jayden, and Rebecca would become friends. He struggled to keep everyone's name in mind and finally just gave up and called those whose name he hadn't remembered either "Ma'am" or "Sir."

"The Pub," as everyone called the restaurant, was huge. It was so much larger than anyone would guess from looking at the outside. It was two levels high with the second level created as a sort of wide balcony that accommodated two rows of tables and chairs and ran completely around the perimeter of the room. This created a ceiling in the lower level that was two stories high in the center. The room was incredibly long which gave the false impression of it being very narrow. Rustic-looking booths of unstained wood with a high gloss varnish finish, lined the walls. Matching wood tables and chairs filled the center of the room.

Since their group was so large, they chose the middle tables, and the wait staff gladly pushed tables together so they could all sit together. After playing musical chairs so everyone could find their niche—moms and dads settling next to their children, some children preferring a booster seat and others requiring a high chair—they settled in for dinner. The menu was extensive, and each of them easily found something that they would enjoy having for dinner.

After they ordered, they all turned their faces expectantly to Ken asking him if he'd explored the campus, asking where his hometown was, when he'd arrived, what his major focus of studies would be, and a myriad of other questions. Ken answered as best he could and felt surprisingly comfortable with this family. They were all so . . . nice . . . and also so, well, happy. He'd never been to dinner with twenty-five people before!

They had a wonderful time chattering about college life, about being young, about choosing a career and trying to find something that one would enjoy doing. They talked about family life and about good friends, and Ken was impressed. Caleb slipped a piece of paper to Ken with the names and cell phone numbers of Kevin, Matt, Wade, Jim, and himself and asked Ken to hold onto it and to call any of them if he or Jayden or Rebecca needed anything or faced a problem. Ken felt that Jayden and Rebecca were awfully lucky to have so many people care about them and carefully pocketed the paper determined to enter the numbers both in his cell phone and into an address book his mother had made up for him to keep at college.

Ken had been surprised when they prayed before the meal. Even the littlest kids bowed their heads and prayed, and what struck him the most was that those children, even the very youngest, added a loud and fervent "amen" when the prayer was finished. He noticed that the prayer included a request that God would look after Jayden and Rebecca . . . and him! He'd been surprised by that too. Yet he'd actually liked it. He never prayed, nor did his family. In fact, his parents weren't churchgoers except for Easter and Christmas and the like, and though they had sent him to Sunday school when he was young, this was new to him. On one hand he was impressed. But he hoped that Jayden wouldn't turn out to be one of those "Bible-totin', hymn-singin', goody-two-shoes" who'd be pushing him to do the same.

Soon they finished their meal and it was time to leave the restaurant, drive Jayden, Rebecca, and Ken back to the dorm, and then drive to their hotel. As they left, Jayden and Rebecca could see that Elizabeth was crying softly with the thought of their separation, and they went to her to comfort her. John too went to Elizabeth and took her hand trying to tell her not to make the kids feel bad. Elizabeth understood what John was signaling to her and was soon herself again. "Hey, I'm just a sentimental old gal and I'm okay, just in need of a hug!"

When they arrived back at the campus, only Elizabeth, Mary, and Kevin accompanied Rebecca to her room while Ruth, Wade, and John accompanied

Jayden. Kevin prayed with Rebecca, Elizabeth, and Mary before they left her room and admonished Rebecca to phone them if anything . . . *anything* . . . worried her, and to remember to pray as often as she could.

Her roommate had still not arrived when they returned, but Rebecca found a note on her bed telling her that she would be back late that night and was looking forward to meeting Rebecca. The note also said "Great decorating job!" and Rebecca was pleased. She too was happy with Aunt Barbara and Aunt Sarah's input for her room. After reading the note, Rebecca peeked into her roommate's bedroom and saw that the closet doors were open and filled with clothes and that a laptop and office supplies had been placed on the desk. A huge, probably four-foot-tall stuffed animal sat on her roommates bed. *Yep, she's here okay!* Rebecca thought and plopped on the bed in her own room to wait for the return of the girl with whom she'd be sharing a suite for the remainder of the year. *Oh, I hope that we can become friends*, she thought and said a quick prayer that God would bless their relationship and make it a good one.

When Ruth, Wade, and John were ready to leave Jayden's room, they asked Ken if he would join them as they prayed. Ken was embarrassed but said, "Yeah, sure," anxious now for them to leave. *What's with these people?* he thought. But when John prayed so beautifully and naturally, Ken felt good about it and was less worried about them being a little too over-the-top about religion. In fact, as he listened, he too became aware of the love that this family had for one another and the trust they placed in God. He also realized that they wanted both him and Jayden to watch out for any bad dudes . . . and even he had to agree that there were plenty out there. Ken was actually glad that, well, if all this God stuff was real, that he'd be protected and helped too. Little did Ken know that he was to play an important role in Jayden's life, that he was about to witness the power of evil, and that he would be making one of the most shocking . . . and erroneous . . . statements of his life.

And so the family left the campus after everyone had said their good-byes and left enough hugs and kisses to last a long time. Jayden and Rebecca were now on their own and hopefully would remember what they'd been taught and would constantly ask God to protect and guide them. The quiet that surrounded the campus became palpable as a thousand vehicles left the campus carrying the parents and friends of those whom the students brought to their first day of college. There was no din of voices and hesitant footsteps, no banging of luggage or grunts from carrying heavy bags of linens. And this quiet found Jayden and Rebecca in their respective dorm rooms knowing that they would now be far from their family and that the family would soon head back home. They were actually—finally—at their university, on campus, no family members close to them, and about to experience a whole new world of acquaintances and professors and classes. They were happy and excited by the prospect of both the challenges and the variety of experiences that were about to unfold. They had no idea that another had watched the family leave, had rubbed his hands together in glee, and was ready to put his diabolical plan into play. Little did they know that for over a year, a plan had been carefully executed, one that had been laid out to begin its nasty work when Jayden and Rebecca arrived on campus. And little did they know that this plan had been formulated by a subtle, patient, and formidable enemy who wanted to destroy them. Chaldeth's plan was about to move ahead.

But Chaldeth frowned when he saw the tiny frames on each of their nightstands. Their minister had given both Jayden and Rebecca a special scripture to read before they left for college, and he had first read it to them. He emphasized the words which told them to continue in what they had learned. He'd copied those words and placed them in a tiny frame for each of them. It was from 2 Timothy 3:14-16 and read, "But continue thou in the things which thou hast learned . . . the holy scriptures make thee wise unto salvation . . . all scripture is given by inspiration of God . . . for instruction . . . that the man of God may be perfect . . ." Chaldeth squirmed when he saw the frames on their nightstands, but nevertheless he was still determined to win this battle.

Chapter 3

Classes and Politics

Rebecca had agonized over which classes she would like to attend. While on one hand she wanted to emulate Jayden and follow a career in medicine, on the other hand she was also interested in law, particularly constitutional law. In the end she compromised by choosing to do a little bit of both, and thus to attend classes in anatomy and physiology, political science, and early American history. The history class covered the time frame during which the Constitution had been developed. Both curriculums allowed for a certain number of electives and also required a number of liberal arts studies, which worked well for Rebecca's choice of classes. She would have until the end of her sophomore year to decide which major she preferred. Her anatomy and physiology class also had an attendant lab where she would learn some of the principles pertaining to how the body worked.

Jayden was also studying anatomy and physiology and would be in the attendant lab, but he had chosen chemistry, psychology, and ethics for his additional classes following the suggested outline of classes for a career in medicine. He'd completed a class about the Constitution of the United States in high school and was glad that Rebecca would be learning some of the fascinating information he had gathered. He looked forward to talking with her about the wonder and magnificence contained in the Constitution and the incredible wisdom of those who developed the liberties it espoused and protected. Jayden felt that those who wrote the Constitution had been inspired by God so this country, filled with people who placed God above all things, would remain safe and free. His enthusiasm about this subject was what had inspired Rebecca to take the class and to consider a career in constitutional law.

The university was comprised of five colleges. Because it was a relatively small campus which was a part of a larger university with other locations, the students in each dedicated study shared the classes in the Arts and Sciences college required by their own curriculum. This enabled students from one area of study to mix with students from other areas of focus and thus allowed Jayden and Rebecca, and their roommates, the potential of taking a class or two together.

Jayden and Rebecca were in the same class for anatomy and physiology and the same lab, and looked forward to attending classes and studying together. On their first day of class, they learned that a requirement of their laboratory instruction was to dissect a frog and a cat. Jayden immediately thought that the dissections would be "pretty cool" while Rebecca had recoiled believing that the experience would be "utterly gruesome." But they were both excited about what they would learn and how it would prepare them for life and possibly for a potential career.

They were nervous about meeting their instructors and the students with whom they would be sharing class hours each week. They'd learned during their registration period that many of their fellow students were licensed practical nurses and medics and thus had already studied much of what would be taught in their anatomy and physiology class. They'd have to work hard to keep up, yet hoped to be inspired by the prior experiences of the other students.

They were also required to attend a one-day, one-hour seminar for freshmen, which would provide them with information about the school, the campus, the extracurricular activities, and where to find assistance for the various problems they might encounter. During this seminar each student would be assigned a counselor should they need advice or assistance. Apparently the professors who could provide this seminar were rotated in the assignment, so neither Rebecca nor Jayden would know who was offering the seminar until it began. All they knew was that they had to be at the gym by 8:00 a.m. on their first day of classes. When they arrived, there was a sea of seats facing a stage containing a podium and a chair in which a man sat who appeared to be studying the students as they walked into the gym and took a seat.

Professor T. Nagorra hated being assigned to conduct the seminar. As he sat on the stage he thought the same cynical thought he had every time he was given this assignment. *There are so many confused kids, with so many dumb questions. Reminds me of a herd of cows so dumb that they require prodding to get them where they are supposed to go.* While he admitted that he was being cynical, to his way of thinking, the seminar was a waste of time; the students would forget what he said, they would ask over and over what to do and where to go, and in the end, all they needed was their assigned counselor with whom they could converse whenever anything came up that another student couldn't tell them. To his chagrin, it was his turn to conduct the freshman seminar, and he had no choice but to do as he was told and conduct it. He was comforted by the thought that it was only for one hour in one day and then he wouldn't have to do it again for quite a while.

He noticed Rebecca and Jayden immediately. He sat on the dais watching the students amble into the hall, wonder where to sit, then finally select their seats. The nerds sat up front and those who would usually try to skip class sat in the back. Most of them looked as if they'd slept in their clothing. They wore jeans and T-shirts, faded and too big for them. Their jeans were often worn hanging dangerously off their backsides and worn, of course, with the prerequisite rips and wrinkles. *Maybe it's some sort of a dress code for the young and uninformed.*

Sneakers, scuffed and often with holes in the canvas, were the footwear of choice. There were the few nerds who wore a tie or a well-pressed plaid sport shirt tucked into belted chino trousers, and who also sported brand-new sneakers or dress shoes. There were a few girls dressed as if they'd come from a disco who wore spike heels and a ridiculously short dress with beads or sequins. But for the most part, the faded wrinkled jeans, the T-shirt, and the scuffed athletic shoes were the predominant outfits. For some reason which he could never fathom, the students chose to wear spiked hairdos with streaks of color and plastered with gel, or conversely, very long straight hair covering their faces. He thought both those hairstyles looked ridiculous and he couldn't understand why so many kids seemed to think it was "cool," or as they said, "rad." Almost all the kids either carried or wore backpacks, which were also ripped, faded, and incredibly unsightly.

Rebecca and Jayden caught his eye because they were so different. They were tall and carried themselves with dignity. They didn't slouch, which was unusual for the tall ones. Rebecca wore dark blue stretch jeans that were unwrinkled and of the proper length. She wore a simply styled unwrinkled white overblouse with an open collar and long sleeves. Not tight, not loose. While her shoes were also athletic shoes, they were stylishly red. They were also clean, low cut and made of leather, and only peeked out beneath the flare of the proper length hem of her jeans. Her hair was long, all one length, shiny, and simply caught back to the nape of her neck with a thin red scarf that matched the color of her shoes. She looked, well, sweet . . . innocent . . . elegant . . . in fact, she even looked . . . intelligent. She wore small round gold earrings and a simple thin gold necklace from which dangled a cross. She also sported a large leather camel-colored shoulder bag which she wore diagonally across her chest and which he guessed was her book and laptop bag. No backpack!

Jayden too wore dark blue jeans which were not faded, had no rips and tears, were form fitting, and were worn just slightly below his waist. His choice of footwear was unscuffed white, leather, low-cut, shoe-style athletic shoes. His shoes too barely showed beneath jeans tailored to the proper length. His shirt was a solid-color safari style with epitaphs at the shoulders and two pockets on his chest. He too wore a gold cross but on a thicker, stronger gold necklace. His sleeves were rolled to expose his wrists. On one wrist was a large leather-banded gold-faced watch and on the other was a thick gold bracelet. His hair was worn just below his ears, curling naturally at the nape of his neck and combed back away from his face exposing his intelligent forehead. Despite his careful combing, one small curl would fall forward and onto his forehead and after a while he would attempt to push it back into place. Jayden also wore a large shoulder bag across his body that apparently held his laptop and other paraphernalia. His bag was of dark brown leather. He carried it well and with authority. He emitted an aura of inner security and strength, and the professor felt a sudden wave of jealousy because he'd never looked that good when he was young.

The professor could see that these two students appeared to be friends, to know one another, and for some reason that too made him feel jealous. He could hardly bear the thought that the girl might be "attached" to the boy. He also noticed that the two students walked into the hall together, sat together, and were immediately joined by another student whom they also seemed to know quite well. That student was not dressed as elegantly, but fit in well with the other two because he did not wear his hair too long, nor his jeans too loose and wrinkled or hanging too low. The professor was intrigued. He was curious about these three, and he wasn't sure why he even cared.

Students came and went, but for some reason he felt impelled to meet these students and to talk with them. He suddenly felt that it was important for him to have these students in the group that he would be assigned to counsel. He panicked for a moment realizing that he didn't know their names so could not adjust the list he'd made of which students would be assigned to which professors. He would have to do some quick thinking. He had to have that stunning girl in his group. He had to.

The idea came almost immediately. It was as if some unseen force knew what he was thinking and gave him his answer instantaneously. Instead of reading the names of the students assigned to each professor as he usually did, and telling them where each professor would be standing at the close of the lecture and asking the students to go to that area to meet their counselor, he would divide the auditorium into sections and assign each section to one of the professors. This way he could make sure that those in the section where the girl sat would be assigned to him. He would tell his group to meet him after the lecture in the balcony section so he could meet the girl and learn her name. Once he had that information, he could track which classes she would be attending. He hoped she'd be in one of his classes. Then suddenly he wondered why he would want such a thing, what was impelling him to care, to behave this way. What did it matter to him?

As Rebecca, Jayden, and Ken settled into their seats in the lecture hall, Ken mentioned how excited he was to finally be starting off on his goal to graduate from college, a goal he'd worked toward all his life. Rebecca and Jayden teased him saying that his goal should be expanded into becoming their class valedictorian. Ken was pleased by their words and wondered aloud if he could indeed attain such a goal, such an honor, and thought that it sure was worth working toward and sure would make a good impression on a resume. Ken and Jayden smiled at one another, pleased that they were so compatible, and glad to each have a new friend.

Rebecca liked Ken, and she too was glad that he and Jayden would be rooming together. She'd not yet met her roommate but hoped that all four of them would become friends. She'd come back from dinner last night with the family to find a welcoming note from her roommate and noted that her roommate had moved her belongings into her room. But Rebecca hadn't seen her. She wanted to stay awake so she would meet her roommate when she came in but was so tired from the events of the day that she fell asleep. The next morning, Rebecca found that the huge stuffed animal had been removed from her roommate's bed and placed on the floor. The bed had been made up, not quite as neatly as it had originally been put together, but on Rebecca's dresser was another note addressed to Rebecca. The note read, "Sorry I missed you. Family emergency . . . but will definitely see you tomorrow tonight."

Rebecca decided to ask Jayden and Ken to join her when her roommate returned tomorrow evening so they could all meet her together. Naturally shy, and even reticent until she got to know someone, Rebecca felt that Jayden and Ken could help break the ice of her first meeting with this new and seemingly busy, vivacious, and possibly stressed roommate. She was so pleased that Jayden had Ken for his roommate and thought how wonderful it would be if she and her roommate could have the same great relationship—and if all four of them could as well.

Rebecca rose early knowing that her first assignment of the day was to attend the one-hour required freshman lecture at 8:00 a.m., and she was ready to go when Ken and Jayden knocked on her door. They walked over to the hall together and then found seats together. The lecture material included information about the grading system, how absenteeism would affect their grades, what options were available for improving grades, when and how they could access the library, and the importance given to their assignments. They also learned about how and where they could use their food vouchers and debit cards, what they could and could not do in the dorm rooms, what nursing and emergency resources were on campus, and the "zero-tolerance rules" which, if broken, would result in an immediate discharge from the school. They were told to seek out the advice of their assigned counselor if they ran into any problems or needed any help. They could also speak with any of the professors, especially if their concerns were about their classes or their performance or grades.

Each of them thought that the professor had provided an informative lecture. The school seemed to genuinely care about helping them move through the learning process of being on a college campus for the first time, doing well in class, and graduating. After the lecture, when they found themselves in Professor T. Nagorra's group, they looked forward to meeting him personally and to the one-on-one that he'd be arranging with each of the students assigned to his group. As each student was given the date and time of their first meeting with him, the professor told each of them to refer to him as Professor T. Rebecca, Jayden, and Ken found that they were the first three students scheduled to meet with him.

"Who goes first?" Rebecca asked the two boys as they left the lecture hall. "Whoever it is has to promise the others that they will give them pointers so we won't be so nervous . . . okay?"

"Yeah, sure," Jayden answered, "but what if you are first?"

"I hope not," Rebecca replied.

"I think I am the first," Ken said. "My appointment is at 11:30 a.m. today . . . just after my first . . . my 9:00 a.m. class, and before my second class, and it may cut into my lunch period a bit if he talks to me for a long time."

"Well," Jayden answered, "Rebecca and I also have a 9:00 a.m. class. We have an anatomy and physiology class together which is combined today with our lab session so we will finish at eleven thirty for a lunch break before our next classes. Rebecca and I will head over to the cafeteria and find seats in the northeast corner shortly after eleven thirty, and then you can join us whenever you finish your appointment with Professor T. Okay?"

"Okay, that's great . . . I'm hoping it won't take longer than a half hour . . . but when are *your* appointments? I wanna get together after all three of us meet with T so we can compare notes."

"Mine is also today. It's after my first afternoon class—psychology—and before a small break I have in front of my Medical/Legal Ethics class, so it's at 2:30 p.m." Jayden added. "When's yours, Rebecca?"

"Mine is after my last class of the day, Political Science, so it's scheduled at four thirty. I will just be getting out of class and will have to hurry not to be late. If there's any way we can see each other after your interview, Jayden, that would be great, but if not I'll just go on Ken's advice about how his meeting with Professor T went. Anyway, even though we'll be meeting for lunch and whether we meet up after that or not, should we meet again at the cafeteria at 5:30 p.m. for dinner, then head over to the dorm by 6:30 or 7:00 p.m. Maybe we can pick up some snacks for us to eat later in the dorm when we relax and talk. We can compare notes about our one-on-one meetings with Professor T. Nagorra this evening . . . and if we break by 9:00 p.m., we'll still have time to tackle our first homework assignments . . . and hopefully we will congratulate one another on successfully completing our first day at college! What do you think?"

Both Jayden and Ken enthusiastically agreed with her plan, and then Ken said, "Jayden, it looks as if you and I have the same ethics class and that Rebecca and I have the same political science class! That's cool! So you guys cannot get rid of me very easily. Gee whiz, I guess we'll just *have* to become great friends or *I* won't help you with your homework . . . great student that I am!"

"Hey, that's perfect! But . . . ummmm . . . it is a question of *who* will be helping *whom* . . . *I* may just be the greatest mind here," Jayden quipped.

"Oh no, you don't. You are clearly demonstrating what absolute male chauvinists you guys are. *I*, being the female here, just may have the *best* mind amongst us . . . so watch out!"

They laughed, happy about their easy camaraderie and the teasing they all seemed to enjoy. It lightened the moment and allowed Rebecca and Jayden to forget the anxiety they felt about . . . something . . . they knew not what . . . but something that seemed to warn them to be careful. They agreed that something caused the hairs on the back of their necks to rise when they walked into the seminar this morning . . . but what? What?

Rebecca had presented them with a good plan that fit everyone's schedule, and so they agreed to meet for lunch and then again for dinner, after which they would spend some time in Rebecca's little sitting room. It would take time for them to get used to their schedules, but it was a good idea to establish some camaraderie and to develop their friendships and with it a support base. Rebecca told them about the note her roommate had left for her, and they too were anxious to meet the mystery woman sharing Rebecca's room. Each of them secretly hoped that she would turn out to be someone super with whom they could all share a friendship. But until tomorrow night . . . they'd still be just Jayden, Rebecca and Ken, and they could only hope that Rebecca's roommate would fit right in with all three of them.

Off they went to their respective classes: Jayden and Rebecca to anatomy and physiology and Ken to a prelaw class. The anatomy and physiology professor wore a white lab coat, half glasses sitting precariously on the end of her nose, and latex gloves on her hands which she kept snapping at the wrists. She was tall and slim, spoke quickly and to the point, and seemed to remember everyone's name immediately. She stood at the head of one of the two long tall lab tables and moved from one to the other as she spoke.

"The first thing you will be doing today is entering the cooler at the back of the room and choosing your cat. It will be on a tray and completely covered, so those of you who might be squeamish need not worry. First you will choose a partner so that one cat will be shared by two people. Please note that in the center of the tables where you are sitting are tags. One of the two partners should fill in the tag with both your name and your partner's name and today's date. When you choose your cat, bring it to the table, in the tray and still covered and then I will explain how to attach the tag. The tag will be used by you to identify which cat is yours. You must always work only on your own cat, not one that bears a tag with someone else's name. You may now choose a partner, put on a pair of the rubber gloves from the boxes on the counters along the side of the room, and then go and choose a cat."

Rebecca was horrified. She hadn't realized that they would be dissecting a cat so quickly, and she'd thought that it would all be computerized somehow, not an actual cat! But Jayden laughed, assured her that she'd soon think nothing of it, and took her hand to drag her toward the cooler. "You choose, Jayden, I don't even want to look!"

When each pair of students obtained a cat, Professor Sendnik continued. "Okay . . . now you have all felt the weight and coolness of the cat and tray and swallowed hard. Now please position your trays so that the bottom or rear legs of the cat are closest to you—not the head—you can accomplish this if you fold back the plastic cover so at least the bottom half of the cat can be viewed."

After the loud rustling of plastic being repositioned, and some grunts and groans and words of horror, the room quieted and the professor again began to speak. "You've made it past the first step. You will only have to uncover that part of the cat upon which you will be working on if you'd prefer, but believe me, you will be okay with all of this within a few weeks. The worst part will be the smell of formaldehyde. If you plan a career in medicine, what you learn here will be invaluable. You will be given your lab assignments and your textbook assignments, and both will entail a lot of memorization. You will be tested every other week on your lab work and every alternative week on your textbook assignments. That means one test every week. If you fall behind in your lab assignments, you can come into the lab at any time . . . provided there is available space for you. Any questions?"

Only one student raised his hand asking, "Where should we attach the tag?"

"Hold the tag so that your names are facing you. The trays should be placed so that the rear legs of the cat are facing you, not the head. Attach the tag to the rear leg on your right by wrapping the elastic around the leg twice, and leave enough slack to allow the tag to overlap the edge of the tray and thus be seen easily when you retrieve your tray again. Place your tray on any available shelf space in the cooler, but be sure to place it where the tag is facing you and the names can be seen. Try to remember where you put your tray so you can retrieve it quickly and easily the next time you attend a lab. Get your cat as soon as you come to class so there is no line or rush to the refrigerator at any one time. Now, you can remove your gloves and place them in any one of the large trash receptacles in the four corners of the room. You will want to wash your hands and can do so in either of the four sinks here in the lab or in one of the bathrooms outside the lab. But before you leave, please copy the assignment that is written on the blackboard, and have this assignment completed when you come to the next class. Are there any additional questions?" And when no one seemed to have a question, the professor finished with the words, "Okay then, you may leave. See you in a few days."

When they met for lunch, Jayden and Rebecca looked expectantly at Ken. "Well, what happened? How did your appointment go? What did he say? What did the professor ask?"

"Well, when I got to Professor T's office, I was a few minutes early. He wasn't yet there, so I sat in one of the chairs in front of his desk, and almost immediately this guy, I think his name was Durk, sauntered in demanding to know what I was doing there. He was a sophomore, not a freshman, and really had a chip on his shoulder. It almost seemed as if he was, well, sort of proprietary . . . I mean, as if he thought that I'd somehow infringed on his territory. It was weird. He was belligerent and asked me all kinds of questions, but when Professor Nagorra arrived, he just sort of slunk out with his tail between his legs, almost as if he were . . . I don't know . . . like . . . afraid of him! I'll point him out to you if I see him again. He was a good-lookin' guy, ya know the type. Usually appeals to the gals because he is tall, athletic . . . he looks as if he works out. He was cocky, sure of himself, and well . . . rude. I think he worked in T's office or something. I mean, he acted as if he was often there and supposed to be there.

"Anyway, the prof was very nice. He said that he wanted me to come to him if I was worried about anything regarding my grades, or about a particular instructor, or even about a personal relationship with another student. I wasn't sure about the 'relationship with another student' thing. I mean, do they do that? I mean, shouldn't it only be if you were bullied or something more serious rather than . . . well, I don't know. It just seemed . . . odd.

"But what was really weird was that he seemed to want to know about both of you. Like how long I've known you, where we met, where each of us came from, and even if the two of you were . . . uhh . . . ya know, boyfriend and girlfriend. I mean, wasn't that too personal a question? And why ask me? How did he even *know* we'd become friends? I was glad that I didn't know a lot of the things he asked me because I could honestly say that I didn't know. But I felt he should ask *you*, not me! But then as soon as I got worried, really began to pull back from his questions, he seemed to sort of sense this and went back to telling me to come to him with problems and that there was very little that couldn't be worked out, and wished me a successful term at the school. Then he stood up, shook hands with me, ushered me to the door, and . . . that was it. That Durk guy was still in the outer office when I left and I feel that he listened to everything that was said and I didn't like that. But then again, maybe this is all paranoia on my part. I don't know . . . it was just a . . . feeling."

"How odd! I wonder why the professor asked you about Rebecca and me. We don't know him, we don't have a 'record' that could have alarmed him, and we only visited the campus once before we all arrived yesterday. I can't imagine why he'd ask you those questions. And it's eerie that he'd sense when you became uncomfortable with his questioning and suddenly pull back. I mean, if someone just *does that* . . . you know . . . *always* talks so personally . . . then they would not have pulled back. Rebecca, when you visit with him, don't give him too much information. Be careful. Remember . . . . there are a lot of kooks in the world, and we can always be more forthcoming after we see 'from whence he comes,' okay?"

"Okay, Jayden. I'll watch what I say. You know, Ken, Jayden and I were talking before you got here and admitted to one another that we'd both had a feeling that something was not right, wasn't as it should be. After we left the lecture hall this morning, and in fact as we first sat down, each of us had that feeling unbeknownst to the other until we mentioned it. And each of us felt that the professor had been staring at us until he started his lecture. We had decided that we'd just ignore those feelings and that it was just because all this was new to us . . . but with what you've just said, well, maybe we'd better listen to that inner voice. We've always been taught to pay attention to feelings like that because the angels that protect us and the spirits that want to harm us could have been activated. The Bible calls it 'discerning the spirits' and tells us to watch, to discern, and to run from anything that seems wrong."

"*What*? I never heard that stuff before. Come on, what 'spirits'? Ya mean ghosts?"

"No, Ken, it's the spirit world. You know, Satan, the devil, and the fallen angels that he took with him from heaven," Jayden replied.

"Oh come on, Jayden . . . come on. You don't *really* believe in that hogwash, do you? I mean, are you trying to tell me that some little guy in a red suit, with horns and a tail and a pitchfork, runs around with a bunch of leprechauns all bent on harming us? What for? Gee whiz. No offense, but that's crazy!"

"No it isn't, Ken. Let me ask you, do you believe in God, do you go to church, do you think that the Bible is the word of God?"

"Yeah, well, sure I do. I mean, my mom would kill me if I said no . . . she's always sent us to Sunday school and stuff . . . went to church for holidays and stuff . . . not much else, I guess . . . but little men in red outfits? Come on, no way! That's really too far out, Jayden."

"Well, then all you need is a short lesson in scripture so you can understand why the guy in the red suit, as you call him, does what he does. It's really interesting, Ken, and something that once you know, really helps you understand why the world is the way it is. It's kinda like having an 'aha' moment once you realize what is happening and why. Rebecca and I will show you when we crash tonight in Becca's "Private Lounge" to talk. Okay?"

"Yeah, okay. It sounds weird and unbelievable, but I'll listen anyway and we'll take it from there. I reserve the right to disagree, however, and if I do, I will have the right to claim to have the better brain here! In fact, I'll have to warn you that I may have to call the funny farm to come and get you . . . both of you! I hope you two don't turn out to be weirdos. It's lucky I like you guys!" Ken said with a grin.

"Okay, we'll take you on, Ken. I'll be glad to take up this challenge and to prove to you that only I, as sole female, have the better brain, and that if anyone has to go to the funny farm, well it might be you!" said Rebecca. "It will be fun, I promise you. Thanks for having an open mind. I'll look forward to our discussion." Wiping the smile from her face and pretending to frown while shaking her forefinger at Jayden, she continued, "But as for you, Jayden, cut out the Becca's "Private Lounge" business or I'll start calling the sitting room outside the room you and Ken share . . . . Ken and Jayden's Hangout for Chauvinists!"

Jayden teased her saying, "Ooh, Becca, we're scared . . . please don't hurt us. We give in . . . we promise that we'll simply refer to *both* our sitting areas as the Hangout and just have to say 'yours or mine' when we plan to meet. *Please* forgive us. *Please* don't hurt us! Deal?" And Ken too joined in the fun and began to look afraid and to pretend to cower from Rebecca and to tremble in fear.

Laughing at how silly the guys were acting, watching their faces and gestures indicating fear and supplication, Rebecca replied, "Good. You *should* be afraid! I *am* quite formidable, you know! But you have obviously learned your lessons well and listened to your queen Becca. I *do* expect my wishes to be obeyed by my subjects, and I will later reward you for doing so with some mango nectar and some cookies when you arrive at the Hangout tonight. I'm pretty sure that nectar and cookies are some of the goodies my mom placed in my fridge."

Their lunch break over, they said their good-byes with a hug for one another and went their separate ways. Rebecca left for her history class, Jayden for his psych class, and Ken to a prelaw class. At two thirty, Jayden went to Professor T's office for his one-on-one interview. The office was empty when he entered, so he sat in the outer office to wait. When the professor arrived, he grunted and waved his fingers at Jayden indicating that Jayden was to follow him into the inner office. Again using his fingers, he pointed to the chair that Jayden should occupy and sat behind his desk and looked at the papers before him.

"I see that you are a straight-A student, Jayden. That's good, but I have to warn you that getting in with . . . uhhh . . . girls . . . will hurt your grades. How long have you known Rebecca? You two seem pretty cozy."

Jayden was shocked by the professor's line of questioning, and for a moment he could not answer. When the professor pressed him, he said, "Rebecca is a long-time friend . . . . my friend and a friend to my family. She is like a sister to me. But . . . uhh, Professor . . . I think it's out of line for you to ask me this kind of a question."

"I'm in this business a long time, Jayden, and I know you—and all the other students—and I am just trying to warn you . . . to stay away from her and stick to your studies. Okay, any questions? If not, you can go now."

Still shocked by the cavalier attitude of the professor, and by the personal things he'd asked, Jayden got up and left. *Something isn't right here,* he thought. And as Jayden left, the professor thought, *I don't like that kid. He's too brazen for his own good. Who does he think he is to question me and to dare talk to me like that? I'll have to teach him a lesson.*

Later that day, Professor T. Nagorra was sitting behind his desk when Rebecca entered his office. When he saw her, he gestured for her to come through the outer room and directly into his personal office. He was once again struck by the simple elegance of her natural style in dress, hair, and makeup. Now he was about to learn whether or not she could back up her aura with any inner substance, or for that matter, with the brains and common sense he callously felt was lacking in many of the other students.

Durk had been standing in the outer office and intercepted Rebecca when she entered. The professor heard Durk ask her what she wanted and then begin to fawn as he realized the quality of the girl who stood before him and answered him with such dignity. He heard Durk say awkwardly, "I'm Durk, what's your name?" and he heard Rebecca reply giving him only her first name. Professor T. Nagorra was suddenly wary of Durk's intentions toward Rebecca, and a wave of jealousy struck him as he imagined Durk winning her favor. He was surprised by the sudden onslaught of words that entered his mind: *Don't you dare try to impress her! She's mine!*

He quickly stood from behind his desk, called out to Rebecca to get her attention, and once again gestured that Rebecca was to sit in one of the chairs in front of his desk. Then he jumped forward to personally escort her to the seat that faced the setting sun so he could see her face clearly. Her skin was flawless and her eyes clear with just a hint of wariness hidden in their depths. For an instant, he wondered how he knew that she was wary of him. He welcomed her to the school using all the charm he could muster and then began to ask her why she chose the school . . . and if she'd been accompanied by any friends, perhaps a roommate? He also asked her how she had come to know Ken and Jayden.

Rebecca was stunned by his questions, especially so soon into the conversation, and she became frightened. His questions were so blatantly out of place. They were too personal too soon, and she remembered what Ken had said. She wished that she had spoken with Jayden to learn what he'd experienced. But she tried not to jump to conclusions. Despite her good intentions, she became frightened and wary and prayed silently for God to help her answer. Her quick mind told her to change the direction of the question, and with a forced exuberance she began describing the entourage of people who'd accompanied her to the campus and had set up her room so beautifully. When she finished her little story about her family's assistance, and before the professor could ask another question, she tried to distract him further by telling him that she seemed to have a mystery roommate and how anxious she was to meet her. Then she went on about their plans to do so the following evening.

Rebecca knew that she was rambling in her monologue, but she didn't know what else to do. She went from one subject to another and even embarked on the anatomy and physiology class she had attended that morning and the concerns she had about the dissections required in her lab classes. She glanced at the clock on the wall adjacent to his desk and saw with relief that she would soon have to leave to meet Ken and Jayden for dinner.

Professor Nagorra watched her, in awe of her facial expressions, her smile, her perfect teeth, and the beautiful proportions of her features. He watched and he listened, never before so enthralled with a student. Warning bells went off in his head, but another force egged him on in thought and encouraged his interest. He'd seen her glance at the clock, and he too realized that she would soon have to leave, and he felt a sudden wave of disappointment.

He heard his next appointment arrive and knew that his time with Rebecca was at an end. Though Rebecca was still speaking, he knew that Durk and the student who'd just arrived were talking and realized for the first time that he'd never shut the door after Rebecca arrived, and whoever was in his outer office would have heard everything that was said. In his most professional manner, he reluctantly drew his conversation with Rebecca to an end and escorted her to the door, reminding her to visit his office at least once a week and to come to him for anything she might need. He could see Durk raise his eyebrows and scowl sardonically at his request that Rebecca visit each week—*that*, Durk knew, was highly unusual. But Professor Nagorra didn't care what Durk thought nor did he look at the student who'd just arrived.

As the professor turned to re-enter the inner office, Durk asked the next student scheduled to meet with the professor to wait in the outer office and followed the professor, closed the door behind him, and sat in the chair just recently occupied by Rebecca. "What's up with you?" Durk asked. "Why all that bull about seeing that girl every week? Who is she? And why did you ask her about her other friendships? You had better not get involved again. What is she to you anyway? Lay off her."

"Durk, you'd better shut your mouth. I've had about all I can take today, and what I do is none of your business. I am a counselor and advisor to some of the students, and that's all you need to know. If you ever talk to a student who I am scheduled to see in my office, I will fire you. And if the door to the outer room is open, I want you to close it. Do you understand? And keep your mouth shut and your thoughts to yourself. Is that clear?"

"Well, you don't have to get on your high horse with me—don't forget, I know a lot—and if you won't tell me what's going on, I'll find out some other way, do *you* understand?"

The professor was taken aback by Durk's words and realized that he'd let their relationship get out of control by allowing too many off the record conversations and casual get-togethers occur between them. He'd have to do something about Durk, get him back in line. "Durk, I've been very generous with you, helped you bring up your grades, helped you out of some ticklish situations, made sure you had enough money for school, and so if I were you I'd be careful about the way you speak to me and the liberties you take. If you want to destroy the hope of continuing to enjoy those amenities, then just keep this up. Got it? Remember, without my help you won't last here."

"Yeah, yeah, I got it," Durk replied, but underneath, he was fuming. *How dare this guy talk to me like that after all the things I've done for him, all the times I've covered for him. Doesn't he realize that I know so much about him that, if he wasn't tenured here, I could get him fired?* But Durk also realized that he needed to be in the good graces of the professor for the next three years if he wanted to graduate, and so it wasn't worth getting on his bad side. *But what was it that made the professor act so . . . so blatantly . . . obvious in front of this girl?* And he determined to get to the bottom of it . . . secretly.

When Durk ushered the next student into the professor's office, he carefully closed the door. Then he also closed the door leading to the hallway. He sat down behind the desk in the outer office, which was used by the secretary who helped the professor twice each week, and began to look for the list of students who the professor would be counseling this semester. He knew that when the secretary came in again she would be entering this list into the computer to forward to the administration office.

After searching through three different stacks of paper, he found what he was looking for: the list of students who the professor would personally be counseling. He searched the names for someone named Rebecca, and from that he learned her last name. With her first and last name he would be able to search a data base from which he could learn which dorm and which room in that dorm she was living. He could also learn what classes she was taking. Durk wanted to find her, to meet her again, away from the professor . . . maybe even warn her. He wanted to get to know her; he wanted to know what the professor wanted with her. He wasn't about to let this go. Something was up. For now, however, he'd gotten what he wanted; and he ran to his next class, not wanting to be late. He'd already missed his earlier class and needed to catch the professor of that class to get the reading assignment. He'd tell him that Professor T had needed him, and it would be okay. They were buddies.

Rebecca too was hurrying. She was to meet Ken and Jayden in the cafeteria. As she walked along the corridors, her thoughts went to her earlier class in political science. She was glad that Ken was attending the class with her and that they could sit together. When she'd walked into the smaller lecture hall where the political science class was being conducted, she saw Ken waving to her from the third row up from the dais from which the instructor would lecture. Ken had saved her a seat and had already opened his laptop so he could take notes. They had greeted one another warmly and then settled into their seats to await the professor.

Quiet descended as the professor walked into the room, and he began the class by saying, "We are going to study the science of politics by working from today's issues backward to the issues faced by FDR. You will be expected to research the topic for each class prior to that class so that each of you will have something to contribute either through a question or an observation. Anyone who has not done their research will be asked to leave class and have their research on my desk prior to the next class. Your grades will reflect your failure to complete that assignment on time. Is that clear?"

Everyone murmured some form of assent as the professor looked around the room expecting a reply from every student. Satisfied by the response he had garnered from everyone, the professor continued taking attendance and then began his lecture. "The most important current political issue, or need actually, is to provide everyone with social justice, not just here at home, but also globally. The role of government is to guarantee and implement this goal. This can only be accomplished by ending a system by which only a few succeed, while others find themselves in poverty. Ask yourself: Do I deserve a home, a job, a car, food, an education, and health care? And then ask yourself, If *I* deserve this, doesn't everyone? Wouldn't that be only fair and just? How we plan to achieve this goal will be the main thrust of what we will be discussing."

When the instructor paused, seeming to expect a rousing positive response, not everyone responded; and the less than enthusiastic reaction of the class caused the professor to frown and say, "It looks as if we have some hardcore capitalists in this class. Am I right?" This time no one responded and quiet descended upon the room. No one dared make eye contact with the professor. "Well," he went on, "you will learn throughout this course how much good government can do for its citizens as it transforms through social justice, reparation, redistribution of wealth, and the demise of greedy capitalists all of which will unite the world in a common goal. Right now many of you are misinformed, but as we move through this class you will begin to understand and support those principles which I will be teaching you. Your assignment for our next class is to read the first three chapters of your textbook. And let me warn you, you'd better read every assignment and come prepared to answer and ask questions. Class dismissed."

Ken had turned to Rebecca asking, "Wow. I guess that we're misinformed and greedy capitalists! What the heck did that mean? How is he so sure of *what* we are? How can he state with such surety that we are misinformed?"

"I don't know, Ken, but he certainly has jumped to a conclusion there," Rebecca had said. "It will be interesting to see what our textbook says. I hope it's straightforward and unbiased. There has been so much turmoil in politics lately, which is what piqued my interest and made me want to learn more about the role of government and thus to take this class, but I am also interested in how our Constitution limits government and assures our liberties. I wonder if my two classes . . . . history and politics . . . .

will be teaching a conflicting viewpoint. But then again, maybe that's a good thing. Maybe that will give me a better idea of the both sides of these questions."

"Well, you could be right. Better to learn both sides rather than one side and be influenced only by that. This should be interesting."

Then Rebecca said, "Well, let's get going. I'll run up for my meeting with Professor T. Nagorra, then I'll meet you in the cafeteria . . . then we'll eat and then we'll talk about men in red suits!" They gathered their belongings and left the classroom.

When Rebecca arrived in the cafeteria, Jayden and Ken were already there. Rebecca told them about her meeting with Professor T. Nagorra and they were once again surprised by his personal line of questioning. Later, just as they had finished their dinner, Durk walked up to their table and said, "Rebecca! Hello again," and nodded to Ken acknowledging that they too had met.

"Hello . . . uhhh . . . Durk . . . right? It looks as though you already know Ken, and this is my friend Jayden. Jayden, this is Durk who I met outside of Professor T's office."

"Hey, Durk. Nice to meet you."

"Yeah, you too," Durk replied. "You guys freshmen?" They all nodded, and Durk added, "I'm a sophomore and will be glad to show you guys the ropes. Ya know, like who are the best profs, the best coaches, the best eating places in town, best pizza delivery, best parties."

Ken quickly answered Durk saying, "That's awfully nice of you, Durk. Sounds great to know who to call about getting a pizza delivered to the dorm when we're either famished or just want to stay in to study . . . maybe we will take you up on that offer someday."

"Why wait? I'll come by tonight and take all three of you to the big sophomore First Day Back Bash. They will have puh-len-teee beer!"

"Thanks, Durk, but we've already made plans for tonight. Maybe another time," Ken said.

"Yeah, thanks, Durk. We'll see you again. Bye now."

"No, you have to come," Durk quickly added. "I mean, you'll meet lots of students and have fun."

"No thanks, Durk, we already have a commitment for tonight which we can't break."

Durk wasn't happy; in fact, he disliked Ken. He was too strong armed about not coming to the party tonight and not even allowing Rebecca to make up her own mind. But at least he'd made contact with Rebecca and could now approach her more easily in the future. He would look for her en route to a class or to her dorm and hope to catch her alone. Durk didn't want to let Rebecca see his anger toward Ken, so he acquiesced as gracefully as possible saying, "Okay, guys, you'll be missing a great time, but I'll let you know when another party time crops up. See ya." Durk wondered why the other dude—Jayden was his name—hadn't said much. Durk knew, however, that Jayden had been sizing him up and he wasn't too pleased by that.

The three friends went back into the line to fill a tray with whatever snacks they wanted for that evening. "Let's not just eat cookies," Jayden suggested. "I'm gonna get myself a thick ham and cheese sandwich on rye bread to bring back to the dorm."

Jayden's mom had packed what she called a "care package" for him and had filled it with lots of things to eat and then had placed those items either in his little fridge or in the kitchen cabinet. But for tonight he'd just thought it would be easier to have something that was already made up and relatively healthy. They needed to stay sharp and healthy.

They commented on the many choices the cafeteria offered to eat. And they liked the list that had been posted that explained the calories, protein, carbs, and fiber in each food. They could choose from salads, sandwiches, and hot items. As they walked back to the dorm, they talked about the classes they'd attended that day, and Jayden teased Rebecca by threatening to psychoanalyze her once he learned some good "stuff" in his psychology class. Then Ken said that Rebecca seemed to have an admirer and went into a vivid and hilarious description of Durk as a movie star. Rebecca interrupted Ken saying, "I first met Durk outside of Professor Nagorra's office, and he seemed sort of aggressive to me, but then in the cafeteria he seemed a little nicer. But come on, he's no admirer . . . come on, don't start that dumb stuff." Then Rebecca changed the subject as they left the cafeteria and began walking back to their dorm.

"Jayden, I was sort of turned off by the professor of our political science class. I wish you were there. The professor seems biased. You know, pro big government, progressive. I really wanted to learn about all sides, all viewpoints, and make my own decisions. Didn't you think he seemed pretty one-sided, Ken?"

"Yes, Rebecca, he almost scared me. But I guess we should give him the benefit of the doubt and just see what happens. I guess everyone has their own point of view, and maybe it's hard to leave that behind if you teach a subject for which you have a strong opinion."

"Well, keep me posted, guys. I'm very interested in that stuff too, and I'd love to know what you are learning and how this guy teaches. If he is biased, Rebecca and I will just bring our Uncle Jim to his classroom and he'll straighten him out. Eh, Rebecca?"

"Oh, Jayden, can you imagine Uncle Jim and any professor of politics? It would be neat to see them in a debate! I love to listen to Uncle Jim. He's so . . . I don't know . . . so patriotic and so well informed and . . . well . . . like a defender of liberty! You'd like him Ken. He's really well informed and a really fun guy. He's courageous, opinionated too, but he usually backs up his thoughts with facts. Don't you think so too, Jayden?"

"You two related then? I mean, well, I met your family and have to say that you guys are really lucky to have such a close-knit and fun family—and from what you say, you are also able to debate some sensitive issues—but are you all related?" Ken asked.

"No, well, not really. Aunt Sarah, Uncle Caleb, and Uncle Josh are siblings, and they are married to Uncle Matt, Aunt Ann, and Aunt Deb. Uncle Matt's sister is Aunt Barbara, and she is married to Uncle Jim. They were the original, uhhh, clan—I guess you could say—eight people strong and they are the people who are related to one another! My grandfather has always attended the same church that they attend and met them there. When Aunt Sarah and Uncle Matt bought their home, they became Aunt Mary and Uncle Kevin's neighbors. And Rebecca is related to Mary. Rebecca and her mom moved into Mary and Kevin's carriage house. My stepdad, Wade, is Uncle Jim's best friend, so my mom, Ruth, also came into their circle. Have I confused you enough?"

"Wow, that will take some practice to remember! But you guys are so lucky to have them around, and to all get along so well."

"You know, Ken," Rebecca added, "it's really love not their matching DNA that holds everyone together, and that love comes from their faith in God. It's so amazing to watch them interact and to see that even when they go through heartbreak they always find something positive in it—some sort of learning experience as a result of what they went through. Sharing their concerns with one another draws them even closer together. My mom, Elizabeth, adopted me when I was just a baby and is the best mother anyone could have. Her husband, my dad, died when I was twelve. Then when I was fourteen my mom got sick and asked me if I wanted to try to find my birth mother. We did and that's Mary. So now, amazingly we are all a family and all so close. Both my moms have such big hearts to love me and now they even love one another . . . so that's my story."

"That's a beautiful story. Many people would have been jealous if they had to share a daughter . . . . Hey, you'd make a million bucks if you could package that kinda love and understanding . . . and friendship . . . and sell it!"

"It's free, Ken, to anyone. It's just a matter of knowing what's available! Want some?

"Ha, yeah, sure, just like that! But sure I'd 'like some' if you'll tell me how to get it . . . and it doesn't cost anything!"

"Okay, you've got a deal. We'll impart our great wisdom upon you as we go along so that you too can become a member of our great and invincible clan!" Jayden quipped.

They laughed together as Ken bowed, first to Rebecca, then to Jayden, and then very formally to the wall in the stairwell, saying, "Thank you, Queen Rebecca, thank you, Jayden, and thank you too, Mr Wall! And now, dear friends, looks as if we've entered the building and will soon be at the door that houses the famous, and has been dubbed as the one and only . . . *Hangout!*

Arm in arm and step in step, they climbed the stairs to the second floor laughing all the way. Ken and Jayden ran up to their fourth-floor room to freshen up and leave their book bags, and Rebecca also freshened up before taking her desk chair from her room into their tiny sitting room where there was a loveseat and one chair already. She wanted to have seating for four in case her roommate arrived sooner than expected. Rebecca placed the sandwiches and some cold bottles of water from the room's tiny fridge on the little table in front of the loveseat and waited for Jayden and Ken. There was a large bottle of mango nectar in the fridge, but she decided to wait and make sure they wanted some before pouring it.

It was still early, just about 6:00 p.m., so if they talked for a few hours, Rebecca would still have time to read her political science chapters and take some notes on it before she went to bed. Today had been her busiest class day, but since she only had three sessions of each class per week, the other days in the week brought staggered classes which would give her plenty of time for reading, research, papers she might have to write, and memorizing what she might need for her exams. Her schedule, except for this one day a week, would be very manageable.

Jayden and Ken arrived noisily, teasing one another about who should enter through the door first since together they were too "broad" to fit. Rebecca was glad that Jayden had a friend in his roommate and hoped that her roommate would be just as nice as Jayden's. She was looking forward to getting together with her roommate, but tonight she wanted to see how Ken would react to what he would probably consider somewhat surprising about the "guy in the red suit"! She worried that Ken would think them "too" religious and shy away from what they thought he should know. *Oh well, we'll just do our best and take it from there. Please, God, open his heart.*

Jayden and Ken played musical chairs for a few minutes before finding "their" favorite seat. "If we're gonna get together like this, we might as well be comfortable,"

Jayden said. "Well then," Ken added, "we'd better go out and buy some man-sized furniture. Could they have made this room or this furniture any smaller? I mean, look at the size of us, and the size of this furniture. If I lay down on this loveseat my feet dangle over the end!"

"Typical males," retorted Rebecca, "never satisfied, always complaining, and always putting off getting down to the work of the moment!"

"What work? We're just here to relax after a hard first day of classes!" Both Ken and Jayden tried to outdo one another in their exaggerated sprawls by extending their legs as far as they would go.

"Okay, see if I care. Sprawl, joke, whatever, and when the little guy in a red suit comes after us and Ken doesn't understand what's happening and therefore has so clue as to what to do, then it will be your fault, Jayden! And if I'm the one attacked and Ken doesn't know how to protect me, you'll feel guilty! So go ahead, waste time, hoard your great wisdom—see if I care!" And then Rebecca, to be sure that they knew she was teasing them, grabbed all the throw pillows, made a bed out of them on the floor, and fell on them and began to emulate making an angel in the snow by moving her arms and legs in and out, and by doing so she took up all the floor space. They laughed.

"Who's gonna attack you?" Ken said. "What the heck are you talking about, Rebecca? That's a scary thing to say. Waddaya mean? What attack? By whom, and how?"

"Okay, here's the deal . . ." Jayden began, "we really *do* have an enemy, really. And there really *is* a devil, Satan, and he doesn't want you or any of us to be loyal to God—ya know, to have a relationship with God—and if we do, or start to, he will attack. And in a lot of situations, he's capable of causing some pretty terrible things to happen by influencing certain people."

"Yeah, right. He's gonna come and whisper in my ear that I should go and punch a professor and get myself kicked out of school, and I'll *gladly* do it? Yeah, right. Come on, Jayden. Get real!"

"Okay, Ken. Let's be serious now. Once I knew that we'd be talking about the devil tonight, Satan, I copied a couple of verses I found through the concordance I have in my computer and will give you the copy but will first read them to you. You won't absorb it all right away, but just keep an open mind and think about it . . . just in case. Okay, here goes:

"Matthew 12:45 says, 'Then goeth he and taketh with himself seven other spirits more wicked than himself, and they enter in and dwell there, and the last state of that man is worse than the first. Even so shall it be also unto this wicked generation.'

"Luke 8:27-36 says in verse 29, '(For he had commanded the unclean spirit to come out of the man. For oftentimes it had caught him: and he was kept bound with chains and in fetters; and he brake the bands, and was driven of the devil into the wilderness.)'

"Matthew 8:16 explains that there were *many* possessed by evil spirits in Christ's time and that He cast them out by his word, and they were healed. 'When the evening was come, they brought unto him many that were possessed with devils: and he cast out the spirits with his word, and healed all that were sick.'

"And last but not least, here's a couple of verses that tells us what Satan is capable of: He can move men to do his bidding (1 Chronicles 21:1), can walk back and forth on the earth (Job 1:7), cause illness (Job 2:7), can take God's word from men's hearts (Mark 4:15), can enter man (Luke 22:3 and John 13:27), can blind the minds of them which believe not (2 Corinthians 4:4), can transform himself (2 Corinthians 11:14), can send messengers to hurt man (2 Corinthians 12:7), can hinder people (1 Thessalonians 2:18), and can produce signs and has powers (2 Thessalonians 2:9). It is important for us to know that Satan is capable of producing signs and has supernatural powers, because that's what convinces us to accept his premises: *'the working of Satan with all power and signs and lying wonders.'*"

"Geez, Jayden, that's heavy stuff. It is *so* far out there, Jayden, that all I can say is . . . . come on. Who really reads that stuff, and how can you apply it to today? You sound as if this really happens. If I didn't think that you were serious, I would never believe this stuff you've just read. In fact, I'd think you needed to be in a funny farm."

"Well, believe it or not, you should read these verses and even look them up in the Bible and mull it over a bit before you jump to conclusions, Ken."

"Yeah, Ken, Jayden is right. Why take the chance that we are right and you are wrong?"

"Well, you both seem so convinced. I don't know . . . are you pulling my leg maybe? Well, okay. I'll look at it again, and I'd like to talk about it again, but for now, I've got to hit my books and computer and get some work done for tomorrow's classes. I will check this out, and honestly, I do want to talk about this again. I guess if any of it is true, it's worth another look anyway. Thanks, Rebecca, for having us over tonight. I hope we can do this often. I learned a lot. See ya tomorrow."

"Okay, Ken, it was great. I enjoyed it too. See ya tomorrow."

"Good night, Rebecca."

"Good night, Jayden."

Chapter 4

Durk and Rebecca

Durk could hardly wait to attend his political science class. He'd learned that Rebecca was in the same class when he'd checked her schedule after locating her name on the student list in Professor T's office. As he approached the political science lecture hall, Durk noticed that he was a few steps behind Rebecca and watched as she entered the classroom and climbed the steps to the third row of seats. He saw Rebecca wave to someone and claim the seat next to him after greeting him with a hug. Then he realized it was Ken whom he'd met in Professor T's office and felt a flush of jealous anger warm his face and cause him to clench his fists.

Rebecca was concentrating on pulling her laptop out of her shoulder bag and didn't see Durk enter nor take the seat directly behind her in the fourth row. When Ken and Rebecca were prepared for class and saw that the professor was not yet in attendance, they began to chat. Durk leaned forward to listen to their conversation and heard them speak about meeting Jayden at the Hangout and about a conversation they'd had concerning some guy in a red suit. Durk was totally confused by their words, but he was curious about why they would need to get together to talk about someone in a suit. He was also confused by Rebecca wanting to go to some hangout. She'd seemed like such an innocent. Yet if these two guys thought that they could get somewhere with Rebecca, why not him? *I'll ask around and find out where the Hangout is. I've never heard of it before, and I've been on campus for over a year.*

In addition to his classes, Durk spent time playing football. He was a member of the football team and a part-time paid assistant to Professor T. When he first came to the college, he'd needed the job for his spending money, and he needed his place on the football team to maintain the football scholarship he'd received which enabled him to go to college in the first place. He'd never required much sleep, so juggling his schedule to accommodate his obligations had never cut into his social life. He loved to party, and he liked the girls.

He and Professor T had become confidants toward the end of the last semester when a sticky matter arose in Professor T's life that Durk helped him cover up. Another professor had accused Professor T of tampering with the records of a female student by increasing her grades and had threatened to bring it to the attention of the dean. Durk developed a plan that would implicate the other professor in a far more "shady" situation and was able to avert the action that had been threatened.

Durk was now aware of many details about Professor T's private life. He'd taken Durk under his wing and reciprocated his loyalty by providing him with term papers and exam questions that would enable him to do well in his classes. He'd also promised that Durk would have a job as his assistant until he graduated. Durk often delegated his office work to one of the volunteers while he and Professor T would relax at Professor T's place for a few beers and a long talk about women or sports or the scrapes they'd been in. Durk's life was going well, and he had plenty of time for personal pursuits.

Women had always flocked to Durk, but while he enjoyed their company, he had never met anyone that he really cared about. Every infatuation quickly became boring and unfulfilling. Some would fawn over his star status on the football team or his position with Professor T, which enabled him to do and obtain special favors. Others seemed vacuous and empty. He felt that not one of his conquests had ever wanted to know the real Durk, and this had surprised him because he saw himself as hip and interesting and did not see that he lacked a value system. He treated others with contempt while demanding better for himself. But he sensed that while he had everything he wanted there was something missing in his life, and he felt a sort of emptiness in his heart that he didn't know how to fill.

He was surprised that after meeting Rebecca he continued to think about her and was actually shocked to realize that he occasionally thought about the kind of life he'd want if he were ever to marry and settle down. He'd never considered marriage, nor had he considered any relationship that might make demands on him. What he'd wanted was to be free to play the field whenever someone piqued his interest. He was aware of some impelling inner force drawing him to Rebecca, making it almost impossible to put her out of his mind. He was also aware that an inner instinct told him that to win Rebecca he'd have to appear different than he really was—more gallant, more respectful, more conservative, kinder. But what was the greatest surprise to him was that he felt willing to become all these things, willing to become someone else to win her over.

Conscious of the elegant manner in which Rebecca dressed, and of her perfect grooming, Durk used some of the money he'd amassed from dipping into the wallets and purses of professors and selling marijuana to students, to purchase two pair of dress slacks, three long-sleeve shirts, and a pair of leather loafers. He also went to a salon, instead of his usual barber, to have his hair cut and styled. Even he was surprised by how terrific he looked. His next step was to ask Professor T to get him the study and exam materials for the political science class which both he and Rebecca attended. He wanted to appear smart and studious and thus impress Rebecca during class with his ability to answer any questions put forth by their instructor.

He'd worn his old clothes to Professor T's office when asking for the materials he needed for class so the professor would not have any reason to question him. Thus, when the next political science class convened, Durk was prepared to be the star of the show by asking all the right questions and giving all the right answers. *And,* he thought, *when Rebecca looks at me, she'll see how great I look!* He'd planned not to enter the classroom until Rebecca arrived and he could see where she sat and choose a seat near her. When he saw her walking toward the door of the classroom, he caught his breath, entranced by her elegance and by how different she seemed when compared to her female classmates. He followed her into the hall, and as he watched her, he saw her face suddenly light up and her hand lift in a wave. He followed the direction of her eyes and saw Ken waving to her and indicating a seat next to him which he'd saved for her. *Well,* he thought, *I guess it will be a regular thing for them to sit together. What is the relationship between these two?* he wondered. *Why should I worry though; he's no competition, that's for sure.*

Durk chose to sit directly in front of Ken so he could watch Rebecca through his peripheral vision if he turned his head slightly toward her. She, on the other hand, would be able to see his daunting profile and perfect grooming, and she could watch him as he answered Professor Emil's questions. He planned to act surprised to see Ken and Rebecca and greet them warmly at the end of class. He hoped to walk out of the room with Rebecca. He might even draw Ken into a friendship so he could learn more about Rebecca.

His plan worked like a charm. He raised his hand when the professor asked a question, he answered the questions accurately, and he even received a few words of praise from the professor. "Good," "excellent," and "right on the mark." When the class was dismissed, he turned, pretended to suddenly notice Ken and gave him a hearty hello, offering his hand for a handshake. He ignored Rebecca until Ken said, "You remember Rebecca, don't you, Durk?" Then he turned to Rebecca saying, "Of course, how are you? It's nice to see you again."

Having overheard some of the conversation between Ken and Rebecca before the lecture began, Durk felt that he understood what their views might be concerning Progressivism, so he turned back to Ken asking, "Ken, I don't know about you, but it sure seems as if this class is leaning quite a bit in one direction. What do you think?"

"That may well be true, Durk. I'm a little concerned about it, but I want to keep an open mind and I like to know both sides of an issue anyway."

"Hey, Ken, are you by any chance interested in football? There's gonna be what I think will be a really good practice game on Saturday morning. Why don't you come? And bring whomever you'd like."

"Thanks, Durk. Sounds like fun. What time?"

"It's at 10:00 a.m., and afterward almost everyone goes down to the Pub for lunch, so plan on doing that too. Rebecca, see if you can round up some of your dorm friends to come to the game to support us. And come to the Pub afterward as well."

"You're on the team then?" Rebecca added.

"Yeah, I try. Since we divided our teammates into two groups to play against one another, I'll be playing quarterback for one of the teams. It won't be easy to play against our star quarterback though, so please be kind to me afterward."

Laughing at Durk's request and impressed by his friendliness and self-deprecating description of his football prowess, they agreed to attend the practice. "Okay, Durk, we'll try to make it, and we'll both ask our roommates to join us. Thanks. We'd better get going now. See you at the next brainwashing . . . oh, only kidding . . . I mean at the next political science class!"

Durk was thrilled by what had transpired. It was almost as if some lucky star was shining over him and helping him. His meeting with them couldn't have gone better! He'd won them over and was on his way to a relationship with Rebecca. He'd watched her carefully as she listened, and he had seen her pupils enlarge and her mouth open when she learned that he was on the football team, and a quarterback no less. Well, he wasn't really the quarterback but was one of the backups. He knew that he was meaner than any of the guys on the team and was pretty sure that he could pull off a good performance on Saturday. *Perfect*, he thought. *My plan is going along perfectly. I'll have her in the palm of my hand in no time!*

Ken and Rebecca hurried to the cafeteria where they planned to meet Jayden for dinner. Afterward they would go back to the dorm, to Rebecca's Hangout where they expected to finally meet Rebecca's mystery roommate. After dinner, they returned to Rebecca's room and saw that the hallway door had been framed with bright multicolored crepe paper. Taped to the center of the door into their dorm suite was an 8 1/2 x 11 sheet of paper:

Hello, Rebecca!

FINALLY we meet!

Enter in

for

lots of fun and laughs!

They were impressed. *What a sweet and thoughtful person she must be!* Rebecca thought. Ken and Jayden told her that they would run up to their rooms and wash up and then be down in a few minutes. "This way, Rebecca, you can enjoy the greeting that your roommate has planned for you. We'll be right back." So Rebecca pushed open the door and walked in. There she was met with a barrage of what almost seemed like sunshine! Feather boas of every vivid color had been hung on the walls of their little den and had been done in such an artful manner that the room looked alive. The throw pillows on the loveseat were also covered in the boas. And a striped throw rug in the same colors had been placed under the small coffee table. Four tall plastic glasses and four dessert plates sat on the little table; one set was in fuchsia, one set in parrot green, one in bright yellow, and another in vivid blue. One pitcher filled with liquid was fuchsia, one large plate filled with cookies was parrot green, one blue bowl filled with cashew nuts, and four yellow napkins completed the picture. Rebecca was stunned by all the work and thought that her roommate had put into their meeting.

Suddenly Kara jumped out from behind her bedroom door, and wearing boas around her neck and streaming down over a long bohemian skirt and white peasant blouse, she ran to Rebecca and threw her arms around her exuberantly, saying, "Finally, we meet! Hi, Rebecca!"

Rebecca dropped her book bag and hugged Kara back exclaiming, "Thank you, Kara! Everything looks so *wonderful* . . . you've done so much . . . you are so thoughtful . . . thanks so much. I'm so happy to *finally* meet you! Oh, and the cookies and drinks . . . wow, you've thought of *everything*!"

"Well, yeah . . . golly gee whiz, but I'm such a good guy . . . yeah . . . shucks . . . and you'd better *remember* that because I want us to be great friends, huh?"

"Absolutely, Kara. That's a deal." And Rebecca stuck her hand out to shake on it, and with that they were instant friends. As Rebecca studied Kara for a moment, she saw a lovely, warm, and genuinely kind young woman who had a desire to please those around her. Rebecca liked her immediately and felt a sense of relief. She wanted them to be friends and wanted Kara to like Ken and Jayden too. She'd seen Kara's inner beauty first and was so pleased by what she felt about Kara. Then Rebecca noticed her outer beauty. Kara was at least a foot taller than Rebecca and very slender—not skinny, just long and lean. Her fingers too were long and slim and her eyes almost almond shaped and deep brown in color. Her skin was smooth and radiant and deeply tanned. Her hair was incredibly long with a hint of curl, and hung almost to her waist. It was a deep shiny chestnut brown with red highlights. Her teeth were straight and very white and her smile quick and contagious. But Rebecca also felt that there was great wisdom emanating from her eyes, and suddenly had the feeling that this was perhaps from past sorrows.

Kara too was assessing Rebecca. She noted her ethereal light blue eyes with their ring of black which matched the deep black of her hair which was twisted into an elegant knot at the back of her head. Her face was a perfect oval. Kara sensed a natural reticence in Rebecca and was happy that she'd seemed genuinely pleased by Kara's welcome, and seemed to genuinely want them to be friends. Kara felt that a true friendship between them would make college life so much better. They'd each have one another's back.

Kara knew the value of a true friend and the pain of false friends. While she appeared welcoming, enthusiastic, and trusting, she was not. She was wary, and she was watchful; she was cautious and could be suspicious, but she wanted this friendship very much and was willing to work for it. She hoped that Rebecca would as well. A one-way street was not worth the pain it could bring. Kara just wanted to know where she stood. If there was not to be that friendship "connection" that she hoped for, okay; and while it would sadden her, she'd rather know up front so she wouldn't have expectations and then be disappointed. It was possible for them to be "passing acquaintances," people who could be civil and kind but would share no secrets and did not watch one another's back. If you knew this up front, there'd be no surprises. But Kara really hoped that Rebecca would be her friend, her true friend.

"Kara, I forgot to ask, is everything okay with your family? I mean, did you have an emergency to attend to?"

"No, not really, same old same old as they say. My family are true worriers and incredible communicators. Everyone has to know everything and form a great wagon train around one another whenever anything, even the littlest thing, happens. So when duty calls, I am never worried. It all works itself out, but they expect me to be there and me to be the one to solve all problems."

As Kara and Rebecca chatted and happily concluded that what they saw in one another they liked, they heard a knock on the door and opened it to Ken and Jayden who bore a box of candy for Kara. "This is a bribe, Kara," Jayden said as he handed her the candy. "It is so that you will *have* to like the two of us! Hi, I'm Jayden, and this is my sidekick and favorite roommate, Ken and we are Rebecca's good friends!"

Both young men extended their hand and were surprised when Kara brushed it aside. "Good friends hug," she said and grabbed them both in a bear hug. Jayden and Ken laughed, already liking this fearless, exuberant roommate of Rebecca's.

"Well, Jayden and Ken, I will open the box and sample one of the candies, and if I *like* it, then I will indeed like both of *you*. But if I don't, well, you might just have to bring candy *again* another time and continue to bribe me!"

"Deal! But perhaps you will sample the candy—like it, like us—but just to get more candy, tell us that you didn't like the candy," said Ken. "Do you think we fell off a turnip truck? We know the wiles of you women!"

Rebecca quickly added, "Kara . . . Jayden and I come from the same town and . . . uhhh . . . . extended family . . . . to attend college together . . . . so I took the liberty of asking Jayden and Ken to join us tonight . . . . I . . . . uhhh . . . . "

"Aha, Rebecca, that's great . . . . you've brought two smart men into our soiree. Why, with these gifts . . . . uhhh . . . . well, of course I will pretend that I do not like the candy, and Rebecca will back me up because we are now buddies. But I foresee that you will have to do more to keep me . . . uhh . . . us . . . in your good graces. Perhaps it was no coincidence that the plates and glasses came in a four-pack!"

"Absolutely!," Rebecca quipped. "Jayden and Ken have become buddies, so the two of us have no choice but to join forces ourselves and will certainly outwit both of them and will have to make them scramble. Although, let's face it, two women against two men? No contest. That automatically tips the scales in our favor!"

"Hah," Jayden quipped, "God made man first and made him superior to women."

"Really? Well, the way I heard it, God made man and then said, 'I can do better than that,' and made woman!"

"Kara's absolutely right, you guys," said Rebecca. "But okay now, take a seat and have some of the cookies and a glass of the great punch that Kara made for us, and look around. Look how Kara decorated the room. Isn't it gorgeous? I was so surprised and so pleased by her thoughtfulness."

"Yeah, it really looks great, colorful, cheerful, and we saw the note and decorations on the door too. That was cool. But then again, come on, if we are to be here on occasion, then how about some guy stuff, huh? I mean, pink? Feathers? Nahh, that's not for us manly men!"

"Ken we do have a TV for you to stare at. That's a 'guy stuff.' And when we come to visit *you*—that is, if we *deign* to gift you with such a visit—we will expect *your* sitting room to be well decorated and in a, ummm, 'guy' theme. It'll be *so* predictable . . . uhhh . . . sports stuff . . . beer logos . . . uhh . . . more sports stuff. Boring!"

"Kara . . . Rebecca," Ken replied, "I have a feeling that Jayden and I will have to make a quick study of 'quips for guys' so that we can even this playing field. You have obviously studied this art because you do a mighty fine job of 'quipping' with us, and so far you gals are winning the quip game! Jayden and I are going to practice though, and we will eventually get the prize. Just you wait!"

Rebecca quickly added, "Oh no, neither of you will ever win this game. We can outdo you two quite easily, but on the other hand, we may be willing to teach you so that you are not left behind in the 'quip field' and begin to feel . . . uhh . . . shall we say . . . uhhh . . . 'inferior'?"

"Inferior? Are you kidding me? What's a few 'quip' words compared to our superior brain, our superior brawn, our superior good looks, and our superior kindhearted intentions?"

"Jayden," Ken added, "there comes to mind a few little ditties that us guys need to remember about women. One is that we should never let women bother us for they know not what they do. Another is that some women are kind, polite, and sweet spirited, until you try to sit in their pew . . . uhh . . . I mean on their mini-couch. And finally, that God Himself doesn't judge a man until he's dead, while women . . . I'll leave the remainder of that sentence to your imagination. So let's just be the manly men we are and forgive these two poor unfortunate women who seek to outwit and outdo the stronger sex."

Both Rebecca and Kara picked up a throw pillow and hit each of them squarely in the chest. "Okay, let's stop kidding," Kara said, "and tell me what classes you have. I'm hoping we have some together. Or maybe that at the very least we have the same lunch period?" And Kara ran through her classes and time periods. "Right now my main major is liberal arts, but I hope to focus on a more specific discipline by next year."

"That sounds like a great idea, Kara. I'm in your early American history class, and I do have the same time period for lunch that you do. In fact, it looks as if we all have the same break for lunch," Rebecca replied.

"And you are in my psychology class," Jayden added.

"Ken? Anything?"

"No, just the same lunch period."

"Well, that's better than nothing. Do you mind if I join you at lunch time?"

"Are you kidding? Of course not. It will be a blast. We meet in the northeast corner as close to eleven thirty as possible and we don't have another class until 1:00 p.m. You?"

"Jayden, that's perfect. I don't have my next class until 1:00 p.m. either, so I will be sure to be there. In fact, on Fridays, my 1:00 p.m. is my only class. Everything is jammed into Mondays through Thursdays, and so on Fridays I'll be studying or writing my papers. Can I take a quick look at the notes any of you have from the classes I take with you so I'll be up to par?"

"Yeah, sure. We all write 'em right in our computers and can just run you off a copy . . . . how's that? Well, gals, speaking of studying, I've got some reading to do for tomorrow, so I'm gonna call it a night. I am so happy to meet you, Kara, and so happy for Becca that she has such a nice roommate. Kara, walk up to our room with us and Ken and I can run those copies right away. See you all for lunch tomorrow, right?. G'night, Becca."

"Yeah, me too," said Ken. "Thanks for a great evening. See you both tomorrow." And with hugs all around, Ken and Jayden left, and Kara went up to get her notes and Rebecca began to clean up the plates and glasses, put away the leftover cookies and punch, and think about how much they had enjoyed the evening. Then Rebecca ran her notes off for Kara and when she returned gave her a warm hug, and each girl went into their own room to catch up on their reading assignments for the next day.

The next day Rebecca asked Kara if she would like to attend the football practice on Saturday, and told her that Jayden and Ken would be there also. Kara was delighted and jumped right into plans to bring a backpack filled with wonderful snacks for all four of them to munch on during the game. "You are so thoughtful, Kara. How do you always think of these great things to do for others and so quickly?"

"I don't know, Becca, but it's sort of just thinking about what *I* would like and so maybe *others* would like it too, but it's also from having a big family and being the oldest. I have a little hot pack that you can warm in the microwave and then put it in a special heat-retaining bag. What if we buy those little pastry-wrapped hot dogs and the cheesy jalapenos that you just heat up. We can put them in with the hot pack and nibble on them at the start of the game. We can also make some sandwiches cut into quarters and eat them as the game winds down. What do you think?"

"Super! And let's ask the guys to bring some cold green tea. Ya know, the ones in the bottles. I think that Jayden has a sort of four-bottle canvas cooler he could put them in. My family is health conscious and said that we should never drink out of plastic bottles, especially if they have ever been in the heat, since the chemicals in the plastic leach into the liquid."

And so when Saturday arrived, off they went to the practice game, arm in arm, friends, happy, and looking forward to spending the day together. Rebecca had explained to Kara that someone they'd met in their political science class named Durk had invited them to the game and that he would be playing, but she hadn't said much else about him. So when Durk ran over to them, dressed in his full football regalia, looking quite splendid, and sneaking a glance at Rebecca while addressing Ken and Jayden, Kara later whispered to Rebecca teasing her about Durk having a romantic interest in her. "Absolutely not," Rebecca replied so indignantly that Kara decided she had better not tease Rebecca about Durk. But to herself, Kara thought of the line from Shakespeare: "*Methinks thou doth protest too much!*"

At half time, Durk came to the sidelines, stepped over the rope edging the field, and this time was properly introduced to Kara. He asked if they had enjoyed the game and invited them to meet him at the Pub after the game. Many of the students and all of the team members and coaches would be there. Kara wanted to go, as did Ken, but Rebecca and Jayden were not convinced. So they asked Durk if they could decide when the game was over and just show up at the Pub if they decided to come. He graciously agreed rather than push them into a definite no.

After Durk went back to the field, Jayden said, "We'll already have eaten—the nibbles, the tea—and in the last quarter of the game we'll be eating the sandwiches we brought, and I'd think we'd have to order something at the Pub, so I don't think that we should go this time. I'm supposed to look after Rebecca, ya know."

"Well, we could each order a coke or something and perhaps just order some fries, or nachos and cheese which we could all share. And if it got rowdy or everyone was drinking a lot, we could leave. In fact, we can invent a signal between us, and if anyone gives that signal, we'll all respect it and leave together. We'll make a pact to stay together no matter what and to leave early."

"That's a great idea, Ken. So let's go and just check it out and even leave after an hour or so. Okay?" Kara replied. "What's the password gonna be?"

"How about 'radishes'?"

They all thought it was a great and innocuous word and agreed that if any one of them said "radishes" they'd all start to say their good-byes and leave.

When they arrived at the Pub, it was packed. It was such a huge place, yet it was full and not just filled by those attending or in the game but by hoards of students. "I guess this is the regular hangout for many of the students," Rebecca said.

And suddenly Durk was at their side, having watched them enter. "Durk, I couldn't believe some of the great passes you made. You are a great player. And how you fended off those guys attacking you was really cool. Seemed as if you got a few punches in when you were double teamed and you scared them off. It was an exciting game. I mean 6-6, then 13-12, then 19-19, and finally you pulled it out with that last Hail Mary to the guy alone in the end zone. What a pass!"

"Thanks, Ken, I didn't do it myself. My teammates did the work." And Durk watched Rebecca from the corner of his eye, not wanting her to know that it was *her* reaction that he wanted, not the others'. He turned to acknowledge something Kara said, and when he unconsciously raked his eyes over her tall frame, she felt her anger surface and she saw something in him that made her wary, something she felt she should warn Rebecca about. Kara had known that Durk was watching Rebecca even when talking to Ken and Jayden and had seen a certain narrowing of his eyes that had alarmed her. She hadn't liked that he'd *sneaked* those looks at Rebecca. Why not be forthright? Durk was *so* smooth, *so* pleasant, that something just didn't ring right for Kara.

Durk sensed Kara's disapproval and wondered at his newfound sensitivity to what others were thinking. He liked it; it gave him power. But where did it come from all of a sudden? Because of his sudden awareness of Kara's feelings toward him, Durk hated Kara instantly. But hating her, or at least letting her know how he felt about her, was not something that would further his plan. He would have to do something to make Kara change her mind about him. He wanted Rebecca, and he could not alienate her friends *just yet* if he wanted his plan to work. Already, thoughts of Rebecca dominated his mind and interfered with the calm in which he could usually create a plan to get what he wanted. He turned back to Kara and looked into her eyes with a smile saying, "I hope you enjoyed coming to the game, Kara, and that you might come again—often, in fact—as we begin our season. My teammates and I are always so grateful for support, and your cheers help us do better on the field as well. Thanks for coming, Kara."

Ooh, smooth, Durk, smooth, Kara thought but smiled outwardly saying, "You're welcome, Durk, we enjoyed it, and we'll be sure to attend many games this year. You really played well." Kara too was thinking that she would be better able to help Rebecca if Durk didn't suspect that she did not trust him, nor trust his intentions. Somehow she felt that his nature was, well, almost evil. And she was horrified by that thought. *Why did I think to use that word, evil? That's certainly too strong a word for what is happening here.*

As Ken and Jayden turned to Kara in conversation, Durk quickly grabbed Rebecca's hand, and turning his body so the others would not see him, he looked into Rebecca's eyes saying, "I am especially pleased that you came to the game, Rebecca. You are truly such a lovely person, and your support means a lot to me." Then he turned away to join in the conversation between Ken, Jayden, and Kara, wanting his words and touch to do its work. He didn't want Rebecca to withdraw because he came on too strong, and by turning away from her, she would not have time to gather those thoughts. He laughed to himself about how easy it was to pretend and to say what women wanted to hear. But Kara had seen what he did.

Chaldeth grinned thinking, *Atta boy, Durk, go get her!* Then he thought, *Kara is right, Durk is smooth, and he will surely be able to pull this off . . . maybe even without too much help from me!*

Jayden and Ken were so enthused by the game, the thought of future games and hearing all the inside sports news from Durk, that without asking Kara or Rebecca, they invited Durk to join them one evening when they gathered in their respective living rooms in the dorm. Durk, not wanting to let them see how thrilled he was to receive this open-ended invitation, replied, "I am really busy with practice, study, classes, and my part-time job, but if I can make it some evening I will be delighted to stop in for a few minutes. Thank you for the invitation."

Suddenly Kara asked if anyone wanted the pickle that was left on their plate of fries, and when Ken reached over to take it, she said, "Gosh, but I sure do wish that they had *radishes*. I love them!" Rebecca, Ken, and Jayden looked at her in surprise, but true to their word, each began to say that they'd better get back to the dorm because they had a paper to write or a phone call to make, etc. Durk hated to see them leave so early, but he was patient; he'd begun to put his plan into play, and soon he'd have them all eating from the palm of his hand.

When they were outside on the street, Jayden turned to Kara asking her what had happened that made her use their code word for leaving. "I'm sorry to burst everyone's bubble here, but there is something . . . bad . . . about Durk. I'm telling you, watch out!"

"Ahh, Kara, I felt the same way about him when I first met him and again in our political science class, and Rebecca felt that way when she first met him outside Professor T's office. But then we realized that we were wrong about him. He's a good guy underneath it all. You just have to give him a chance," Ken replied.

Jayden then added, "I don't know. Perhaps we should heed Kara's warning and heed Rebecca and Ken's *first* impression. I mean, let's not avoid him, but why not take it slow, give him the benefit of the doubt for now, but be careful . . . watch. Even the Bible warns us always to be watchful against being deceived. Matthew 26:41 says, "Watch and pray, that ye enter not into temptation; the spirit is indeed willing but the flesh is weak." And 2 Timothy 3:13 warns, "Evil men and seducers shall wax worse and worse, deceiving and being deceived . . .""

"That's judging, Jayden, isn't it! I like him. I admit that I didn't like him very much at first, but now I find him to be very respectful and attentive and caring, so I don't think badly of him at all. He's been very kind to all of us," Rebecca exclaimed.

"Yeah, Rebecca, you just think he's a 'hunk,' that's why you like him. And that kind of thinking can get you into trouble, believe me," Kara said sardonically.

"That's not true, Kara. Come on, I just don't think it's fair to prejudge. When we first met him, we didn't like him, but maybe he too was being cautious about us. And maybe he had a bad childhood or something and this is what you are sensing. Let's just give him a chance, okay?"

"All right, Rebecca, but let's take Jayden's advice and at least *watch*, so if something isn't quite right we will not be caught unaware and open ourselves to harm."

They walked back to their dorm talking about their classes and their professors, and Rebecca wondered aloud why so much material in her teaching guides seemed to leave out details that she felt made a difference in how one viewed the subject. "What I learned in high school about American history and what Uncle Jim taught us about the so-called politics of the founding fathers is so different than what I am now being taught. Let me give you two examples. My textbook contains a copy of the Declaration of Independence, and wherever a reference to God, to the Creator, to Divine Providence, or anything relating to faith was written in the original document, it's been removed and replaced with a few dots in the textbook. I think that's outrageous. I mean, isn't a document a document? Imagine if we tampered with all documents! And I remember reading hundreds of references George Washington made about how important it was for us to acknowledge that it was God who protected our country, that Divine Providence guided our founding, and without elected officials who espoused Biblical principles we would fail as a country. My current teaching is that George Washington was a deist, and that's just plain wrong! There is no doubt, just by what he wrote, that he was a devout Christian who was well versed in the Bible. I mean, almost everything he ever wrote contains quotes from the Bible. He didn't acknowledge them as quotes, but they were . . . . you can see that many of his statements and writings are taken almost word for word from the Bible, so it's evident that he knew his stuff . . . was a devout Christian!"

"You're right, Rebecca, and I think it was John Adams who said our Constitution was made for a moral and religious people, and Samuel Adams said something to the effect that we had to be a virtuous people to enjoy the gift of Heaven. James Madison spoke of 'the finger of the almighty' being extended to our country. But in the textbooks we now use and the lectures we receive nothing is said about the faith of any of these men, of how they prayed, or why they felt it so important that we be a religious, virtuous, honor-bound people," Jayden added.

"I never knew that," Kara added. "And it sure is good to hear. But if all this is really our history—I mean, if it is factual—why then isn't that what is being taught now?"

"I'd guess that not allowing God and religion into the picture, therefore not referencing the importance of morality, integrity, honesty, honor, prayer, and all that stuff, the politicians get away with being ungodly and corrupt," Ken added. "And another thing that I don't like is that what is taught seems so biased. I mean, isn't teaching sort of like journalism where ethically you are supposed to present both sides of an issue and allow students the freedom to make up their own minds?"

"Yeah, well it should be like that and I'd sure like to know both sides so I can have all the facts and then be equipped to debate an issue openly and honestly," Jayden added. "If someone hides the truth, well, then I tend not to believe *anything* they say."

"It isn't right to withhold the opportunity to learn the truth and to teach a bias, especially for political gain. I feel sorry for kids who believe that what is taught is correct and then go out in the world and fight for the wrong things."

"Rebecca, isn't that really like . . . uhh . . . uhh . . . brainwashing . . . or maybe propaganda?"

"Yeah, Kara, it sure is. It's actually indoctrination. What a shame. I want to learn both sides to everything," Ken added.

They arrived at the dorm, wound down their conversation, and separated—Kara and Rebecca to their rooms and Ken and Jayden to theirs. But little did they know that Durk had also left the Pub and headed out to see Professor T. Durk had formulated a plan so that he could see Rebecca alone, and he would need the professor's help to make it work.

On Monday, Durk waited until Ken and Rebecca were seated in the political science lecture hall and quickly moved to take the seat next to Ken. Rebecca was on Ken's opposite side. He greeted Ken warmly, and after nodding with a smile to Rebecca, he engaged Ken in a conversation about sports until the professor began his lecture. About a half hour before the class was to end, a student entered the lecture hall, spoke to Professor Emils, and then walked to Ken and handed him a note. The note was from Professor T. Nagorra and requested that Ken meet him in his office immediately. When Ken left, Durk slid over to sit next to Rebecca, but did not say anything to her.

When class ended, Durk asked Rebecca to accompany him to the tiny coffee shop outside of the cafeteria which catered to "quick takeouts" for students on the run but also had a few small tables inside. Rebecca had plans to meet Kara and Jayden in the cafeteria, but since the professor had dismissed them a little earlier than usual, she acquiesced. Durk had succeeded in convincing Rebecca to join him with the words "just for a minute, Rebecca, because I am worried about something and need your help."

When they sat down, Durk explained that he could sense Kara's reticence about him and told Rebecca that he was worried because he wanted Kara to approve of him. He asked Rebecca if she would be willing to tell him what he could do to change Kara's mind about him. He talked about his terrible childhood and how his escape to college gave him an opportunity to move on and to meet people who could help him become a better person. He said that he looked up to Ken and Jayden for the example they were to him and that he hoped they would allow him to be their friend.

Rebecca's natural compassion made her assure Durk that Ken and Jayden liked him and that he would be welcomed in their circle. Durk gently placed his hand on top of Rebecca's hand as it lay on the table, and he smiled gently into her eyes, thanking her. He asked her to tell him if ever there was anything he needed to change or to do so he would not lose their favor and then asked if she would keep their little meeting today a secret because he would be embarrassed if the others knew about his insecurities or suspected his intentions. Rebecca did not want to keep anything from her friends, in fact, was surprised by his request, but nevertheless she agreed.

As they parted, Durk faced Rebecca, took her hands in his, and leaned down to kiss her on the cheek. Then with a hint of tears in his eyes—pseudo tears—he whispered, "Thank you, Rebecca, you don't know what this means to me."

Walking to the cafeteria, Rebecca relived the previous half hour and all that Durk had said and done. Her face flushed with the memory of his twice taking her hand and then kissing her. He seemed so alone and so forlorn, and he seemed so genuinely in need of a friend, and more so, in need of a friend who could also be a role model for him. *He is gentle and kindhearted, and under his bravado, he is so very vulnerable. How sad to lose your mother at a young age and then to have a drunk father who beat him. That must hurt him very much,* Rebecca thought.

And with Chaldeth's help, Rebecca began to fall in love for the first time.

Immediately after leaving Rebecca, Durk went to Professor T's office. He wanted to thank him for getting Ken out of his way. As he entered the office, Durk was delighted to bump into Ken just as he was finishing his meeting with the professor. *Bumping into Ken here and so soon after class will give me additional cover,* Durk thought, *they'll never suspect that I spent time alone with Rebecca.*

As Durk settled into the chair opposite Professor T's desk after Ken left, he began to thank him for sending the note to Ken to get him out of the classroom and allow Durk to make his move. It had worked like a charm and had cleared the way for him to approach Rebecca. He also wanted to describe his meeting with Rebecca. As he spoke, another idea seemed to suddenly formulate in his head, and he asked the professor if he would give Rebecca a part-time job. "This way," Durk said, "I can see her often, and we'd have the privacy of your office whenever we needed it and . . ."

The professor interrupted Durk asking, "And what do I get out of all this?" He looked at Durk for a long moment and then added, "Now . . . remember when I brought that friend here and you uhhh . . . . took pictures for me from the outer office? Well . . . ?"

Durk was uneasy by what Nagorra wanted him to do because he liked Rebecca and could see that she was very naïve, innocent even. Rebecca wasn't . . . like that. But then, because he wanted this job for her, wanted to see her often, Durk rationalized his concerns away by telling himself that even if he agreed to what the professor was asking, later he would be able to put the professor off . . . for a while anyway. Right now he needed his help. "Okay, deal . . . but I have to work on her a while. It won't happen overnight."

When they gathered in the cafeteria, Ken told Rebecca that Professor T had called him away from class because he needed to redo some of the student paperwork for Ken. Evidently, his original paperwork had gotten lost in the shuffle. He explained that the professor wanted him to join some of the extracurricular activities that would help him further a career in law. "Isn't it great Rebecca? I mean, it's sort of like he's taken a special interest in me and wants to counsel me toward what will be good for my future, for my resume. He said that he especially wants me to get on the debate team since this is great practice for future lawyers!"

The next day, almost at the end of her history class, Rebecca too received a note from Professor T. When she heard his offer, she was thrilled by the prospect of working in his office for four hours each week, and thereby not only earning some spending money, but also having, as he explained, a job with a long list of responsibilities that would be excellent for her resume. She was to work for two hours, twice a week in the early evening after dinner. She would be primarily entering data into the professor's computer. This schedule would still give her time to study and work on any papers she needed to create.

It wasn't long before Durk convinced Rebecca that, whenever he was scheduled to work during the same hours that Rebecca was scheduled to work, they would take a little time to sit and talk. And it wasn't long after that when Durk was able to convince Rebecca that he was falling in love with her. This declaration then led to Rebecca allowing him to hold her and then to kiss her freely.

At first Durk gloated over his conquest, but then he realized that he was falling in love with Rebecca. He would look at his calendar and his watch often to calculate the days or hours until he would see her again. He reveled in stroking her thick black hair, and was unable to stop thinking of her when they were apart. He hadn't planned on this and tried to convince himself that it would pass, that she was just another girl, that he would never be serious about such a Goody Two-shoes. Sadly, Durk knew nothing of God and had dabbled in many ungodly activities and was therefore a slave to what Chaldeth wanted.

Chaldeth had also filled Professor T's mind with thoughts of Rebecca, and on many occasions, without Durk's knowledge, the professor had watched them through the doorway between the inner and outer office. The professor had long ago carefully tampered with the door's closing mechanism, so it was open just enough to accommodate his needs. The professor was struck by Rebecca's delicate features, her ridiculous trust in Durk, and her almost unbelievable innocence and he was surprised by her unwillingness to succumb to Durk. She was still worth watching because he loved the smoothness of her Dresden doll-like unblemished white skin and the widening of her ethereal blue eyes when she was surprised by something Durk said. He began to daydream that it was he rather than Durk who was with her, and thoughts of her began to emerge both day and night. From these thoughts rose an unreasonable and demanding jealousy that filled his heart and mind, and a resolve that he would eventually share Durk's involvement with Rebecca. But for now he would bide his time, perhaps wait until either Durk or Rebecca would be obligated to him. Then he would strike.

Rebecca too had thoughts constantly racing through her mind. She was plagued by her moral outlook on life. It demanded that love and intimacy and marriage be all wrapped up together. And it demanded honesty about her activities, and she knew she was not being honest with anyone, not even her mother. She loved the sensation of Durk's kisses and of his hands through her hair; she loved it when he gently stroked her back and told her how much he needed her. But she hated the fact that she was not sharing the news of her relationship with Durk with her closest friends. In fact, with no one at all. And she was uncomfortable with always having to fend Durk off even after clearly stating her unwillingness to do more than kiss one another. *Why?* she asked herself. *Why am I not jumping for joy wanting to shout to the whole world that we are getting serious, that we love one another?*

Rebecca had no idea that sharing her news about Durk was not something that Chaldeth could allow. It could put a stop to his intricate plan for Rebecca. With secrecy, Chaldeth could maneuver Rebecca into the fall he'd planned. With secrecy, she would not have the fellowship of other believers to help her back onto the right track, and she could be made to fall into the trap that Chaldeth had set up for her.

Nevertheless, Rebecca tried, when in conversation with Durk, to bring up her uneasiness with not telling her family or friends about their relationship, but he would always convince her that the time was not yet right, to wait a little longer, to be sure that she loved him before telling anyone. He convinced her that she would be embarrassed if she changed her mind about him, and others knew that for months they'd been secretly meeting. Durk's arguments seemed reasonable, but then she would ask herself, *Why do I have these terrible doubts? Why do I feel so guilty?*

And so time passed, and with it, Rebecca's opportunity for honesty passed and with it her guilt and shame increased. Just as Chaldeth had known, with each passing day Rebecca became more isolated, more vulnerable and more prone to his whispers, and all because she had agreed to subterfuge that first time.

Rebecca didn't understand the power that came from having friends who were of like mind. She'd forgotten that God works through people, not by writing on the wall with a bolt of lightning coming from the sky. She'd forgotten that friends who love you and have faith and integrity will try to help you, advise you, protect you, and support you, and most of all will pray for you. Even Rebecca herself had stopped praying about her circumstance. She felt that God would not approve, and because she could not stop seeing Durk, she felt that she could not ask for forgiveness for keeping it a secret nor could she ask for help. And with that failure, that one all important failure, the spirit of self-doubt entered her heart and weakened her resolve, and she found herself following Durk's lead more than ever before. She became enslaved to her sin of omission and rationalized her guilt by telling herself, *Durk needs me, he loves me, he would never do anything to harm me.* She consoled herself with the thought that she loved Durk with all her heart and did not want to let him down. She believed that he'd been so hurt in life by people who he had wanted to love him that it was her duty to be someone he could count on. And so she chose Durk over Jayden, Kara, and Ken, and even over her mother; and sadly, she was learning how to deceive them, the very people who truly loved her and who would have given her the right advice. Though fully aware that she was deceiving her family and her friends, she could not bring herself to tell them the truth. She was in a catch-22. Rebecca had forgotten the power of godly love and its attributes of forgiveness and grace when someone was honest. The spirit of self-doubt had helped her forget the very things that could have helped her. And Chaldeth gloated.

Kara, Ken and Jayden talked often about Rebecca when she was working and shared their concerns about her. Kara told the others that Rebecca seemed to have become reticent, very quiet and withdrawn, and rarely wanted to talk about herself. She wouldn't go into detail about her job other than to say that it was simply a boring two hours of data entry. She had mentioned that Professor T was never there when she was working, so they'd assumed she was alone in the office.

Jayden and Ken more easily accepted how quiet Rebecca had become, chalking it up to the fact that she was busy with her job and her studies, but Kara continued to worry, to watch, and to try to draw Rebecca into a deeper conversation when they were alone. She also watched Durk for any signs of untoward or overt behavior but hadn't seen anything that worried her. She decided, however, that one night when Rebecca was at work, she'd drop in just to say hello and see what Rebecca's duties were.

Meanwhile, Durk, aware of Rebecca's fears, began a campaign to completely win her over. He wanted to be successful; he wanted to feel that he was in control. He wanted to stop worrying that Rebecca might suddenly have a bout of conscience and leave him, or that she would tell her wimpy friends and they would somehow stop her from seeing him. He had to do something to ensure that she was his. And that left him only a few avenues to explore.

He finally decided to prey upon her sympathy, her compassion, to make her love him so much that she would choose him over anybody else if push came to shove. He planned to tell her of a lonely and abusive past and of his hopes for true love and decency and understanding in the future. He felt that he would accomplish his goal by being kind and gracious, by making her feel that without her he would be lost. He would play on her emotions and her natural sense of loyalty.

For a while even Durk began to believe that all the things he said were true, that he did love her and want a future with her. But when reality struck, he knew that he would never be able to limit himself to one relationship for the rest of his life and that in the end he would feel trapped and burdened by her narrow-minded belief system. Sometimes he felt as if there was a "good" Durk and a "bad" Durk inside him and that they battled one another. He understood why he preferred to see himself as "bad" because bad represented the ability to put yourself first, to go after what *you* wanted, even to hurt anyone who stood in your way or hurt you, and of course, it enhanced the drive to *win*! He considered many of the guys he met to be wimps; they were people who walked away from a fight, who took your bad mouthing, who would rather study than steal the test answers, or lose a football game rather than simply yank a face mask. What for? What did this get them in the end?

And so little by little, with gifts and loving words, with kindness and gentleness, with sad stories of a hard life, Durk won Rebecca's heart, and with it her loyalty. He began to look forward to the love he saw in her eyes, to the joy she expressed when she saw him and the feel of her arms hugging him when he told her stories of a made-up past, and of a grandmother who was an angel to him and the only person that had ever loved him. He told her that she reminded him of his grandmother because of how she loved him. When he saw her admiring glances when he was talking with others, it felt good, and for a while Durk did wonder if he could really love Rebecca. Even he had to admit that she was a good person, that she was incredibly trusting and wonderfully innocent. And, although quiet most of the time, and although extremely naïve in the ways of the world, she was very smart. In fact, he'd never met any one person with all the attributes that Rebecca had. *Maybe I should think about a serious relationship with her after all.*

Durk's ambivalence, however, ended soon enough when Rebecca scolded him for his savage attack on a teammate while on the football field. Rebecca had come to one of his practices because Jayden and Ken were in a debate forum and Kara was meeting with her guidance counselor about the courses she would need to take the next semester. Durk had been playing quarterback and had been blindsided by this teammate who'd tackled him from behind and made him fumble the ball. Durk was furious, and holding his teammates face mask, had yanked his head, cruelly wrenching his neck, and pulled him to the ground, jammed his spiked shoe into his stomach, and laughed. Durk was reprimanded by the coach and ordered to run laps around the field for the remainder of the practice.

Rebecca asked him why he was so cruel to his teammate. She told him that the young man had only been playing the game as he was supposed to, to stop the play by bringing down the quarterback. "What you did, Durk, was unconscionable," she'd said. Durk was furious with her and left without her at the end of the practice.

Rebecca was devastated when Durk walked away from her. She tried to replay her words and actions to understand why he was now so angry with her. She'd only been trying to help. *Maybe I was too hard on him. Maybe I hadn't seen everything that took place. Maybe the boy who tackled him had said or done something that I didn't see that made Durk react as he did.*

She began to worry that she would never see Durk again, worry that he was so angry with her that he might not want their friendship to continue. Her self-doubt made her wonder if she was the one at fault, not him. *Maybe I should have given him the benefit of the doubt . . . maybe I assumed too much and he was not as guilty as I thought . . . perhaps Durk was suffering right now because he thinks that I have betrayed him and did not stand by him.*

But Durk was not suffering. His anger at being tackled and his anger at how Rebecca had spoken to him filled his heart so completely with rage that there was no room for anything else. He vowed that he would make her pay for what she'd said. *No one speaks to me that way. No one!* He knew that he had her wrapped around his finger, so he planned to just sit back and let her suffer for a while, let her worry that he'd walked out on her. Maybe, after a few days, he'd begin to exact his revenge.

When the time was right, Durk approached Rebecca pretending to be remorseful. But beneath his smiles, his acknowledgement that he'd behaved badly, and his apology, he seethed with the memory of what Rebecca had said to him. Rebecca was now in the category of his mind where many resided: those from whom Durk would extract his pound of flesh. But another part of Durk had missed Rebecca, and her sweetness caused his anger to subside. He wanted to continue to see her and make sure that he was just as important to her now as he had been before the "incident."

In fact, Durk himself began to experience some self-doubt. He fought his feeling for her and for her way of life and hated it when he felt protective of her. He wondered how she could be so loving and forgiving all the time. He remembered that Rebecca had once said that prayer and scripture was a wonderful healing tool as well as a guidance tool. She'd said that her friends and family turned to the Bible for the answers to all their needs. If Rebecca had done this after their breakup, then could it be possible that she would not want him anymore, that she was only being kind to him now? Could the Bible have done something like that to her? *Nah, impossible,* Durk thought, *it just told her to forgive me.* And Durk was right, but not just for that reason.

Rebecca was a victim of a plot initiated a long time ago—a plot to separate man from God by any means possible. While God had given mankind specific instructions for their journey back to Him after falling into sin, the minions of fallen angels, like Chaldeth, worked diligently to cause the misunderstanding of God's instructions. They worked to cause men to misinterpret all things good and then fail to administer God's instructions properly. Evil was the master of perversion—just a tweak to a few words could cause confusion and confusion inspired the natural complacency of men.

Thus, instead of running from Durk, fleeing from all things evil immediately as God had advised, Rebecca felt it was her Christian duty to remain, to forgive, to understand. It was a mistake that would almost destroy Rebecca and a mistake that, in this day and age, so many made. In fact, it was one of the most important weapons that the spirits of the world used to their advantage. Time and time again the spirits manipulated personal guilt or a perverted idea of how to offer help to others to trap those they targeted. Evil understood that they could entice certain people to believe that they were not in danger; rather, that they were "righteous," "forgiving," "understanding," when in reality they were feeding their personal ego. Evil knew that they could cause some people to remain in a dangerous circumstance because it gave them a "feel-good" sensation to think they were helping someone. Evil could make them feel superior by telling them that they "knew better" and were thus charged with *being* better by not running away. It was a far cry from what God really meant for them to do. In 2 Corinthians 6:14, God warned His people of these situations saying, "Be ye not unequally yoked together with unbelievers; for what fellowship hath righteousness with unrighteousness? And what communion hath light with darkness." But His children did not always listen. And Chaldeth smiled.

Chapter 5

Temptation

If Rebecca had shared her thoughts and actions with Jayden, he would have talked with her about the mistake she was making—not just in regard to Durk, but in regard to the instruction God gave men through scripture. He would have told Rebecca that God understood man's fallibility and thus advised that they share fellowship with one another. He would have reminded her that when one shares their concerns with those who know God's words they would explain God's instructions in such matters.

Jayden felt that it was a gift, a precious gift, to truly know what God said to them. Listening to the many conversations between his grandfather and his mother as he grew up, he'd learned that God covered every circumstance of life through the words given to men in scripture. God had provided these words to teach and protect His children. But Rebecca did not seek the safety of the shared wisdom of her brothers and sisters in faith; she had gone out on her own, and she was deceived. She'd forgotten that, if left unprotected, she would be attacked . . . . subtly, slowly, and insidiously . . . . and that all her remaining armor would be chipped away inch by inch until that armor could be easily penetrated.

Rebecca understood that she was not thinking rationally, but following a course that seemed to direct itself. She felt as if she was on a roller coaster that insisted she stay put until it had completed its run. Sometimes she was afraid and asked God to help her, other times she was impulsive and rebellious and followed the path of least resistance because it pursued what she wanted, whether it was good for her or not. She'd hidden her relationship with Durk from Jayden, Kara, and Ken, and even from her mother because she instinctively knew that the others would not approve of his lifestyle. Neither did she. But then she would justify her actions by telling herself that they knew so little about Durk and didn't see, as she did, all the good in him. Sometimes a little voice would tell her that she was making a mistake, but she didn't care; she was in love for the first time in her life, and she wanted to be with him so badly that she buried her natural caution and ignored everything she had been taught.

A few days after their argument, Durk decided to approach Rebecca when she was working in Professor T's office. He'd gotten over his rage and was now able to plan more carefully once again. He'd gotten his hair styled, polished his shoes, sprayed on his favorite cologne, and dressed in his most flattering outfit to impress Rebecca. When he walked into the office shortly before Rebecca was to leave the office for her dorm, he stopped in the doorway between the inner and outer office and stood with his arms open, inviting Rebecca into them. She rose from her desk chair and ran to him, so happy that he had come to see her and appeared to still care about her.

He looked wonderful! *So tall and lithe, such a strong presence, such a wonderful smile,* she thought, *how lucky I am that he loves me.* He led her to the loveseat in the outer office, and they murmured their apologies amidst touches that seemed to Rebecca to express his love. So relieved was Rebecca that they were together again that she gladly gave Durk some leeway in how intimate an embrace he demanded. Rebecca was sure that Durk had thought things over and would now begin to mend his ways.

Durk was fully aware of Rebecca's relief that he was here to see her. She was delighted that he'd come to the office to reinstate their relationship and was immediately willing to put their differences behind them. He was also fully aware that Rebecca easily succumbed to the more intimate embrace he'd boldly initiated. From that, he knew that it was just a matter of time before he gained complete control of her. He'd get his revenge and have Rebecca as well!

But what Durk didn't know was that Kara had also witnessed their embrace. She'd clearly seen the fleeting look of conquest cross his face as he turned to lead Rebecca to the loveseat, and she was frightened for Rebecca.

Kara's original plan had been to drop in on Rebecca and walk back to the dorm with her when she finished her work. But as she neared the building that housed the office where Rebecca worked, she'd seen Durk walking toward the same building. She became suspicious and slowed her pace, crossed to the other side of the street, and followed him from a distance wondering if he too was going to see Rebecca. She followed him up the stairs and watched from the stairwell door as he entered the office. She approached the door to the professor's office quietly and stood in the outside hallway straining to hear the conversation inside. She carefully peeked around the door and saw Durk standing with his back to her and his arms outstretched. Then she saw Rebecca run to him and realized that they had initiated a romance. They were so engrossed in one another that they had not seen nor heard Kara's presence. She quickly withdrew, hiding herself, then peeked again, and then again, all the while listening to what was said. Her fleeting glimpses of their embrace gave her far more information. She knew now that Durk and Rebecca's relationship must have been going on for quite a while, and she was stunned that Rebecca had kept it a secret. *What should I do? Should I confront them? Should I just go back to the dorm? Should I tell Jayden and Ken? Should I keep Rebecca's secret? Should I just talk to Rebecca about it when she comes back to our dorm?*

Finally Kara decided to make some noise from further down the hall, maybe bang the stairwell door, then hum a tune as she walked toward the office so they'd know that someone was approaching. Then she planned to walk into the office and watch and listen carefully for what they would say and do. She would act surprised to see that both of them were together. *Let's see how they react to my raised eyebrow at catching them together . . . let's see if Rebecca tells me the truth!* Kara retraced her steps and loudly slammed the stairwell door down the hall from Professor T's office. Humming loudly as she walked toward the office, then calling "Rebecca! Rebecca? Rebecca!"

When she entered the door to the professor's office, Rebecca was sitting behind the desk in the inner office working at the computer. Durk was in the outer office sweeping the floor. Durk greeted Kara with a warm and loud hello, gave her a hug and pointed to the inner office saying, "Rebecca's in there, Kara, still working. Go on in." *Durk is completely composed. No sign of nerves, of guilt. Just as smooth as ever,* Kara thought. *You weasel!* But when Rebecca greeted Kara, it was different. Rebecca was nervous; she looked forlorn, caught, guilty, remorseful, and Kara felt sorry for her. "Kara! What a surprise to see you! Come on in. Sit down. I was just finishing up, getting ready to leave."

"I decided on impulse to visit you and to walk home with you, Rebecca. Is that okay?"

"Of course," Rebecca replied, smiling outwardly. But both Rebecca and Durk were disappointed because they'd planned to spend more time together. It was, after all, their reunion, the first time in days that they were together after their argument. Rebecca had been so happy that all was well between them again, and she wanted to be sure that Durk still cared for her and that he was implementing her suggestions to change his life. But Durk was disappointed for another reason. He'd had lots of plans for Rebecca, lots of plans for laying the groundwork for full control.

Sometimes Durk had a pang of guilt for the way he so easily calculated, planned, and executed his actions; for the way he manipulated people to gain the upper hand; for his need to win, to compete. Sometimes he was uneasy with the rage he felt that made him seek revenge when someone hurt or criticized him. Sometimes he wondered where that trait had come from. He'd never heard of original sin, or as Rebecca's Aunt Sarah called it, "generational" sin where the sins of the forefathers were visited upon the generations after them. He'd never been to church, to a Bible study, or anywhere else where he might have learned those principles and how to overcome the traits that made him somehow uneasy. He didn't even know that he was supposed to try to overcome them.

Usually Durk shrugged off those fleeting thoughts and returned to his usual gloating over what he considered his superior ability to outwit others. Without understanding what he was doing, he welcomed those spirits into his life who helped him gain his immediate desires. He never allowed his questions, his softer feelings, or his guilt to linger. He justified his actions by thinking, *I've had a hard life and had to struggle to get where I am, and Rebecca was born with a silver spoon in her mouth, so she deserves what she gets. In fact, it will do her good to learn about how life really is!* Despite those thoughts, when he was with Rebecca he'd soften a bit . . . but that was before she'd been disloyal to him. All he could think about now was that disloyalty must be punished, broken, destroyed. *Why should I risk everything I've worked so hard for just to end up catering to the whims of someone as simpleminded as Rebecca? Well, she isn't really simpleminded. In fact, she's incredibly smart . . . but so naïve . . . so unaware of the real world.*

When Kara walked into the office and had looked at Durk, he suddenly sensed another threat that must be stopped in its tracks. Kara. He knew that she distrusted him and that she saw through him somehow, and he hated her for it. *But can I win her over? And if so, is it worth the effort?* He wondered if perhaps he could strong-arm her, force her, bribe or threaten her some way. He'd have to think this one out, think about what he would have to do about Kara. *What if she tells Ken and Jayden about her suspicions? What would they do? What do I need to do about all of this?* And suddenly, as if some unseen power had helped him, Durk began to form a diabolical plan to silence all of them.

While Rebecca began to tidy her desk and prepare to leave, Durk quickly penned a note to her. He needed to ward off an attack on his credibility that might come from Kara, and he needed to make sure Rebecca stood against Kara. So he penned a note to slip to Rebecca that read, "Remember that I love you . . . remember that they will try to turn you against me . . . remember that I love you and I need you. You are my only hope . . . please stand by me. XXX Durk."

That should do it, Durk thought. With a quick look around both the inner and outer office to make sure all was in order, Durk locked the door to the hallway and walked the girls down the stairs and out into the night. He offered to walk them back to the dorm, but Kara quickly said that they'd be fine alone. He gave Kara a quick hug, and when giving the same quick hug to Rebecca, he slipped his note into her hand. Then they all said good-bye and separated.

As they walked back to their dorm, Kara purposely kept the pace slow so she could talk with Rebecca. "How do you like working in Professor T. Nagorra's office, Becca? Does it get lonely or scary to be in that office alone?"

"No, actually, I like the peace and quiet, and I like to get my work done as quickly as possible, and I often finish early if I start right away."

"You never come home early, Becca. What do you do when you finish ahead of schedule?"

"Oh . . . ummm . . . I . . . keep busy. I can always find something to do."

"Is Durk always there when you are working? I noticed that he was sweeping. Does he work there when you do?"

"Uh, yeah . . . uh well . . . not always . . . just sometimes. Gee, Kara, why all the questions? I just kinda bump into him from time to time."

"Oh, I understand that, but it's just that you never mentioned seeing him, and we always worry about you being alone in the building."

"Well, sometimes some of the professors work late, and sometimes students meet with professors in the evening, and there's always the janitor around . . . oh and . . . and the watchman comes in at least once. So I'm okay."

"But it's not like you not to mention seeing him. I mean, we all hang around together from time to time, and you and I see each other all the time because we room together, so I just thought that you'd have mentioned it. Are you uncomfortable with him there when you are alone? I'd be glad to come over and study in the outer office while you work."

"*No*! I mean, no thanks, Kara. I'm fine, and Durk is hardly ever there. Don't worry . . . and come on . . . let me handle my own life, okay?"

"Okay, Rebecca," Kara replied softly, "I just wanted you to know that I'm here if you ever need me." With that said, and Rebecca feeling guilty about lying to her friend, and Kara worrying because Rebecca wasn't being truthful, they walked home in silence. Rebecca felt terrible about her lie. *Why do I hide my relationship with Durk? Why not just tell them?* she wondered. *I know that something is wrong, I know that the way I am acting is displeasing to God and goes against everything my mother would want me to do, but I don't know why I'm doing this, and now I don't know how to fix it.*

When they arrived at their rooms, they found Ken and Jayden looking for them. "Where'd you go? We thought that Rebecca was at work but that you, Kara, would be here."

Rebecca hoped that Kara would not mention seeing Durk with her, but Kara spoke and Rebecca could not stop her without sounding as if she had something to hide. "Well, I had been thinking about Becca and wondering what it was like for her when she was working—you know, what the building was like at night, if she was ever scared to walk home alone in the dark—so I decided to surprise her and walk over and see for myself and then walk her home!"

Rebecca jumped in hoping that that was all Kara would say. "Yes! It was such a treat to see her and to be reminded of what a thoughtful friend she is!"

"But guess who I ran into over there?" Kara continued. "Durk! He works in the same office!"

Kara knew that Rebecca was dismayed by her words, but she felt strongly that the others should know, and so she'd taken the chance and blurted out everything even though she knew Rebecca wished she hadn't.

"Durk?" Jayden exclaimed. "Rebecca, why didn't you tell us? Has he been bothering you? What's going on? I don't understand why you would not have mentioned this."

Ken and Kara exchanged looks that told each of them that they understood why Rebecca hadn't said anything. Durk was up to no good, and Rebecca was afraid to tell them!

Rebecca was mortified. She too could see that they would automatically think that Durk would be unwelcome company while she worked. If she said otherwise, they would think that something was going on and would quickly assume a relationship between Durk and herself. *Well, they'd be right, wouldn't they?* she thought. *Oh, why didn't I tell them in the beginning?*

"I'm sorry, there was really nothing to tell at first . . . I mean, I thought that Durk's being there . . . I mean the first time . . . well, that it was a fluke and he wouldn't come again . . . and I knew that if I said something you might be angry with him and maybe say something that would hurt the new friendship you'd all been building."

"What friendship?" Jayden replied angrily. "We're friends, the four of *us*. Durk is an acquaintance who, over time, and as trust built, might have *become* a friend. But this . . . this . . . subterfuge . . . isn't right, Becca. I'm supposed to look after you. I mean, what if Durk had made a pass or something? We need to at least know who you expect to be with. Gosh, Becca. I'm disappointed in you for not telling us. That's all . . . just tell us!"

"I said I'm sorry. I mean . . . well . . . we don't meet every time I'm working . . . well, I mean . . . well maybe . . . most of the time . . . but I am a grown woman, and I have the right to some privacy, don't I? Don't I?"

Crying, Rebecca ran into her room and shut the door. The others stood looking at one another, shocked to realize that Rebecca was seeing Durk regularly and had never told them. "Gosh," Ken whispered, "not saying a word may mean that she was afraid, or ashamed, and either way I blame Durk. Do you think that he coerced her into not telling us? I'm really worried. What should we do?"

"Kara, you go in to Rebecca and stay with her until I return. Ken, you sit out here and wait for me or my phone call. I'll be right back. I'm going to make a visit to our so-called friend." And before Kara or Ken could stop him, he was out the door.

When Jayden knocked on Durk's door, Durk knew instantly that it would be about Rebecca. He opened the door, and with his most hearty smile he asked Jayden to come in and sit down. He noted right away that Jayden's fists and jaws were clenched and asked what was wrong. "Wrong?" Jayden yelled. "Wrong? Come on, Durk, you've been sneaking around behind my back trying to make time with Rebecca. Nothing would be *wrong* if you'd been up-front about it, but when you sneak it, then yeah, something *must* be wrong. And I wanna know about it."

"Calm down, Jayden. Nothing is wrong. You are jumping to conclusions. I was just as surprised as Rebecca to find that we were working on two of the same nights in the same office, that's all. Over time as we talked we became friends. I really care about her and hope it moves further, but that will be up to Rebecca, won't it?"

"Why didn't you or Rebecca say something, Durk?"

"Well, I personally believe that Rebecca is afraid of you, Jayden. And that's sad. I too thought that the both of you were friends, but obviously if she can't confide in you then you are not friends. And remember, it isn't my place to tell you, it's Rebecca's."

Jayden was stunned by Durk's words. He was suddenly insecure, suddenly afraid, suddenly thinking more about his friendship with Rebecca than Durk's friendship with her. Durk gloated as he clearly recognized Jayden's confused thoughts and sudden inaction. *Oh, it's so easy with these country bumpkins,* Durk thought. *I've won again, and so easily too! I can do almost anything I want and get away with it because I am so much smarter than these idiots. But I will get even with Jayden for this after I get Rebecca, and I'll get even with Kara for telling them. They will pay for this . . . this . . . minor inconvenience.*

Jayden returned to his dorm, and Ken saw immediately that his face was ashen. In fact, his entire demeanor reflected that he'd received a crushing blow. Ken wanted to know what had happened and said, "Gosh, Jayden, you look as if you've been hit by a Mack truck. What happened?"

"Nothing, Ken. That's the trouble: nothing. Once again, Durk turned the circumstances to his advantage. He intimated that Rebecca was afraid of me, afraid to tell us that they were seeing one another. Ken . . . that means that she doesn't trust me, or us! Durk said that if she didn't tell us she didn't trust us, and that meant that we were really not friends at all. He even intimated that they were pretty close and that it wasn't his place to tell us . . . it was hers. And he was right, Ken . . . darn it but *he was right!* I had no argument; I was done, dead in the water, and could do nothing but leave. Durk turned the tables on me so efficiently that I was left with nothing to say. Gosh, Ken, Rebecca is no match for him. Maybe we aren't either."

"That's pretty scary. Geez, I hope that Rebecca isn't in over her head. This is rotten . . . boy, I can't stand that Durk anymore. I thought that we were friends . . . he knows that the four of us are friends . . . I mean, it's almost as if he welcomed this . . . secret . . . knowing that he could break us up. You know, separate Rebecca and us!"

"Ken! That's it! It isn't Rebecca! It isn't me, or us. That's what he wants us to think! He's a conniving no-good rat fink, and *Becca is* in big trouble. But she will *never* listen to us. She will have to see this for herself to believe it. What can we do?"

Kara walked out of Rebecca's room just then and told them that Rebecca had fallen asleep. Ken quickly filled Kara in with the details of Jayden's visit to Durk and what was said. As Kara began to respond, he silenced her so he could explain what they'd concluded, and then she responded by saying, "I knew that Durk was no good. I sensed it from the very first time I met him. So did you, Ken, until you were blinded by the glory of a football quarterback! We need to stop him from whatever his plans are for Rebecca."

"Yeah, but we'll only alienate Becca. We need to be just as sneaky as Durk. We need to figure out a way that Durk will trip himself up so Becca will see him for what he is. Let's not let on to either of them what we suspect. Let's pretend nothing unpleasant happened, and let's watch . . . carefully. But, we now know that Durk is far more formidable than we had suspected. I mean if he could so callously say those things to you—he knew full well that what he said would upset you—then he's dangerous."

"Kara, Ken, you're both right. You made some good points," Jayden added. "We can't just accuse Durk of something for which we have no evidence. He's smart and unscrupulous, and we might not be able to outwit him. So we will have to be patient, although that's gonna be tough to do. We have to watch over Rebecca without her knowing, and we have to 'get the goods' on Durk, find out who the real Durk is. Thinking back on the finesse he used tonight to try to stymie us, he may be a really *serious* threat to Rebecca . . . maybe to us too. Should we tackle the job of finding out what Durk is really up to?"

"Absolutely! That's a deal!" Ken and Kara agreed. "And we'll get the answers we should have gotten long ago."

When Rebecca awoke the next morning, she was surprised to see that Kara was not angry with her, was in fact cheerful, and chatted away about plans for the weekend. Later in the day when Rebecca saw Ken and Jayden, they too seemed just fine and gave her a hug as if nothing had come between them. *Maybe they decided that I have the right to make my own choices in life. Maybe they realized how wrong they are about Durk, even realize how good Durk is*, she thought.

So Ken, Kara, and Jayden put their heads together when Rebecca was once again at work and began to make plans. Each of them came up with a number of ideas about how they could gather information about Durk, and how they would watch over Rebecca. Ken suggested that they try to learn from others; perhaps Durk had a "past" that would give them some insight, perhaps there were past relationships or situations they could uncover. Kara wondered if perhaps there was something they could learn from Professor T since Durk seemed to use his office so freely.

Their final plan was that each of them would tackle a different area of sleuthing, and before anyone became suspicious of their questions, they would switch areas and then they would compare notes and try to separate truth from gossip. They agreed that Ken would approach Professor T, meet with him as if he needed some advice, and then switch the conversation to how fortunate Durk was to have his job with the professor, and then perhaps talk about football and what an asset Durk was to the team. Kara would surreptitiously watch Rebecca and Durk and listen carefully when the three of them were together, and when Rebecca and Durk were alone together, she would try to monitor them as best she could. Jayden would spend time with Durk's teammates who usually stopped in at the Pub after practice to have a few beers and discuss the events of the day. They always talked about sports and what had occurred on the field that day, but sometimes they spoke about an incident that had angered them, or about the various girls that they dated. Jayden would see if he could get them to talk about Durk.

In the meanwhile, Durk couldn't believe his good luck that Ken, Jayden, and Kara had seemed to back off. He'd worried that they'd keep at him and certainly would try to influence Rebecca to stay away from him. But his ego prevailed, and he began to believe that they simply could not stand up to him. *I probably intimidated the little dorks*, he thought. Emboldened by his sudden sensation of power, he too began to make plans, and those plans included his decision to move ahead and finalize his control over Rebecca. *It's time for me to pay more attention to Rebecca and get her to be a little more pliable. I'm tired of playing games with her, tired of waiting. Maybe I'll bring her to the beer party this weekend, get her to smoke a little pot. That'll lighten her up.*

Rebecca was thrilled that Durk had invited her to a party, thrilled that she would meet his friends and be a part of his life. She too felt emboldened by the sense of freedom she'd felt when she dared to speak up to Jayden, Kara, and Ken, and they'd apparently realized that she had the right to live her own life. A part of her was excited by the idea of stepping out into a new arena, a new way of living, apart from the constraints placed on her by her mother and friends and her limited ideas of what she could and could not do. Nevertheless, a small part of her heart was filled with the worry that she was wrong, that she was opening the door to trouble, that she was allowing the spirits of the world to lead her rather than God. She remembered her mother's warning and Jayden's as well, and for some reason Ken's words to them one day in the cafeteria rang a bell in her mind. He'd told them of the various drugs that could be slipped into their drinks. He'd also told them that his parents had admonished him that if he were ever at a student party to never to accept anything to drink that he hadn't made or gotten for himself. They'd even told him to carefully check bottle caps for their seal as well.

However, the spirit of rebellion was so strong and so overpowering that Rebecca brushed those thoughts aside. As she did, she found that she could no longer pray; she didn't seem to have the time for it. At night before climbing into bed, she'd always prayed, always asked for God's guidance and protection and thanked Him for His help in her life. But recently she was so tired that it was an effort to pray, and even if she forced herself to begin, the words just wouldn't come. She worried that this was because she was keeping so many secrets. She knew, way down deep in her heart, that to want to hide her relationship with Durk and keep it a secret from her mother, her family and Jayden, that something wasn't right. But because she didn't want to face the answer to that question, she would brush those thoughts aside. *After all*, she thought, I *want to be with Durk . . . I love him.*

Rebecca convinced herself that what she was doing was right, that she was in a learning curve where, in order to make the right decisions, she would need life experiences; she would need to date, to go to parties, to meet people, and to learn how to have fun. There was plenty of time later in life for being, well, a fuddy-duddy who just spent time with family and church and stuff. *After all, how could anyone say that their favorite color was blue if they had never seen red and green and yellow?*

Rebecca's frame of mind was perfect for Durk's purposes. Though she had not shared her thoughts with him, he sensed that after her altercation with Kara, Jayden, and Ken, Rebecca became less cautious. She seemed to want to get out, to have fun, and not to worry any further about what Jayden, Kara, and Ken would think if she did not spend her free time with them. When he invited her to the beer party, she'd accepted immediately. Durk thought, *Ahh, now we're getting somewhere,* and also thought that he would find an empty room at the party where he could bring Rebecca.

In the past, Durk had shared many thoughts and plans with Professor T, and they laughed together at the stupidity of freshman girls—in fact, of all college girls in general. To both of them, these girls were naïve, hungry for attention and affection, and trusted everyone and everything. *How dumb!* Durk had quickly acquiesced when the professor said that he wanted to be in the outer office when Durk entertained the girls, but with Rebecca he'd hesitated. They had laughed together remembering episodes where Durk had sweet-talked the girls, but for some reason he did not want the Professor to laugh about Rebecca.

As Durk recalled the past and the good shows he'd provided for the professor, he remembered that he usually loved the fact that the girls had no idea that they were being watched. Durk was excited to think that, between the beer party and the next few nights when Rebecca was working in the professor's office, so many opportunities would present themselves for him to bring Rebecca into line and to get her to be like everyone else—not so uptight, not so incredibly frigid. But then he also recalled that when he'd first met Rebecca he'd been impressed with her dignity and had been jealous of the way the professor seemed to fawn over her.

Suddenly Durk recoiled at the idea of the professor watching Rebecca, and he wasn't quite sure why. Rebecca was . . . different . . . not like some of the others. But then a wave of anger rushed through him as he remembered the way she'd threatened him and the way her friends had looked at him, and suddenly the idea of the professor watching was exciting again. And Chaldeth chucked to himself. He knew why Durk had again changed his mind: it was Chaldeth's influence over Durk. It had taken some time, but even though God warned these silly people through scripture, they simply did not pay attention to the fact that Chaldeth had the power to move men's hearts and to make right wrong and wrong right just as he was doing with Durk.

The next day, as Jayden and Rebecca walked over to their anatomy and physiology class, they avoided the subject of Durk and discussed the cat that they would once again have to dissect in the laboratory section of their studies. Once in the lab, Rebecca allowed Jayden to slide the cat out of the plastic bag while allowing the bag to retain the liquid that resulted from its slightly defrosted state. They could feel the cold arising from its body and were almost surprised that it was always just defrosted enough for them to slice easily into its skin with the scalpel. Its fur was wet, long, and tangled, and its knees were bent with its legs splayed outward. Its gray green tongue was hard, unyielding, and it protruded from the side of its mouth seeming to try to distance itself from the globs of red and blue wax emerging from its throat. The "wax," actually a dye, had been injected into its jugular vein to provide color to the veins and arteries so the students could follow their course and learn about the circulatory system.

As they cut, they had to move and discard the greasy yellow globules of fat found under the skin. They also had to use their probes to pick away the hardened fecal matter that had seeped from the colon after death. When Rebecca learned what they were removing, she had to leave the room until she could compose herself enough to return. The smell of the formalin, used as a preservative, also contributed to Rebecca's discomfort and made her gag. They wore latex gloves to protect their hands, but the wet fur stuck to their gloves, their scalpels and probes, and even found its way to the manual they had opened to guide their exploration. "Oh, Jayden, the cat has no dignity left. He's so vulnerable, and if he knew what was happening to him now . . . well, it would be terrible."

But Jayden encouraged her by explaining that, to become a good nurse or physician, they would have to know how the body worked, what happened in life and in death, where the organs were located and what they looked like, and how the skeletal and circulatory system worked. When Rebecca finally removed her gloves, she saw that she'd somehow pierced the two index fingers of the gloves and that fur from the cat had lodged under her nails. Horrified, she scrubbed her hands in the lab sink but could not dislodge the hair without using the probe. It seemed as if no matter how hard she scrubbed, she could not rid herself of the feeling that she had not removed every cat hair from under her nails. The instructor explained that it was best that everyone keep their nails very short for the duration of the class so their nails would not penetrate the gloves.

In time they were to identify the individual teeth, the glands, muscles, vessels, organs, and nerves. As the cat was "skinned," they saved the skin to cover the cat when they returned it to the refrigerator to help preserve the remaining carcass. In time, they completed their studies with the cat and were delighted to finally finish with it. But then, as they reviewed their dissection manual and their textbook, they realized how much they had learned. They were amazed by their greater understanding of how the human body worked from what they had discovered through their work with the cat. They memorized, and memorized, and memorized. And as they studied together, and as Jayden helped Rebecca learn and seemed to have so much wisdom and patience, Rebecca acknowledged once again what a very fine person Jayden was. She hoped that they would be friends for life.

Rebecca also began to open to Jayden about her concerns regarding Durk. "I love him, Jayden. I've never been in love before, so I don't really know what to think or feel or do. And I feel so guilty that I hold him off and that I don't see him as often as he'd like. But I have to do my work. I have to get good grades because my mom is paying for all this, and because I want to have a good career either as a doctor or as a nurse. I want a life where I can marry and have lots of children and be a part of our family . . . and sometimes Durk frightens me. Sometimes I can't see him being happy with my family."

"Rebecca, you are right to be cautious. Love is a very important thing. Everyone wants to be loved and to love, and we have so much to learn about love. But when I think of the future, and of being closely involved, I ask myself, will that person always love me? Will I always love that person? Will they love my family and will my family love them? Do we and will we share our faith and our love of God? I guess another question we have to ask is . . . are they honorable and trustworthy. And you know . . . that's a lot to learn about someone. It takes time, lots of time. Just remember that whatever decisions you make, you must always ask yourself if God would approve, and if the answer is yes, then you will be okay."

"Thanks, Jayden, thanks for being so understanding. I will do what you say, and I am so glad that we are such good friends. I don't know what I'd do without you." But Rebecca did not follow Jayden's advice. The thoughts that filled her mind were of how Durk would be once they married and had a family. She did not connect his *current* thoughts and actions with the future thoughts and actions she imagined he would have. She believed that, in time, she could change him. Thus she looked forward to going to work that evening and seeing Durk once again.

Durk rushed to Professor T's office in anticipation of being with Rebecca. He'd showered and shaved, splashed cologne over his face and chest, and had dressed carefully. Rebecca too had looked forward to their meeting and had washed her hair, had added a special perfume to her neck and shoulders, and had worn the blouse that Durk said he liked. She'd gotten to work early and worked fast and furiously to finish her work so she would have more time to spend with Durk. Her heart was hammering, her mouth was dry, and she felt as if the love that she felt for him would overwhelm her.

Kara had watched Rebecca get ready to leave their dorm. She'd chatted incessantly about their various professors, the food in the cafeteria, and some of the papers she was trying to complete for class. She wanted Rebecca to think that she was unconcerned about what Rebecca would be doing for the evening. Rebecca was pleased that Kara seemed to accept her plans for the evening without any admonitions and without asking her when she would be back. She was also pleased that she and Jayden had talked more openly together, and he too had seemed supportive. It was liberating, but then again, she also felt a little more responsible for herself. She could no longer blame them for anything.

Kara waited about an hour after Rebecca left, and then, dressed in black from head to toe, feeling like Sherlock Holmes must have felt when he was sleuthing, she made her way over to Professor T's office. She waited outside until she saw Durk enter the building and again waited to implement her plan. She would enter the building herself about fifteen minutes after Durk. As she was about to move from her position across the street from the building where Rebecca worked, she was surprised to see that Professor T was walking toward the entry door. She was relieved to think that Durk and Rebecca would not be alone, and she was about to leave and go back to her room when something about the professor made her uneasy. He looked, or moved, almost furtively. *Why?* He'd looked left and then right, he'd hesitated at the door to the building, peeking in the glass before opening it, then he'd closed it softly as if he didn't want anyone to hear the door open or close. Then he seemed to pause at the foot of the stairwell and appeared to be listening before climbing the stairs. A sudden sense of fear filled Kara's heart, and she was determined to follow Professor T to see why his actions appeared so furtive.

Meanwhile, Durk had greeted Rebecca and had led her to the couch in Professor T's inner office. He'd partially closed the door to the outer office and also left the door to the hallway partially open so that the professor could enter without making any noise. He'd turned out the lights in the outer office. Only the two lamps on the sides of the couch where he and Rebecca sat were lit. From past experience he knew that this was the best lighting to hide the professor and to highlight what took place on the couch.

Durk sat next to Rebecca and began to tell her how beautiful she was and how much he loved her. He held her hand and stroked her hair, combing through it with his fingers. He gently ran his hand up and down her back. He kissed her neck and her ear, and then turned her face toward him. He could hear her short breaths and see her chest move up and down, almost in gasps, just before her lips met his. He rested his hand on her thigh and slowly began to stroke her leg. As his touch became more intimate, Rebecca squirmed and moved out of his reach. But Durk persevered telling her over and over again how much he loved her, and how desperately he needed her. As he thought about the professor watching from the inner door, his excitement mounted, and he was inflamed by a desire to prove his prowess once again. His ego made him determined to put on a show and to make this conquest.

The professor stood in the dark outside the door between the inner and outer office. Only the light from the outer hall filtered through the transom in the top of the doorway to the hall joining the sliver of light from the partially open hallway door. Another sliver of light from the partially opened inner door penetrated the outer office. This provided the professor with just enough light to move freely and quietly through the outer office. It was also just enough light for Kara to see the professor. Kara, however, was in full light in the outer hallway. Her heart pounded with fear. *What will I say if they see me? Oh God, please protect and help me,* she thought.

Kara had carefully moved along the hallway wall until she reached the partially open door to Professor T's office and had waited, listening for any sound. Then she moved slowly, quietly, to the door opening and quickly looked inside. She saw the professor at the inner door and, frightened because he was so close to her, she quickly pulled back, trying to calm her breathing and quiet her pounding heart. With everything still silent, she moved again to look into the small door opening knowing full well that she was in full light and the professor was in very little light, making her a perfect target should he turn around.

But the professor never heard Kara. He was engrossed by whatever he was watching through the inner-door opening. This helped Kara grow bolder in her own sleuthing, and slowly she began to understand what was happening. A sense of profound horror ran through her body causing her to gag, and she quickly put her hand over her mouth hoping she'd made no sound. She pulled back from the door, and when she could control her fear, she looked again. The professor was still at the inner door but had now pulled up a chair so he could watch in comfort. Then Kara saw the camera. *Oh, how disgusting,* Kara thought. *What should I do?* She had to stop this. But if she just barged in and told Rebecca, Professor T would deny it and Rebecca would have to choose sides, and then both the professor *and* Durk would know that they were spying on them. *Oh, what should I do? Should I try to grab the camera and run? But if they caught me? We'd have no proof, and they'd know we were spying. Please, God, show me what to do!*

Suddenly Kara knew what she should do. She would move down the hall to the stairwell. She would phone Rebecca, pretending to be at the dorm, and tell her that there was an emergency and that she would have to come right to the dorm immediately. *Oh, what emergency? Okay, think, Kara, think!* Then Kara did have an idea: she would tell Rebecca that Ken was hurt and that she needed to come home immediately. Then she would hang up before Rebecca asked any questions, so Rebecca would think the worst and leave quickly. Then she would phone Ken and tell him to get back to his room, if he wasn't already there, and to bandage his ankle or something right away and come up with a story about how he'd gotten hurt. If Ken didn't have a first-aid kit that had those wraparound bandages, she'd tell him where hers was. If he wanted to know why she was telling him to do this, she'd simply say it was a life-or-death matter for Rebecca, so just *do* it. She'd have to run fast, so Rebecca wouldn't see her if Rebecca did leave immediately.

Kara ran down the stairs, and at the front door she made her call to Rebecca. *Oh, what if she doesn't answer?* But Rebecca did answer and sounded very concerned and said she'd be right there. Kara began to run back to her dorm, and while running she phoned Ken. Ken heard her puffing, understood that she was running, and somehow knew that this call was urgent. He agreed to do what she said, no questions asked. And Kara ran as fast as she could and tried to stay in the shadows so Rebecca would not see her if she too was running. Kara calculated that unless Rebecca was held up by Durk or the professor, she could be only a few minutes behind and Kara could not risk being seen by Rebecca.

Jayden was out, presumably meeting with some guys from the football team, so when Ken hung up the phone after talking with the puffing Kara, he ran down to Kara's room, grabbed the entire first-aid kit she'd mentioned, ran back to his room, and climbed into his bed to apply the stretch bandage. He placed pillows at his back so he could sit up, then quickly placed a bottle of aspirin and a glass of water on his nightstand and waited for Kara.

Story . . . what will be my story? he thought. *Okay, calm down . . . what's plausible? Okay, okay, ummm, I was, ummm . . . I was going down to the Pub to meet Jayden . . . no, no, that won't work . . . we don't want Rebecca to know that Jayden was there. Oh, think . . . Okay, I was going to the library—yeah, the library—and on the way home, carrying a lot of stuff and trying to cut across the lawn, I fell over one of the sprinklers, and the pain was so great that I lay there for a while unable to move. No, that's no good because I have no books here from the library. Okay . . . I was coming home from the library—no mention of books—and tripped over the sprinkler and lay there in agony, then hobbled here, figured I needed to go to the hospital, but then aspirin helped and I'm okay. It's just a sprain. Yeah, that's good.*

Kara ran into Ken's room. She was out of breath but began to blurt out her story as quickly as she could. "I saw the professor standing in the dark of the outer office peeking into the room where—presumably—Durk and Rebecca were . . . alone. I got scared. I think it was like some kind of, you know, like a voyeur does. I mean, he had the lights out in the outer office so he wouldn't be seen and even brought a chair to the crack in the door so he could sit and watch what was going on. Oh, Ken . . . oh . . . then I was going to barge in and tell Rebecca . . . but then I thought that then they'd know we were spying and that maybe we wouldn't be able to convince Rebecca that they were bad, not us. But then I saw the camera in the professors hand . . . and was gonna try to grab it and run . . . but then I . . . I thought that maybe he hadn't taken any pictures yet or maybe he'd catch me and then . . . then I thought that we need evidence so I . . . Oh, Ken, they *are* bad . . . oh, Ken, I am sickened by this. So I phoned Rebecca to get her outta there . . . telling her you had an accident . . . to come right away . . . and hung up. Oh, Ken, did I do the right thing? Can we pull this off? I just needed to get Rebecca away from that . . . that disgusting voyeur!"

"Yes, Kara, you did *exactly* the right thing. If Jayden comes in, we'll have to make him believe that I was really hurt and didn't call him because, by that time, I began to feel better. Then when Rebecca is gone, I'll fill Jayden in about what really happened. Maybe we have to change our strategy. Geez, I'm shocked. I can hardly believe that they'd do something like that. I mean, Durk had to be in on it, don't you think?

"Yeah, I'd think so. Ohh, how could he do that to Rebecca? In fact, maybe they've done this kind of thing before."

"Geez . . . that would be horrible . . . I mean . . . it's already horrible . . . but . . ."

Rebecca burst into the room, out of breath and visibly shaken. "Oh, Ken, what happened to you? Are you all right? I came as soon as I could after receiving Kara's phone call. What happened? Do you need to go to the hospital?"

"No, no, Rebecca, it was so nice of you to come, and I'm sorry if I worried both of you. Kara just came running in as well. At first I did think I might have to go to the hospital—it hurt so much that I could hardly walk, and I just laid on the lawn. But now I think it's just a sprain. Aspirin took away the pain, and I can walk on it, gingerly, but I *can* put weight on it now. I called Kara from where I fell thinking I needed help to get back to the room, but before Kara even got here I'd hobbled back to the room already, wrapped it to keep down any swelling and took some aspirin."

"Good. I was so worried . . . made me think all the way over here how much I love you guys and how devastated I'd be if anything happened to any of you." Ken and Kara were so glad that Rebecca had come right away. That meant that she'd been right behind Kara and had perhaps avoided what Durk and the professor had in mind that night.

Jayden walked in at just that moment totally unaware of the drama that had just taken place. He noticed that Ken and Kara exchanged a look of relief and seemed to be signaling to him with their eyes. He didn't understand what was happening. Rebecca was home, she seemed safe and whole. But then he noticed Ken's bandaged ankle.

"Ken, why are you in bed? What's wrong with your ankle? What happened? Are you all right?"

"Yeah, Jayden, I'm fine, but I think I overreacted. I fell over a sprinkler when I was cutting across the lawn and called Kara because the pain was so bad that I couldn't walk. But then it began to subside, and I hobbled back to the room, and after aspirin and a bandage, I realized that it's just a sprain. But I'd frightened Kara and she phoned Rebecca and here we all are. Sorry."

"Don't say sorry. We're all friends—special friends—and we help one another. We're just glad that you are okay, that's the important thing. You did the right thing to phone. It may have been very serious and you could have needed to go to the hospital. Right, Kara? Right, Rebecca?"

"Absolutely! Yeah, and look, it brought us all together again!" Kara quipped.

The four friends spent about a half hour together, and Jayden poured them some mango and cranberry juice, a combination they all liked, and they talked about their classes for a while. Ken and Kara did not want Rebecca to go back to work so they continued to talk to keep Rebecca distracted and too worried about Ken to think of leaving. Later, after watching Ken walk on his ankle and satisfied that he did not need to go to the emergency room, Rebecca and Kara left for their own rooms with plans that they would meet again the next evening for dinner in the cafeteria.

When the girls left, Ken hopped out of bed once again and took off his bandage, telling Jayden to sit down while he told him what had really happened and to hold onto his hat and his temper when he told him. Jayden was stunned. *Why had Ken lied about hurting his ankle? That isn't like him. I wonder what could have happened to cause him to do that?*

And as Ken told his story, Jayden's blood began to boil. "How dare they do such a thing . . . how dare they try to compromise Rebecca that way . . . and you are darn right that Durk had to know what was going on. I'm gonna kill him. In fact, I'm going to the head dean and tell him about this. Geez . . . a camera? Isn't that against the law?"

"No, Jayden, you're not going to the dean. Now think about this. Slow down and think. We're gonna get them, trip them up, catch them somehow, but we have to find a way to make Rebecca think about what dangers are out there. We have to do something to protect her while we are getting the evidence we need. Otherwise, *if we don't have evidence*, it's just our word against theirs, and that won't hold up. If we let them know what we are doing, they will close up shop and we won't be able to put a stop to this . . . this . . . a permanent stop to this . . . behavior. We have to think of the others they may have harmed, think of the women they might harm in the future! Going after them now won't help. They'll just deny it. It might alienate Rebecca from us, and worse, it will make them hide what they do. Now that we *know* beyond the shadow of a doubt that they are up to such . . . filth, we know that we can find evidence of it. Hard cold evidence will put them away for good. We have more hope of getting them than we ever had before."

"How am I supposed to let this go, Ken? I need to protect Rebecca from these animals. Now!"

"Yeah, but you'll only win the first round. She may not believe you. She believes Durk. She loves him. She'll side with him thinking you are jealous, or interfering, or you hate Durk or something. She'd never believe you, that's *why* we need evidence. I know it's tough, and maybe we'd better speed up our plans, but we can't tell Rebecca right now. We can't if we want to put these guys away for good."

"You're right . . . darn . . . but you are right, Ken. But you know what, maybe we can make up a story about this type of operation—you know, voyeurism—like maybe something we read in the newspaper about a girl who was seduced while the guy's friend watched from the 'outer office'!"

"That's a good idea, Jayden, but we'll have to do it subtly—you know, talk about some other things we read first—then about that. Maybe if Rebecca hears about stuff like that, she will take note of her surroundings. And you know, Jayden, as strange as it seems right now, I really trust Rebecca. I mean, yeah, she's naïve and all, but I think that when it comes right down to the wire, that she'd pull back from taking that final step over the cliff. You know what I mean?"

"Yeah . . . well . . . I guess I do too. She thinks she's in love, and she wants to please the bum . . . and I think she'll go to great lengths to please him . . . but I think I agree with you that she will keep her wits about her. Maybe we do have a little time, because I think Durk will have a hard time making her do anything that really goes against what she was taught. She does love God, respect His instruction, and she loves and respects her family and would never want them to be disappointed in her. She also knows the heartache that her birth mother went through, so from that perspective she might be extremely careful. And I guess that she would be a better person if she does make the decision on her own—you know, to follow what she has been taught and what she's always felt was right and what would lead to *real* happiness. But it's so hard for me to let her . . . well . . . you know . . . experiment . . . with all the spirits that are out there. I want her to be happy, but I don't want her to get hurt. I will have to trust her, I guess . . . and pray that God will protect her. But we have to work fast, okay? She could be in great danger if they trap her somehow . . . or . . . or . . . force her."

And with those words Jayden suddenly began to cry. Ken was shocked. He didn't know what to do. But then it dawned on him: Jayden was in love with Rebecca. Not just as a friend, but he was *in* love! *Boy, no wonder this hurts him so much,* Ken thought. *He loves her so much that he lets her go . . . wants her happiness above his own . . . geez. I'll bet that was one of the most difficult things that Jayden ever had to do. Boy, I wish I could do something to make this easier on him.*

Jayden had turned from Ken not wanting him to see him crying, so Ken pretended to busy himself at his desk until Jayden got hold of his emotions. Jayden recovered quickly, embarrassed and glad that Ken had been busy at his desk and may not have seen him break down. When Ken casually asked him if he was okay, he assured Ken that he was fine, just worried about Rebecca.

A few nights later, Rebecca was to see Durk again and planned to attend a beer party with him. None of the others had been invited, nor knew that Rebecca was even going to a party. But the fact that she was going out without them worried Ken, Jayden, and Kara even though she'd said that she would only be gone for two or three hours. They had been glad that Rebecca had stayed close to them during the last few days but were now worried that they would not know where she was and would not be able to watch over her when she left. They had read aloud a number of things that college kids should watch out for and had added their little spiel about voyeurism. But they were still worried and decided to spend the evening together and wait for Rebecca to return. They wouldn't be able to sleep anyway, so they might as well stay up until she came home.

The party was at Professor T's house, and it was prearranged that Durk could have free access to any room in the house if he wanted to be alone with Rebecca. Beer and wine ran freely, and there was also a stash of hard liquor that only a few had access to. Rebecca would only accept a Pepsi, and this had made Durk angry. But she was adamant, and he figured that he'd wait a while and ask her again later . . . maybe even just hand her something that was sweet claiming that it contained no liquor.

Rebecca had never been to a party like this before and was somewhat surprised. Everyone was drinking and getting pretty rowdy. Many couples were dancing, others obviously in love and impervious to kissing in public. Some were telling jokes and others recounting football plays and scores. Professor T seemed to be the only nonstudent in the group and roamed the rooms watching everyone as they partied. He especially seemed to enjoy watching and flirting with the girls in their incredibly short skirts and halter tops. The girls appeared to know him well and sometimes allowed him to kiss or caress them and easily walked away from him when he went too far. Rebecca was appalled. She also saw that Professor T appeared to watch the couples who were deeply engrossed in one another.

When Durk brought her a sweet-flavored drink, she had no idea that it contained liquor, but within a short time she felt dizzy and felt a warm wave of relaxation flow through her body as the alcohol entered her blood stream. She lazily contemplated whether or not Durk had inadvertently added liquor to her drink, but she didn't want to fight with him so she simply sipped rather than drank the delicious nectar. Durk drew her through the crowd telling her that he wanted to talk with her, and that they needed to find someplace quiet for him to do so. He led her to the stairway, took her empty glass from her hand, and replaced it with another glass filled with the sweet pink liquid before climbing to the second floor.

When they entered the bedroom, suddenly Rebecca was afraid. She turned to Durk telling him that they'd better go back down the stairs because she was uncomfortable being in a bedroom alone with him. He promised her that he'd only brought her upstairs to talk with her, but needed a "hug and a kiss" before he told her what he needed to say. He said that he understood that she would not want others to hear what he was saying, or to see him kissing her. Her heart melted because he was so considerate and deciding she had misjudged him, she acquiesced and remained in the bedroom. They sat on the bed, perched at the foot of the bed. Durk turned her face to his, told her how much he loved her, and began to kiss her.

As the liquor flowed through her veins and reached her brain, and she listened to his loving words, saw how tender he was and so sweet, she relaxed, trusting him completely. He kept murmuring how much she meant to him and how much he needed her. His weight pulled her backward until they were lying flat on the bed with their legs dangling over the edge. He continued to kiss her, and she kissed him back. Emboldened, he ran his hands down her rib cage and over her hip and back up again and continued to do so. Rebecca was frightened by how much she wanted him to keep touching her and how soothing his touch was.

But then Durk moved her skirt and ran his hand up her thigh, and though she moaned with the pleasure of his touch, she suddenly pushed him away and sat up, struggling against his attempts to hold her down. She began to cry. Feeling contrite, an emotion quite foreign to him, Durk took her in his arms and apologized. "I'm sorry, Rebecca, it's just that you are so beautiful and you feel so good . . . I wasn't going to do anything wrong . . . honest." And Rebecca believed him, deciding that he'd meant no harm. She wanted to believe that Durk had just been carried away by the moment and meant her no harm.

Durk gently brought her back down on the bed once again and began to stroke her, and Rebecca, trusting him again, relaxed under his touch. But then she saw a reflection in the dresser mirror. She could see Professor T at their door watching them. Two mirrors, one in the hall and one in the bedroom, had given him away. Rebecca gasped and said loudly, "Durk, I want to go home right now. Professor T is watching us."

Durk was furious. He'd almost gotten Rebecca to relax, and then that stupid, idiot of a professor had messed him up. Chaldeth too was furious thinking, *These men are so dumb! And that stupid professor is too impatient.* Chaldeth would now have to start over and work a little bit harder to bring about the completion of his plan.

The professor, realizing that he'd been caught, walked into the room pretending to be sorry for interrupting them. "Oh, I'm so sorry, I guess you two wanted to talk privately. This is my bedroom, and I'd just come upstairs to get something. Please forgive me for barging in. I do apologize."

Rebecca was confused. Had she imagined that he'd been watching? Perhaps that drink had made her imagine crazy things. Her upbringing made her respond cordially, and she said, "We should apologize for being in your room. We'll leave now . . . sorry." And Durk could do nothing but follow her out the door with a parting scowl at the professor.

Good save, Professor, thought Chaldeth. *I can make that save work for me.*

By the time Rebecca reached her dorm, she'd convinced herself that it was her fault that she'd even allowed Durk to bring her upstairs and that Durk meant her no harm and the professor had not been spying on them. *It was probably those silly stories Ken, Jayden, and Kara were telling me about voyeurism and that terrible drink that caused me to be so suspicious. It was the professor's own room after all, and he had every right to be there. How ridiculous I was. I hope he doesn't fire me.*

Chapter 6

Chaldeth Plans

As he reviewed the events of the past month, Chaldeth saw that he had made progress . . . but not enough. He wanted results, and to obtain them he was going to have to make things happen at a faster pace. The only way to accomplish this goal was to cause Rebecca to become more acquiescent and Durk to be more assertive. But how? If he inspired Durk to bring greater harm to Rebecca's friends to prevent them from interfering, Rebecca might flee. Therefore, whatever he chose to do to correct this situation would have to be done subtly.

He was angered by their feeble efforts at spying, but he also laughed at those efforts because he knew that he could outsmart them. They were like a buzzing fly circling his head, that's all; certainly not a real threat. There was only one thing . . . . their faith . . . that could become a threat, but with Jayden and Rebecca far from their church, not receiving Holy Communion every week and forgetting to pray, he felt that even that threat was nothing to worry about.

Chaldeth had experienced a short tremor of fear when Jayden told Ken about the power of entities like Chaldeth. Chaldeth remembered their conversation—in fact, he could recall their exact words: "Okay, here's the deal," Jayden had said, "we really do have an enemy . . . really. And there really is a devil, Satan, and he doesn't want you or any of us to be loyal to God—ya know, to have a relationship with God—and if we do, or start to, he will attack. And in a lot of situations, Satan is capable of causing some pretty terrible things to happen by influencing the people around us."

But Ken hadn't taken Jayden seriously and had replied, "Yeah, right. He's gonna come and whisper in my ear that I should go and punch the professor and get myself kicked out of school, and I'll *gladly* do what he says? Yeah, right. Come on, Jayden, get real."

Jayden had come right back at Ken by telling him about the scripture that explained the dangers of the evil spirits governed by Satan and he had gone to his computer to retrieve the information he was looking for. When he completed his search, he turned to Ken and began to read. "Matthew 12:45 says, 'Then goeth he and taketh with himself seven other spirits more wicked than himself, and they enter in and dwell there, and the last state of that man is worse than the first. Even so shall it be also unto this wicked generation.'

"Luke 8:29 says, '(For he had commanded the unclean spirit to come out of the man. For oftentimes it had caught him: and he was kept bound with chains and in fetters; and he brake the bands, and was driven of the devil into the wilderness.)'

"Matthew 8:16 explains that there were *many* possessed by evil spirits in Christ's time and that He cast them out by his word, and they were healed. 'When the evening was come, they brought unto him many that were possessed with devils: and he cast out the spirits with his word, and healed all that were sick.'

"And last but not least, here's a couple of verses that tells us what Satan is capable of: He can move men to do his bidding (1 Chronicles 21:1), can walk back and forth on the earth (Job 1:7), cause illness (Job 2:7), can take God's word from men's hearts (Mark 4:15), can enter man (Luke 22:3 and John 13:27), can blind the minds of them which believe not (2 Corinthians 4:4), can transform himself (2 Corinthians 11:14), can send messengers to hurt man (2 Corinthians 12:7), can hinder people (1 Thessalonians 2:18), and can produce signs and has powers (2 Thessalonians 2:9). It is important for us to know that Satan is capable of producing signs and has supernatural powers, because that's what convinces us to accept his premises: 'the working of Satan with all power and signs and lying wonders.'"

Chaldeth seethed with anger as he recalled that conversation because this knowledge could be a danger to him. Ken was considering what Jayden told him, and so was Kara. Chaldeth's challenge was to make them forget or ignore the warnings God provided about him and those like him; in fact, he hoped to make them think that statements such as those were ridiculous. He needed Jayden and Rebecca to be complacent about what the Bible taught and Ken and Kara to think that it was impossible for such activities to exist.

Chaldeth knew full well that God had developed a perfect and all-encompassing plan for every person who was ever born, conceived, or died. Chaldeth hated the fact that this plan demonstrated God's powerful, loving, forgiving nature. He hated that God had placed His plan of salvation into the physics of this world to help mankind overcome evil and bring them into an eternity of righteousness with God. He was jealous of what God offered these . . . these . . . people and angry that he was forced to battle the natural laws that faith and love ignited.

Those who understood God's plan and used their faith were under some kind of special protection which Chaldeth could not penetrate. He and all the others who had followed Satan had to win this war, had to stop God from fulfilling His plan . . . or they would die. No evil of any kind would be allowed into the new heaven and earth that God wanted to create for those who would remain faithful to Him while on this earth.

But Chaldeth and his friends had one thing going for them. There were a certain number of people that God wanted for that new heaven and earth, and no one but God knew what that number was. Only if Chaldeth and his friends could prevent God from reaching that number, could this world and all its evil continue to exist.

Chaldeth knew that Jayden and Rebecca's family . . . and even their friends . . . were a part of that special number that God wanted for His Kingdom. If Chaldeth could break them, even some of them, he and his minions would be assured of more time, many more days and months and years in which they could continue to live.

Chaldeth remembered the moment when he had decided to join Satan in his rebellion against God. During their war only once did he wonder if he'd chosen the right side. He had worried when they had lost the war and God banned them from heaven and they had come to earth to continue the war in a different manner. They became terrorists. In fact, they were very much like the terrorists who Satan himself now inspired and worked with. The fallen angels could not succeed openly so they had to hide, plot, inspire others to hatred, hit hard, and then go into hiding again. But the battle they now fought would be their last if they didn't win this time. This was a fight for their life. This one had to be won. This one could only be won if people were unaware of the presence of their army, or of the consequences of allowing themselves to be inspired by those in that army. Chaldeth and his cohorts needed to prevent them from turning to God, learning God's words, and knowing that it was them who caused their agony, not God.

This is why the things that Jayden had said to Ken were a danger to Chaldeth. This is why Chaldeth wanted to bring Jayden down along with Rebecca. And what a wonderful twist it would be if Chaldeth could inspire Ken to turn against Jayden! *Yes! That was it! That could be the icing on the cake! Now . . . how can I accomplish this?*

Chaldeth adjusted his former plan by simply adding a few tidbits to it. Distrust, jealousy, envy, perceived hurt, revenge, anger, power, greed, these were but some of Chaldeth's tools, and he could use them in his quest to break those who followed God and to inspire those who did not. He could cause man to hurt man so easily when they did not know that this was the way the evil ones worked. *Sometimes it was so easy!*

But Rebecca and Jayden were not as easy a target as Chaldeth had first imagined. They had been brought up to know about evil and how it worked. They could become suspicious if Chaldeth wasn't subtle enough, and that suspicion could cause them to run for cover . . . to God. They also knew about the protections God offered against the work of the entities of evil. So Chaldeth had to be subtle, patient, move slowly, create benchmarks for his progress that the average person would not recognize . . . cause a *slow* erosion of their integrity. *Ahh, what a challenge,* Chaldeth thought, *but I am up to it. I can do it and I will!*

Chaldeth had to keep them focused on Durk or even the professor and not on evil or God. He had to cause them to focus only on the problems and to make them think that they themselves could solve those problems. His final plan, if everything would work just as Chaldeth planned, was to break Rebecca through her association with Durk; and he was considering introducing drugs and alcohol to achieve his goals more quickly. Then he would incite Jayden and have him make huge mistakes that would entrap him and he would cause others to accuse Jayden of harming Rebecca. He would place doubt and anger, even some kind of fear in Ken's heart so he would choose not to help Jayden, perhaps even blame Jayden for what Chaldeth would make happen.

He'd leave Kara to stew over her inability to help any of them and let anger fill her heart. Then he would cause that anger to turn to hate and produce an unforgiving heart. It was funny, really, that God had placed power into the act of forgiving. No one seemed to understand that concept. And to Chaldeth, that was incredibly odd. If they forgave, if they loved the soul who committed the evil, they would be protected and could even win in the long run. It was a very strange concept, but it was what God had put in place and what so few people understood.

Chaldeth laughed to himself. How many people knew that he and *every one* of Satan's minions had read the Bible from cover to cover and *fully* understood every passage? They had actually watched and experienced what the Bible related. Almost no one understood that! And this was such a great advantage to Chaldeth, and others like him. Those . . . people . . . were so stupid. Didn't they ever ask themselves how Chaldeth and his kind—in fact, all the spirits of this world—understood that they had to stop God from obtaining the number of souls He wanted if they didn't know what the Bible said? Or that they knew what their end would be? How would Chaldeth's kind know how to fight if they didn't know what to block in the hearts of men so they could convince them to do their bidding?

One of Satan's greatest triumphs was the perversion of truth. All truth could be found in God's words, and to pervert or change those words or the interpretation of them was so easy for the spirits of this world; just a little tweak here and there, and voila, either a new "religion" was born or wrong became right—perfect! It was such fun for Chaldeth and the other spirits of this world to cause these perversions because those they nudged into a false doctrine *believed* that stuff! They believed that their "new" way, the direction in which Chaldeth and his friends had nudged them, was the *right* way. They even thought that they were doing God's will. *Oh, that's such a thrill for us to watch, especially when we can say that we were the cause of the little tweak that sent those weaklings spiraling in the wrong direction. We can do so much; even cause God's children to become complacent about Christ!*

Whenever Chaldeth became discouraged by the slow pace of his progress, he would think of the incredible success of his cohorts who'd inspired the extremists groups in the Middle East to believe, *actually believe,* that if they murdered everyone who disagreed with them, God would reward them. It was also amazing that they believed, *really believed,* that their reward—to be with beautiful women in eternity—was a *godly* reward! That was an amazing feat! But they had done it, and it had brought great success to the underworld.

The people that Chaldeth found the easiest to convince were those who either did not know, forgot, or ignored what God explained in Matthew 22:37-39, the greatest commandment: "Jesus said unto him, Thou shalt love the Lord thy God with all thy heart, and with all thy soul, and with all thy mind. This is the first and great commandment. And the second is like unto it, Thou shalt love thy neighbor as thyself." And Matthew 25:40, "Inasmuch as ye have done it unto one of the least of these my brethren, ye have done it unto me."

They had also created doctrines that taught that if someone believed that Christ had died for their sins, there was no other work for them to do—they were automatically saved. Even the Bible told them that faith without works was dead! Chaldeth proudly quoted the passage that these people ignored. James 2:17 says, "Even so faith, if it hath not works, is dead . . ." and again in James 2:26 God told them, "For as the body without the spirit is dead, so faith without works is dead also."

He gloated over the perversions of faith and the false interpretations that they had created and had instilled in so many people. Chaldeth knew that throughout the Bible God tells His people that they need to overcome thoughts, impulses, and deeds that are not pleasing to Him and tells them to continue in the struggle to overcome these things throughout their lives. Chaldeth was overjoyed that they had been able to pervert those statements as well. Many believed the perversion that if they just had faith all would be well with their soul. But in Revelation 2:7, God said, "To him that overcometh will I give to eat of the tree of life, which is in the midst of the paradise of God." And God even told them *how* to overcome!

So all in all Chaldeth knew that they were making progress. He believed that if they kept hacking away at God's words, at people's true faith and good works, he and his cohorts would ultimately win the battle in which they were engaged. Undermining faith was easy if they could break someone's hope, make them doubt that God really meant what He said in the Bible, and cause them to doubt the promises God made to His people. Chaldeth felt that they were winning this war through those whose inability to interpret every nuance caused them to believe that the Bible was not to be taken literally. Why believe one part and not another?

Chaldeth laughed aloud at that conclusion because he knew that man's ego was so great that they could not admit that their minds could not grasp the incredible and true meaning, so instead they said that the Bible was, after all, written by fallible men! That had been a great victory for them. Chaldeth and his friends had laughed together saying, "Well, they are only one step away from totally negating the Bible. Soon they'll be saying, 'It is impossible for us to literally eat and drink of Christ's body, so it's all just metaphor. None of it can really be understood.' And then they will no longer believe at all, and God will never reach the number of souls He is looking for."

So as Chaldeth thought about his plans for Jayden and Rebecca, he fully understood that he'd have to interfere with what God would try to do for them. Rebecca would have to want her relationship with Durk so badly that she would throw away all caution. *Perhaps*, Chaldeth thought, *I can do this by making her defend "poor, misunderstood" Durk from "mean, judgmental" Jayden. This will surely incite Jayden and push him into making mistakes so I can trap him and cause others to accuse him of being the one who harms Rebecca.*

Chaldeth believed that Jayden would wonder why God didn't help him, and this could break his faith. As for Kara, well, she wasn't a Holy Roller, as he called the others, so he could probably make this whole situation cause her to believe that God didn't ever help. And as for Ken, if he placed fear in Ken's heart, it was possible that he, like many others would turn to God. Many ran to God only when they were afraid. Chaldeth would have to be careful about how he dealt with Ken and finally decided that he would take it step by step and adjust his plan as it evolved.

One thing was for sure: he had to make his plan work. If he did he would not only break Rebecca and Jayden, but possibly their whole group of family and friends. They would rush to help when they learned of the troubles Chaldeth would cause, and they would pray. They'd get their ministers to pray, they'd tithe a little more just for Rebecca and Jayden, and they'd keep at it. But at some point, they'd begin to doubt; and if Chaldeth was lucky and God waited to send help in order to test them, then maybe Chaldeth could get all of them, or at least many of them. That would put off his own destruction for quite a while.

It was strange that these humans didn't know what God said in Revelation 16:14 where He warned, "For they are the spirits of devils, working miracles, which go forth unto the kings of the earth and of the whole world, to gather them to the battle of that great day of God Almighty." Not only did Chaldeth know the Bible from cover to cover, and understand its every word, he also knew God's plan. He knew that God's plan of salvation had to be stopped or Chaldeth and all evil would die a terrible death. Luckily, once again, he and his friends had successfully prevented many from seeing how simple and easy to learn God's plan actually was. They'd worked to block men's minds, another of their abilities, so that people would find God's plan complicated and be unable to explain it. They'd blocked the minds of many ministers as well, so they would not lay it out to their parishioners in simple terms. And it was, after all, very simply explained.

Chaldeth thought of God's plan and its simplicity, and in a sudden desire to be sarcastic and to mimic those who preached God's plan, he said aloud, "God longs to fill His kingdom with souls who will truly love Him and His Son and also love one another. He wants these souls to understand the value of love, trust, and loyalty, and to choose to practice these attributes voluntarily. God began His plan by creating the earth in its limited universe. Then He created Adam and Eve to live happily in the Garden of Eden, walking and talking with Him.

"But the beautiful and powerful angel Lucifer, later known as Satan, rebelled against God because he was jealous of Christ, and of the new being, man, that God wanted to bring to fruition. As a result of his rebellion, Satan was thrown to earth with the angels who chose to follow Satan and had thus also disobeyed God. These numbered one third of all the angels. Satan knew God's plan and understood that, when the plan was completed and God obtained the number of faithful loving souls He longed for, Satan would be thrown into hell for what he had done. To prevent God's plan from moving forward and thus forestall his own destruction, Lucifer destroyed God's relationship of trust and loyalty with Adam and Eve by enticing them to sin through disobedience. God then banished Adam and Eve as he had banished Satan.

"But God, knowing what Satan would do to them, provided a way for Adam and Eve, and the generations to follow, to escape the captivity Satan proposed for them and return to God. Christ offered Himself as the perfect sacrifice by which the sins of man could be forgiven.

"At every turn, Satan interfered with God's plan, trying to break those who would follow God. He had to, because when God collected the number of souls he wanted for his new creation, Satan would be bound forever. Thus Satan is fighting for his life when discouraging the faithful. But many of those tested by Satan are strengthened through these attacks, becoming like gold refined in the fires of tribulation. From these faithful, God is building what the Bible calls the Bride of Christ.

"God even provided for those who died in sin by creating a means of testimony in eternity, but only while grace is still available on earth. Christ entered hell after His death to give testimony of His triumph to those who had died in their sins before He could bring His perfect sacrifice. He told them that now they too could find forgiveness.

"God has allotted a certain amount of time for His chosen ones to be made ready, and when that time is up, His Son will return to earth for the First Resurrection to take to heaven both those from eternity who have obtained forgiveness and those alive who are faithful. When they are gone, grace will also be gone, and a great destruction will begin where one third of all the people on earth will die. When the destruction ends, God will send His Son back to earth with those He had taken at the First Resurrection. They will have celestial (perfect) bodies and will reign as kings and priests for one thousand years of peace to bring testimony to everyone living or dead who was not taken in the First Resurrection. Satan will be bound during this time, unable to influence mankind, so all mankind will learn about . . . and accept . . . God.

"But after the one thousand years of peace, Satan will be loosed again for a little while so those who have now accepted God can be tested. Satan will wreak havoc on those not firm in their faith. Then will come the day of judgment when everyone, except those taken by Christ for the First Resurrection, will be judged. Some, which the Bible calls the "goats," will be cast into hell with Satan forever, while others, called the "lambs," will inhabit God's new kingdom where there will be no sorrow and no tears. Those taken for the First Resurrection will continue to reign as kings and priests in the new kingdom. They will never have to be judged because their sins had been forgiven and entirely wiped away by God. Only those from the First Resurrection and those remaining faithful after the thousand years of peace would share the new heaven and earth."

When Chaldeth finished speaking, he felt drained and said to himself, "If God completes His plan, all evil will be destroyed forever." His voice sounded bitter and angry as he recited the plan that would destroy him. He hated God's plan and the simple sound of its inevitable conclusion. That hate made him more determined than ever to move ahead with his own plan and move as quickly as he could. His first move was to fill Durk's mind with a need to dominate Rebecca and to make Durk believe that he could only achieve his goal by being more aggressive.

Rebecca noticed that something had changed in Durk. He had become cavalier about their relationship. He didn't talk with her as often as he had in the past. But he held her more often, and she could feel the passion in him. When she became frightened by its intensity and would pull back from his embrace, he'd be terribly angry and she would try to calm him by entering back into his embrace. Usually her reticence slowed him down and allowed her to maintain the line that she worried she might cross. She wondered what was troubling him and wanted to make everything all right for him. Her heart went out to him believing that he was suffering in some way.

She would often wonder why she could not be more like him and allow herself the freedom to enjoy life and to engage in some of the activities so many of the students seemed to easily accept. She recognized that she held different opinions about politics and religion and even about simple things like work ethics and the role of government. She was often persuaded by the arguments that some of the students gave to support their position. Her confusion about these matters added to her confusion about her relationship with Durk.

Even the professors seemed to truly believe that their way of thinking, so different from her way of thinking; was the right way, the only way. Chaldeth had successfully planted the first seeds of doubt in Rebecca's heart, doubt that the teachings she'd grown up with were correct. Sometimes she'd discuss her thoughts with Jayden and Ken and Kara, but they never felt that what she worried about was worth the worry. They told her to stick with what she'd been taught and she'd never go wrong. This alienated her from them, and she began to seek out the company of new friends who understood her questions and were willing to explore these different avenues of debate with her and help her find the answers she sought.

Jayden noticed that Rebecca had taken on many extracurricular activities but was glad that she was venturing out, meeting new people, and debating various issues. He felt that if it took her away from Durk, it was good for her. But Jayden had no clue that those debates were influencing her in such a negative manner. He was busy trying to keep his grade average perfect so he could go on to medical school. He was also blinded for some reason to his old worries about Rebecca, and that was unusual for him. Chaldeth chuckled. It had been so easy. He'd made Jayden think that as long as Rebecca didn't mention Durk she was okay. Chaldeth had successfully drawn Rebecca away; he'd placed some of his key people near Rebecca . . . and there was more to come.

One evening Chaldeth arranged that Kara, Jayden, and Ken would be elsewhere when Rebecca was feeling (due to Chaldeth's influence) very lonely and confused. He'd arranged for a student from one of Rebecca's classes to knock on her dorm door and invite her to a political debate. Rebecca agreed to go hoping to assuage her loneliness and her sense that no one understood her confusion about the many pertinent issues in her life. By the end of the evening Rebecca decided to join this group and soon began to enjoy their lively debates and discussions. They spoke about life's choices, their personal responsibilities to society, and today's emerging political scene.

Sometimes her Uncle Jim's remarks about these subjects came back to Rebecca as she sat listening to these debates. She marveled how both arguments appeared to have merit yet each conclusion was diametrically opposed to the other. What was she to believe? She suddenly understood that rhetoric itself carried a lot of weight in convincing people to believe a certain point of view and she marveled at the inherent danger in that.

Durk, having joined this group when he learned of Rebecca's involvement, sided with the opinions given during the debate that opposed those Rebecca later expressed. When she spoke of her uncle's political views, Durk said that he must be a raving conservative, whereas most people were liberals. "Don't you know that, Rebecca?" And rather than sound uninformed, she simply nodded her head in assent.

Chaldeth wasn't interested in politics, only in how someone viewed religion as a whole. He wanted a confused and liberal view to be considered and accepted by Rebecca. Many of her fellow students were engaged in exploring New Age religions. Some touted tarot cards or astrology, numerology, feng shui, the glorifying of nature, and non-Christian religions as the path to heaven. Every approach, even radical Islam and atheism, was considered acceptable in the mind of many. Rebecca was at first shocked, but then as she listened to the arguments in support of each of these positions, she felt that each appeared logical. In a few fleeting instances, Rebecca remembered that God said in Malachi 2:8, "But ye are departed out of the way; ye have caused many to stumble at the law; ye have corrupted the covenant of Levi, saith the Lord of Hosts." Despite the warning bell that went off in her head, she was fascinated by what she heard. It was so different than what she'd heard at home.

Sitting in her dorm room a few evenings later, Rebecca was thinking of these debates and went to her computer to search the Bible and concordance. She searched for words and phrases that might help her learn what she should believe. She didn't want to judge; she wanted to follow the truth and be pleasing to God, but what she was hearing was so confusing. It all sounded so, well, right somehow. She prayed and asked God to help her and to guide her to the words in scripture that would tell her what to do.

Almost immediately she found Matthew 24:28 where Christ spoke about the Pharisees, the priests in the time of Jesus, and Jesus to them, "Even so ye also outwardly appear righteous unto men, but within ye are full of hypocrisy and iniquity." Then she was led to Acts 20:29-31 that warned, "For I know this, that after my departing shall grievous wolves enter in among you, not sparing the flock. Also of your own selves shall men arise, speaking perverse things, to draw away the disciples after them. Therefore watch . . ."

That's what Jayden said, she thought. *He said to watch and be careful because Satan is devious and subtle and we'd have to be careful not to lose God's words, have them stolen from our heart. It is true that the words I am hearing sound . . . . just like it says in Matthew . . . . as if they are righteous. And it is true that nothing is ever said in these groups about God or the Bible or about living as God asks us to live. But on the other hand, what they say seems so . . . so . . . caring. . . so concerned about the welfare of others and about making opportunity and acquisition equal for everyone. Yet they never talk about Christ or about grace or sin. But on the other hand, they speak about helping others. Conversely, they do judge and speak of taking vengeance. God doesn't advocate that! I am so confused. Oh well, there is no harm in just listening.*

Chaldeth breathed a sigh of relief. His hardest task was to refute the word of God, and while he wasn't yet home-free with Rebecca, he was on the way. She was confused, and doubt had begun to rear its powerful head! Just a little more brainwashing and she was his! Now he'd better get Durk on the job again. Chaldeth was getting impatient. He wanted to see a breakthrough with Rebecca.

Chaldeth visited Durk and made him think of Rebecca. He caused him to believe that Rebecca was playing with him, mocking him, play acting at being a little Goody Two-shoes. *Maybe,* Chaldeth hinted, *she is even bragging about how easily she controls you, Durk. Maybe, Durk, you're simply not man enough to succeed with Rebecca.* It was that final thought that made Durk succumb to the cruelest part of his nature and made him determined to show Rebecca that he *was* man enough and that *he* was the one in control—certainly not her.

There was a party planned at the house Durk rented with three friends. The house was located just off campus and gave them more freedom than they would have had if they lived in the dorm. At first, Durk was not going to invite Rebecca to the party because there would be a number of other girls attending who were a lot of fun to be with. But instead he decided to ask Rebecca to attend after all and planned to get her alone . . . ostensibly to discuss a serious matter. It was strange to Durk that he still wanted Rebecca since so many others caught his fancy—girls who were more pliable and easier to deal with. Some were even gorgeous. But there was something about Rebecca—her quiet dignity, her ethereal eyes, her pitch black hair and lithe figure, her way of dressing, the elegance with which she held herself . . . . that kept drawing him to her. In some ways she represented what he really wanted in life but believed he could never have—a sort of stability and goodness. But then he would laugh, reminding himself that he would never be the type to stick around in a so-called stable environment where everyone always acted like a bunch of Bible-spouting nerds.

As he thought about it, he realized that he could almost hate Rebecca for what she stood for, and he was not about to let her take him for a fool. His friends were aware of his attachment to her, and there was no way that he would allow them to believe that he'd failed with her. His reputation was, after all, very important to him. He would prove himself once and for all at this party.

Meanwhile, Jayden had been associating with many students who were acquainted with Durk in the hope of gaining information about him. He listened to those who were on Durk's team or spoke of him by reputation. What Jayden learned was not good. The students joked about Durk, and most of them disliked him, although they never let Durk know that they felt this way. "Durk is a ladies' man, the love-'em-and-leave-'em type," one student said. Another added, "Well, I'd hate to get on his bad side because I think he's capable of anything. His temper can be so violent that he will do anything to get even and do so with no remorse." One student laughed and said, "Well, he sure is a good source for pot! I don't know where he gets his stuff, but he's always got it. I'm amazed that he's never been caught selling . . . it's common knowledge that he's the man." And another added, "I heard that Professor T is a good friend of Dean Peerca, who is always coming around to talk to the prof, and that he's the one who holds the purse strings to the goods. Durk's the go-between to reach other students that sell . . . and buy." Jayden replied to what was said by adding, "That doesn't say much for Durk's integrity or for the professor or even the dean's integrity either."

"*Integrity?* Are you kidding, Jayden? None of those guys ever thinks about that stuff. I mean, you've seen Durk on the field, haven't you? Well, he'd sooner grab your face mask and break your neck if you cross him and would blame his mother as his source of drugs if it got him off the hook. He has *no* integrity. And Professor T *sells* grades and test answers, and he gets away with that stuff. And sometimes he sells them for . . . uhh . . . favors . . . if you know what I mean!"

Jayden felt sick when he heard these statements. And because these things were said in a group of other students, and no one had refuted what was said—in fact had contributed even more information—Jayden believed what he heard. Rebecca was mixed up with these . . . these . . . these . . . dirtbags. *Could she already know these things?* Jayden felt that he had to do something to protect her. *But what?* If he said anything about this, she'd think he was lying and that might send her more quickly into danger.

When Jayden told Ken and Kara what he'd learned, Kara shared with them what she had learned. She'd held back from telling them what she had learned over the past few weeks because she knew that they would worry. "Rebecca has joined that left wing political group, and she never told us. The never telling is what's scary. I am afraid that they will influence her negatively. I mean, so many of them laugh about God and religion and support the fight to remove God from schools and government despite what our founding fathers tried to instill in our government and our way of life. And the speakers they invite from outside the campus encourage them to demonstrate against certain businesses, and against certain political figures or positions. I know because I've followed Rebecca and stood in the back of the room and listened to what she listened to."

Jayden suddenly thought of a verse from the Bible and was surprised that he knew it so well. Isaiah 29:13-15 says, " . . . this people draw near me with their mouth . . . but have removed their heart . . . behold I do a marvelous work . . . The wisdom of their wise men shall perish . . . Woe unto them that . . . hide their counsel from the Lord, and their works are in the dark, and they say 'Who seeth us? . . . '"

The others, not knowing the Bible well, were however struck by how fitting those words were to Rebecca's situation. Jayden went on to explain that many people wondered why those who oppose God seem to prosper. "So many ask," Jayden said, "why doesn't God strike them down? But God allows a lot of this stuff to go on so that His plan can move forward and reach its culmination. It's through all this . . . stuff . . . that God's people demonstrate their loyalty, are seen by God and others, and even by themselves, as faithful. Being tested is a strengthening in and of itself, and those who remain faithful through it all are the true followers of God. Going through these things teaches us right from wrong and helps us use our free will to choose between good and evil; between God and Satan."

"Jayden, you're so good at explaining these concepts. I mean, we're only a little bit religious maybe, and so we don't really know about all these things you mention—like evil, like spirits, like a plan that God has—about why certain heartaches occur. It's all so interesting and you really help us when you explain it. I for one have never been given an explanation. Choosing or not choosing to be . . . religious . . . never seemed that important. Yet when you tell us the meaning of the words in the Bible, I'm sort of . . . impressed . . . sort of seeing that I'd better get with it . . . get off the fence and choose."

"Thanks, Kara, but maybe God brought us together so you could learn. I think He works in some of the most unusual ways, but He always gets the job done! God says that everyone, *everyone*, will eventually hear what He says and what He offers. Those who listen and follow will become those who He will share a future with, and those who will not . . . well . . ."

"Yeah, Kara, we really should try to learn more about this stuff. I agree," Ken added. "I don't want to miss out just because I didn't know—well, I guess I'd better say didn't *listen*, so I do want to learn. Jayden, you told me the night after we first met what Satan does. You even said that there are lots of evil spirits around to trip us up, and you gave me a list of the stuff they do. I've kept the list and have been meaning to talk to you again about it." Pulling a wrinkled piece of paper from his jeans, Ken read, "Satan and his guys can make men to do his bidding (1 Chronicles 21:1), walk back and forth on the earth (Job 1:7), cause illness (Job 2:7), take God's word from men's hearts (Mark 4:15), enter man (Luke 22:3 and John 13:27), blind the minds of them which believe not (2 Corinthians 4:4), transform themselves (2 Corinthians 11:14), send messengers to hurt man (2 Corinthians 12:7), hinder people (1 Thessalonians 2:18), and produce signs and has powers (2 Thessalonians 2:9). Is this really true? Why would they, and how do they have the power to do this, and why doesn't God stop them and . . ."

"Wow . . . that's scary, Ken," Kara said. "I guess they must do it so subtly that I for one can't spot it. Jayden, do you think that Satan has entered Durk and blinded his mind and makes him do his bidding? But geez, does the fact that Durk is . . . well sort of . . . forced to do this stuff . . . uhhh . . . exonerate him?"

"Well . . ." Jayden explained, "that's what forgiveness is for. Sometimes, perhaps many times, God will present the truth to Durk, and it will be up to him—you know, free will and stuff—to make his choice . . . his own personal choice. But he will be told, as everyone eventually will be, and he will have the opportunity to change . . . but he may not. I guess that's why we aren't supposed to judge. But judging doesn't mean that we do not act to help one another escape from evil and to run from those who are evil and to pray for protection against evil. That's being careful, not judging."

"So what should we do?"

"I don't know. You asked a lot of questions, and there are answers for you that we can go over a little at a time. But right now, I'm feeling pretty bad. I am sick with worry about Rebecca, and I don't know what to do. We've been down this road before and decided to wait and watch. Well, we have waited and watched . . . and we've obtained quite a bit of information and all of it points to a danger for Rebecca. But where do we go from here? Dragging Rebecca kicking and screaming from associating with Durk and dear old Professor T. Nagorra won't stop this. And I'll bet that his crony, the dear Dean Peerca—and I wouldn't be surprised if dear sweet Professor Emils too—are also involved in this! If they aren't stopped, they'll be hurting even more students! I am thinking about calling my Uncle Jim and asking him what to do. I know that if he were Rebecca's parent, he'd come and get her and take her out of school and expose those . . . rats. I think he'll want to protect Elizabeth, Rebecca's mom, but he'd still probably get Rebecca, and probably me, outta here right away."

"But if you call him and then your family does take her out of school, and take you too, how will they stop what's going to happen to other students? There's no proof we can use to stop these guys and they will harm others."

"Yeah, that's true. So right now, I guess that they would probably get off scot-free and keep on doing what they've done. Another thing . . . . we're so close to finishing this semester and I'm getting great grades and want to go on to medical school so don't want to leave right now and . . . gosh, that sounds selfish doesn't it?"

"No, not at all. You and Rebecca have worked hard to get good grades, and to give it all up—maybe lose all credit for the semester if you leave now—well, it's a quandary. But how about if we really get the goods—you know, obtain real, concrete evidence against Durk and Professor T and could get *them* off the campus, and maybe the others too. Rebecca would learn the truth, thank us, and the campus and all the students will be better off for it . . . and neither of you would have to leave."

"Kara, that's a great idea," Ken said.

"Yeah, Kara, it is!" Jayden added. "But we're taking a risk. Rebecca might be in danger. We'll have to work fast and hard if we do that, and we should set a deadline for completion so we don't jeopardize Rebecca in case we can't do what we set out to do within a safe time frame."

"Okay," Kara said, "let's do it. We'll set that timeframe and do it! First of all, one of us will watch Durk, one of us will watch Professor T, and the other will try to watch Rebecca so we can barge in if anything is about to come down. If we hear anything about pot, we'll all try to get some info about where, how, when, and who. Maybe we should even switch these assignments—you know, change who watches whom—so if we are seen, it's a different person seen each time. This way they won't know we are onto them. What do you think?"

"A stroke of genius, Kara. Let's get that calendar with all the spaces under each date and write in our assignments . . . but let's use a sort of code so if Rebecca sees it she won't understand what it means."

"Great idea, Ken, another stroke of genius. Here's the calendar. What do you say we give our sleuthing two weeks, and if we haven't gotten some answers by then, we'll phone my Uncle Jim and tell him what has happened."

Thus Ken, Jayden, and Kara, armed with what they had learned, made their plans and then hit their books so the time they would spend on bringing this problem to an end would not interfere with their grades. Chaldeth hadn't liked what he heard. Nevertheless, he grinned believing that he could easily thwart their plans. He'd just have to complete his own work within that two-week span of time. He'd overheard their conversation, and he laughed at them. "They'll never pull it off. They'll fail. They have no idea that there will be a party at Durk's place, and that's when I will have Durk strike."

The night of the party arrived, and Kara noted the excitement in Rebecca's demeanor and also noted how carefully she dressed, discarding one outfit for another. Kara knew that tonight was an important night for Rebecca. Ken and Jayden were not yet back at their room, so Kara made a note on their calendar to indicate that she would be tracking Rebecca tonight. Their plan was that they would phone when possible to let one another know where they were and what they were doing.

Kara dressed in her usual black to follow Rebecca, hoping that Rebecca would walk to where she was going and not be picked up by car. Sure enough, Rebecca headed toward the wide cement walk that led around the campus buildings and down the hill toward the town. She appeared to be following directions written on a piece of paper. Kara kept her in sight and tried to keep a tree, a building, or a parked car between her and Rebecca should Rebecca turn around and look back.

Within ten minutes, Rebecca arrived at a small house just a few blocks from the huge brick buildings of the main campus. It was an area of homes that had been converted into student rentals. Durk shared the house with three other students and had a room of his own. But neither Kara nor Rebecca knew that. All Rebecca knew was that there was a party at this location and that Durk would be there waiting for her. True to his word, Durk had been watching for Rebecca and came out onto the porch to wave her in. Kara saw him walk onto the porch and knew then that Rebecca and Durk would be spending the evening together. She also realized that there was a party going on because she saw the many people, heard the loud music, and watched some students walk into the house carrying a six-pack of beer. She quickly telephoned Jayden to tell him where she was and what was happening. When Jayden relayed the message to Ken, Ken offered to walk over and simply crash the party, hoping to remain unnoticed by Durk or Rebecca.

As they considered Ken's suggestion, they realized that he was their best bet, because if either Durk or Rebecca saw Kara or Jayden, they would immediately suspect their presence. Whereas with Ken they might think that he had been invited to the party. Kara waited outside the house and walked halfway up the block, then turned and walked halfway down the other side of the block as she waited for Ken. When Ken arrived, probably not ten minutes after she'd phoned them, Kara walked back to her dorm and sat with Jayden, both working on term papers halfheartedly as they waited for word from Ken.

But Chaldeth had a plan as well. He could easily thwart Ken's efforts in a crowd of malleable people . . . so that's what he did. A drink, intended for a girl who had just broken up with her boyfriend, had been tampered with by that boyfriend in the hope of luring her back to his dorm where he could talk some sense into her and have her give up the idea of not seeing him again. Chaldeth simply had someone move the drink and someone else hand it to Ken. Unsuspecting, Ken slowly sipped the drink from a corner of the room where he could observe and remain somewhat anonymous. While he looked around, he listened carefully to the conversations around him in case anything of interest to their "case" was mentioned.

When he'd sipped less than half of his drink, he began to feel dizzy and his eyes felt terribly heavy. Without his being aware of falling, he slipped sideways off the chair and lost consciousness. His friends gently lifted him from the floor to the nearby couch laughing and telling him to sleep it off. When he awoke, everyone was still busy with their personal interests and had never even considered that he might have been drugged. He remained supine on the couch for about one hour, then lay still, focused his eyes and woke fully suddenly realizing that he'd been asleep. *How long did I sleep? Is Rebecca still here?* he wondered. And at that moment, he saw Rebecca walking down the stairs with Durk directly behind her. He heard Durk tell her that he would walk her to her dorm. Ken stayed quietly on the couch but turned his face so they would not recognize him and they left. He frantically phoned Jayden, who was at first angry with Ken because he hadn't phoned earlier.

"Why didn't you call? We've been frantic. Is everything okay?"

"I don't know, Jayden . . . here's what happened. Someone must have done something to my drink. I had sipped less than half of it when I passed out. But listen, Durk is walking Rebecca home right now, and I will be there shortly thereafter. I'll take a different route home so I won't bump into Durk on his way back. But I do have some good news. I learned that a big shipment is coming to the campus . . . to Professor T! I'll tell you the details when I get back."

Kara was already in bed but not asleep when Rebecca walked in, and she was relieved that she was home. Rebecca walked quickly into her room, head down and carefully avoiding any glance toward Kara's bedroom. She would have been mortified if Kara noticed that she'd been crying. She didn't want to answer questions; she just wanted to think, to understand what had happened and why. She needed to figure out what she was going to do and needed to do this on her own. "*Oh God, please help me make the right decision.*"

Rebecca didn't sleep the entire night, but neither did Ken and Jayden two floors above them. Ken's words were jumbled from the mickey in his drink and from wanting to blurt everything out as fast as he could. "I was listening to the guys . . . I wasn't watching the drinks . . . someone handed me one . . . I just sipped . . . all of a sudden I passed out . . . I'm so sorry . . . Gee, Jayden, I never even thought . . . anyway, Rebecca was upstairs though 'cause I saw her come back down when I woke up, but I never saw her go up. I mean, I never saw her at all until she came down the stairs . . . but what I heard . . . oh gee . . . this is our chance, Jayden . . . what I heard before I passed out was that everyone was excited about a so-called big shipment of stuff . . . and not just marijuana . . . coming to the campus . . . to Nagorra . . . but some heavier stuff as well! They were all talking about the Feds and the chances that T was taking . . . they laughed about it . . . and . . . and . . ."

"Slow down, Ken. Okay, we might have some info with which to trap the professor, but think, think about Rebecca and Durk. Did she appear drunk or "mickied" herself? Was she laughing? Crying? Think! It was a little over one hour from the time you went into the party and then called us."

"Yeah, I'd looked at the clock too when I woke up and not too much time had passed but I don't know. I mean, Durk was kind of murmuring to her as they walked by. He offered to walk her back to her dorm and . . . well . . . in fact . . . come to think of it he did seem to be trying to comfort her . . . and yeah . . . I think she was crying. Maybe not crying outright, but kind of like sniffling as if she had cried or been upset earlier . . . but she definitely wasn't drunk or out of it."

"I wish I could call Kara, but I'll just have to wait until morning to talk to her. She needs to take a really good look at Rebecca to see if she's upset or troubled, maybe even pump her for info. Gee, Ken, what if . . . I mean, what if Durk gave her a mickey . . . or if he . . ."

"Calm down, Jayden, Rebecca isn't easily taken advantage of, and Kara's got a good head on her shoulders and she will definitely be watching Rebecca for signs of . . . anything! And she will let us know right away. In fact, she'll be dying to know what happened to me and what I saw . . . or didn't see as was the case. Sorry, Jayden."

"Aw, it's okay, Ken, it wasn't your fault. I know that I shouldn't worry so much, but if you were given a drink, well, I wonder who your drink was really for . . . I can't believe that people do that kind of thing. That's one of the things that my stepdad Wade rammed into my head before I left for college. He's seen a lot of bad stuff—you know, Iraq and all—and he's not too trusting of the world. He told me never to drink anything I didn't make myself—*never*. And he said that if I walk away and then come back, don't drink that same drink either!"

"I guess that's smart, Jayden. Today's world is different than our parents' world when they even left their houses and cars unlocked . . . and made binding deals with a handshake."

Ken and Jayden spent most of the night studying so they could spend extra time sleuthing to find out about the drug delivery. They dozed and woke occasionally, but both were too worried to sleep.

Kara phoned as soon as Rebecca left for the day. "What happened, Ken?" When Ken gave her a short version of what he'd learned and of the little he'd seen of Rebecca at the party. Kara told him that she saw Rebecca return last night but hadn't talked with her and then this morning only as she was leaving. She told Ken that she thought Rebecca had been crying because her eyes were puffy. "She was very reticent, Ken, and didn't want to talk. It seemed as if she'd stayed in her room until she was almost late to class just to have an excuse to rush past me and have an excuse not to talk."

Ken, Jayden, and Kara agreed to meet to talk about how they would approach their latest information about the "shipment." They wanted to learn more and then come up with a plan that would accomplish two objectives. They hoped to gather enough information to convince Rebecca that the type of people she was dealing with were dangerous and to find a way to stop them. But how? That was the question.

As they talked, they agreed that Kara would continue to be on the lookout for whatever she could learn about Rebecca, and would call them if they could help in any way. Ken and Jayden would listen everywhere they went for more information about the shipment, most importantly when and where the exchange would take place. If Durk was involved and could be caught, that would solve another problem. Kara said that she too would listen and explained that sometimes guys did not pay attention to what they said if a girl was near them as much as they might if it was a guy they didn't know. She also said that sometimes the girls knew a great deal more than they let on, especially if they were privy to information through the boyfriends. They agreed that they would confront Rebecca that night, all three of them together.

Chaldeth was furious that Ken had overheard the conversation about the drug shipment. Now he had to implement some changes to his plan. He decided to cause a rift between Ken and Jayden; that would solve a lot of problems for Chaldeth. He hadn't yet worked all that out and would need to put on his thinking cap for that one. It would have to be done quickly and with one fell swoop. Then he thought of something that might work. If Jayden could suddenly begin to judge some of Ken's actions and spout religious stuff, Ken would be turned off; in fact, he'd suspect Jayden of being a religious zealot. And if Ken could feel that Durk was being unjustly judged and develop a soft spot for him, that would work to separate Jayden and Ken as well.

Chaldeth arranged that Professor T would call Ken to his office and tell him to wait for him if he were late. Of course Ken would jump at the opportunity in the hope of learning something about the drugs. Chaldeth also arranged for Durk to be working in the outer office when Ken arrived and inspired Durk to speak with Ken before the professor arrived. He actually planted into Durk's mind the exact words he wanted Durk to utter—all the right things to tug on Ken's heartstrings.

Ken sat in one of the two chairs opposite the professor's desk. The note that the professor had sent him said that if he were late Ken should wait for him because he had something important to discuss with Ken. Durk entered the inner office to pick up some papers that needed to be filed in the cabinet in the outer office. He greeted Ken warmly and sat down on the second chair that was opposite the desk and next to Ken.

"Ken," Durk began, "I need some advice. I am really head over heels in love with Rebecca. Honestly, I respect her wishes and treat her like a sister—honest. In fact, I want to marry her someday. She's all a guy could ever want. Sometimes we sit together for hours and she tells me about her family, her upbringing, her faith, and I just listen, awestruck by a lifestyle I've never known. You guys would probably think that some hanky-panky was going on, us being alone and everything, but really, I just listen and I wish I could be like her, like you guys, and I want to try. But Jayden hates me. I know he's jealous. I know that he's in love with Rebecca, and she knows too and is afraid to upset him. But without you guys accepting me and helping me learn, I'll never be worthy of her. Will you put in a good word for me with Jayden?"

Ken was completely taken aback by Durk's words. Durk sounded so sincere, and looked as if he was close to tears. *Why, he really does love Rebecca,* Ken thought. *Maybe we have misjudged him; maybe he's just a pawn in Nagorra's hands. Maybe I should warn him. At the very least, maybe we better give him a chance to prove he's an okay guy. Jayden is in love with Rebecca, and maybe this does skew his view of Durk.*

But wisely, while Ken felt sorry for Durk and believed him, he said nothing of what he and Jayden knew about the drugs. *Just in case,* Ken thought. But Ken agreed to help Durk by talking to Jayden and trying to get Jayden to see that Durk really loved Rebecca and would take good care of her. Durk was so thankful that Ken almost felt guilty holding back the information he had. After Durk thanked him profusely, he said, "Well, I'd better get back to work because I have to keep this job so I have some money to spend on Rebecca. I also have to keep in the good graces of the professor since he can help me choose the right classes to prepare for a good career with which to support Rebecca someday." And he turned to go back to the outer office, but turned back and held out his hand to Ken wanting to shake hands and saying again, "Thanks, Ken."

Ken was impressed by how Durk had acted and by what he'd said. He'd tell Jayden. Then the professor walked into the office full of apologies for keeping Ken waiting. "Ken," he began, "I need a favor for which you will be paid. I have a terribly busy schedule next Tuesday, one week from today. There are a lot of things I have to attend to, and I am scheduled to post grades from the midterms that day. That requires that I go into three buildings, open the glass cases in the main hall of each building, tack up the lists for that building, relock the cases and the doors. And it has to be done early in the morning. Can you . . . will you do this for me? You can pick up the keys and the papers that need to be posted—the buildings where they need to be posted are printed at the top of each sheet—and you can pick them up either the night before or that morning from my office. But you must return the keys that afternoon."

"Certainly, I'll be glad to do that. You'll be away . . . off campus?"

"No . . . well, yes . . . actually, I'll be in town and in and out but not to my office until later in the day. I have some business to attend to and have to meet some people and take care of some personal matters. Can you post the grades for me?"

"Yeah, sure, I'll mark it on my calendar and I'll be here that morning to pick up the keys and then return them when I finish my classes. Anything else?"

"No, Ken, that's all . . . and I really appreciate your doing this for me."

Ken left, anxious to get back and report the day's events to Jayden. But when he returned to their room, Jayden wasn't there so Ken made himself some cheese and crackers and poured himself some juice. Then he opened one of his textbooks and studied until Jayden came back. But before Jayden came in, Kara knocked and sat down to listen while Ken relayed the day's events to her.

When he told her about his conversation with Durk and his personal response, she snapped at him. "Oh come on, Ken, you don't really believe that . . . that . . . garbage that Durk was handing you, do you? What's the matter with you? Weren't you the first one of us to have a bad feeling about Durk . . . or was that Professor T? But anyway, come on, get real. Durk was putting one over on you, and you fell for it."

"You sound pretty insensitive, Kara. You're making disparaging remarks about my ability to perceive what someone says and means. That makes me wonder if you have the wrong perception about *all* the people who don't fall under your spell!"

"That's unfair, Ken. I just think it's pretty dumb to suddenly begin to trust Durk now, after all we've uncovered about him. I am surprised that you could be that gullible."

"So now I'm dumb *and* gullible as well?"

"What you've just said sure points in that direction."

"Well, I guess I know who my friends aren't."

"You know what I meant, Ken. Anyway, let's not argue. You're not in the greatest mood, so I think that it's best if you stop talking gibberish about Durk. Maybe I'd better leave, and we'll just talk again later."

"Sure . . . fine. Have it your way," Ken replied curtly and Kara left.

Shortly thereafter Jayden returned, and Ken began to tell Jayden about his day and about his talk with Durk. As he extolled Durk's virtues, Jayden responded exactly the way that Kara had responded, and Ken was annoyed. Not only did Jayden rebuke Ken for his thoughts about Durk's good intentions, but he also laughed and accused Ken of being on some joy juice if he believed Durk was so innocent. When Ken tried to convince Jayden to listen to his point of view, Jayden laughed sardonically, telling Ken that he had been hypnotized by Durk. This angered Ken so much that he walked out of the room, slamming the door behind him.

Chadeth chuckled. It had worked. He'd turned them on one another.

Chapter 7

The Attack

The rift between the four friends was never openly discussed, but each felt slighted and misunderstood and each carried a hurt in their heart that translated into anger. When they came into contact with one another, they were cordial but cool and hurried off to attend to their studies or to some other errand. Kara wasn't aware that Jayden felt as she did about what Ken had said about Durk, and Rebecca was so engrossed in her own concerns that she didn't realize that a rift had developed. The end result was that the friends stopped discussing weighty matters. Thus, Kara, Jayden, and Ken no longer spoke to one another of their concern for Rebecca even though they worried individually. Chaldeth was delighted.

Durk, on the other hand, buoyed by his success in drawing Ken to his side and possibly even to standing against Jayden, decided to use the same tactics on Rebecca. He began to play on her sympathies by telling her how badly he felt that Ken and Jayden and even Kara seemed to think he was not good enough for her. He asked Rebecca for advice about how to change their minds, how to please them. He spoke about his childhood and the pain he'd endured when his mother left and his father beat him. He said that he dreamed of a happy life with someone who would stand by his side even if the whole world turned against him. He told Rebecca that despite his never having someone loyal to him in his life, he had always been loyal to others. "It's built into me, Becca."

Because Durk had another life outside of Rebecca, he also concocted a story about obtaining a job after classes and some evenings delivering merchandise for a caterer, a florist, and a book shop. This story allowed Durk to move freely and to party and date without questions from Rebecca regarding how or where he spent his time. He lowered his head as if unsure of himself when he told her that he was also saving money so that at some point he would have the funds to make their commitment to one another "official." That stunned Rebecca . . . but she believed him. She believed everything he told her.

Rebecca thought often about those words from Durk—about them having a future together—and she felt a great sense of responsibility toward him. She wanted his happiness and well being. She felt that she needed to protect him from harm, from those who misunderstood him, those who did not see the kind and gentle heart that he possessed. She also felt that she should try to understand his point of view on some of the issues that she'd earlier disagreed with.

Rebecca also thought about that last evening before leaving for college when her mother had given her a small double frame. It was hinged in the middle to allow it to stand freely or to open or close. Her mother had used her computer to print some verses from the Bible in the dimensions that would perfectly fit the frames. She'd chosen a beautiful French script font and centered the lines of the verse before printing it. Elizabeth had read the verse to her and then tried to explain how these verses would help Rebecca through all she was about to experience at college. They'd cried together remembering when they'd done something similar for Rebecca's father just before he died. One side of the frame listed the highlights of six different verses and the other side of the frame listed three verses from 2 Corinthians.

On the left side of the frame were the verses:

> For we wrestle not against flesh and blood, but against principalities, against powers, against the rulers of the darkness of this world, against spiritual wickedness in high places. (Ephesians 6:12)

> Be sober, be vigilant; because your adversary the devil' as a roaring lion, walketh about, seeking whom he may desire. (1 Peter 4:8)

> Ye therefore, beloved, seeing ye know these things before, beware lest ye also, being led away with the error of the wicked, fall from your own stedfastness. (2 Peter 3:17)

> Put on the whole armour of God, that ye may be able to stand against the wiles of the devil. (Ephesians 6:11)

> For the eyes of the Lord are over the righteous, and his ears are open unto their prayers . . . (1 Peter 3:12)

> And they shall teach my people the difference between the holy and the profane, and will cause them to discern between the unclean and the clean. (Ezekiel 44:23)

Elizabeth explained that these verses would remind Rebecca about the power of evil and that she may have to wrestle with the spirits of evil. She warned Rebecca to be careful and to always "discern the spirits," which meant that she needed to look carefully at the people, the circumstances, and the activities around her so she could identify the spirits God warned against. She explained that it was through scripture that God helped mankind, and that one of those warnings was that she must remain stedfast in her faith and put on the armor God provided so she could stand against that evil when it came. Elizabeth's final words to her daughter that evening was that no matter what she encountered, God would always hear her prayers.

The other side of the frame contained words from 2 Corinthians 6:14, 17, and 18. The scripture, centered in the frame, was encompassed by a lovely chain of tiny leaves and rosebuds and read:

> Be ye not unequally yoked together with unbelievers: for what fellowship hath righteousness with unrighteousness? And what communion hath light with darkness. (2 Corinthians 6:14)

> Wherefore come out from among them, and be ye separate, saith the Lord, and touch not the unclean thing; and I will receive you, and will be a Father unto you, and ye shall be my sons and daughters, saith the Lord Almighty. (2 Corinthians 6:17,18)

"But Mom," Rebecca had asked, "wouldn't we want to help an unbeliever, and to do so, wouldn't we have to stay around them, not run away from them?"

"Oh, Rebecca, of course we would. It's okay to have friends and associations who do not 'believe' or believe differently than we do. Sadly, many people do not know what the Bible says, nor understand God's plan for them, and therefore they find it difficult to recognize the role that faith should have in their life. We have a wonderful opportunity to be a role model, and we can teach others about the incredible wonder of what God offers them. What our Heavenly Father means by these verses is that we must watch for evil, for the sin it encourages, and we should run from it before it has a chance to overwhelm us, become a yoke for us. Do you know what the word yoke means?"

"Yes, Mom, a yoke is that big wood or leather thing that fits around the necks of two oxen or horses to hold them in line with one another so their strength to pull a cart or a plow is equally dispersed. It kind of makes them work together."

"Exactly! Well, just picture a yoke that is made just for humans, and then imagine that you are yoked together with someone who does evil. You would be forced to "work" together, perhaps go where they go, do what they do, witness or even engage in what they do, and not be able to escape. The yoke can envelope you when you least expect it, and when it does, it will have power over you. So God tells us to flee when we see that the circumstances we find around us, or the people we are with, are engaging in evil things. This is why God tells us to wear the armor He provides, and to only be yoked to believers. The armor protects us by helping us recognize when to flee."

As Rebecca stood, now in her dorm room and looked at the beautiful little frame and read the words it contained, she began to cry. She thought about her mother and wished she were here, wished that she hadn't been so secretive about her relationship with Durk. *Oh, Mom, what should I do? How do I know when I should stay and try to help someone and when to flee? How do I make my heart stop loving someone? Doesn't loving someone mean that we should always stay by their side, help them? Oh, Mom, I just don't know what to do. Oh, why couldn't God just tell me what to do? If He did, I'd do what He said . . . I would! Oh, why am I so confused?*

Chaldeth smiled. This was the dilemma that he so easily caused humans to face. Their egos made them think that they could be the saviors of the world, and that opened the door for minions of spirits to attack. Chaldeth mimicked Rebecca's thoughts, "*Oh, Mom, I need to save Durk . . . only I can do it . . . Oh, Mom, look at me, by my great faith and perfect conduct I have the power to beat the armies of Satan!' How ridiculous these foolish humans are, so filled with their mistaken concepts, their self importance, so unsuspecting of the danger they put themselves in!* And Chaldeth was glad—glad that they were so stupid, glad that he could manipulate them through their foolish notions! Chaldeth mimicked Rebecca again, thinking, *Oh, Mom, why let God do it when I can do it?*

It had been so easy with Rebecca. He'd used her ego, her self-importance, to drive her decisions. He'd used the love she felt, the empathy that lived in her heart, the kindness she employed, her foolish trust, and even her desire to bring God's words to others to make her overlook Durk's shortcomings. He'd used her friends to make her believe that indeed Durk was misunderstood and falsely maligned. He'd also used her natural need to love and to be loved—and of course, her natural response to being caressed—to bring her to where he needed her to be. She had gone to the party at Durk's house completely unaware that his party would be so wild. *Was she so naïve that she thought that the party at the professor's house was an anomaly? How stupid!* Chaldeth had even been able to use her dismay to nudge her even further into his plan of destruction.

Rebecca thought about what had happened that night at Durk's house. She had followed Durk into the living room and saw that some of the students were very obviously drunk, others were acting as if they were in a stupor, and she wondered if they were using drugs; others engaged in acts so openly affectionate that Rebecca had to turn away. The air was permeated by a smoke that had a sort of sweet pungent odor that irritated her lungs and made her cough. She knew she should leave, flee, but she did not. She was, however, terribly uncomfortable and looked for a niche where she could turn her back to what was happening and simply ignore it. She wanted to focus on talking to Durk, but the music was too loud for them to engage in any real conversation.

When Durk suggested that they go upstairs to escape the craziness downstairs, she readily agreed, hoping to forget what she'd witnessed downstairs. Durk apologized to her about what she'd seen, saying that he had been unaware that the party would be so out of control. He'd told her that he wanted to protect her and that once upstairs, they would be away from those influences and could talk. She truly had not realized that they would be going into Durk's room, nor that his room would be a private room and not shared with another student.

Chaldeth chuckled to think how easy it had been with Rebecca. But he'd had to work a little harder to bring Durk to where he needed him to be. He'd placed a wedge between Jayden, Kara, and Ken—even between them and Rebecca—and opened a soft spot in Ken toward Durk that would serve him well in his plan to harm Jayden. *Oh, it was such a good plan!* But now he needed to bring Durk around and cause him to become more aggressive toward Rebecca.

Earlier Chaldeth had arranged for Durk to encounter a series of setbacks. His car broke down and required expensive repairs, the compressor in the small refrigerator Durk kept in his room failed, the last sale of the marijuana Durk sold to cover his rent was sold "on credit," and the new supply was delayed. Durk was now out of money and felt pressured. His rent was due, and his credit card was maxed out.

What worked so well for Chaldeth was that Durk's predicament made him uneasy, fearful, quick to anger, needy, and impulsive. Chaldeth had noticed the tender feelings, wishful thinking, and curiosity about Rebecca's faith Durk had been feeling on occasion, and he needed to end these immediately. Putting financial pressure on Durk would move him in the right direction.

Months earlier, Chaldeth delayed the drug shipment by causing its confiscation higher up along the pecking order. Now Professor T and Durk were waiting for this new shipment and were anxious to obtain the monies from the sale of the drugs that would begin as soon as they got the shipment. The professor was actually a distributor, not only of pot but also of other more potent drugs including sedatives and amphetamines. He deposited money from the sale of his drugs to an overseas account and planned to use it for an early retirement. He also knew that with such a stash he could run if something went wrong and he could easily relocate if necessary. The professor sold only to four students, and his main business emanated from two colleagues on the campus and one shop owner in town. Seven was his lucky number. The others took most of the risks because they actually had all the customers. The money just rolled in. The professor, however, had made one mistake. He'd begun using himself.

Chaldeth had opened the door for Nagorra to engage in this extra little side business. Even before he'd come up with his plan to destroy Rebecca and Jayden, he used the professor and his little business to harm as many students as possible.

Chaldeth knew that it was through the young ones that he could do the most damage to God's plan. It was a tremendous effort to bring anyone out of an addiction. Chaldeth's goal was to prevent these students from having the ability to sustain a religious life. His threat came from the twelve-step programs that encouraged them to tap into God's help. If Chaldeth could stop the younger generation from believing, stop them from becoming one of those so-called numbers that God wanted, he'd live longer!

Rebecca and Jayden were not his only tasks. All of Grandma's family and friends—Sarah and Matt, Caleb and Ann, Josh and Deb and Barbara and Jim, and all the others associated with them—were also part of his assignment. The younger ones were the easiest targets—the easiest ones to destroy, addict, and draw away from God! They were vulnerable. Many parents had no idea about what *really* went on in the world, especially the underworld and its battle with God, and had no idea how to teach their children these truths. It was amazing to Chaldeth that God, knowing what they would face, told them what to do, how to stay safe, yet they didn't seem to want to know. They didn't know how to use God's words even when they heard them. That was Chaldeth's salvation: they had no clue! Again Chaldeth mimicked his enemies by imagining them saying in a loud and falsetto voice, "Oh . . . evil spirits? Never! That's only in the movies! Oh . . . 'things' that attack us? Oh, how ridiculous! And these spirits use drugs just to keep our children from God? Nonsense . . . spirits can't do that!"

Chaldeth knew full well that scripture clearly warned mankind about him. Revelation 12:9 explained, "And the great dragon was cast out, that old serpent, called the Devil and Satan, which deceiveth the whole world: he was cast out into the earth, and his angels were cast out with him." And Matthew 12:45 warned, "Then goeth he and taketh with himself seven other spirits more wicked than himself, and they enter in and dwell there, and the last state of that man is worse than the first. Even so shall it be also unto this wicked generation."

Even Luke 22:3 and John 13:27 told them clearly that Satan and his angels can enter man, could blind the minds of them which believe not. *Funny*, Chaldeth thought, *they are even told in Acts 28:27 that God said, "For the heart of this people is waxed gross, And their ears are dull of hearing, and their eyes have they closed . . ."* He couldn't help but wonder why they were so complacent, so stupid, especially those who had read or heard those words from the Bible!

But this was fine with Chaldeth because it allowed him to do his job, enjoy some amazing and easy conquests, and most importantly, to prolong his life. *Funny, though, that if people knew and practiced their faith, their suffering would have ended a long time ago because God would have gotten that special number of people He wanted and they'd all be in their new Heaven and Earth where there was no more sorrow or tears. Odd*, Chaldeth thought. He could never understand why mankind would not pull together to help themselves, save themselves from their sorrow. *Here it is my job to cause sorrow and make these idiots forget about God. Steeped in the pain and troubles they face, you'd think that they would listen to what God clearly tells them about how to avoid, even end, their troubles.* Chaldeth laughed, knowing that in Revelation 21:4 they were told, "And God shall wipe away all tears from their eyes, and there shall be no more death, neither sorrow, nor crying, neither shall there be any more pain; for the former things are passed away."

All they had to do was call on God, learn what He said, and do what He taught them! God tells them in 1 Peter 13, 14, "And who is he that shall harm you, if ye be followers of that which is good? But and if ye suffer for righteousness sake, happy are ye, and be not afraid of their terror, neither be troubled."

They were really stupid, these people, Chaldeth thought. *But back to work. It is time for me to see my plan through to the end, time for me to show God that He does not control these people—I and my cohorts do!*

And so Rebecca had gone to the party, had gone upstairs with Durk, and Ken had tried to protect her. But Chaldeth had made short shrift of Ken. The joke was that the very words Ken had used to warn Rebecca about what she drank when she went to a party, Chaldeth had turned back to bite Ken. *Ah, the irony of it . . .* and Chaldeth did like to make jokes once in a while . . . *Yeah . . . . especially when they spotlight the fallibility of these peons.* There hadn't been a mickey in that drink as Ken thought; it had simply been a small amount of sedative. Chaldeth now wished he'd used LSD so he could cause a psychotic event, one that could be repeated without warning at any time in his life. *That would have been like planting a spirit right into Ken's mind—one who'd stay there and cause havoc whenever it wanted!*

Chaldeth had long ago, when Durk first moved into his private quarters, inspired Durk to be prepared for any event, especially those attached to the women Durk often brought to his room. Durk had his own stash of weed that he never let go below the minimum he might personally need; he had a camera set up and ready to go whenever he chose. He had a sweet margarita mix in his refrigerator and tequila and the triple sec that made that drink taste so good. He could drop anything into that drink, and it would never be detected because the taste of the margarita overpowered anything else. From the date rape drug to LSD, to the newer mood enhancing drugs, to a simple sedative, Dirk usually had one dose of each stashed in his room. Music, mood lighting, mirrors, and a king-sized bed completed the accoutrements he'd wanted on hand.

Durk didn't use most of what he called his "props" very often; in fact, most of the women he'd brought to his room were more than willing participants, but it fed his sense of power to own these items and he often bragged about them to others. Sometimes this had acted as an aphrodisiac both to him and to those he brought to his room. But after a year of having the freedom to engage in these activities, Durk became aware of a sense of disgust that he'd feel after allowing his need for power dictate his actions. He'd never been in love, but he'd loved his mother and grandmother and knew that he wanted someone good, someone like them, to be in his life—not someone who he would never be able to trust nor who made these poor choices for their lives.

He often felt that he was in a catch-22, not knowing where to turn except to the instant gratification that allowed him to forget. *What?* he'd wonder. *What am I trying to bury? What am I really searching for?* He didn't know. He could vaguely recall thinking that his mother and grandmother were like angels because they were good, and his father was the epitome of evil. When he'd met Rebecca, he'd thought of his mother and grandmother. He wanted Rebecca to become them. He wanted her to snatch him away from his current life and bring him back to where he'd been when his mother and grandmother were alive.

But because Durk did not understand how to fill the void in his life, and because he knew nothing that negated his present lifestyle, he reverted back to what he *did* know and what *did* bring him relief even if that relief was temporary. Chaldeth had had to work a bit to eliminate Durk's thoughts that his mother and grandmother and Rebecca were one. He had to keep Durk angry, keep him focused on revenge, think that Rebecca judged him like his father had, think that she would hurt him as his father had, and make him believe that she, like his father, would betray his affections. Chaldeth needed Durk to react toward Rebecca the way he'd finally reacted to his father. Anger, resentment, jealousy, insecurity, revenge, hatred, fear—especially fear—and insecurity were the forces within people that allowed Chaldeth to be so successful.

When Durk brought Rebecca to his room, his motives were to somehow force her to be his, to love him beyond anything she'd ever known and to need him in her life. He'd gone back and forth between feeling his need for her and feeling that he'd discard her after a while; but that night, Durk wanted her to love him, wanted her to renounce everyone else in her life to be his. He wasn't quite sure what approach he should take, aggression or kindness. He understood that if Rebecca came to him of her own free will then somehow he would be able to trust her—a bit anyway—but if he tricked her or forced her, she could take flight. His ego could not endure such a blow; if she spurned him, Ken would know, Kara would know, Jayden would know, his teammates would know, and even the professor would know and he would lose face. That must not happen. Chaldeth, displeased by Durk's gentler thoughts about Rebecca, *was* pleased with his thoughts of failure and the ridicule it would bring him. Chaldeth had placed the idea of that ridicule in Durk's mind.

Durk, seeing how nervous and skittish Rebecca was about what was occurring downstairs and then from suddenly realizing that she was sitting on Durk's bed, made an instant decision, inspired of course by Chaldeth. He would place a small amount of sedative in Rebecca's drink so she would calm down and focus on him. He gave her only the sweet margarita mix as she requested—no alcohol—but laced it lightly with the powdered sedative. He sat with a small distance between them and simply held her hands after placing a small tray table at the foot of the bed on which they could rest their drinks and a plate of chocolate covered strawberries he'd bought to please her.

They talked, and Durk told her more about his childhood—he even spoke about his mother and grandmother and how much he missed them—and of course, he spoke about the cruelties he'd lived under with this father. He told Rebecca that he wanted to be more like his mother and grandmother but couldn't seem to make . . . the connection . . . to such a life. Rebecca's heart went out to Durk. She reached over to him and held him and told him that she wanted him to come home with her for Christmas break to meet her family and that together they would help him. For a moment Durk had hope—hope that he *could* change, that he *could* move into a different kind of life. But then Chaldeth's influence began to raise its ugly head once again, and as Rebecca leaned into him, Durk could only think of bonding her to him in any way and by any means possible.

Rebecca felt sleepy, but she also felt more relaxed than she'd ever felt. Durk's hands stroking her hair and rubbing her back became so extraordinarily wonderful to her that she leaned into him with a greater trust and with a desire that he never stop making her feel so cared for, so loved, so cherished. His kisses were warm and sweet, his murmurings so loving. Her body and her mind became relaxed from the sleeping drought. It seemed so easy and somehow so right to allow Durk to carry her downward to a supine position on the bed. She was so close to falling asleep that she had to force herself to stay awake. She thought that her sense of relaxation came from how wonderful Durk's touch was and how much she was in love with him.

Rebecca suddenly wondered if she'd nodded off for a moment, but then she decided that she'd just been so relaxed that her mind had wandered. Durk was still murmuring to her, but now there was music playing and the lights were off except for the small yellow light that came from a bedside lamp. She thought that perhaps Durk had turned on the music and only put the one lamp on after he placed the table at the foot of the bed. Maybe she had been too nervous to notice. She was still being lulled by Durk's hands through her hair and his kisses over her face and neck, and once again she felt a wonderful sensation move through her and a wave of sleepy contentment as she relaxed even further.

She felt an overwhelming desire to sleep and simply give in to her sense of well-being when she suddenly realized that Durk was unbuttoning her blouse, that one of his hands was moving to the uppermost part of her thigh, and that his breathing was labored. She was terribly frightened and pushed Durk away from her, mortified that she wasn't aware of what had been happening! *Did I fall asleep? How was that possible? What happened? How much time passed?* She was terrified. She'd never thought that this terror and guilt could be a part of love. *What would my mother say? How will Durk ever respect me again? What have I done? Has anything happened . . . really?*

She did the only thing she could think to do and acted on impulse and out of fear. "*Stop,* Durk! Don't *ever* touch me like that again. Get *away* from me! I trusted you . . . oh, I *never* want to see you again!" Running for the door, she bolted down the steps barely able to button her blouse before reaching the bottom of the stairs. With Durk right behind her, telling her he would walk her home, she ran out into the night.

What Ken had seen in his slightly fuzzy state was Rebecca and Durk walking down the stairs together, somewhat in a hurry, and Durk telling her that he would walk her home. As they left the house together, he'd realized that something was amiss but hadn't been able to connect it to anything specific. He'd looked at the clock and noted that only about an hour had passed since he'd arrived. Then Ken telephoned Jayden and left the party and took a different route back to their dorm.

Outside, Durk tried to comfort Rebecca by telling her that nothing had happened. But she was crying saying over and over again that she was so embarrassed, that she didn't know what had happened to her to make her behave that way, to let Durk "have so many liberties." Durk had truly been sorry at first, but then he felt angry, felt that Rebecca was blaming him, judging him, dismissing him. *How dare she?* "You are a two-bit tease, Rebecca. You egged me on. You wanted me as much as I wanted you," he retorted. Then he begged her, not willing to lose her, and apologized telling her again how much he loved her and what she meant to him and that she was his only hope for making changes in his life.

By the time they arrived at Rebecca's dorm, she had calmed down and had once again believed Durk's pleas and forgiven him. Her thinking had shifted, with Chaldeth's help, into phrases like, "Maybe nothing bad had happened after all. Maybe I did stop everything before it started. I really do love him. Maybe it was my fault as he claims . . . maybe I led him on, and maybe some evil force wants me to leave him because I might be the only one who can help him toward a life that is good and filled with God and faith and all the things he's never been taught. After all, if I leave him, there would be no one to teach him and he would fall back into all those things he needs to escape. I must help him. He really doesn't know how to do things differently, and after all, he really loves me too."

And so they made up. However, Rebecca fell into a deep depression. She was plagued with indecision, with guilt, with not really knowing what had happened. She was afraid that perhaps she had fallen asleep and that Durk was just trying to make her feel better by saying that nothing had happened. She hated the secrets she kept from her mother, from Jayden. She hated not making progress with Durk in terms of his turning to God or wanting their relationship to be above board.

Rebecca kept her thoughts and her fears to herself. In one way she didn't want to know what had happened, and in another way she felt embarrassed, humiliated, and she felt as if Jayden and Ken and Kara would hate her, scorn her if they knew that

Durk sold marijuana, and evidently wanted to be intimate with her. But now, however, Rebecca was drawn even closer to Durk because of her misconception about what she should do. She felt that the only way she could forgive herself and exonerate Durk's actions was for them to truly be in love and eventually marry. Therefore, without understanding her motivation, without acknowledging her need to justify her actions, she decided to try and win Durk to accepting *her* feelings about life, *her* beliefs, the way *her* family interacted with one another, *her* ideas about the sanctity of marriage, what to *her* true love was really all about. To Rebecca's way of thinking, because of her inexperience and inability to seek advice, it was now her *responsibility* to bring Durk's life into her way of life or she would forever have to admit that she'd been so wrong, so foolish, so . . . easy. Only love would exonerate her.

If Rebecca had confided in her friends, Kara would have explained that Rebecca was laboring under guilt and Kara would have said that Rebecca needed to learn from these experiences and move on. Jayden would have told her to move on as well and he would have suggested that she obtain the forgiveness of sin and Holy Communion to give her the strength to leave Durk. But like so many people, Rebecca carried her guilt and thought that, whether God forgave her or not, she would need to beat herself up with her mistakes. Her self-inflicted guilt brought depression and lethargy, it brought hopelessness and fear, and it interfered with everything she did. Her guilt, evil knew . . . and used against her, could eventually separate her from God.

Chaldeth laughed a scornful, knowing laugh when he saw how Rebecca reacted to a single one-time action that was a pretty normal part of the learning process for so many young people today. *Let her imagine the worst,* Chaldeth laughed and thought. *Let her worry and be filled with remorse and run to Durk, and maybe then she'll run to other ways to alleviate her guilt. Guilt is one of my best weapons! They are so stupid not to realize that they downplay the value of Christ's sacrifice when they do that! Christ is willing to forgive them, yet they can't forgive themselves. Do they think they are more important than Christ? It's a joke! But then again, I love it when they do this because their inability to accept forgiveness and the harboring of their guilt makes them putty in my hands! What egos they have! A little humility would go a long way with them.*

Chaldeth's plan was to make Rebecca sick with her guilt, but sick in a way that would make her believe that Durk was the only person in the world she could turn to for solace. If Chaldeth could make her feel guilty about one thing, she would then conclude that it made no difference to step a little further over the line, and then a little further, and even further. He wanted her to decide that guilt was guilt and sin was sin and how much no longer mattered! On many occasions, he'd been able to get the so-called children of God to believe this, and before they knew it, they allowed all *kinds* of sin into their life thinking that after they worked things out themselves, *then* they'd ask for forgiveness, and *then* they would stay on the straight and narrow! How ridiculous . . . how convenient for them that they justified continuing what they knew was displeasing to God!

As Rebecca and Durk continued to spend time together, they also began to include Ken in some of their activities because Ken had been showing signs of accepting Durk into Rebecca's life. Rebecca felt that Ken would be a good influence on Durk and when Ken was with them, Durk couldn't try to be more intimate with her. Durk was pleased by Ken's acceptance, and when he realized that Ken's actions had alienated Ken from Jayden and Kara, he was not only pleased but also felt that he could trust Ken.

Despite their rift with Ken, Kara and Jayden still talked and still suspected Durk of all kinds of clandestine activities. They witnessed how depressed and withdrawn Rebecca was and saw that she'd excluded them from participating in her life. Still loving her and believing that Durk was behind Rebecca's attitude, they continued to watch and listen for ways to help her. When Ken and Rebecca were out, Jayden and Kara often sat together in Kara's little living room and studied or talked.

Kara had been brought up in a large loving family, but being the oldest of her siblings and having a mother who worked full time, she'd been the major care giver. That's why she was so adept at preparing special little snacks for them when Jayden came to talk. She'd make delicious spreads for crackers and wonderful dips for raw veggies and sometimes, using her blender, would prepare healthy fruit-laden smoothies for them with a dash of tasteless fiber and perhaps even some powdered protein. She was very health conscious.

One evening Jayden asked her about her faith, and she told him that she believed in God and wanted to do what was right. She told him that she'd learned a lot about the Bible in Sunday school, but that her family did not pray nor did they, as far as Kara knew anyway, know all that stuff about evil spirits that Jayden had told her. Kara admitted to thinking that Jayden was a bit of a religious kook at first, but that she'd later looked up the verses that Jayden had given her and had been surprised to see that Jayden was right after all. *What else could those parts of scripture mean?*

"What are you supposed to do, Jayden, to prevent those spirits from harming you? Is it possible to stop them?"

"Yeah . . . well, maybe not for the short term, but you can stop them for the long term and stop them from letting what they do have a permanent effect on you. I mean, God uses some of the things the spirits do or cause, to become a blessing to you—you know, a benefit! He actually turns the bad into something good for you."

"How's that possible? I mean, if they cause some terrible thing, how can it be undone or be turned into a benefit?"

"Well, there's one verse that almost everybody knows. It's in Romans 8:28, and God says, "And we know that all things work together for good to them that love God, to them who are the called according to his purpose," and then there is another in Matthew 10:29-32 where Christ says, "Are not two sparrows sold for a farthing? And one shall not fall to the ground without your Father . . . Fear ye not therefore, ye are of more value than many sparrows."

"There are lots of others, Kara, but what I've even witnessed *myself* is that things happen that seem *impossible* to fix, *impossible* to bear, and then somehow God shows us *why* we lived through that experience and how it actually *benefits* us, and it also teaches us what to avoid or what to do in the future! Every person in my family can tell you stories that support these kinds of miracles—from a divorce, to someone's seemingly unjust death, from a devastating seventh-month miscarriage to a little one-year-old losing a foot because of a market bomb in Iraq. These terrible experiences turn into a blessing and are what we call mini-miracles that keep on happening and keep on giving us strength in bad times. Through them we also learn that we can trust God to make all things okay."

"Well first of all, again, do we have any protection against the work that these spirits do? And second, how can someone develop enough faith to trust God when things do go south?"

"God tells us to wear the armor of God that He provides for us. Wait a minute, let me get my computer. I have the concordance and the Bible in it and can find the verses where God says this. I just have to enter a few phrases to begin the search. When we use everything God gives us and do what He asks of us, God refers to us as an 'overcomer.' Okay, here's one in Revelation 3:21 where God says, 'To him that overcometh, will I grant to sit with me in my throne . . . '

"God often describes an overcomer as someone who put on a clean robe, or washed his robe, meaning that they washed sin away by following what God asked of them which includes asking for forgiveness when we make mistakes. The robe is a symbol of that forgiveness. Revelation 7:13-14 explains who the overcomers are: 'What are these which are arrayed in white robes? . . . These are they which came out of great tribulation, and have washed their robes, and made them white in the blood of the Lamb.' Scripture goes on to assure us that *nothing* is too difficult for God. Jeremiah 32:17 says, 'Thou hast made the heaven and the earth by Thy great power and stretched out thy arm, and there is nothing too hard for Thee.'

"God also lets us know that to be an overcomer isn't easy. We know this because He tells us in Revelation 7:17, 'And God shall wipe away all tears from their eyes.' We understand and believe that God is all powerful, that we may suffer for a while, but that we need to stand firm in faith to be an overcomer. The words in Ephesians 6:13 tell us, 'Wherefore take unto you the whole armour of God, that ye may be able to withstand in the evil day, and having done all, to stand'. God reiterates in Romans 13:12, 'The night is far spent, the day is at hand: let us therefore cast off the works of darkness, and let us put on the armor of light.'

"The light is God's words. It is the teaching and sacrifice of Christ and the promises God gives us. Revelation 4:20 promises, 'Behold, I stand at the door, and knock; if any man hear my voice, and open the door, I will come in to him, and will sup with him, and he with me.' And in Matthew 11:29, God says, 'Take my yoke upon you and learn of me . . . ' And in 2 Timothy 2:7, we are told, 'Consider what I say; and the Lord give thee understanding in all things.' And we are warned in Hebrews 3:7, 8, 'Wherefore, as the Holy Ghost saith, Today if ye will hear his voice, Harden not your hearts, as in the provocation, in the day of temptation in the wilderness.'

"While our armor is found in God's words, in what He asks us to do, it is also found in the sacraments. Holy Baptism, Holy Communion, and Holy Sealing all give us an inner power and certain gifts . . . sort of like getting a passport to Heaven and a little angel who sits on our shoulder and warns us in times of danger and pulls us back if we begin to be drawn away."

"Wow, Jayden, that's a lot to remember. But then again, I guess you are saying that if we just *learn* these verses, understand what we're up against, *choose* to believe and *follow* God's ways, then God, I guess, does the rest . . . right?"

"Exactly."

"So why do we need to help Rebecca? Won't God do it?"

"Yeah, sure He will. But we also have a responsibility to our brothers and sisters in faith to help where we can, and especially to pray for them. Remember that God not only uses His angels to help us, but He uses human beings—I mean, think about the apostles and all our ministers or the stranger that walks by and rescues someone from a bad situation. God kind of nudges them toward accomplishing what He needs to have done as He looks after His children. So we should be willing to help if He can use us. But we still have to be careful and know when to flee too."

"Well, that makes sense I guess. Okay, I'm willing . . . and thanks, Jayden, for teaching me so much. I honestly just didn't know . . . and that kind of bugs me. I mean, my parents are good people—my whole family is—but I don't think that they know any of this stuff. Does this mean that they can't be children of God?"

"No, not at all. God will reach everyone at some point in time. And you can help them too. The only thing is they have to accept what they hear when they do hear it. Some will have to go out on a limb to accept what He offers. But in 2 Peter 3:9, we are told 'the Lord is . . . not willing that any should perish, but that all should come into repentance.' And God tells us in Psalm 91:15, 16 what we can expect if we do the things He asks of us: 'He shall call upon me, and I will answer him; I will be with him in trouble; I will deliver him and honor him. With long life I will satisfy him, and show him my salvation.'"

Jayden and Kara had many conversations about the faith that Rebecca and Jayden shared, and Kara wondered how Rebecca could walk away from all the beauty she shared with Jayden. Kara's heart was kind and understanding, and she was so enthralled by Jayden's words that she began to pray for Rebecca every night asking God to help her break away from whatever might not be good for her. She also asked God to make any experience Rebecca had, good or bad, "work together for good to them that love God."

Chaldeth knew, of course, about the conversations between Kara and Jayden, but he wasn't really concerned. He'd break Jayden through the plan he had to entrap Jayden, have him blamed for something that he could not escape. Kara would fall when she saw that God hadn't helped either Jayden or Rebecca nor had answered Kara's prayers. So Chaldeth moved away from thoughts of Kara and Jayden to concentrate on obtaining the drugs for Professor T and to keeping his plan on track. His next step was to make sure that the professor got to his meeting safely and on time.

Ken had gone to Professor T's office on Tuesday morning as he had promised and found the papers that he was to post. They and the keys were where the professor said they would be. He went off to the buildings to take care of his obligations.

Later that afternoon, after running all his personal errands, the professor drove to a location just outside town in a small building off the main road. He was waiting for his contact, waiting to pick up his long-overdue merchandise. He was usually nervous at this juncture, afraid of a raid, of someone who'd ratted on his contact and would be following or waiting, and if any of this occurred, they could be caught. This was the only really dangerous time as far as he was concerned. He would rather have sent someone like Durk for the delivery, but a lot of money was at stake and his contact did not want another person to know who he was, what they were doing, or when and where they met. So the professor had to make the exchange himself.

Finally, one-half hour late, the black Cadillac with tinted windows arrived. *So typical*, the professor thought cynically, *don't you know you are only advertising something shady when you drive that car, dress as you do, and have those goons accompany you?* Three huge men emerged from the vehicle, looked around, went into the building, and then signaled the professor's contact to leave the vehicle. In typical dark sunglasses, fur collared well-cut overcoat slung over his shoulders, and dressed in a sharkskin black suit and tailored black shirt with a white cravat tied fashionably around his neck, the professor's contact walked into the building and greeted him perfunctorily. "Got the money? Let's see the money."

The professor handed him the briefcase, which one of the burly goons took from him, brought to a nearby table, opened and counted the money it contained. "All here, boss."

The man in black snapped his fingers and said to the man standing guard at the door, "Get the stuff."

The professor asked if everything was there—the pot, the LSD, the sedatives, and all the other items he wanted. He didn't want to have to meet again soon; he wanted to keep his exposure at a minimum.

"Yeah, of course, what do you take me for? Think I was going to stiff you? That would be like taking candy from a baby. But, you better remember that if you ever think you can stiff me, you're a dead man. Got it?"

"Yeah, yeah . . . I mean . . . no. No, of course not," the professor stammered. "I'm just anxious to get it. My people have calls for it . . . that's all."

Three large boxes were brought inside the building, and the professor, without examining them, asked if the other men would help carry them to his car. With the snap of his fingers once again, the deed was done and everyone climbed back into their vehicles with the understanding that they would meet again when either the professor or his dean called for more.

Professor T drove swiftly back to his office. He'd always used his office to stash his merchandise, taking what he wanted from the boxes to his home as needed. This way if anyone checked his house they wouldn't find anything . . . much. The office, with its inner and outer rooms, had two doors that could be locked, and the building itself required an access card to enter. The professor had reasoned that if his office was raided he could claim that someone was framing him. He was sure, however, that if anyone checked his office they wouldn't be able to find anything.

A few years earlier, looking for a place to store his merchandise, he'd noticed that the walls of his office were unusually thick and he had carefully removed the plaster and lathing from the lower part of the wall behind his desk chair. He saw that there was enough space between the two walls for the merchandise. After installing shelves, he'd paneled the bottom half of the walls of the entire inner office, and only he could spot where a portion of the panel behind his desk chair could be removed.

As he pulled into his reserved parking space in front of his building, he thought, *Now, I need help to get this stuff into my office. Where's Durk, I wonder* . . . And at that moment, the professor saw Ken walking toward his office carrying the keys he'd promised to return and quickly called out to him. "Ken! Hey! Can you help me a minute? I bought a couple of things to decorate my office a bit and need to get them up there."

"Sure thing, Professor. Here's your keys. I was just on my way to return them. What do you want me to carry?"

"I have three boxes in the trunk of the car. Can you manage two of them while I carry one and then open and hold the doors for you?"

"Yeah, I guess so. Are they heavy?"

"No, not really. Certainly not for a young man like you!"

The professor removed the boxes, piling two into Ken's outstretched arms and one on top of the car while he closed and locked the trunk. Then he took the box from the roof of the car and walked toward the outer door of his building. They decided to climb the stairs rather than walk around back to the elevator. While climbing the stairs and balancing the boxes, Ken tried to be careful. He did not want to drop any of the boxes, but the two stacked upon one another partially blocked his vision. He believed that the boxes contained fragile decorative items and therefore he wanted to be careful with them. Suddenly the top box slid toward Ken's face, and he lowered his arms and dipped his nose down to steady until he could shift the boxes back into position once he reached the stairwell at the second floor. As he stuck his nose firmly into the box to steady it, he smelled the pot. Distinctly. He knew what pot smelled like, and this was it. He was sick with fear that someone would know what he was carrying and think he was a part of this . . . crap.

Ken hated drugs. His brother had suffered for years until he finally got free of their hold on him, and Ken had vowed never to go near them; in fact, he'd been so angry about what had happened to his brother that he vowed to kill anyone who tried to bring them into the lives of those he loved. *Why would the professor have this stuff . . . so much of it. There's a lot of kilos here. Does the prof sell the stuff? To students? Oh geez . . . to . . . Durk? Is he the one who gives it to Durk? Oh boy, what if Durk has offered it to Rebecca? No,* he thought. *Durk would never harm Rebecca. But then again, Rebecca has been so . . . uhhh . . . withdrawn lately. Isn't that one of the lasting symptoms of the stuff . . . unless you are in the midst of a hit? Ohhh no . . . this is that shipment I heard about at the party . . . This is it!"*

Ken pretended that he hadn't noticed anything odd; in fact, even asked the professor if he wanted help unpacking his knickknacks. The professor laughed and told Ken to go on home, that he'd take care of everything. He thanked Ken for his help and turned to busy himself at his desk.

As Ken walked back to the dorm, he thought about the pot and wondered what he should do. *I wish I could talk to Kara or Jayden,* he thought, *it'd be a lot better to share this with them, but I can't . . . they are still so down on me because I asked them to trust Durk. They were so unfair to me, so why bother? And Rebecca knows better than to get into that stuff.* And so Ken remained quiet, but he was terribly worried.

Meanwhile, Rebecca had been learning more and more about Durk. He'd confessed to using drugs on occasion and to selling them. Rebecca was terribly upset by this news, but Durk told her that by the time Christmas break arrived, he'd quit doing both. He'd said that he needed to earn enough money to stay in school, and there was no other way he could accomplish that goal. Rebecca hadn't come up with a solution to Durk's money problems—she certainly wanted him to stay in school—but she also knew that he was playing with fire and that what he was doing was wrong.

More easily influenced by Chaldeth now that she was further removed from Jayden's guidance and her own prayers, Rebecca initially accepted what Durk told her. But finally she decided that she would tell Durk that they could not see one another again until Durk agreed to dump his drugs into the river or toilet or somehow get rid of them without giving them to anyone else and she planned to say, *You must do this because what you are doing is wrong. It's dangerous to you, it's dangerous to those you sell it to, it's even dangerous to me now that I know about it; and now that I've carefully explained this to you, surely you will do what is right and ask God to help you with your money problem.* In fact, Rebecca was going to ask her family to lend him the money he needed until he could get a larger student loan.

When Durk arrived at the professor's office the next time Rebecca was scheduled to work there as well, she confronted him. She believed that by being adamant and by being strong and having the courage to stand up for what was right, she would help Durk recognize that she was doing the right thing, for his sake, by asking him to stop and to discard the drugs he had in his possession. But what Rebecca didn't know was that Durk had already picked up his share of the professor's new shipment and was now responsible for providing the professor with his share of the proceeds. Durk fully understood that the professor had laid out a lot of cash to complete this transaction and would extract a pound of flesh, or more, if Durk didn't come through with the money.

When Rebecca confronted him and acted so high and mighty about what he was to do, and demanded he do it, and even spoke to him in what he deemed a shrill and loud voice as if she was *his* lord and master, he lost control. He'd been worried sick about his true feelings for her and about the fact that he'd been cheating on her; he'd been constantly torn between guilt and pride, and he was under a lot of stress to pay back the money he owed.

When Rebecca made her demands, he felt that he had been blindsided. He'd planned to spend a nice evening with her and touch her and smell her clean lavender-scented hair and glory in her kind soft words and in how much she loved him. Maybe it was the surprise of her shrill demands, maybe it was the stress, maybe it was his sudden fear that he would lose her, but whatever it was, Durk reacted.

First, just as his father reacted in anger to him, Durk struck her hard across the face, she reeled backward in shock. He grabbed her and shook her telling her that she was killing him, that he'd planned to get out, but that he couldn't until

Christmas. He told her that she was destroying him, and that she had no real love for him, for if she really cared she would help him ease his way out and not want to bring him so much harm. "Don't you realize, Rebecca, what the gangsters who sell this stuff *do* to anyone who runs, anyone who gets out, anyone who doesn't pay? Do you want me killed . . . brutally?"

He knew that he was playing on her sympathies, scaring her, but he wasn't about to let her lecture him or lay down *her* terms or *make* him give up what he was doing. *How dare she order me around,* he thought. And so he reacted the only way he knew how to react and with the same venom his father had spewed. "Don't you realize that you are involved in this and that I'm trying to protect you by paying them back before I get out? What more do you want from me, Rebecca? Do you want to risk me going to jail or risk me being dead? And maybe you'll go to jail with me . . . maybe even your precious little Jayden . . . do you want that?"

Rebecca was truly frightened. She hadn't understood these elements of his involvement. *Oh, I am so dumb, so naïve . . . I've read stories, I've seen TV shows like this, but I have never been up close like this.* And so she slipped into the worst response she could have and said, "Okay, Durk. I'm so sorry. I didn't realize the danger. I will help you, and together we will get out by Christmas . . . like you said. Please forgive me." Durk smiled; he'd won. And Chaldeth sneered. *How stupid she is.* It had been easier than either of them thought it would be; in fact, now Rebecca was even better primed for Durk to exercise more power over her in the future. Now she too was caught up in what he was doing; she was in fact now an accessory.

Durk too was primed for destruction whenever Chaldeth decided to give him up. Durk was unaware that entities such as Chaldeth existed or that they could influence so many thoughts and actions. Chaldeth knew that God would bring his vengeance down on Durk at some point in time for what he'd done to Rebecca, for there was a verse in the Bible that made a direct threat against anyone who harmed one of God's children. Chaldeth was untouched by the threat—at least at this point anyway—but Durk would surely be, and Chaldeth, knowing this, could only laugh and think, *Durk's destruction will only be part of the fun.* And he thought, *if Durk only knew that God warned in Mark 9:42, "And whosoever shall offend one of these little ones that believe in me, it is better for him that a millstone were hanged about his neck, and he were cast into the sea."* Chaldeth would not acknowledge that the scripture he'd just recited was also meant for him.

Chapter 8

The Fall

Rebecca worried incessantly. She began look at every student she passed in the halls wondering if they were watching her because they too were involved in the drug business. She feared that there was someone following her who had become suspicious of her or of Durk. She couldn't sleep, she could barely eat, and the stress bore into her heart and produced a constant and debilitating fear. Durk told her that she was an accessory now because she knew and didn't report the drug activities. What would happen if they were arrested? How could she ever face her family? She began to look at her professors differently because Durk had also told her that some professors were selling drugs.

The only highlight in her week was the anatomy and physiology labs and lectures. She trusted the professor who taught those classes, and of course she still trusted Jayden. Jayden recognized that something very serious was bothering Rebecca. He saw it in her pale, thin, and unsmiling face and in the lackluster quality of her eyes. He noticed that she jumped in fear if someone spoke from behind her or accidently brushed against her when they passed, and he suddenly made up his mind that he needed to have a serious talk with her. He needed to find out what was wrong.

That day in their lab class, having long finished the cat dissection, they were to dissect a frog. Both he and Rebecca were shocked by its size. It was huge, probably two feet long when its legs were fully outstretched. The body itself was close to a foot long and about eight inches across. It was bright green with huge bumps on its body and glazed frightened eyes. There was one frog for every six students, and the professor told them that they would be performing some important experiments while the frog was alive but brain dead. She went on to say that the frog would feel no pain from or after the pithing process which she herself would perform on each of the frogs.

As she made her rounds to each student group who'd donned the usual aprons, goggles, and latex gloves, she would hold the squirming frog by its neck, legs dangling downward, and bend its head forward holding it firmly as she pushed a metal probe into the back of its neck and up into its brain. "By rotating the probe after insertion", she explained, "the brain will be completely destroyed and the frog will lose all sense of feeling and understanding about what is happening." When the frogs continued to squirm after this process, the professor explained that the frog's nervous system was reacting and this could be stopped by removing the probe and reinserting it, this time in a downward thrust into the spinal column to destroy those nerves. The frog was flaccid and limp after this last procedure.

The students were instructed to follow her lead and dissect the leg of the frog. They removed a leg muscle called the gastrocnemius, and the sciatic nerve and the femur bone, and kept them wet with Ringer's solution to simulate the body fluid. They placed the muscle on a machine that could measure and chart the contraction and relaxation of the muscle according to what chemical was placed in contact with the muscle. The students were stunned to see that the muscle, cut out of the frog, still worked on command according to the chemical with which it came into contact.

The professor explained, "Always remember that there are many substances that cause a reaction, sometimes a chain reaction in the body, and that some are beneficial and others are detrimental. And remember that the heart is also a muscle. Muscles perform by electrical impulses, and certain chemicals can simulate those impulses." She looked slowly around the room and then said, "Certain chemicals, drugs, will create all kinds of reactions in humans and can actually stop the heart from beating and cause death. Some chemicals cause hallucinations or brain damage, and others cause long-lasting debilitating or addiction problems." Rebecca was frightened wondering if the professor was talking to her because she knew of her association with Durk. But she told herself that she was being paranoid and concentrated on the lab work.

Rebecca had hated the plight of the frogs, but by the end of class she was amazed by what she'd learned and she felt that she'd been given a gift of understanding that perhaps someday she could translate to helping others. As she looked around the room and saw the light of comprehension and dedication on the faces of her fellow classmates, she understood suddenly that she'd been sticking her head in the sand, afraid to face the tough choices to champion what was right. *Every student here may have to choose right from wrong when helping others.* Rebecca realized that she would have to make tough decisions every day to be a good physician. She'd have to stand up for her patients, for the humane treatment of her patients, and stand up for those who could not fight for themselves like the elderly or the infirm. *How will I do that later if now I cower from the truth and refuse to fight for what's right?*

Filled with fervor, Rebecca felt almost out of control with the exhilaration she felt, the sense that she would finally do something right. She was filled with the desire to *do* something *soon*, to take a stand somewhere, and at least show *herself* that she hadn't lost her courage. As she and Jayden walked from the lab to the cafeteria, she bubbled over with her determination to be a good physician and a courageous person. "Jayden, it was as if something special opened for me, some wonderful bit of wisdom. It was the frog . . . well, it wasn't *really* the frog . . . well, yes it *was* . . . because instead of feeling squeamish, I *wanted* to learn. I really *wanted* with all my heart to understand these incredible occurrences . . . to use them, apply them, to go out into the world and be all that I can be . . . and get *better* all the time . . . not worse!"

Jayden was so happy and relieved to see that Rebecca was once again herself. Maybe now she would see things differently, as they really were. But as she chatted on, he felt a little warning bell go off in his heart. *Was Rebecca a little bit too fervent? Was there some underlying situation she was talking about under the guise of medicine? Had she been frightened by something or not stood for good against her fear somewhere along the line? Was she instead talking about rectifying some earlier stance she'd taken?* But then Jayden dismissed his thoughts, afraid that he was jumping to conclusions and could cause Rebecca to turn back into her shell if he voiced his foolish concerns.

But Jayden had been right and would later regret not taking his own stance and speaking to Rebecca about his gut reaction. But now he thought, *Wow, I am so quick to point out the splinter in Rebecca's eye and not see the beam in my own!* And he recalled how God warned them of this inclination and that they should watch for it, and correct it. When he could, he looked for the verse through his concordance and found that it was in Matthew 7:3 and said, "And why beholdest thou the mote that is in thy brother's eye, but considerest not the beam that is in thine own eye?"

When Rebecca walked into her American history class, she was still filled with fervor and wanted to prove to herself that she was ready to take on the world and at least make an effort to right the wrongs of the past. About halfway into the class, Professor Doog asked for the students' input, and Rebecca raised her hand to ask a question that she felt might bring some serious consequences but needed to be addressed. "Professor, I have two questions that have really been bothering me and for which I'd like an answer. The first is why do history textbooks omit the fact that our founding fathers were very devout, that the majority were Christians, and that their speeches and other writings actually use words and guidelines directly from scripture? My second question is why do history textbooks also omit the fact that so many African Americans were instrumental in the founding of this country, were highly respected and admired, often as friend and confidant working alongside the founding fathers?" *Boy, that felt good,* Rebecca thought.

The classroom was so quiet that they could hear a pin drop. The professor gazed at Rebecca for a long moment, then walked back and forth behind the lectern for another moment before turning to answer Rebecca's question. He looked directly at Rebecca, squared his shoulders, and spoke softly and almost sadly. "Rebecca? Is that your name?" "Yes, sir, it is." "Well, Rebecca . . . class . . . I am going to be honest with you and give you a lesson that may make your eyes bulge out of your heads. We have fifteen minutes left so I will try to be brief, but if any of you want to go further into depth during another class about what I'm going to tell you, I will be glad to do so." The professor took a deep breath and began a story that shocked the students and caused many to seek additional information about what he told them.

"President Woodrow Wilson was the person most instrumental in promoting an ideology that *continues today* to eat away at the fundamental principles of our Constitution . . . and to destroy what our founding fathers intended for our country. A man born in Chicago named Saul Alinsky, who was a self-proclaimed Communist/ Marxist, wrote a book in 1946 titled *Reveille for Radicals*, and twenty-five years later he wrote another book titled *Rules for Radicals*. These books laid out a plan for an underground revolution that would, slowly and insidiously, erode our country's principles and the Constitution that our founding fathers created and espoused. In time this erosion of principles opened the door to a revolution that brought about the change that Alinsky suggested.

"Having no patience for those who were simply 'liberals,' Alinsky favored a more radical approach to bringing about a transformation of our country. Believing that people loved drama, he assembled activists under the guise of community organizers as a way to achieve his goal. His premise was that if people were beset by crime, unemployment, inadequate housing, malnourishment, disease, demoralization, racism, discrimination, or religious intolerance, they could be brought together to force the changes he espoused. Thus his plan was to create these conditions to further his agenda.

"Alinsky admitted that his plan was a manipulation, but that the end result justified the means they used to achieve it. Identifying the enemy, singling them out and pointing to any different agenda as evil and the cause of the people's plight became Alinsky's plan to crush any opposition. The total destruction of faith in our country, especially a faith that was not radical or did not encourage destructive actions, was an important part of the plan. Faith was to be replaced by a certain carefully engineered morality that attacked the opposition.

"Massive inflammatory protest rallies were used to intimidate those who opposed Alinsky's ideas. Redistribution of wealth was a part of this plan, except of course for those deemed the 'intellectual elites' who would rule our country once Alinsky's plan was in full swing. In the meanwhile, change would be brought about internally, quietly, and insidiously until it was too strong and too late to stop.

"The intellectual elites that Alinsky spoke of were encouraged to become professors, lawyers, authors, and speakers and to run for public office, even at the lower levels of government. By working together through various venues, they influenced the content of newly published textbooks, and had all religious references removed, even from original writings. They campaigned to remove religion and

God in any form from schools and government buildings. They supported the development of community organizations to champion their cause. Union leaders espousing their plan gained power and further incited people against their targeted enemies . . . often by accusing their opponents of racial discrimination. In time this became known as the Progressive movement and many Progressives openly admitted their goals, and many acknowledged their affiliation with Communist and Marxist ideologies. Some were and are politicians or closely affiliated with politicians.

"But as this movement gained strength and the general population began to understand the Progessive's ideology and the agenda that they had for this country as outlined by Saul Alinsky's plan, something happened . . . a miracle if you will. Another movement began that gained incredible momentum and did so very quickly. It was called the Tea Party, and through various means these citizens began to uncover more information about the Progressive Party. They identified those who were Progressives, uncovered their ideology, and questioned their systematic acquisition of power. The citizens who supported the Tea Party fought back and vehemently opposed the ideology based on Saul Alinsky's *Rules for Radicals*. They began to educate others about the Progressive ideology and fought to bring back textbooks which accurately portrayed our history, and pushed for those ideals and principles that our founding fathers intended for our country. They fought to put God back into people's lives and into the schools and government, and to expose the true agenda of some of the politicians in power. The Tea Party inspired a religious movement that openly espoused a conservative, Bible-driven method of engagement and responsibility, and a true patriotism that touched the hearts of the people. The people began to demand that their elected officials also genuinely espouse these values . . . not any particular religion . . . but the Judeo/Christian values outlined in the Bible . . . . and be willing to fight corruption and fight to 'get their country back' and out from under the Progressive Party's control." At that moment their time was up and students had to leave for their next class. Many stayed to shake the professor's hand and to ask him to continue to teach them about this turn of events. Many told the professor that they felt privileged to meet someone with his courage. Rebecca stayed and thanked the professor for what he had done. Once again she was filled with confidence, filled with the thought that, if she confronted what was wrong, she could perhaps help make it right. The professor told her that he admired *her* courage!

Later that day Rebecca entered her political science class and sat between Ken and Durk. She planned to ask a similar question so the students could hear the other side of what this professor had taught them. But everything suddenly turned ugly when she asked this professor the same questions she had asked Professor Doog. Professor Emils was furious with her and verbally attacked her in front of the class, and Durk recoiled from her remarks as if she'd struck him. Ken looked at her with his mouth open.

Professor Emils replied, "Tell me, young lady, that you *support* the capitalists who want the people poor and starving, living on the streets, beset by racism *such as yours*, kept from an education and denied healthcare. Tell me, young lady, if you truly *want* the rich richer and the poor poorer and the larcenous pleasures of a materialistic society be the rewards of only the rich, greedy, and powerful. Tell me, oh you of the privileged few, if you *enjoy* human suffering and that you *dare* to deny reparation to American Indians and former slaves who *your* kind exploited. Tell me that you *support* the wide disparity of wealth, privilege, and opportunity in this country."

Rebecca fired back, "All the Progressives are doing is *transferring* that so-called wealth, privilege, and disparity to *their* own elites. They *need* to keep the people poor, and in need to achieve their end—which is to gain power—they *want* the masses under control so they will vote the way they are *told* to vote. What *you* offer will lead to a dictatorship and take *away* freedom and faith. How can the destruction of our God-inspired, and blessed, Constitution be the right thing to do? And if your way is right, then why the subterfuge? Why not present it to the people? Are you afraid to let the people decide for themselves? Are you so afraid of faith, of God, that you have to ban it? Should I seek reparation because my ancestors were once indentured? I've read all about Saul Alinsky, your mentor, and what the Progressive party, which took over the Democratic party, is all about, and I wonder why you . . ."

Recovering from the shock of Rebecca's outburst, Professor Emils, furious with Rebecca, interrupted her, and with incredible venom loudly told her to sit down and shut up. "This country was *thoroughly* corrupt before the Progressives came along. Banks, businesses, churches, and all *conservatives* are the manifestations of a capitalistic society bent on waging war, stealing and wasting resources, creating economic injustice, unequal opportunity, prejudice, bigotry, imperialism, and the neurotic assumption that this is a 'good' country and that its people are 'good' and that God looks after them. Saul Alinsky was right to say that we have to rid the country of these disgusting ideas and the power that you *erroneously* believe your faith provides. That's utterly ridiculous and so are your ideas of creation."

"What, so someone *else* can create their set of vices by creating a country where people will be forced under their thumb? Or where power becomes your god? People are imperfect, yes, but I'd sure rather have my God and the Bible's direction about what is good and right." Rebecca shot back surprising herself.

Another student called out, "By your refusal to allow God and biblical principles into people's lives, *no one* will stand as 'good' . . . so your argument isn't valid." And his remarks brought applause from more than half the students.

Professor Emils was livid with anger and told everyone to get out. "Every one of you . . . get out . . . and if you ever pull a stunt like this in my classroom again, you'll fail the course." As the students began to shuffle their belongings and ready themselves to leave the classroom, Professor Emils called out a parting shot to

Rebecca. "And *you*, young lady, can expect an *F* for this class, so don't bother coming back. Is that clear? Do not ever come back into my classroom."

When they reached the hall, Durk turned to her saying, "What have you done, Rebecca? He's gonna have it in for you now. He might not let you back in class. Why couldn't you just go along?"

"Well, Durk, I'm tired of 'going along,' and I am going to make *lots* of changes and make things *right* in my life . . . *every* facet of my life." And as Durk looked into her eyes, he saw the fire and the determination, and he knew that she was referring to him, to the drugs, to their relationship.

Ken stood with them listening to their exchange, and he too knew that Rebecca was putting Durk on notice for something. But he said nothing other than, "Way to go, Rebecca. You sure told him, that old bigot! You had him frothing at the mouth!"

What Rebecca didn't know was that her words had sent many of the students to the library and to their computers to research who Saul Alinsky was. Their research also led them to read about Richard Cloward and Frances Fox Piven and what the Progressive party espoused. What they learned was to make a difference. And as they shared what they learned with others, it brought huge numbers of young people to help in the fight to stop the Progressives from reaching their goals.

Later that evening, Durk was to meet Rebecca at Professor T's office, but earlier he'd met the professor and had accidently blurted out what Rebecca had said in their political science class and also what she'd said later when they were out in the hall. Durk was hoping for some reassurance from the professor about what Rebecca might do. Instead, the professor panicked and told Durk that they would have to rein Rebecca in. He confided that the man who taught the political science class was one of the professors who ran the drug sales on campus, and if he learned that Durk had compromised their operation by telling Rebecca, he might do something drastic. They needed to keep Rebecca quiet.

Professor T, fully believing that Durk had already compromised Rebecca, told Durk that he should perform well that night because he planned to film them. He said that if Rebecca learned of the film, she would remain quiet. Durk wasn't happy with this plan for two reasons. One was that he hadn't yet compromised Rebecca and didn't want to admit this to the professor, and two, he knew that if she ever learned that he had any part in filming her he'd never see her again. He wondered if he could prevent the camera from getting anything really worthwhile, and then if it ever came out and Rebecca learned of it, Durk could tell her that he'd protected her.

That evening Rebecca came to work armed for bear. She felt good again for the first time in a very long time, and she was determined to make Durk give back the drugs. Her plan was to seek a better paying job with more hours of work so she could help

Durk pay his debts. She would bring Durk to church with her when they were home for Christmas, and she would ask her minister to pray with him to help him make the changes in his life which would be required to get him back on the right path.

But when Rebecca went through her plan with Durk, he felt as if he'd been hit by a ton of bricks. *Why should I change? I like what I'm doing . . . my life is lucrative and exciting . . . I'm important and sought after and . . . free to follow my inclinations wherever they lead me.* Rebecca, thinking that she was doing what was right, kept talking, kept insisting; and when Durk turned away from her, she pulled on his shoulder to turn him back to her. Durk pushed Rebecca down onto the couch in a fury, and in doing so ripped her blouse. He held her hands above her head with one hand and tried to assault her with the other intending to gain control of her. He no longer cared whether or not the professor was filming them. He only wanted to stop Rebecca from talking and from thinking that she was in control.

But Rebecca kicked and screamed and pulled away from him with every ounce of strength she had. He was infuriated by her resistance. He purposely tried to hurt her with his hands, but Rebecca screamed and Durk put his hand over her mouth to quiet her. Furious, Durk pulled her off the couch to a standing position and then half dragged her toward the desk where the hard surface would allow him to more easily hold her until she calmed down and stopped fighting him. As he released his hand from her mouth, she began to beg God to help her; and this outburst frightened Durk, and for a moment he was immobilized and for some unfathomable reason he was stopped in his tracks. He turned away from her unsure of what to do.

Suddenly he saw that Professor T was standing next to him close to Rebecca, and Durk heard Rebecca scream. As Durk turned back to look at Rebecca, she slumped to the side of the desk then fell, hitting the back of her head on the knob adorning the arm of one of the chairs in front of the professor's desk, then again as she struck the floor. She didn't move. One arm was in a grotesque position and seemed unnaturally bent. Durk panicked but the professor continued to stand over her, glad that he'd silenced her.

Durk thought for a moment that Rebecca was dead. "What happened?" he asked. "I turned from her, and then I heard her scream, and when I turned back to her, she was falling. What did you do?"

"Shut up, Durk. Don't forget, I have the film. You are involved here too—up to your neck. We have to make this look like an accident . . . wait, no . . . we'll make it look like someone else did it. Jayden, that's who. Call him, Durk, right now. Pretend you're Rebecca and crying . . . and tell him to come here immediately."

Durk couldn't, or wouldn't move, so the professor grabbed the phone. After leafing through the student phone directory, he phoned Jayden. In a falsetto voice supposedly fraught with fear he pleaded, "Please Jayden, help me . . . Professor T's office."

The Professor quickly placed a bag of marijuana in Rebecca's hand and was about to drop some money near her when he decided to move her into the hall. It wasn't the best idea to have her right in his office. He dragged Rebecca by the feet into the hall two offices down from his, quickly unlocked the door to that office with his master key, and positioned Rebecca half in and half out of the door. Then he repositioned the marijuana in her hand and placed the money all around her. He quickly lit a joint, and putting his mouth over hers, blew smoke into her mouth hoping it went into her lungs. He took a quick look around to make sure that everything was in order. Then he ran back to his office to make sure that all was in order there as well. He grabbed his camera, locked both the inner and outer door, and dragged Durk, who was still in shock, down the hall and into the rear elevator to the first floor, then out into the open air. Pulling Durk along with him, they ran to the professor's car and quickly drove to his house where the professor immediately placed dishes on the table, adding whatever cold cuts and pre-made salads he had. He brought an open bottle of wine to the table and crumpled two napkins. He opened one of the textbooks Durk was supposed to be studying and laid it on the table near where Durk was sitting. Satisfied that he'd created their alibi, he sat down next to Durk to wait. He spoke sharply to Durk so he would understand what he was to say. Durk seemed almost catatonic and sat quietly, unresponsive to anything the professor said.

Meanwhile, Jayden, receiving the professor's phone call and believing that it was Rebecca who had phoned, hung up the phone, was very obviously distraught by what he'd heard and ran out of his dorm room. Ken knew something had seriously upset him. As Jayden left, Ken was sure that Jayden had yelled something to Ken about Rebecca needing help at Professor T's office. Ken continued to work on one of his class assignments but he couldn't concentrate. Finally he phoned Kara and told her that Jayden had run out of their room after receiving a phone call and seemed unusually distraught. He told her that he thought Jayden had said something about Professor T and that Rebecca needed help.

Immediately, Kara told Ken to come to her room; that they needed to get to the professor's office themselves. "Now!" she said loudly. She reminded Ken about their worries over Rebecca and about Professor T's voyeurism. Ken gasped, suddenly afraid, suddenly wondering why he hadn't reacted to Jayden's hurried and frazzled departure more quickly. When Ken arrived at Kara's suite, Kara was ready to go, and together they ran to the building that housed Professor T's office. "His office room is dark," Kara said as they neared the building. "I can usually see a light when someone is there."

"Maybe Jayden went somewhere else, Kara. Should we go back in case he phones?"

"No, dummkopf. We have our cell phones with us. Let's go up . . . I mean, we're here anyway. Let's see if we can discover anything out of the ordinary."

And so they quietly climbed the stairs and opened the door from the stairwell into the hall of the second floor. They immediately saw Jayden, bent over a body. They stood quietly, transfixed, as they watched Jayden and they heard him say, "I told you not to get involved, Rebecca. I told you . . . and now look what has happened . . . I warned you . . . Oh, Rebecca . . . Gosh, I didn't mean for this to happen. I didn't want you to get hurt . . . Oh, Rebecca, I'm so sorry." And Jayden broke down and sobbed.

Kara and Ken ran up to Jayden. When they saw Rebecca lying motionless, Kara quickly phoned 911. Then Ken saw that Jayden had a bag of marijuana in his hand. As he stared at Jayden, he also saw a wad of money with the bills haphazardly hanging half in and half out of his chest pocket. Jayden was incoherent and kept telling Rebecca that he was sorry, that he didn't mean for this to happen.

For some reason, Ken's mind filled with the picture of Professor T. Nagorra's three boxes of marijuana and for the moment thought that Jayden might be involved. His mind imagined Jayden striking Rebecca because he had seen her with Durk, and filled with jealousy, he'd reacted with anger. For some strange reason, even though Ken knew better, his mind pictured Jayden grabbing her, pushing her, taking the marijuana from her hand, and Durk running away to avoid coming to blows with Jayden or perhaps running when he'd seen Jayden hurt Rebecca. Maybe the drugs also had something to do with why Jayden had lost his temper, why he'd hit her.

Chaldeth had placed those images in Ken's mind and then began to cause a raging anger against Jayden to rise in Ken's heart. *After all,* Chaldeth hinted, *Jayden had gotten pretty nasty with you, so why not with Rebecca? After all, you saw Nagorra bring the drugs in, and now Jayden is standing here with drugs in his hand . . . and money.*

Two police cars with lights blazing and sirens blasting arrived outside the building, and shortly thereafter an ambulance also arrived and dispensed the paramedics with their bags and gurney. They charged noisily up the stairs, and the paramedics pushed everyone aside to minister to Rebecca. The police separated Ken, Jayden, and Kara, took them to different areas in the hall, and began to ask them questions. The police officer who had taken Jayden aside noticed the bag of marijuana and the wad of money and called another officer to join them to witness what Jayden had in his possession and what he said. They took the marijuana and money and handcuffed Jayden, dragging him roughly down the hall, down the stairs and into one of the police cars. Jayden seemed to be in a stupor which the officers believed was from the use of drugs.

The police questioned Ken and Kara separately, and suspecting that they were also involved in selling drugs, pushed them unmercifully for answers. Both were terribly frightened by these sudden accusations against them. Their first instinct was one of self preservation, and as Chaldeth knew, that often caused people to point the blame toward someone else. Ken and Kara gave their statements, and those statements were totally different.

In Ken's statement, he blamed Jayden for everything: the drugs, Rebecca's injury, jealousy, spying on Rebecca and Durk, and after the words left his mouth he wondered why he'd said what he did and why he felt that what had happened was entirely Jayden's fault. His thoughts plagued him afterward as his mind asked the question, *Even if Jayden had harmed Rebecca, why would I so openly and bitterly accuse Jayden without any facts?*

But Chaldeth knew why. He himself had inspired Ken's words and had planted that immediate and condemning thought in Ken's head when Ken first saw Jayden leaning over Rebecca. In fact, Chaldeth had planned the entire episode. He'd wanted Rebecca completely compromised, and although that hadn't happened, this was good enough. Rebecca's injury had been in his control and was to work toward harming all the others. Chaldeth was pleased. Now his only worry was to block any help that could come for, to, or from Jayden or Rebecca's family. Chaldeth knew of another part of scripture that promised such help, and he had to somehow stop it from occurring. The words that worried him were from Hebrews 13:5 where God promised His children, "I will never leave thee nor forsake thee."

A similar promise could be found in Malachi 3:10 where God said, "Prove me now herewith, saith the Lord of hosts, if I will not open the windows of heaven and pour you out a blessing, that there shall not be room enough to receive it."

Chaldeth remembered that Sarah had once used scripture to comfort Mary when she was suffering, and it had brought Mary from disbelief into belief. That was a worry and risk that Chaldeth was always aware of. The words he hated most in this context were found in Isaiah 43:2 and said, "For He hath said, 'When thou passest through the waters, I will be with thee; and through the rivers, they shall not overflow thee: when thou walkest through the fire, thou shalt not be burned; neither shall the flame kindle upon thee.'" And one more found in Zechariah 13:9 read, "They shall call on My name, and I will hear them: I will say, 'It is my people,' and they shall say, 'The Lord is my God.'"

But Chaldeth had a few tricks up his sleeve, and knew that his plan was a good one. He would—he must—win this battle. He wanted Rebecca and Jayden to suffer, to find no way out, and the others to give up hope and wonder if God *really* was with them after all. Doubt was a particularly potent weapon in Chaldeth's arsenal. He'd also known that Peter had thrice denied Christ and that Judas had devastatingly betrayed Christ. This had given Chaldeth the idea to have Ken deny his relationship with Jayden and to betray him. Chaldeth was also toying with the idea of having Ken hang himself over the matter as Judas had; that would haunt Jayden every day of his life and could cause him to give up on God.

The police charged Jayden with battery with the intent to kill and also with possession of a controlled substance with the intent to sell. He said nothing in his defense, so they assumed that he was guilty, especially given Ken's account of what the underlying situation might have been.

The paramedics took Rebecca to the hospital, and as soon as the hospital obtained Rebecca's next of kin information, they phoned the police department in Rebecca's hometown. The chief of police personally drove to Elizabeth's house to tell her that her daughter had been injured. Elizabeth ran to tell Mary, and Kevin. The three of them along with Teddie drove to the hospital as soon as possible. En route to the hospital, Mary phoned Sarah who promised to call everyone else and told Mary that they would all pray and then they too would drive to the hospital.

Meanwhile, Kara asked the police officer why Jayden had been arrested and told the police that Jayden had simply rushed to Rebecca's defense when she phoned him. But they did not believe her. She was later to learn that no call had been made from Rebecca's cell phone.

When Kara and Ken finally arrived back at their dorm, after giving signed statements to the police, Kara spoke with Ken and learned from him what he'd initially told the officer who had questioned him which then found its way into the statement he'd signed. She was furious with him and told him that he'd he done something terrible and that he'd out and out lied.

"Why did you *say* such a preposterous thing? You *know* that Jayden didn't hurt her . . . you *know* that Jayden doesn't use or sell drugs . . . what have you done? *Why* did you say those things? You should be ashamed of yourself. What you did was absolutely inexcusable."

Ken couldn't answer. He didn't know why he'd said the things he'd said ; it was as if something had made him say those things, think those things, see those images, just as he began talking with the police. He felt terrible. "But, Kara, I really did think all those things when I first saw Jayden standing over Rebecca."

"Well, Ken," Kara continued, "we are marching *right* down to the police station and telling them the truth, and *then* we are going to tell them of our suspicions about Durk and the professor and the camera. We will tell them *everything!*" Then Ken told Kara about the boxes he'd carried into Nagorra's office and how they had smelled of pot. "Well then, we will tell them this as well. Why didn't you tell me . . . us . . . about those boxes? What has gotten into you, Ken? You have really let me down. In fact, you've let all your friends down."

When they arrived at the police station, the police questioned Ken gruelingly when he tried to retract his original statement. They asked why he'd lied in the first place. Then they asked him why he was lying now. They asked him why he did not call them when he'd seen the boxes and smelled the pot. Was he hiding the fact that he too was involved with drugs? Who else was involved? Why did he point his finger at Jayden if they were friends? Ken was exhausted from their intensive questioning and became incredibly frightened. As he began to understand that Jayden was charged with something he hadn't done, he was afraid that he too would be charged with something he didn't do. But one good thing happened. When he told the police about the packages he'd carried into the professor's office, their ears perked up. When he explained that Rebecca and Durk met often in the professor's office as well, they immediately phoned the narcotics squad, and Ken felt that perhaps some good would come of this after all.

Two narcotics officers spoke with Ken, reviewed the reports, and obtained a court order to search the professor's office and home. But neither department accepted Ken and Kara's statements that Jayden was innocent of any wrongdoing. The only thing that Ken had going for him was that Kara's story matched his later story almost word for word. The police remained suspicious because of what Ken had initially said, the things that Ken now realized was his unfounded and erroneous first impression.

The professor had always felt secure in the belief that his merchandise was well hidden behind the dark walnut paneling. But he'd never thought that there would be a court order to search his office or home, and he did not know that the narcotics division might employ the use of a drug-sniffing dog for such a search. He thought that dogs were only used at the borders for cars and trucks, or in huge buildings and terminals.

Thus, Professor T. Nagorra's stash was located in his office, and another search took place quite unexpectedly at his house. He was arrested. He was shocked by the sudden turn of events and quickly blamed Durk, pretending that he hadn't known that the drugs were there. He said that he had always suspected that Durk used and sold drugs. He claimed that Durk must have placed the drugs in his office.

Durk's room was searched and his merchandise found, and he too was arrested. When he learned that the professor claimed that Durk had purchased and planted the drugs, he in turn blamed the professor. Both denied having anything to do with Rebecca being hurt or found in the building, and both blamed Jayden telling the police that he was in love with her and always in a jealous rage over the attention she paid to Durk. Both denied any knowledge of the drugs found in the office, and both claimed that the merchandise found in their houses was used only for their private consumption.

The police report stated that Jayden had attacked Rebecca out of a jealous rage and that he was one of many student pushers. Durk was charged with possession and intent to sell and the professor charged as the possible distributor of the drugs. Investigations were continued in the hope of uncovering additional affiliations with

Durk, the professor, and Jayden. If Rebecca died, Jayden would be charged with murder. Durk's attitude was that if he was going down, then so were Jayden and the professor—maybe even some others he could name in exchange for a plea bargain. But strangely, no one told Durk that Rebecca had been seriously injured.

Rebecca lay in a stark white hospital bed in a pale green room that also housed a night stand, a rolling tray table and two straight-back uncomfortable chairs. She was in a special bed that turned completely upside down so that its unmoving occupant would not receive pressure-point lacerations on her skin. She was in a deep coma. She did not respond to any voice or any touch. Tests demonstrated that her brain was still functioning and all else was in good working order despite the two serious blows to her head. Her right arm had been broken—just one bone, not two—and now had a heavy cast over it, making it more difficult to turn her and requiring special positioning when the entire bed was turned.

Her family and family friends came and asked if she could be moved to a hospital closer to their home, but the doctors felt that it was best to wait a few weeks until some of her injuries were stabilized. They prayed day in and day out, reminding God of His promise to help them through every difficulty. When Elizabeth first saw Rebecca, she was devastated by how frail her daughter appeared. She left the room to cry and then returned with a determination to stay by Rebecca's side until she woke up. Mary too came and tried to comfort Rebecca and Elizabeth. She understood that Elizabeth was afraid because she had lost her husband despite many prayers and pleas to God.

Elizabeth held Rebecca's hand and stroked her hair as she said, "Remember, Rebecca, how God tells us that in all things we should continue to trust in Him? Remember the verse from Psalm 62:8, "Trust in Him at all times, ye people; Pour out your heart before him: God is a refuge for us." Elizabeth used this quote as much to help herself as to help Rebecca.

Later when Mary went to sit with Rebecca and give Elizabeth a short break, she too reminded Rebecca that God promised them strength and help, and she recited from Isaiah 25:4, "For thou hast been a . . . strength to the needy in his distress, a refuge from the storm, a shadow from the heat . . ." But Rebecca never responded.

A week later, when Jayden had been released on bail and into the custody of his parents, he too came to sit by Rebecca's side. Worried about their circumstances, he had been looking through the Bible and found an especially comforting verse which he read to her. "Rebecca," he said, "neither of us should worry because in Acts 15:11 the early apostles said, 'But we believe that through the grace of the Lord Jesus Christ we shall be saved . . . ' We both have to hang onto those words, and if we do, we will be okay. I know it seems tough. I mean, we're really both in a mess right now, but God will see us through it, I know." But with that said, Jayden broke down and sobbed, wishing that he'd phoned his family earlier and He and Rebecca had left the school before such harm had been done. Chaldeth saw and thought, *Good. Soon his faith will give out and he'll blame God and I'll have him! In fact, I'll have made a pretty good catch. I'll have Ken and Kara, the professor and Durk, Jayden and Rebecca through what they will have to face, I'll get every one of their friends and their family members. Good catch, if I have to say so myself.*

So Chaldeth stood in the corner of the room watching what went on, who came in, what they said, and when they left; and there seemed to be nothing occurring to cause him worry. With wings comfortably folded back and arms folded across his chest, Chaldeth, with the strength of his angel's body, stood for as long as he wanted to watch over his prey. With each conquest in his long cruel life, his face had gained just a little bit more of the ugly qualities of sin and lost more and more of an angel's original beautiful and glorious countenance. By now Chaldeth was terribly ugly, but like so many entities filled with their own importance, he saw only what he could have been and not what he really was, what he had become.

It bothered Chaldeth to think that these . . . humans—well, those who followed God anyway—would be higher in stature than any angel and would later be given perfect, beautiful celestial bodies. Chaldeth was angered by this and thought, *God insulted the angels by wanting to make man higher than angels and made that insult public by admitting this in scripture! How dare He make these humans better than an angel when angels have been around for so long!*

Celestial bodies were described in scripture, and the kingdom God prepared for these humans was also described. They would rule with God and Christ, and they would rule the angels. *How preposterous! Why should they rule us? Just look at the weak frail failure that lay in the bed, or look at the worried peons that come to her bed expecting a miracle. Are they greater than me, greater than Chaldeth?*

There was also a nurse that came every day to Rebecca's bed whether she was assigned to Rebecca that day or not. She was young, and she was evidently someone who had a great deal of faith, so Chaldeth decided to attack her in some way too. Maybe he could even accomplish this in a way that would involve and destroy her faith. He hated anyone who supported this entourage of "loving" souls. So Chaldeth plotted and arranged for Jane to meet one of the physicians in charge of Rebecca's case and try to get them both to give up on Rebecca. Chaldeth realized that if he could confuse the doctors, maybe have them leave the case, leave because they lost hope, perhaps there would be less chance for Rebecca's recovery.

The doctor was someone who prayed at the bedside of his patients when no one else was around, and Chaldeth had been drawn to him. Chaldeth hated that he prayed and hate was like an aphrodisiac to him. But so far his plan regarding the nurse and the doctor was backfiring. Both of them began questioning Rebecca's friends and family members as they witnessed their devotion and were listening to their open, trusting, loving prayers. Chaldeth had wanted to use them to bring further harm to Rebecca, but instead he saw that they, like the family he hated, were protected by their faith, their dedication to helping others.

Jim and Wade had taken their turn to sit by Rebecca and continue to talk to her. The physicians had explained to the family that coma patients could hear what was said, and hearing familiar voices and comforting words often kept such patients from disconnecting and often brought them back to full consciousness. This was why Elizabeth had made a schedule of visiting, and they all were making a concerted effort to rotate their visits so that Rebecca always had someone nearby. They'd brought extra chairs to Rebecca's room and left them so that a large group could assemble at one time.

That day, Jane walked into Rebecca's room after her shift ended and sat quietly to listen to the conversation that Wade and Jim were having and directing toward Rebecca. "Jim, do you remember the in-depth discussions we used to have before you joined the church? You know, about religion, about scripture, about the plan God laid into the physics of the world, about generational sin and the debate about creation and evolution?

"Yeah, Wade. Sometimes when I think of those days, I'm embarrassed by how much it took for me to finally understand and to finally accept and grab the gift God was offering me. I sure was a stubborn one back then!"

"Ha! And you're not now?" Wade laughed, teasing Jim. "You know the one thing that I still need to learn more about is that generational sin thing. I mean, I know about the sin of Adam and Eve and how what they did, their sin, impacted all of mankind, but the stuff where the actions of our ancestors impacts us personally . . . well, I'm not sure I understand that, Jim. I have questions about how we combat those inclinations we may inherit and how we inherit them."

"Well, you know, I'm pretty new to all this, Wade, but here's how I think it goes: It's because of the battle between good and evil that we are living through. The sin of Adam and Eve resulted in the *requirement* that mankind learn of good *and* evil. Their disobedience to God allowed sin to enter our world and gave Satan the right to influence us. God warned them, and they did not listen, so sadly, that single act of sin now allows Satan to use sin against mankind for a certain amount of time. God, because of His righteousness, *cannot* interfere unless man asks for His help. And believe me, God *has* provided us with all kinds of help to get through—even overcome sin. It's complex, but all a part of an incredible plan to perfect love, an environment in which evil cannot exist, and which will eventually allow God to create an untainted new world."

"Well, yeah, that's the part I get. But the part where we inherit and pay for the sins of our own personal forefathers, even one, two, or three generations ago . . . well, I'd never heard anything like that. I mean, is it in our DNA or something?"

"You know, Wade, I've been thinking about that lately, and you wanna know why? Durk. I went to see that boy, and I've talked to some of the people who know him, especially Ken and Jayden, and you know Ken made a remark that stuck with me. He said that he felt sorry for Durk because he was raised to fail. Ken said that Durk's father was an abusive drunk. I wondered about Durk's father's family and then wondered if Durk ever wished that he could break the chain of those traits. If generational sin—inherited sin—caused Durk's bad behavior and there was any chance that he wanted better for himself, then if he understood what his problem *really* was in a spiritual sense, maybe there'd be a chance for him to redeem himself."

"Wow, what a forgiving heart you have! But then again, you're right. He is only a kid after all and if he never had a good role model, Jim, I can see how he may have made a lot of bad choices."

"I was so concerned by these thoughts that I actually looked up some of the things that God tells us about the sins of the forefathers. Wanna hear them?"

"Yeah, sure, I wanna know too."

Jim pulled a slip of paper out of his chest pocket and unfurled it. "Okay, here we go. For example, in Jeremiah 11:10 it says, 'They are turned back to the iniquities of their forefathers, which refused to hear my words . . . ' and in Exodus 20:5 the Bible says, 'Visiting the iniquity of the fathers upon the children unto the third and fourth generation . . . ' And in Numbers 14:18, we are told, 'And by no means clearing the guilty, visiting the iniquity of the fathers upon the children unto the third and fourth generation.' That sure seems as if what an uncle or father, grandfather or great-grandfather or any of their spouses did behind the scenes could impact a life pretty badly. . . and that's only a few of many verses like that."

"It does seem as if that would impact a life. But at what point do we excuse someone's behavior because of the behavior of their ancestor? We do need to take responsibility for our own actions at some point, don't we?"

"You're right Wade, at no point can we really excuse certain behaviors, but we can begin to understand and then overcome them. We are and must remain responsible for the harm we personally cause or the bad or illegal deeds we commit. What I am saying is that maybe some people would think about this information if they were provided with it. We can't change something when we don't understand it, but if we begin to understand why we have these tendencies, these impulses toward behaviors that are not pleasing to God . . . and certainly not pleasing to good men, we can decide to change. I mean, if we don't know, don't look for, don't watch for, don't pray for the help we need to fight it, how can we ever be okay? But if we want, really want to be okay, maybe we'll listen, believe, and then learn how to make some drastic and wonderful changes in our life."

"That's true, Jim. But how do you get this information out there? I sure never knew. In fact, I'd never even heard of it before. But how does someone beat that rap? You know, crawl out from that . . . uhh . . . that curse of what their ancestors might have passed to them as a tendency toward some terrible action?"

"I'd like to know more too," piped Jane who'd been sitting quietly in the back near the door.

"Me too," added Dr. John who'd slipped in behind Jane and had been enthralled by the discussion between Jim and Wade. "That's so interesting. To tell you the truth, I'm a churchgoer, and I never heard anything about this either, just about Adam and Eve. Yet it makes sense that if we are impacted by the sin of Adam and Eve, then why not be impacted by ancestors who are closer to us in age?"

"Exactly," Jane added, "I agree. This is something we should all learn and then share with others. I mean, if I were, for instance, a compulsive shoplifter, I'd never think that maybe I had an ancestor who stole or did something to pass such a . . . a . . . tendency . . . . a gene maybe . . . along to me! But then my scientific mind asks, if it is a gene like some say alcoholism or drug addiction or even homosexuality is, then can God help us overcome that too?"

"Yeah, I guess so, "Jim replied. "That's why I call the one from Adam and Eve inherited sin and the other generational sin, because there may be a significant difference. I mean, if it's true that we are 'wired,' as many say today, to be an alcoholic or addicted to drugs or drawn to homosexuality or anything else someone feels they can't live without, maybe there's a reason. We see so much evidence of drug users and alcoholics overcoming their addiction despite their so-called wiring. Through programs that take a faith-based approach, many overcome drugs and alcohol addictions, so why not all other addictions? Why not overcome anything else? You know . . . . why not be able to free ourselves of any other spirit as well through faith, through God."

"Sometimes," Jim explained, "I think that rather than a gene or being 'wired' for a certain tendency, we actually do inherit a kind of change to our DNA that allows a certain kind, or kinds of, spirit to enter a person and cause him to thirst after what he shouldn't want. Matthew 8:16 explains that there were *many* possessed by evil spirits in Christ's time and that He cast them out by his word, and they were healed. 'When the evening was come, they brought unto him many that were possessed with devils: and he cast out the spirits with his word, and healed all that were sick.'

"Luke 8:29 says, '(For he had commanded the unclean spirit to come out of the man. For oftentimes it had caught him: and he was kept bound with chains and in fetters; and he brake the bands, and was driven of the devil into the wilderness.)'

"So it seems that these spirits can be made to leave just as they often do when someone goes through the twelve-step program. The Bible also tells us that some spirits really hang on, and that the only way to get them to leave is if we starve them by prayer and fasting. Fasting, in this context, would mean to stay away from . . . . abstain . . . . from spirits or activities that the Bible tells us are not pleasing to God. Run from them! We associate the word fasting with meaning denying ourselves food, but here I think that it means to deny the spirit what it needs to live. That could be the drug addiction, the alcohol, the homosexual activity, the pedophilia, anything.

"When the apostles complained that they had been unable to cast out a certain spirit, Christ told them that only by prayer and fasting could they be cast out. Matthew 17:21 says, 'Howbeit this kind goeth not out but by prayer and fasting.' Well, again, most people think that means not eating—you know, going without food for a while—but I think it means 'going without' that activity . . . running away from any temptation, staying away from the temptation itself. Then maybe that spirit starves, and leaves that person to look for a more satisfying, easily directed person. The bottom line is that God finds certain activities 'an abomination' or 'evil,' and therefore we should try to overcome them. It doesn't mean someone can't be forgiven or loved, just that they need to understand that they cannot keep on thinking it's okay because they are wired to drink or do drugs and such."

"Gosh this is so interesting. I have so many patients thirsting to know how they can fight their addictions, and this knowledge could help them," Jane said.

"Yeah, and it provides hope and direction. Many would give their last dollar to find out how to break their addictions. Another thought is that if someone overcomes their inherited tendency, maybe their "wiring" or "gene" or "DNA" changes once again so their own kids won't be plagued by, won't "inherit", won't suffer the sins of their forefathers. Ya think that's possible too?" added Dr. John. "Great point and maybe we can all go home and read more of what the Bible says about this subject and discuss it again in depth. Maybe we can come up with some really fascinating direction for this problem," Jim replied.

Chaldeth squirmed. He hadn't liked that conversation at all. He'd have to stop these stupid people from these fruitless conversations. But the conversations had not been fruitless because already Jane and Dr. John had plans to share their newfound information with others, and wondered if this could help those patients who'd given up, who felt they were trapped by their addictions. Both felt that if a patient understood why they were held hostage, they might have the will to fight back. It made sense, and if it worked, well, wow, it was a *major* breakthrough.

Before Jane left, she told everyone about a verse her mother often used. It was in Proverbs 3:5 and said, "Trust in the Lord with all thine heart; and lean not unto your own understanding." And the others thought that that verse was so important for them to remember and to share with others.

One's own understanding often trips us up, Jane thought, *whereas God's words will always work for us!*

After they left, Jim continued to speak to Wade about the incredible yet somewhat confusing connection between original sin, generational sin, and unclean spirits that can attack and dwell in mankind. They determined to learn more and see if they could come to a conclusion that would help them explain it more eloquently. "I really would like to speak with Durk. Something draws me to him, Wade . . . something that wants me to give him one more chance. If he doesn't know about the power of Satan and his cohorts, or realize how he has become trapped by them, and if he doesn't know about God's grace, he cannot make an informed decision about his life."

At that moment, Jim thought that he felt Rebecca's fingers tighten on his . . . just a little bit, just one frail little squeeze. But maybe he was wrong. He looked into her face and saw no movement and watched her hands and her slender frame covered by the white blanket and still saw no movement. But he did tell the nurse, and she came to examine Rebecca explaining, "Sometimes the body gives a light tremor, but it is unconscious. But then again, some of these patients awaken abruptly, and we don't know why. Sometimes they even awaken and then slip away again to awaken again at another time. Keep up your hopes . . . and keep praying."

Jayden came in just then, and Jim decided not to mention that he thought Rebecca might have responded to something he said. But he did tell Jayden about the conversation they'd had about generational sin. When he described what he'd read in Matthew 17:21, Jayden told him that a similar verse could be found in Mark 9:29 and quoted, "And he said unto them, This kind can come forth by nothing but by prayer and fasting."

"Jayden, in these verses God is talking about rebuking unclean spirits and making them leave those who they invaded. What do you get from these particular verses in regard to that subject, especially the part about fasting?"

"I am not sure . . . I know that it can't be correct to assume that God means, you know, dieting exactly . . . I mean, I guess you could refer to those who carry the spirits of gluttony or anorexia, but I think it means something . . . more than that. I think it has farther-reaching implications, don't you, Dad? What do you think?"

Wade replied by asking Jayden to think of another meaning for the word fasting, and Jayden understood what Wade meant and said, "Yeah, yeah, it's like dieting, isn't it? It means staying away from . . . not partaking of . . . abstaining from . . . . wow!"

Jim added, "That's what we were thinking too, Jayden, and that teaches us that while some spirits are easily rebuked, others cling within an inch of their lives. But by not 'feeding' them, by abstaining from what they want and need to live—by abstaining from what they 'feed' off of—they have no choice but to leave!"

"So if someone just sort of 'dabbles' in drugs or alcohol, or something potentially addictive, maybe even pornography or pedophilia or homosexuality, the spirit that enjoys that activity can enter and cause that person to want more and more and then finally control them and force them to feed their needs. Is that what you mean, is that right ?"

"Jayden," Wade said, "that's right, and that's something I can grasp and accept too. And by golly, I'm gonna tell everyone I meet who had or has a kid involved in stuff that destroys their life how to be free of it. This method still takes an awful lot of willpower, but by golly, it sure gives people hope and it provides a specific direction for them to take."

"Yeah," Jim added, "and it sure debunks the opinions of those who say, 'Oh they are just wired that way and can't help it!' And then their own kids are "wired" to commit the same acts and suffer the consequences. So many people, including college kids, drink way too much and simply excuse themselves by saying that they are wired that way—they claim to have an addictive personality and like to drink. Many use drugs or move into homosexuality thinking that they cannot change because it's the way they are. That's heartbreaking because with *each* encounter into any of these addictions that spirit gets a stronger hold over them and becomes excruciatingly difficult to remove."

"Well, Jim, 'tis a puzzlement to many, that's for sure. But for us and others who try to gain a better understanding of scripture, God leaves no question unanswered. The sad thing is that parents don't know this stuff and can't teach their kids properly, and without this knowledge these poor kids succumb to those spirits and then pass them on to yet another generation."

Wade stood and stretched and said, "I feel so badly for kids today. So many kids don't know what evil is or know how to protect themselves from evil. I'm so glad we have one another to discuss these things. We are so blessed. I guess this is one of the reasons that God asks us to know His words and to remain in constant fellowship with one another. Breaking bread together . . . . meaning talking with one another about God's admonitions . . . . is so crucial. I wish we could provide every parent and every child with this information. My favorite scripture of all says it all. It's from Joshua 24:15 and says, 'As for me and my house, we will serve the Lord.'"

"Good one, Wade . . . I like that too, and another one I really love is from Psalm 27:1 and says, 'The Lord is my light and my salvation; whom shall I fear? The Lord is the strength of my life; of whom shall I be afraid?'"

Speaking of scripture," Jayden said, "I'm not going to let you guys outdo me. I've got a good one too, one that Mom gave me to take to school with me and read every night. In fact, it's actually a combination of two different verses, but they go well together. And . . . I've pretty well kept that promise to read them once every day, missing only a few times.

"They are from Psalms and Romans. Psalm 1:1-3 says, 'Blessed is the man that walketh not in the counsel of the ungodly, nor standeth in the way of sinners, nor sitteth in the seat of the scornful. But his delight is in the law of the Lord; and in his law doth he meditate day and night. And he shall be like a tree planted by the rivers of water, that bringeth forth his fruit in his season; his leaf also shall not wither, and whatsoever he doeth shall prosper.'

"And Romans 8:25 says, 'But if we hope for that we see not, then do we with patience wait for it.'"

Chapter 9

The Challenge

It was a difficult time for the family. They had the responsibilities of homes and children and jobs in an area about a four-hour drive from the college Jayden and Rebecca attended. The hospital where Rebecca lay in a coma was in an area not too far from the campus, and thankfully there were plenty of hotels and restaurants that could accommodate them when they arrived to keep their vigil with Rebecca. The families babysat for one another when one or two couples were scheduled to spend a few days with Rebecca. They took turns visiting with her, wanting someone in addition to Elizabeth and John or Mary and Kevin there for support at all times. Juggling their schedules was a challenge.

Each of them prayed that Rebecca would awaken well and whole and Jayden would be exonerated from the charges against him.

As the drama of circumstances unfolded, and they became aware of the troubles that Rebecca and Jayden faced, they realized that the campus was not a place without problems; and for Rebecca and Jayden to stay on, these problems would have to be fully resolved. Until they were, they would not sanction Rebecca and Jayden's return to the campus. Rebecca would need to understand the danger she was in and the danger she had put Jayden in by her friendship with Durk. They believed that she must have been aware of Durk's involvement with the drugs.

Jayden needed to be exonerated from the charges against him. If they were not dropped, Jayden would be expelled, and most likely, so would Rebecca, and this could hamper their acceptance into another school. To address this challenge, the family wanted to gather all the facts, and consider retaining a good attorney. They believed without question everything that Jayden told them, and they listened carefully to what Ken and Kara told them. They were convinced that none of these youngsters had done anything wrong other than exercising bad judgment and for not phoning them right away. Rebecca might have misplaced her affections, and she, Jayden, Ken, and Kara may have not responded properly to the seriousness of drug use and sales on the campus, but the family knew that they were innocent of any complicity in the drugs.

As the entire story unfolded, the family recognized that Rebecca and Jayden had been under spiritual attack. Their first reaction was to admonish Jayden for not alerting them when he first began to worry about Rebecca. But Jayden was already so filled with regret, so devastated by the harm that had befallen Rebecca, that they focused instead on giving Jayden every support they could and uncovering the source of the campus problems.

They were pleased that Jayden's faith superseded the fear he could have had about the charges against him. He knew that the charges were false, and he fully believed that in time God would bring the truth to the surface. The family too trusted God to help them. "If God brings us to it, He will bring us through it," was a little saying that Grandma had used and which they'd all adopted. But they were also practical. The charges were serious.

As the family discussed the problem of drugs on the campus, the men decided to try to uncover some of facts behind Professor T. Nagorra's actions, especially the part Kara had mentioned in regard to the camera she had seen. They decided that the women would alternate between staying at Rebecca's side and supporting Elizabeth and Mary and babysitting for the children. The men decided that after a few hours of sleuthing each day, they would join the women in Rebecca's room to share what they had learned. Both the women and the men wanted the charges against Jayden dropped. And they wanted those who perpetrated the sale of drugs, harmed others through their unscrupulous acts, and destroyed the safety of the campus punished and removed from the university.

"We need a plan . . . not only for which of us drives up here and when, but also for getting to the truth. We need to identify *everyone* involved. We need to know who did what, who worked for whom, and why Jayden was framed. We still don't know who made that phone call to Jayden and why. We need to learn what the students know, what the professors know, how long this has been going on, and even if there is some outsider involved, and if so, who he is. By getting to the bottom of this and being sure it's been taken care of—eliminated—is the only way that we'll ever feel that the campus is safe for Rebecca and Jayden. And that's a tall order for us."

"Jim, that's true," Wade added. "If we do tackle these problems, we will need to talk to lots of students, maybe talk to professors, learn where to find the people who will open up to us. This is gonna take some time, especially since we will have to gain the trust of those who we hope will talk freely."

"Is it possible for us to sit down with a calendar," Caleb added, "maybe even plan to take some vacation time so we can tackle this together and get it done quickly? We can follow Elizabeth's schedule of who will be up here together and form sleuthing teams to get to the bottom of this."

"Good idea, Caleb," Josh interjected. "If we want to establish trust so people will open up, we need to let them get to know us, understand what we are trying to do, and thoroughly believe that we are not looking to point the finger at anyone who may have tried a joint or gotten drunk or looked the other way. No one will open up if they are afraid of getting into trouble with the law . . . or with any of their professors!"

"Hmm, good point, Josh, and that is gonna take time. Anyone got any ideas?"

"Well, what if we made up some flyers that describe our plight and our goal and just ask for help? Clean, simple, and to the point. Maybe the majority of professors and students *want* a safe haven on campus, *want* right to win over wrong."

"I don't know, Matt. There are a lot of campus professors nowadays who are extremists—left-wing radicals entrenched in college life by the fact that they are tenured and can't be fired! Years ago these guys banded together claiming that, for them to have *real* freedom of speech, freedom to opine a potentially explosive subject, they *had* to be protected against being fired by an administrator or board of directors who disagreed with their views. Just like *every* ploy ever initiated that ended up a bad influence, this one sounded reasonable at the time, and *voila, tenured* professors who can say and do *and teach our kids anything* they want!"

"Yeah, now parents not only have to teach their kids about God, about all the things necessary to being safe, but also the truth about all kinds of subjects that some of these profs have perverted. I think about evolution and creation and can't believe that only evolution is taught. I think about our Constitution, some teach that it's outdated. I think about how many of these guys teach that socialism and Marxism should be adopted as a way of life in the United States! It blows my mind!"

"Kevin makes some good points. We will be up against the . . . uhh . . . well . . . we'll be up against what the Bible has told us are the powers and principalities of evil, the spirits that push these guys into believing such hogwash and acting in other harmful ways, like pushing drugs. Remember Ephesians 6:12? 'For we wrestle not against flesh and blood, but against principalities, against powers, against the rulers of the darkness of this world, against spiritual wickedness in high places.'"

Jim went on to add, laughing, "Well, I guess dealing with me when I fought against God will do you guys some good now. You already know how to handle someone who is 'stiff-necked'! Do you remember when Barbara got so mad at me when I just kept on revisiting God's words but refused to accept them? She stood up shaking her index finger at me saying, 'In Acts 7:51, God warns: *"Ye stiff necked . . . in heart and ears, ye do always resist the Holy Ghost: As your fathers did, so do ye."'"*

The other men laughed with Jim. "Yeah, she really told you off that day—and let's face it, you were a hard nut to crack, Jim—but look at you now!"

"Don't make light of this, guys. Jim was stiff-necked, but what we are going up against now is a strong and dangerous force that might fight back with a vengeance . . . and we'd better not forget that."

"Good point, Caleb. Well, the only satisfaction we can get right away is that we know the end for those who have joined forces with evil. The Bible talks about how evil seems to prosper and good seems to suffer. But in the end evil will be punished, and if I hadn't read about that in scripture, I could easily get discouraged. Remember that verse?"

"Yeah, Jim, I know it well. It's in Matthew 23:23-25 and says, 'Woe unto you, scribes and Pharisees, hypocrites! For ye pay tithe of mint and anise and cumin, and have omitted the weightier matters of the law, judgment, mercy, and faith: these ought ye to have done, and not to leave the other undone. Ye blind guides, which strain at a gnat, and swallow a camel. Woe unto you, scribes and Pharisees, hypocrites! For ye make clean the outside of the cup and of the platter, but within they are full of extortion and excess.'"

"That's a good point, Matt, but that's not the scripture I was thinking of. There's one about how evil people prosper and how easy it is to be envious of them."

"Oh, okay, that one is in Psalm 73:2, 3 and does speak of the prosperity of those who are evil. It says, 'But as for me, my feet were almost gone; my steps had well nigh slipped, For I was envious at the foolish, when I saw the prosperity of the wicked.' But remember God also says in Psalm 73:17, 'Until I went into the sanctuary of God, then understood I their end.'"

"Yeah, that's it. And the one from Matthew is also good to remember. Well, anyway, we've gotten off the point here. Our goal right now is to find those who, even secretly, want good for this campus and will talk to us. So how do we do this?"

"I like the idea of a schedule of who works with who and what areas each twosome should tackle."

"Me too. Everybody?" Everyone grunted their approval, and they began to draw up a tentative visitation schedule. After a short discussion, they decided that they would go in twos to look for people who would talk. By going in twos, one might catch a nervous look or pick up on something the other hadn't noticed, or redirect a line of questioning or even soften the conversation if needed. This plan would also allow them to talk to two people at once if they happened upon friends who admitted to knowing something.

Josh added, "Let's hold off on the flyer for now. We'll be tipping our hand, and those who are involved in this . . . dirty business . . . will just go underground. Let's just mingle for now, stay undercover so no one knows what we are seeking or who we are."

They agreed with everything that Josh said and thought that they could always create a flyer after they'd obtained some of the information they needed. They planned to visit and talk with Durk. He was still in jail because no one had made his bail. They also felt that a visit to Professor T. Nagorra, who was being held without bail at this time, might bring them some new tidbit of information. Perhaps if they angered him he'd say something he hadn't meant to say. He wasn't the big kingpin in all this trouble; he had to have connections to someone outside of the campus.

They also discussed the potential of and danger in uncovering a big drug dealer off campus. They knew that they might be opening Pandora's box and facing great danger if they went after a big drug dealer. The police might tell them not to interfere with the case, probably tell them that they needed to stay out of it because they could be in danger if they tried to get involved. Maybe they would even order them to stop interfering.

They decided to keep their activities a secret for now . . . at least as best they could. They acknowledged that the "bad guys" would pass the information to others, warning them that they were out questioning people, so in time what they were planning to do would be exposed. Thus at some point they might have to deal with the police or the campus administrators, especially if they spoke with people who might report their activities. They tried to anticipate every roadblock and every problem they might face. One of their main concerns was to protect the women. While the women would be the ones who would stay with Rebecca, it was possible that someone would try to use them to silence the men. They could not come up with a solution for that concern except to tell the women, who would also be in twos, to stay together and to wait for the men to drive them to the hospital and pick them up at night. John would also be with them.

"Maybe we're being paranoid. Maybe we are overreacting, and maybe we should rely more on God. Let's be sure to put this plan in God's hands . . . ask for His blessing, His help, His protection. And then trust in that," Matt said. "Nevertheless, we must be careful and not take any foolish risks."

"True . . . but by discussing as many of the contingencies as possible, we will be better prepared."

They decided that they would use some of their vacation time, taking it in two- or three-day intervals rather than in weeks. This would allow them to follow a lead more efficiently. They planned to assemble notes at the end of each day, so whoever took up the torch would have a full briefing, and know who to revisit if necessary. With their plans made and their hearts at peace, they prayed together and then began to implement the steps they'd outlined.

Durk seemed to be the one who might know the most. Since Rebecca had wanted to help Durk, appeared to have spent time with him, then maybe there was a streak of good in him that they could bring to the surface. All of them liked to give people a second chance, but they all knew that for a second chance to work, to really be effective, it had to be based on honesty, on a real desire to change, and if possible, a desire to make restitution for the harm that had been done.

Since Jim hoped to find the good in Durk for Rebecca's sake, they decided that Jim would be the one to try to establish a deeper relationship with Durk. Jim felt that if Rebecca had been attracted to Durk there must be something good in him. He did after all have a tough life, never had anyone in his life that he could count on or anyone who was a role model for him. Secretly, Jim had always hoped that Rebecca and Jayden would get together; he saw how much Jayden loved her and wondered how much Rebecca's involvement with Durk may have hurt him. On the other hand, trying to help Durk might remove Rebecca's desire to help him herself, and she could step out of that role and become more objective. There were a lot of women who had so much empathy in their heart that it could blind them and allow them to enter into a situation that would not be good for them.

For now, Jim decided that he'd give Durk the benefit of the doubt. He felt that perhaps Durk hadn't known that there was a better path to take. He thought of a scripture that encapsulated those thoughts and remembered the verse because he'd once felt that it had applied to him. The words were found in Romans 3:11 and 18 and said, "There is none that understandeth, there is none that seeketh after God. There is no f ear of God before their eyes." If someone didn't understand, as he himself once hadn't understood, then how could they make the right decisions . . . ever?

Thus, before the men lay the challenges of rearranging their lives for a while to help Jayden and Rebecca, and to expose the evil that stalked their college campus. Clearing Jayden's name, and keeping home and hearth safe while doing so, was another challenge. Before the women lay the challenges of changing their already busy schedules, keeping their vigil at Rebecca's bedside, and keeping the family focused on their prayer life and their trust in God. Rebecca's challenge was for her to heal, to awaken, and awaken to a loving family with a thankful heart and with no fear or anguish over the past. For Jayden it was to find the discipline to maintain his grades without the benefit of attending classes. There were only two weeks of the semester left, but he could not attend classes because of the charges against him. The college had a zero-tolerance policy.

But given the circumstances of Jayden's perfect 4.0 average grades, the fact that he'd never been in trouble before, and suspecting that Professor T. Nagorra and Durk were more involved in the charges against Jayden than they had admitted, they hoped that the school would allow Jayden to obtain assignments from his professors and work independently off campus. Later, Jayden's anatomy and physiology professor, convinced that this fine young man had little to nothing to do with what had happened, would personally tutor Jayden and tell him what materials he needed for the final exam. Rebecca had done well in her classes, so the family hoped that she could also make up the work if she recovered from her coma.

Chaldeth was beside himself with wrath. He'd not considered that these . . . men . . . would take such a position, try to chase everyone down, and try to . . . fix . . . everything. *They will be no match for me,* he thought arrogantly, *this is just a little glitch. I'll figure something out.* Chaldeth, however, was so angry that his feelings overwhelmed him and caused him to act irrationally and tip his hand. Giving in immediately to his hatred and desire to hit back, he'd acted rashly by causing flat tires, dead batteries, a head cold, a boss that didn't want to grant vacation time during the month of December, and a host of other little inconveniences. He laughed to watch their frustration and watch them struggle to right all these situations. But later, when they'd gotten together and shared their latest experiences, Matt had an "aha" moment and said, "Well, well, well, we must be on the right track. The spirits have attacked in full force . . . all of us!" And the others laughed too, agreeing. "We'd better pray every time we walk out our door and every time we climb into a vehicle and every time we hit a lot of traffic. Those . . . powers and principalities . . . and their mangy little minions . . . have obviously declared war on us, so they must be worried!"

Chaldeth was highly indignant and thought, *These arrogant little humans. How dare they laugh, how dare they take this lightly, how dare they make fun of my attack. I will make them pay!*

Although they had laughed, they clearly understood the seriousness of their situation. They knew that God was on their side, and that gave them courage. But they also knew the hatred and the power of their enemy. Caleb read them the verse from Isaiah 54:13, 14 that assured them, "And all thy children shall be taught of the Lord; and great shall be the peace of thy children . . . for thou shalt not fear: and from terror; for it shall not come near thee."

They embarked on their various duties, and since they all carried cell phones, they agreed to check in with one another regularly and to lend assistance whenever needed. And so these men, each one a role model and a defender of their families and their friends, stood staunchly together to support those they loved and try to right the wrong that had been done. God looked at them, at their courage, at their love for Him and for one another, and at how steadfast they were to Him and to their brothers and sisters in faith, and He smiled on them. God knew that this would not be easy for them, but He would see them through this; and in the process, they would prove their trust in Him, and He would prove His love and power to them. They believed that God would help them because in Malachi 3:10, God told them, "And prove me now herewith, saith the Lord of hosts, if I will not open you the windows of heaven, and pour out for you a blessing that there shall not be room enough to receive it."

Rebecca too had to face her challenges. She'd been living in denial before her descent into her coma, and she'd been suffering because of it. Deep in her heart and soul, she had known beyond a shadow of a doubt that not telling her mother or Jayden, or even Kara for that matter, about her activities meant that she felt the need to hide those activities from the eyes of others. And if she did this, then what she was doing would not stand their scrutiny, not gain their support. She'd struggled with the choices she'd made, knowing they were not good ones, but she wanted to be with Durk so badly that she made every excuse she could for holding onto him and therefore she had kept their relationship a secret. But God knew that His children could be nudged into rationalizing and justifying doing those things about which he'd warned them. He also knew how and when He would nudge them back toward the truth and that through their experiences they'd grow stronger in faith and wiser in their knowledge of the power and danger of evil.

Rebecca had not been aware of the stress she'd brought on herself. Instead she operated on the high levels of cortisol that gave her the energy normally reserved for a fight-or-flight reaction. But when these levels remained constantly high, they played havoc with the body, wore it down, and produced increasingly high levels of inflammation that further damaged her body. As she denied the reality of her errors, her stress levels had climbed. It was not that she simply made a mistake; it was because she'd turned her back on her family, their teaching, their admonitions, every friend, every warning, even everything God had taught her. She had wanted something and had selfishly gone after it regardless of the consequences. Her guilt overwhelmed her, and her mind did not want to acknowledge her wrongdoing. She longed for comfort, for forgiveness, she longed to go back and start over, she longed for everything to somehow right itself, but she was afraid of the pain that this would bring to her and to those she loved. And so she retreated; she hid in the safety of denial. She had focused only on Durk, had believed that she loved him and that, when he changed, all would be all right. Now she hid in her coma.

The truth as God saw it was simply that Rebecca had indeed made some mistakes, but He knew that the learning process for His children took a long time and required a great understanding of His love, of the power and devastating effect of evil, and of the plan that He had laid into the physics of the world to help His children. Rebecca's family would also forgive her even if they knew all the circumstances. But Rebecca, like so many people, could not forgive herself. Her ego first had to die so that the sacrifice made for her could emerge as so much greater than her personal need to not be found lacking.

Mankind's fallibility was that they did *not* fully admit to the depth of their sinful nature, nor acknowledge a *daily* need for forgiveness, nor step up their efforts to live as God asked them to live, and this was their primary stumbling block. They made excuses. They put off doing better. They justified unkind reactions. They blocked out the *constancy* of their sin and their limited capacity for love. But God loved them nevertheless. And in time, He knew that while they could not always escape the traps that Satan and his fallen angels laid for them—and that they sometimes even enjoyed them—there was a seed within them that if nourished would bring them *out* of that captivity and into striving for good, acknowledging God's love, choosing good over evil, and being thankful for all that God had taught them.

God did not ask for perfection; He asked for the constant and dedicated *striving* for that perfection. Their striving demonstrated how much they loved Him and how much they hungered for what God offered them. Guilt was actually a good thing if it brought remorse and a re-dedication to getting back up, brushing oneself off, and trying again. But as in all good things, Satan usually turned the good guilt into a perverted version of guilt which brought only hopelessness, languor, and self hate.

God watched over Rebecca, but she herself would have to make the decision to climb out of her coma and face the truth that roamed her subconscious mind. The two blows to her head had produced a coma caused by a large subdural hematoma lodged against the fragile covering of her brain. The doctors had drilled into her skull to drain the blood from the hematoma in order to relieve its pressure against her brain and felt that in time, as the swelling diminished, Rebecca would awaken. But a coma is a very interesting condition; it can be a curse and it can be a blessing. It can be a mechanism that provides the body with time to heal, but it can also be a mechanism that allows the mind to retreat, avoid facing what might be too traumatic to re-live. Coma patients could often hear the conversations of those gathered around their bedside, and sometimes those conversations could bring them back to consciousness.

Rebecca could hear the voices around her. Sometimes she fell asleep while they spoke, but often she listened even though she couldn't bring her consciousness to the surface. Sometimes the message in those conversations seemed garbled to her sleepy mind, but other times she strained to listen because something stirred her heart toward the words she heard them say. She heard their plans to gather information, and she wanted to warn them, but her subconscious mind and that protective mechanism in her heart knew that she was not yet strong enough physically, mentally, nor spiritually to face her own role in what had happened to her. She could only listen, and even then she couldn't always gain a complete understanding of what was said. But Rebecca's life depended on her receiving and accepting what would draw her conscious mind to the surface.

Chaldeth *wanted* Rebecca to die and the others to find her death unjust and blame God, as Jim and Grandma had once done because of the injustices they suffered. Jim had once argued, *If there is an all-powerful, loving God, why would He let His children suffer?* This argument, however, showed a lack of understanding of God's plan. God worked to extricate His children from the grip of evil, but they had to know of evil to know that they must avoid it. They would need to choose sides. They would need to trust God explicitly if they chose righteousness over evil. Jim had once made the argument that asked how one can make the right choice without knowing what the Bible states. How can someone *trust* if they don't understand *who* really causes their pain? And how can they be helped if they don't know that they must ask for help? But in God's plan, everyone who ever lived or ever died would have the opportunity to know these truths and to make their own choice out of their free will. Even this was a process, a path that sometimes ran straight and other times curved so much that it hid truth for a while. Rebecca listened when she could and often struggled to rise from the abyss of captivity that held her.

Elizabeth stayed in town indefinitely and was almost always at Rebecca's bedside. Mary too came as often as she could. Juggling Teddie's needs and the demands of her job was a challenge, but she too came for a few days every week and was content to know that Elizabeth was always there. She and Elizabeth spoke by phone twice every day as well. Even though John stayed with Elizabeth, the other women helped keep her company. They would also look after Rebecca when they could finally coerce Elizabeth and John to go out for a breath of fresh air, go to the cafeteria for a meal or for coffee and a snack, and once in a while to go to a nice restaurant for dinner. When the men came to see Rebecca, usually when dropping off or picking up their wives, they would talk together about Rebecca and Jayden.

Josh, being the youngest, had planned to hang out at the pub. He wanted to blend in with the students to learn what they said about the "big incident" at the school. Matt and Kevin would do the same on the alternate dates that they were scheduled to be at the pub or on the campus. When Matt and Kevin let their hair grow a bit longer than usual and donned jeans and a T-shirt, they looked young enough to pass as one of the students, and the three were teased unmercifully by the others. Jim, Wade, and Caleb approached students wherever they saw them and simply asked questions. Jayden was to study and stay away from any potential problems arising from what the men were doing. John would stay with Elizabeth as a support, and if a student came to visit Rebecca, John would try to elicit information from them out in the hall.

Josh had uncovered their best lead. He'd been at the Pub and had started a conversation about Professor T and his "merchandise." Another student began talking about how difficult it was to obtain any joints because the professors and students who sold the "stuff" had stopped selling until the police finished their investigation. "Yeah," one student said, "but the supply is gonna dry up. Without T gettin' it from the big guys, there may not be any in the future."

Josh made sure that he had the student's name right and passed the information to Jim who, a few days later, visited that student and told him that he'd better tell him what he knew rather than have to tell the police. When Jim assured him that no one would know it was he who'd told him, the student provided the name of who he knew was selling . . . and using. Jim then told the student to pass the word that they would not involve anyone who gave them a lead, anyone who could help them find who were the big guys—not the students—selling the stuff.

Jim tracked down the professor the student had named, but Wade was the one who went to see him. When Wade, Jim, and Josh had discussed Josh's information, they decided that they might cause confusion and thus learn more from those they contacted if the same person never talked to them twice. They also felt that a description of the person tracking them would be almost impossible to provide if it changed each time. They agreed to not implicate any of the students involved if possible, but amongst themselves had decided that they would visit them again after the investigation and give them a good talking to.

When Wade married Ruth, Jayden's mom, they'd decided that Jayden wouldn't take Wade's last name. Jayden was already seventeen years old when they married, and he still had hopes that his real dad would "straighten out" someday. This was now an asset because not having the same last name as Jayden allowed Wade to be in on this search for the culprits.

Wade made an appointment to see the professor the student had named, and as he sat in the outer office to wait for him, Wade thought, *This prof better talk to me or I might really lose my temper and drag this guy into a back alley. He's scum in my opinion, harming unsuspecting kids this way. I wonder how many have become addicts because of his lies that it was "safe" to use and never caused an addiction?*

Wade could not bring himself to address the professor by his title and simply started his conversation by saying, "Emils . . ." The professor, seeing the size of Wade and assessing his obvious sense of self-esteem, assertiveness, and even fearlessness, assumed that Wade was someone of importance, someone worth knowing, and accepted the slight believing he'd been addressed as one peer to another. He beamed at Wade, wanting to be liked. "What can I do for you, sir?" the professor asked as he walked from behind his desk to greet Wade in the middle of the room.

Wade walked directly to him, claiming as his own the safe zone most people required. Towering over him, looking directly into his eyes, Wade said, "I wanna know the *exact* involvement *you* have in the drug dealing, and I wanna know *now!*" Emils recoiled and stepped back, but Wade took another step toward him closing the gap entirely and grabbed his shirt collar. "*Now,* you mealy mouthed little worm, talk or you will never *walk* again, do you understand?" Emils looked around for help, and seeing the door closed and no one to turn to, he began to babble. "Are you from . . . I mean . . . did they send you to collect . . . I mean . . . I'll be paying, honest . . . it's just that things happened on campus and we have to be . . . you know . . . careful. But I'll get the money to you . . . I will." Wade realized that the professor thought that Wade was there to collect money and therefore sent by one of the leaders of this pack of rats.

Professor Emils realized that security would not be making the rounds of the building until evening. Any students who might be passing in the hallway would never enter his office because they were afraid of him—he'd made sure of that so they wouldn't nose around. But now, recognizing how alone he was and how vulnerable, he was deeply frightened. He had to know who this . . . this . . . hulk was . . . he had to know if he'd been sent by the kingpin. *How dare this bully accost me this way?*

"Sir, I beg your pardon, but you must have mistaken me for someone else. I am, after all, the professor of the political science classes here in the university, and I have an excellent standing—tenured, you know of course. And who might you be? And please take a step away from me." Emils sounded quite arrogant and unafraid, but he was terribly afraid of this hulk of a man, of what he might know, and of what he might do, of who had sent him. His mouth was so dry that his tongue clicked against the roof of his mouth as he spoke.

Wade picked up on Emils's fear, and from what he'd already said Wade knew that this professor was deeply involved in the drug trade. Wade had been in Iraq and learned about fear. He also now knew that this man was as guilty as could be and that he could provide Wade with a great deal of information. With one hand he began to twist the two sides of Emils's shirt collar. As the collar tightened around his neck and he felt the pressure building to choke off his air supply, Emils's eyes filled with fear.

This idiot is going to kill me, he thought, *he doesn't even care!* But he didn't speak, and Wade, with his one hand still around the shirt collar still exerting pressure against his neck, brought his other hand to Emils' eyeglasses and removed them, dropping them to the floor saying, "It would be easy for me to take your eyes . . . one at a time." Wade began lifting him off the ground by the shirt collar with one hand as he placed the knuckles of his other hand into one eye socket. Wade would never inflict permanent damage, but he knew that this could hurt, and more importantly, he knew that the threat of eye damage was very intimidating. That fit his purpose well.

"Stop! Wait! All right, I'll tell you! It wasn't my fault. I was coerced. It was Nagorra. He bought the stuff and he . . . he . . . yeah, he forced me . . . to be one of the people who took the money from the rich stupid little brats . . . he made me give them some weed to sell in exchange for the money he wanted. I was forced into it. I didn't want to do it. I was forced. Put me down, you're hurting me!"

"That's a start," Wade said "just a start. Where did he get it, and why couldn't you say no? How did he force you?"

"Well . . . he . . . he gets it from . . . I can't tell you anymore . . . they will kill me . . . Okay, okay, some guy in a black coat and a black Cadillac . . . every month or so . . . they meet in a shed or something outside of town . . . he made me take him once . . . and he *makes* me sell it . . . honest, I didn't wanna do it."

"What does he have on you then? And what shed? Where? And who's the guy in the black coat and Caddy?"

"I don't know . . . I mean . . . well, I can't . . . . because . . . . well . . . . Nagorra has some films . . . of me . . . and . . . with . . ."

"What kind of films?"

"Uhhhh . . . well . . . uhhh . . . with a student . . . I mean, it just sort of happened. Her grades were bad and . . . I mean . . . it wasn't my fault. She . . . uhhhhhh . . . she . . . uhhhh, yeah, she came on to me, we partied. You know, a little alcohol, a little mickey . . . you know how it is . . ."

"You dirty, filthy weasel, I ought to kill you." Wade was suddenly afraid of how much he wanted to hurt this disgusting excuse of an educator, this filthy self-gratifying dirty worm who would coerce, blackmail, drug, and seduce a young female student and think nothing of getting a bunch of trusting students addicted. Wade wanted to hurt him. But he also knew that there were bigger fish to fry; there was more that he needed to know. What was this film bit? Why would Nagorra have films . . . who were they of and when and how were they taken?

"I could easily kill you now, and if you are lying to me and you are the one who did the coercing, which you already admitted to doing to your female students, I will make your death slow and painful. You are *now* going to take me to wherever these films might be stashed. Understand? If you *don't*, after I finish with you, I'm going to carry your damaged body right to the *police station* . . . and let them find the films. Remember, that's *after* I do some damage—a lot of damage to you—got it?" And to make his point, Wade lifted the professor off the ground by his collar until he began to choke and his face began to turn red.

"Yeah, yeah, okay . . . okay . . . but please don't hurt me . . . please don't call the cops . . . you'll ruin me . . . we can make a deal . . . okay? I'll tell you what I know if you don't involve me . . . please . . . I have a key to Nagorra's office . . . I mean, I think some of the office keys are alike, but I don't know if the one to his house is still in the box at the back door. I'll do it . . . but only if you promise not to call the cops and to give me all the films with me in them . . . yeah, you can keep the others . . . just give me the ones of me and . . ."

Wade felt sick to his stomach. *Now the guy was talking about films, plural, more than one. Were these all films of students . . . different students?* The thought made him sick. *These two professors are pushers, stalkers, rapists, pornographers, pedophiles even. They are inhuman. They are dogs preying on the innocence and vulnerability of kids!* Wade was determined to bring these . . . these . . . arrogant rats down.

Holding the professor's arm tightly, Wade walked him out of his building and into the building that housed Nagorra's office; and using a master key, they were able to enter. When Professor Emils saw the paneling off the wall behind Nagorra's desk and the empty shelves between the new two-by-fours in the wall, he panicked. "The police know . . . the police know . . . What am I going to do? Maybe they have the tapes too? Oh, what am I going to do?"

Wade too saw that the police had rummaged thoroughly through Nagorra's office and realized that they knew more than they'd told the family. *Good,* he thought, *maybe they will get to the bottom of this and rid the University of this scum. It will probably not be prudent for me to enter Nagorra's home, because if the police found something hidden in this wall, they would certainly have searched Nagorra's house.* Instead, Wade walked the hysterical Emils back outside the building and to the parking lot where Wade had left his truck. He forced Emils into the passenger seat where he activated the child-safety locks preventing Emils from leaving.

"Where are you taking me?" Emils screamed.

"To the cops," Wade replied. "If you talk to them, they may consider a plea bargain, and it will lessen your jail time. If you don't, you'll have the book thrown at you. And if they do that and your fellow prisoners learn that you preyed upon children, your life inside will be . . . . well . . . . you can imagine what they will do to you. The police probably already have the films of you . . . so your goose, *professor,* is already cooked. You are going with me to the police station, and once there, you are giving them a full confession . . . in front of me. Got it?"

Emils began sobbing, worrying about his job, his prestige, his salary, his life. "I'm ruined," he exclaimed. "I'll be ruined!" When they arrived at the police station, Emils begged Wade to reconsider, begged him to let him go. "I have some money . . . I'll give it to you . . . just let me go . . . I'll even leave the country . . . I didn't do anything *really* wrong. I mean, if the kids didn't buy from me, they'd just buy somewhere else . . . and the girls . . . well, they . . . wanted . . . I mean . . . their grades . . . made them . . ." But before Emils could complete that sentence, Wade punched him to prevent him from ranting about how he'd taken advantage of these kids and then justified his actions. That was what made Wade want to hurt the guy. Wade couldn't stand him but he knew that without his testimony, the others might not be caught. *This guy wants to justify what he did, won't admit culpability, doesn't see himself as the small worm that he is. Worm? Hah, he's the same wily selfish serpent rat that went after Eve!*

Aloud, Wade told Emils that if he did not confess to his own actions, or tell the police all he knew about the others involved in this filth, they would throw the book at him, but if he cooperated he'd get a lighter sentence and maybe get some protection inside the jail. As they climbed from the vehicle when they reached the police station, once again Wade lifted the little pip-squeak off the ground by his shirt collar and said, "Unless you confess right now to the cops, I will *personally* find you—in jail or out—and make *sure* that you never do this crap again. I'll make *sure that the guys inside know what you did*, you understand? You realize what they will do to you?"

Wade walked Emils into the station and told the desk sergeant that he wanted to speak with someone who was working on the campus drug case. The two men were almost immediately seated at the desk of a detective. Wade told the detective that Emils had something to say, that he, Wade, would add something when he was finished, and then he would turn Emils over to the detective. Wade said that he wanted to make sure that the detective understood Emils's part in the case and wanted the confession made before the detective right away. He had only a short window of time to give the detective enough ammo to really nail Emils. His main fear was that Emils would clam up, lawyer up, and then possibly even be released. Wade's stomach lurched with this fear, and he silently asked God to help him get the confession on tape right away.

Wade told the detective that Emils was the mastermind of a huge drug ring and also of a pornography ring and that he had recruited Nagorra to work for him. Wade winked at the detective to let him know that he was baiting Emils. His plan worked . . . Emils, shocked by the accusations that Wade was making was quick to defend himself and sang like a bird blaming everything on Nagorra while incriminating himself and others. His confession was recorded, and when it was done he signed the confession, was booked, and locked into a cell.

Before Wade left, the detective thanked him for his clever ruse—a ruse that had allowed them to obtain a signed confession—perhaps incomplete but nevertheless one that would give them some bargaining room to keep Emils and Nagorra incarcerated and even help them obtain additional information.

The detective admitted that they'd found films but said that he could not elaborate on that just yet because the information they had gleaned involved minors who they wished to protect. Wade was glad about that. "This will really help us nail these guys, because what we have on tape is, in one case, statutory rape! We want to protect that child." He asked Wade not to say anything about the tapes and asked him not to speak to the press under any circumstances. He also warned Wade that he was not to interfere with their detective work, that it would be dangerous for him to do so, and that he didn't have the expertise that the police did.

As soon as Wade left the police station, he telephoned Jim to let him know what had happened, not mentioning the tapes. Jim phoned Josh who called the others. Josh had won the day for them with his excellent lead. But they still had more work to do. They needed to clear Jayden's name. But they now had a great deal of hope, especially if Nagorra would sing because Emils had. While they hoped that this arrest would mean that Jayden would be exonerated and that they would find out who was responsible for hurting Rebecca, they also knew that the police might not look any further.

Chaldeth was beside himself. His hatred boiled over. He couldn't believe that his perfect plan was being sidetracked so easily. He was determined not to give up but to make things even worse for this interfering family. *"I'm not done with you yet,* he thought raising his fist at these men. *I'll get you yet, and you'll wish you'd never started this fight with me!*

When John told Elizabeth about Wade's success, and that a Professor Emils was now in prison, Rebecca heard too. A part of her brain struggled to understand why this was important for her to assimilate. *Professor Emils? Why, isn't he my political science teacher? Isn't he the one who threatened to fail me? He's the one who recently sent me a note demanding that I meet with him to discuss my failing grades!* But then that part of her psyche—the protective subconscious—determined that she could not yet bear to put these clues together. She wasn't yet strong enough to face the truth about what she'd allowed to enter her life, or almost enter it, and without her conscious assent she slid back into the comfort of the deep abyss of sleep.

Challenges also faced Kara and Ken. Kara visited Rebecca every day. As she looked at Rebecca, she was filled with a sense of helplessness, but she also became aware of how much she loved her friend and respected her quiet dignity and her faith in God. She realized that she'd thought of Rebecca like she would a loving sister and had hoped that they would be friends for their entire lives. She understood how fortunate she had been to have had a roommate like Rebecca and to meet Jayden and Ken and have the privilege to call them her friends as well. She wondered why a tragedy had to occur before she could come to appreciate what she'd been given. She was filled with remorse because she hadn't taken Rebecca aside and forced her to talk about what was bothering her.

Kara realized that to be a good friend, a true friend, sometimes you had to risk everything to help someone understand when they were in danger. She commiserated about not knowing enough about God to have the courage to reach out to Rebecca using the words from the Bible that Rebecca would have understood. *Oh, Rebecca, what really happened? Who hurt you? Why did they hurt you? Why didn't you talk to us? Why did they put that bag of marijuana in your hands? Were you attacked from behind? Were you afraid? Oh, Rebecca, if only I'd have stuck by your side.*

Kara began to cry, and since she did not want to distress Rebecca, she left Rebecca's side and walked into the hall where she could let her emotions run free. If she didn't, the lump in her throat would be too painful to endure. As Kara sobbed, shoulders heaving, head bowed and her hands at her face, Elizabeth moved to her side; and after a minute or so she put her arms around Kara and turned her into her shoulder. "Cry, honey, go ahead and cry and let it all out. You will feel better. But then we will pray together, and God will help you. You will be amazed by what He can do and how all this will turn into a blessing."

Elizabeth stroked her hair, patted her back, and encouraged her to cry. Soon Kara's tears began to ebb, and her sobs became short little gasps until they too stopped. Since there were others in the room with Rebecca, Elizabeth led Kara to a private little sitting room across the hall from Rebecca's room. "How can I help, child? Why are you so sad?"

"I've let Rebecca down . . . I love her like a sister . . . I'm so lucky that she's my roommate . . . I mean, she and Jayden, Ken too, are such good people . . . and I've let them down. I should have done more to stop Rebecca from seeing Durk, or at least insisted that all of us got together, not just Durk and Rebecca alone. I made some mistakes . . . I suspected Nagorra . . . and Durk too . . . but I didn't do enough . . . maybe I should have called you, but I was afraid that if you knew you'd take Rebecca out of school . . . I just don't . . . but if it hadn't been for my . . . my . . . indecision . . . my lack of action . . . Rebecca wouldn't be in this fix."

"Oh, honey, you are wrong about that. It is *not* your fault at all. You did what you could, you did what you thought was right, and believe me this will turn into a blessing in the end, you'll see. You cannot carry the weight of the world on your shoulders. How can you know everything when you are still so young? How can you stop someone from making their own choices? Do not blame yourself. Not one iota of this is your fault. Rebecca is blessed to have you for a roommate too, and especially to have you as a friend. She is going to be okay, believe me, Kara."

"Really, are you sure?"

"Yes, I am, Kara. And we are going to get to the bottom of what happened and also learn what evils are taking place on the campus and get that cleared up. We want all of you to have a happy, healthy campus life, one that lifts you up, not one that brings you harm. Have you talked with any of the men yet? Anything that you can tell them about Durk or Professor T. Nagorra, or anything else that you think might aid them in getting to the bottom of this, will help them. You might know one little thing, one tiny detail, that could lead them to uncovering a host of other things. They need to clear Jayden's name, you know."

"Jayden didn't do anything wrong, I know that. In fact, he got a call for help from Rebecca and ran out of the dorm to help her, and we ran after him . . . probably only three to five minutes afterward. I called 911 as soon as we saw Rebecca lying . . . oh, I wish that Rebecca would wake up and tell us what happened. But Jayden did nothing wrong, only ran to help Rebecca when she phoned. And now they are saying that she didn't use her cell phone, that the call came from Professor T's office, and I know that she wouldn't use his phone when she had her own phone."

Elizabeth saw Matt and Sarah walking up the hall toward Rebecca's room. She asked Kara if she would talk to them and Kara agreed. Elizabeth ran to the door to intercept them and call them into the tiny waiting room to talk with Kara. Then she said, "I guess it's time for a shift change. One group arrives and another leaves after their 'briefing'! I want you to talk to Matt and Sarah as if they were your own mom and dad. You can tell them anything, and they will keep private anything you ask them to."

"Okay." But Kara was a bit nervous, afraid that Sarah and Matt might be angry with her for not looking after Rebecca properly. As Matt and Sarah sat, Elizabeth excused herself to go back to Rebecca.

"Hi, Kara, I'm Sarah, and Matt is my husband. We live across the street from Mary and Kevin, and Rebecca and Elizabeth live in the carriage house right behind their house. I guess you already know that there are a bunch of us who are neighbors, friends, or relatives. So we are so happy to welcome you to our zany but loving group! We hope to see a lot of you as you and Rebecca visit us on holidays and we visit you when we come to the campus."

"Hi, Sarah. Hi, Matt. I'm pleased to meet you. I guess you know that I'm Rebecca's roommate . . . and, I hope, her friend . . . for life. I would love to visit you but . . . . but . . . . ."

"Friends for life? That's a wonderful statement, Kara. I know that you and Rebecca really hit it off. Isn't that such a great gift? God puts people in our lives who can be such a blessing, and I can see that you have been a blessing to Rebecca. We are so happy that you could room together."

"That's the problem . . . Rebecca and Jayden were a blessing to me. I mean, they taught me so much about . . . well . . . loving one another . . . about the fun people can have when they share their hopes and dreams and wishes. They even taught me so much about the Bible . . . and it was fun to learn. We also helped one another with our studies . . . but I don't know if I was a good enough friend to Rebecca to have let this happen. I feel so . . . . so guilty."

Sarah and Matt heard the catch in her voice and knew that for some reason she was blaming herself. "Kara," Matt said, "sometimes we have no control over our circumstances even when we have taken every precaution. Sometimes things just . . . happen. Please don't blame yourself. Look how you came running when she needed you? And just you watch, something good will come out of this. You just wait and see."

"All of you have so much faith. It amazes me."

"There is evil in this world, and we cannot always circumvent the plans that evil lays out for us, but God always brings us through it. You'll see. You will be so overjoyed by how all this will turn out and how God can turn these difficult circumstances into a blessing."

"Jayden explained, to Ken and me, about the evil spirits, and we were shocked. I mean at first we really didn't believe him, but we finally read all the scripture about it and . . . well, then we came to sort of accept it . . . but it's weird and scary and it is hard to believe."

"Yes, it is. Did Jayden also tell you about God's plan and how evil works to prevent His plan from moving forward?"

"Yeah, and he told us that those evil spirits really can't stop it anyway, but that they can prolong its completion time. That's good that they can't stop it. Is that why you believe that Rebecca will be okay?"

"Yes. But I'm starting to believe that what happened to Rebecca is related to a terrible and spreading sickness within this campus. Drugs, pornography, corrupt professors . . . and that for any of you to stay here, the campus will have to be rid of all these influences. I'm starting to believe that God has His hand in this for many reasons. Kara, do you know anything—anything at all, even the most bizarre or inconsequential thing—that could give us some clues about where to look and what to look for so we can correct what is happening?"

"Maybe. Uhhh . . . I'm not sure. But okay . . . here's what I know . . . some professors have incredibly liberal political views and don't teach both sides . . . just their point of view. Conversely one professor is ostracized because he does try to tell the truth, and maybe you should talk to him. Rebecca loves him. He's her early American history prof. He'd tell the truth if he knew anything.

"The other professor, the one with the really liberal views, threatened to fail Rebecca because she called him on what info he did and did not give the students, and then he wanted her to come to talk to him about how they'd handle her failing grade. But he wanted her to come alone at night, and she was afraid to go because she didn't trust him. There is pot for sale on campus, but I think that's pretty much on all campuses. But there's also something that makes you pass out. Ken picked up the wrong drink and passed out for a couple of hours. So you should talk to him. I think that Professor T and Durk were involved with pot and that Rebecca was trying to get Durk out of all contact with that stuff."

"Thanks, Kara for being so open with us. We are all working to get to the bottom of this and making good headway. We will fill you in when we can. Right now, it's got to be sort of hush-hush so we don't tip our hand. Can you give me the name of those two professors? I'll catch Ken next time he visits Rebecca to see if he knows anything that might help us. If you think of anything else—please, please, even the smallest thing—please let one of us know. Okay?"

"Okay. And thanks. Thanks for caring and for working so hard to make this campus safe and good. Oh, and the good professor is named Professor Doog and the bad one is Professor Emils . . . and ya know, that Professor Emils said he would fail Rebecca even though she had straight As!"

Kara, feeling so much better, walked with Sarah and Matt to Rebecca's room, said good-bye to Elizabeth and the others, kissed Rebecca, and returned to her dorm to study. She made herself a hot cup of green tea, added her healthy Stevia sweetener, and opened her books.

Matt had written down the names of the two professors Kara mentioned and relayed the information to the others. "Maybe Professor Doog, who Kara and Rebecca really like, would be willing to tell us if he's seen any bad stuff going on around the campus. If we promise him that we will not give his name ever, maybe he'll tell us what he's seen or suspects. The other guy, the one that threatened Rebecca, is Emils. He's already in jail. It's a good thing that Wade didn't know what he did to Rebecca when he caught up with him. Emils would be mincemeat!"

As the men talked and exchanged ideas and had conference calls with the others, they decided that both Matt and Sarah should try to speak with Professor Doog, the professor who Kara said tried to teach honestly and who they both liked. If Sarah and Matt could convince him of their good intentions and he felt it safe to open up to them, perhaps they could gain an ally in their goal to rid the campus of the wrongdoing that had spread like wildfire. They decided to make an appointment to see the professor as soon as possible.

Ken too had his challenges. Over time, and when the initial shock wore off of seeing Rebecca so . . . so fragile and unmoving in the hospital bed, he'd realized that Jayden would never have harmed her; he loved her too much. Ken felt terrible that he'd betrayed his friend by allowing the police to believe that Jayden may have been responsible for what had happened. He'd tried to retract his statement, but the police would not allow him to change it thinking that he only wanted to protect his friend and roommate. The police officer had said, "There'll be plenty of time to set the record straight, son. You can do that when the trial comes up and you have to testify. By then there will be a lot of things unfolding, and the jury can decide who's telling the truth."

Ken felt bad and felt that he'd really let Jayden down. He did not want to see Jayden because he feared that Jayden would be furious with him. But what Ken didn't know was that Jayden had not been told what Ken said, only that the police had statements that incriminated Jayden. Jayden assumed that those statements came from Durk or Nagorra. But with Ken avoiding contact with Jayden and with Jayden assuming their earlier disagreement was still active, there had been little opportunity for them to work things out.

Ken understood that he would have to talk with Jayden, explain what he'd done, apologize, and ask what he could do to help him. He'd have to hope that Jayden would forgive him. Ken also wanted to speak with Wade, Jayden's stepdad, and explain to him the mistakes he'd made. He wanted Wade to know about Durk and Nagorra, and about the mickey that had been put into the drink he'd taken even if the drink had not been meant for him. He also wanted to tell Wade about the smell of pot that rose from the packages that he'd carried into Nagorra's office.

And so it began that everyone acknowledged the role that they would be playing in this drama and the challenges that they faced to bring out the truth. They could not anticipate what the future held for them, and so it was a time of anxiety and reflection, but it was also a time where each of the players got to look inside their own hearts and learn more about themselves. God knew that, as they had to enter the fire that would burn away their impurities, their faith was what could protect them and leave them unscathed and allow them to emerge purified.

Caleb had posted a scripture on the wall next to Rebecca's bed that should she awaken she would see right away. All who entered Rebecca's room could see it as well. He'd copied the verses onto an 8 1/2 x 11 piece of paper and centered the writing. Then he decided to omit the last sentence because it spoke of their need to repent and he did not want Rebecca to think that this was the focus of his intent in providing her with this verse. He'd chosen it so they would all remember that sometimes they had to enter the fire, but when they did, they would be refined, purified, molded into the kind of person that God wanted them to be. And that God gave them His beautiful promises about what that meant. Caleb had placed the scripture onto a hard sheet of cardboard and into a chrome frame. It read:

And I will bring forth the third part through the fire,
will refine them as silver is refined, and will try them as gold is tried:
I counsel thee to buy of me gold tried in the fire,
that thou mayest be rich; and white raiment, that thou mayest be clothed,
and that the shame of thy nakedness do not appear;
and anoint thine eyes with eye salve, that thou mayest see . . .

Revelations 3:18, 19

Chapter 10

Healing

Elizabeth was beginning to feel the rigors of staying by Rebecca's side sometimes for as long as sixteen hours a day for almost three weeks. She was also exhausted from the struggle to believe that God *would* bring Rebecca out of her coma and back to full health, and that all would be well once again. She could not help but remember the similar struggle she had with her faith when her husband had died. She had trusted that God would allow the surgeries her husband had undergone—then the radiation treatments, then the chemotherapy—to *cure* her husband's cancer. She remembered feeling that he was too young to die and that she and Rebecca were too dependent on him for God not to cure him. But then God took him despite her hopes, her prayers, and her trust.

When her husband died, Elizabeth had to wrestle with her pain in order to accept God's will. She *wanted* to believe that He knew best, that someday she would understand why, and that in time all would be well again. But it had been a constant battle not to keep asking why and not to feel angry and hurt and let down. She'd had to hide her true feelings so she could help Rebecca live through her own grief at losing her father. If she doubted God or expressed anger or disappointment, then so would Rebecca, and Elizabeth knew that that would not have been the right thing to do. It had been so difficult. She had cried herself to sleep on many occasions, and she had struggled to appear energetic when she was, in fact, filled with a lethargy so debilitating that she wished she could go back to bed and stay there. But it had gotten better over time, and while the missing of him never ended, she had finally gotten used to his empty place in their bed, at the dinner table, and in the big easy chair he'd always preferred in the living room.

We can't know God's exact plan, she thought, *we can only hope and pray, trust and then accept the will of God. Sometimes it simply cannot be the same as our will. Sometimes we cannot see why something must occur that is so difficult, but we must acknowledge that God is never wrong. I understand and fully believe that God's will is perfect and that it might be necessary for it to be different than mine, but understanding does not take away the loss . . . or the pain. It only helps me to cope with them. I can comfort others with these words, but I can't comfort myself. I cannot stop feeling afraid . . . and alone . . . . and I don't know how to balance my fear that God will take Rebecca, with my trust that He will not.*

Elizabeth realized that she felt the best when she was helping others. *Maybe it's because I don't think of myself at those times,* she thought. *Rebecca needs me now, and after all, I did help Kara a little bit, didn't I? Maybe I was wrong to let Rebecca go away to college rather than ask her to attend a college nearby where she could come home every night. She might have talked to me then, shared her worries, and maybe I could have helped her . . . and then maybe this would not have happened.* Elizabeth felt guilty and worried that what had happened was her fault and she chided herself. *Now I'm thinking the way Kara was thinking.*

When she was with John, he could always sense her mood. He knew somehow when she was in the throes of what he called her "if I had, then it would" agonies, and he'd say, "Elizabeth, you pray, you tithe, you go to church, you know and continue to study God's words, you accept God's offer of Holy Communion and truly strive to overcome, so why not just 'let go and let God'? Stop trying to second-guess Him." And then he'd tease her or dance around her to make her laugh, and for a while she *would* laugh. She'd be angry at him for calling her on her misguided worries, but then when he tried to make her laugh, her anger would dissipate and she'd realize that what he said was right on the money.

Once again John sensed the turmoil she was in. He broke into her reverie saying, "Elizabeth, what are you thinking? Please talk to me." Elizabeth was startled but turned to John and asked, "Why does it seem that everyone around me can accept whatever happens to them and go on in perfect harmony while I put on a happy face as if I am just like them when I am not? I'm carrying the pain in my heart. I feel as if I am very different than other people are and it makes me feel as if I am a misfit."

"Elizabeth, you are no different than anyone else. *Everyone* carries something in their heart that troubles them, but they, like you, also try to put on a happy face. Some are devastated by the loss of their job, by money problems, by marital problems, by a cruel boss, by a nasty neighbor. Whatever it is, everyone has their cross to carry . . . today or tomorrow or yesterday. No one is exempt, especially the children of God. But we are brothers and sisters in Christ, and that's why we need to have fellowship with one another. We can let those who love us share our burden, and it becomes lighter for us. Oh, I don't mean that we have to blurt out every grizzly detail, but we *can* tell others that we are struggling with fear or loss . . . and they will comfort us and they will add their prayers to ours. And remember that even the apostle Paul carried something that he wished he could overcome, and God let him know in no uncertain terms that he had to carry it so he'd remain humble! Remember that verse? It's from 2 Corinthians 12:8-9 and says, *"For this thing I besought the Lord thrice, that it might depart from me. And he said unto me, My grace is sufficient for thee; for my strength is made perfect in weakness."* And then in verse 11, Paul admits, *"I am also become a fool in glory."*

"That's a good point, John. I guess if we didn't see ourselves make mistakes every day of our lives, we'd be pretty self-centered and strut in our own glory . . . then we could begin to think that we didn't need God. I have been following your advice, John, about asking for the peace that Jesus left for us. I have memorized that scripture about peace and use it over and over again, not only when I pray, but when the fear comes. It gives me comfort, and I do believe that slowly it is working. Do you remember it? It's in John 14:27 and says, "Peace I leave with you, my peace I give unto you; not as the world giveth, give I unto you. Let not your heart be troubled, neither let it be afraid."

"Just hang on a little while longer, Lizzie, and you will see the miracle of God's love."

Jayden walked into the room, greeted his grandfather with a hug and Elizabeth with a kiss, then he walked over to say hello to Rebecca. He always spoke to her as if expecting an answer, and he told her of his day and his experiences. He spoke with inflections in his voice that one would use when the person they spoke to would be responding. He pulled one of the chairs up to the edge of the bed so he could hold Rebecca's hand as he spoke.

"Hey, Becca, I aced two of my exams so far and have only two more to go. I'm studying for my psych exam tonight and tomorrow, so wish me luck. I sure wish you'd wake up and help me study . . . you're so good at making me concentrate and also in picking out the areas of study that you think the most questions will cover. Hey, did you know that Uncle Matt and Aunt Sarah are here for the next day or two, so they will be popping in to see you and expecting you to jump out of this bed and give them a hug. You up to it? In fact, I'm missing my hugs a lot too, so come on, sleepy head, wake up for good ole Jayden and the rest of us. You've been laying down on the job for too long. Joke, get it? Joke."

At that moment, Ken walked into the room. He too greeted everyone warmly and leaned down to kiss Rebecca's cheek saying, "Hey there, I was missing you in that wonderful political science class and for the big exam. But guess what . . . we have a substitute teacher now. Dear old Prof Emils is out and probably not coming back to campus. Good news, eh?"

Ken greeted Jayden tentatively not knowing what to expect from Jayden since they had their falling out. Jayden greeted Ken warmly, and they both turned back to Rebecca. But then Ken turned toward Jayden, again deciding that he'd put off leveling with Jayden for too long. He really wanted Jayden's forgiveness and his friendship. "Jayden, would it be okay if I talked to you for a few minutes? Can you spare about ten minutes? In fact, would it be okay if we talked in the small waiting room across the hall?"

Jayden agreed readily and nodded to Elizabeth and John to make sure that they knew he was leaving and that one of them should come to Rebecca's bedside to continue talking to her.

Ken waited for Jayden, and then they walked together across the hall and into the empty waiting room. Jayden chose a seat, and Ken pulled a chair over so he could face him. Jayden sat with his knees splayed, his elbows resting on his knees and his hands folded just above his knees. His shoulders were hunched, allowing his body to lean forward. His head was slightly bowed, and as he waited for Ken to speak, his eyes were looking toward his hands. His body was relaxed, giving a submissive yet saddened appearance. He did not say anything, just waited patiently for Ken to speak.

Ken felt a sudden despair, a sudden terror that Jayden would never again be his friend and that he'd perhaps lost one of the best friends, best role models he'd ever had. Ken, unused to praying, silently asked God to help him; and then slowly, he began to tell Jayden of how he had betrayed him. When he did begin to speak, Jayden kept his head bowed and his eyes on his hands and Ken could not read Jayden's immediate reaction. But he persevered, understanding Jayden's reticence.

"Jayden, I want to ask for your forgiveness and want to explain why I did what I did . . . but I want you to know before I start that I now realize how lucky I was—am—to have you as a friend . . . and I am hoping that if I can make this up to you . . . that you'll let us remain friends."

Jayden didn't move and did not say anything, yet Ken felt no animosity, no denial of his heart, no rebuff—just a quiet, serene patience—and realized that Jayden probably would not speak until he'd heard Ken out. "Jayden," he continued, "when we started to have all those suspicions about Durk and Professor T, I was really down on both of them. I still am. To this day I have *no* idea why I suddenly wondered if Durk was really an okay guy and if you were being too hard on him. I've been beating myself up with questions about what I could have been thinking, and I can't figure it out. Maybe because Rebecca cared for him it was wishful thinking on my part. Maybe I wanted the bad guy to only be Nagorra. I don't know, and I don't like that I don't know. I've even been thinking about what you said about the activities of evil spirits here on earth, and I have been wondering if I was . . . uhhh . . . well . . . you know . . . sort of *taken over* for a while. I know that sounds crazy . . . and maybe I'm just looking for something to blame other than myself . . . but . . .

"Well, anyway, when you got that phone call from Rebecca calling for help and ran to Professor T's office, I just kind of stood there for a while, not knowing what to do. But then I phoned Kara, and she acted immediately . . . and berated me for not acting immediately. 'You could have helped Jayden and phoned me later,' she said. And here again I later wondered if this was a part of the master plan of some evil. Anyway, Kara and I ran over to Nagorra's a few minutes after you left. When we saw you standing over Rebecca, holding the bag of weed, money hanging out of your pocket, saying 'I'm sorry' to Rebecca over and over again . . . well . . . my mind just went completely in the wrong direction, and I thought that *you* . . . thought that maybe you and Nagorra had . . . I'd suspected Nagorra of having a lot of pot and so seeing you holding that bag of weed . . . I know it was wrong, I know that what I thought was disloyal . . . but I know you are in love with Rebecca and I . . . I don't know. I thought that you had argued with Rebecca, I judged you wrongly . . . . I jumped to a ridiculous conclusion when I saw you. I made a *huge* mistake, and I did something that I shouldn't have done."

Ken got up from his chair and began to pace nervously around the room. "But the *worst* part was that when the cops came . . . when the cops came, I . . . I . . ." Ken's voice broke, and he struggled to continue talking. He paced even more nervously, wringing his hands. "When the cops came, they separated Kara and me and asked us what happened. Of course I didn't really know. I hadn't been there . . . but I . . . well I . . . I said something about my first impression . . . of you . . . you know . . . loving her . . . being jealous . . . maybe angry . . . I don't know. But what I said really, really incriminated you. Oh, Jayden, I don't know even today *why* I said what I said. I know you. I know that you would never, *never* hurt anyone . . . I . . . I . . . honest to God, Jayden, I tried to retract my statement . . . but . . . but even though what I'd said diametrically opposed what Kara said, they wouldn't let me change it . . . said I could do that in court . . . and I will. I mean, I sure will . . . but I guess that's why they charged you. Oh, Jayden, I am so sorry, I wish I could undo what I've done . . . and I will when they call me to the stand. I will. I mean, I'm gonna tell them what a great guy you are and that I musta been . . . I don't know . . . *possessed* or something. I'm gonna tell them what a jerk I was and that I was not only wrong but . . . . stupid and irresponsible. Is there a chance that you could ever forgive me?"

Jayden was quiet for a minute. When he looked up, he saw that Ken was standing, wringing his hands, looking incredibly forlorn. Inside, Jayden felt a heavy burden lift off his heart. He loved Ken as a brother, and he hated them being at odds with one another. He felt that some of this was his own fault because he had allowed himself to carry his hurt feelings for so long. He should have been man enough to make up with Ken the next day. His feelings and his withdrawn attitude toward Ken had probably been the opening for that spirit, and Jayden was sure that it was indeed the work of a spirit that had made Ken react as he did with the police.

Jayden wanted to say the right things to Ken. This was a serious matter, not only because of the charges against him, but this could impact the newfound understanding of God that Ken was developing; and it could impact a friendship that was not only important to Jayden, but perhaps was also important to Ken.

"Ken, first of all . . . don't worry. I know how those spirits operate. I also believe in you, and I'm sorry for holding onto a grudge when I chose not to understand your concern for Durk. At the time I only 'heard' that you sided with Durk. That wasn't right for me to do, and even if I got angry for the minute, I should have made it right as soon as I could . . . I'm sorry. But I kinda believe that there's something *more* going on here. My dad . . . uhh, stepdad . . . and Uncle Jim said that they believe that God was . . . is . . . well . . . sort of . . . cleansing . . . the campus somehow, and that all of this . . . *all of it* . . . is serving a greater purpose. I kinda think that they're right. And if they are . . . then your part in this is greater than just jumping to conclusions. You probably were, as you said before . . . although that word is kinda weird to use . . . *possessed* . . . for a little while anyway. I'd rather use the word blinded because that connotation is more easily understood."

"I was devastated by my arrest and the incredibly unfounded charges against me and . . . well, the Blackberry that I carry has a Bible and concordance in it, and I turned to it out of . . . desperation . . . fear. I sorta needed a word of reassurance, you know? And it was weird, but I ended up with something out of the Book of Psalms, in fact the entire third Psalm. It really helped me. The first and second verse said, 'Lord, how are they increased that trouble me! Many are they that rise up against me. Many there be which say of my soul, There is no help for him in God.'

"But as I read further in that same Psalm, it said, 'But thou O Lord art a shield for me; my glory, and the lifter up of my head. I cried unto the Lord with my voice, and he heard me out of his holy hill.' And the sixth verse was the kicker. It said, 'I will not be afraid of ten thousands of people that have set themselves against me round about.'

"I was calm after that Ken, and I was not afraid any longer. I seemed to understand that something greater than me was afoot and that I needed to trust and wait it out. Then, I decided that on my own I would finish out my semester—I mean not attend classes, but do the work and see if I could later find a way to take the exams—and I felt that everything would be okay . . . even Rebecca . . . and it was such a relief.

"I'm glad that we talked today, Ken. I should have been the one to initiate a talk with you and I'm sorry, but if it's okay with you, let's pick up from those first few weeks and let the other stuff go. Deal?"

Ken was thrilled and grabbed Jayden in a bear hug, then, slightly embarrassed, he backed off, but Jayden laughed and grabbed him back in another bear hug and all was well between the two friends. Ken was impressed by what Jayden said about turning to the Bible and finding just the right words to help him through his shock of being arrested. *There really is something to having faith, and I want whatever it is too,* Ken thought.

They walked back to Rebecca's room smiling, and when they were at her bed, they told her that they'd made up and that now she'd have to put up with both of them. Ken suggested that Jayden read something to Rebecca from the Bible so she too would have some special words to hang onto. Jayden took the Bible from Rebecca's night stand and let it fall open naturally, and then he placed his finger on a verse without looking. His finger fell on Isaiah 12:2 which said, "Behold, God is my salvation; I will trust, and not be afraid: for the Lord JEHOVAH is my strength and my song; he also is become my salvation."

"Do ya think that that would work for me, Jayden? I'd sure like to find something in scripture that we could all hang onto together. What do you think?

"Sure, Ken, try it."

"Well, here goes." And Ken too let the Bible fall open and without looking reached to touch a part of the page with his index finger as Jayden had done. "Look, look, it's . . . ahh . . . now how do you read it? Oh yeah, the name, the chapter, and then the verse. Okay, it's in Isaiah 55:12 and says, 'For ye shall go out with joy, and shall be led forth with peace: the mountains and the hills shall break forth before you into singing, and all the trees of the field shall clap their hands.'

"It worked!" Ken said joyfully.

"Well, now, Ken," Jayden said, "what you read is true. God will honor that . . . but . . . don't pin all hopes on that. I mean, there's a lot more to faith . . . and the elements of faith work together to bring about the miracles we seek. We have to have a real . . . a really deep trust in God. Our hearts have to be right . . . we have to know what God asks of us . . . what His plan is . . . and then . . . well . . . then he opens a lot of stuff to us, and He really piles on the blessings too!"

And so Ken and Jayden's friendship was healed, and Chaldeth again could not understand what had gone wrong. Chaldeth paced in rage, and his thoughts ran rampant. *I had Ken . . . I had him in the palm of my hand . . . I'd blinded him . . . led him . . . turned him against Jayden . . . made him say what he said. And now look what happened. Why, Ken won't even make a good witness now. How did he slip away from me?* Chaldeth tried to get Ken to take offence with Jayden's words, to think that Jayden was upbraiding him when he said not to pin his hopes on just opening a Bible, but it didn't work. Ken was still too happy with the mending of their friendship to take umbrage.

Way down deep in Rebecca's subconscious, she recognized that the words between Ken and Jayden meant that they were still friends; and while she could not quite put everything together about what their rift may have been she could feel her body suddenly relax. *It's like when my shoulders suddenly slump and I hadn't even known that I was holding them in a tense position.* She felt somehow . . . happier. *If only I wouldn't keep drifting off to sleep.*

Jim, in the meanwhile, had gone to visit Durk. Durk was still being held because he'd stubbornly refused to work with the public defender who been assigned to his case and Durk had refused to accept the terms required for a bail bond. The only statement he'd made was that, if they wanted to know anything, they should ask Professor T. Nagorra. Durk was sullen and angry and felt that, as usual, he was getting a raw deal. He knew that he was on his own, that there were no family members to help him, and most likely no friends. Durk had turned twenty that day, and he was alone . . . in a jail cell . . . bolstered only by his anger at the injustices of his childhood . . . of his entire life.

Jim had been in many places that screamed of despair and in many situations fraught with danger and hopelessness, but a jail seemed even worse. With walls of dirty concrete and cold iron bars with peeling paint everywhere, and floors that echoed the sound of heavy boots and foul words, the jail accosted the senses with its lack of empathy and its blatant display of confinement. When Jim was ushered into his cell, Durk first thought that he was just another lawyer. When Jim explained who he was, Durk exploded. "How *dare* you come here. You . . . of the lofty, educated, *privileged* class . . . holding hands with your precious little wimp Jayden who doesn't even have the guts to fight me for Rebecca . . . you're all a bunch of dim-witted jerks."

Jim sat down on the edge of the small hard mattress on Durk's bed but remained silent. Durk looked at him for a minute and then said, "What, cat got your tongue, simpleton? Now just get outta here and leave me alone."

When Jim continued to sit and not respond, Durk asked, "What do ya want? What didya come here for, huh?"

Jim answered quietly, "Durk, I just wanted to tell you something that I thought you would want to know. I believe that you really care for Rebecca and would like you to know how she is."

"Yeah, well how is she? Back with her precious little family, laughing at her little play-acting at being with one of the 'bad' guys? Laughing at playing innocent while making a fool of me?"

"No, Durk, she's been in a coma all this time."

Durk was shocked. Jim had delivered his news so simply and quietly that it took Durk a while to absorb the horror of what Jim had said. Suddenly Durk felt weak in the knees. His mind raced to the last time he'd seen Rebecca. He hadn't known exactly what had happened . . . just that suddenly Rebecca had screamed, the professor was at her side, and then she was on the floor. Then the professor was dragging her into the hall wanting Durk to get outta there fast. Durk had thought that the cops were coming or something. He hadn't known that Rebecca was really hurt, or had something else happened to Rebecca?

Durk felt so weak that he too sat, and Jim noticed that the fight seemed to go out of him. A minute or so of silence ensued, and then Durk asked, "Is she gonna die?"

Jim told him that they did not know yet, but there was a good chance that she could still come out of her coma. He explained that the doctors had drained the blood that had put pressure on her brain but that the swelling was still there, still interfering with a recovery.

"Geez, what happened? I didn't ever mean for Rebecca to get hurt . . . I mean, really hurt. I thought she was okay. I mean, like that she had fainted or something. She infuriated me with her demands . . . wanting me to . . . well . . . change my life . . . but she had no clue that I have to . . . I have to . . . stay in school . . . or I'll end up like my old man. I've *gotta* get out of that rut, or I'll be just like him, and then I might as well be dead. I have no choice. I mean, I'm not privileged like you . . . I gotta do this on my own . . . ya know, go to college, get a decent job . . . a real job. I don't want to live on welfare and all that crap and then beat my own kids. Oh boy . . . if she dies . . . I'll . . . I'll . . ."

Durk had a sudden recollection of the professor dragging Rebecca from his office and realized that even though he'd seen that Rebecca hadn't moved, hadn't resisted, had been unconscious, he'd done nothing to help her. Durk's mind couldn't fasten onto the exact moments leading up to the professor's entrance into his office, and he was suddenly terribly afraid. *What had happened? Did I hurt her? Did the professor hurt her? The professor did say something about having to keep her quiet.* Durk couldn't remember all the details, but suddenly he felt terrible, felt that ultimately, what had happened to Rebecca was his fault.

Jim watched the emotions move across Durk's face, and as Durk turned to look at Jim, Durk embarrassed himself by starting to cry. Once he started he could not stop. It was as if every feeling he'd ever suppressed, every anger, every hurt, every crushed hope and dream, every one of his father's cruelties suddenly came crashing down on him, and he sobbed, finally released from . . . something . . . something he'd held at bay for a long time. He was filled with a distinct vision of all the things that he'd experienced and all the things he'd done that he wasn't proud of. He cried and with those tears came remorse.

Neither Durk nor Jim understood that Chaldeth's hold over Durk had slipped in the wake of Jim's kindness and his soft, understanding, nonjudgmental tone. It was through Jim's love that God had stepped in to offer yet another chance for Durk to learn the truth and change his life. It was painful for Durk to see himself as he was, and yet it was the only way that Durk could make the decision to change.

Chaldeth pushed against his opposition . . . . God's love . . . . as best he could. He *would* not, *could* not, let this force win. He struggled to stop Durk from seeing himself as he was, and he tried to place hate in Durk's heart for Jim. But despite his efforts, Chaldeth could not break through the love—the unconditional love—that Jim carried to Durk which was far stronger than Chaldeth.

Watching and straining in his effort to retain his power over Durk, Chaldeth tried to make Durk stop crying and he tried to strengthen him with the hate, resentment, anger, envy, jealousy that could be so powerful. But the love and compassion coming from Jim toward Durk was too strong, and Chaldeth could not—for now anyway—break its greater power. Furious, Chaldeth decided not to use up his energy, but to wait and strike again. If Jim could be made to feel anger toward Durk, he would lose the power with which Durk had been drawn. Chaldeth would wait for any sign of anger, or better yet, any sign of hate, on the part of Jim or Durk.

Before Jim set out for his visit to Durk, he had opened his Bible and it had fallen open to Jeremiah 31:9 which said, "They shall come with weeping, and with supplications will I lead them: I will cause them to walk by the rivers in a straight way, wherein they shall not stumble . . ." These words gave Jim direction and hope where Durk was concerned. Remembering those words, Jim watched Durk's tears and knew that he cried over his concern for Rebecca and his remorse over his past deeds. But Jim had also listened carefully to Durk's words about his childhood, his father, the beatings he'd received, and even how desperate and alone Durk was as he struggled to get an education. He understood why selling pot was so important to Durk, and suddenly he also understood why Rebecca wanted to help this young man.

When Durk stopped sobbing, he found Jim's arm around him, and with his anger abated and his guard down, he stayed close to Jim and quietly asked, "What can I do?" Jim moved so Durk would not be embarrassed by their contact. Still close to him, however, Jim told him that he understood why Durk might have chosen the path he was on. Jim explained how he'd opened the Bible before visiting him and how God had provided a special word for them. "What word ?" Durk asked. And Jim repeated, "They shall come with weeping, and with supplications will I lead them: I will cause them to walk by the rivers in a straight way, wherein they shall not stumble . . ."

"Oh God," Durk said sobbing again. "Oh my God." But then Durk's cynicism, long engrained in his heart from years of struggle and abuse, arose again and Chaldeth saw his opening and planted the thoughts in Durk's mind that caused him to say to Jim, "Yeah, sure . . . it sounds good, but what has that to do with reality . . . my personal reality. Nothing will work for me, nothing can help me now."

"A lot, Durk, a lot can work for you. Here you have a promise from God that He will help you, that He will prevent you from stumbling, but there's also a special meaning in the part that describes you as coming to Him with weeping and supplication. It means that you've emptied your heart of hate and anger and will listen to Him, learn what He wants you to know, and then be able to accept what He sends you."

"That isn't so easy, is it?"

"No, but if you will accept Rebecca and Jayden and their friends and family as your friends—and that includes me—and trust us, we'll help you learn how to do it and God will be at your side."

"Yeah . . . *bull* . . . you don't know anything about me . . . and if you did . . . well . . . forget it."

"Durk, let me tell you something else. There is not one single child of God who is not a sinner. There is not one single child of God who does not *continue* to slip from time to time."

"Yeah, but not sins like mine."

"Wanna bet? I don't know if you know anything about the Bible, but David . . . King David . . . was one of God's favorite people, and he murdered someone so he could steal his wife. Another man named Jonah didn't want to do what God asked of him and tried to hide from God, and another, Noah, sometimes drank too much, and Jacob lied to his father. Samson was a womanizer, Rahab was a prostitute, Job went bankrupt, Peter denied Christ, and there are more. So if God loved them and brought them out of *their* stuff, he can do the same for you, but He will do it only if you really want it."

"Yeah, but will He rain money down on me too?"

"Yeah, Durk, He can. It might be in the form of an excellent student loan and a great part-time job, one that He would approve of, but yeah, He can do that too! In fact, God will guide you through every step and through every circumstance. The first step is explained in Proverbs 23:26 and says, 'My son give me thine heart, and let thine eyes observe my ways.'"

Jim's words had caught Durk's interest and caused him to think, *If this stuff is true, and certainly Jayden, Rebecca . . . and now it appears Jim too . . . seem to thrive in it . . . then maybe I should try it. Certainly the path I've taken has failed, and I'd be lucky to find someone who would really give a darn about me . . . someone who does not have an ulterior motive for helping me.* And so Durk asked how someone could give their heart to God. What exactly did they have to do? Jim told him about how he himself had been drawn to God and how he had been taught and finally learned. He explained the necessity to have a real relationship with God.

"Let me tell you, Durk, about a church service I attended when I'd adamantly told my girlfriend, now my wife, that I'd never believe! In fact, what the minister said actually made me angry at the time because I thought—in fact, I was sure—that he was saying those words just to me to point out my failures . . . and in those days I sure didn't want to hear that!

"The minister addressed the congregation, asking us if we would be happy in relationships where we were treated with indifference, where the people we loved were uncommunicative, acted neither hot nor cold, neither caring nor uncaring. Would we feel loved, would we feel that we were important to them, would we feel that they cared? Would our love for them cool and become lukewarm? He then went on to ask if the relationship each person had with God was intimate and open and loving. He asked if we conversed with God as a loving couple might converse. Did we speak to God each day of our difficulties and our triumphs as a couple in love might speak with one another? Did we trust God and ask His advice as such a couple would with one another? He asked if we sought to do something each day to show God how much we love him as a couple in love might do and learn what pleases God as a couple might learn to please one another."

Jim explained that the minister had gone on to say that if we did not do these things—the things all good relationships require—we hadn't yet developed the kind of relationship with God that would allow Him entry into our hearts and minds, nor our spirit or future. And if we hadn't yet developed that kind of a relationship, we really didn't know Him and would be classified as being lukewarm toward God. Being lukewarm is a state that God warns us about.

"God wants to develop a bride for His Son and inhabitants for His new heaven and new earth who will be capable of giving and showing love, and He cannot accept those who are not willing to work for the kind of a relationship that existed between the couple that the minister had described. If we are to live together for all eternity, we need to learn to live with love and kindness in our hearts as God and His Son live.

"The minister concluded with the words, 'Only we can answer the question about what kind of relationship we have fostered with God. Only we can answer this for ourselves. Once we've heard or read what He asks of us, the rest is up to us. God has given us free will.'

As Jim was talking, Durk suddenly felt exhausted. He felt a sense of despair which was quickly replaced by anger. He felt as if his thoughts had jumped from wanting to hear what Jim had to say to hating the things he said. He was filled with a sudden resentment toward Jim so strong that he was surprised by its force and wondered why he felt this sudden anger. He wanted Jim gone. He wanted Jim to stop talking. He wanted his old life back. He knew he'd never be the kind of person Jim spoke about, and that sense of defeat upset him.

Durk was torn. Intellectually he'd believed Jim and wanted what he had. But out of the blue and rising from his sense of inadequacy, he felt the old hate, born of the fear that had governed his thoughts ever since his father began to beat him without cause. He felt the anger burst into his mind, and with it, the need to blame someone else for his failures. Even more fervently he felt the need to be strong—not vulnerable—so he could fight against what was happening to him. He needed anger to help him get out of the ghetto that his life had become. He couldn't do it if he succumbed to the namby-pamby approach Jim was suggesting.

But Durk didn't know that it was Chaldeth who'd placed those thoughts into his mind and Chaldeth that had caused his fear and resentment to bubble up to the surface and attack the life that Jim was describing. Chaldeth began to sweat from the effort he had expended in order to break through the shield that Jim's love had erected around Durk. Chaldeth's hold on Durk would have to be weakened before Durk could break free of him, but Durk did not understand any of this and fell once again—and quite easily—into the old ways . . . the only way he knew.

"Yeah, well. That's not for me. I've already used my free will to get where I am, and while it may not be the way you'd do things, it's all I know. I've had a lot of time to think, and I am the way I am, good or bad. I'm selfish, I guess, and that's the way it is. I've had to fight for everything I want in life, and it's made me . . . well . . . bitter, I guess. Anyway, I've been around so much and seen so much that I could never change. I appreciate your offer, but no thanks. I'll get myself out of this one way or another, and I will never be able to accept your way of life . . . or Rebecca's. That's a fantasy life . . . and it's for the privileged few."

Jim heard the sarcasm and bitterness in Durk's voice, and he'd also heard the sudden anger. He could sense the change in Durk. But Jim also knew that the evil which had infiltrated Durk's world was not about to let go. In fact, Jim clearly saw that it had now dug its heels in and wanted not only to engulf Durk but to attack Jim and stop Jim's access to Durk. Jim realized that it was time to go. But he would return, and he would, with God's help, tackle the spirit that was fighting so hard to keep its hold on Durk.

"You may think this way now, Durk, but let me leave you with something to think about—and I am coming back again so we can talk some more because I feel that it is important for you. I want you to think about what God says in Psalm 5:11, 'But let all those that put their trust in thee rejoice: let them ever shout for joy, because thou defendest them: let them also that love thy name be joyful in thee.' If you trust Him, God promises in Jeremiah 3:3, 'Call unto Me, and I will answer thee, and shew thee great and mighty things, which thou knowest not.'

"But here's my parting thought. I see something good in you, Durk, and so did Rebecca. I don't think that you pursued a relationship with Rebecca because she was to become the love of your life. But I do think that you pursued a relationship with her because you were attracted to her goodness, and that's because something in you hungers for that goodness. That means that there is still a chance for you to turn your life around. I believe in you. I believe that you can still make a good and honest life for yourself. I believe that you will find the love of your life someday, but only when you are worthy of that kind of love . . . and I believe that you will be someday. Think about it. I'll stop in again tomorrow if it's okay with you, Durk."

"Yeah, sure, but don't think I'm gonna be this 'new' person you seem to think I'll be. That's bull . . . we are what we are."

"No, we're not, Durk. We are what we want to be if we are willing to work at it. And you, young man, are a fighter, not a quitter!"

Durk tossed and turned all night. His thoughts ran rampant thinking about the jam he was in, why his life was in the mess it was now, and he was overcome by a raging anger at Jim for upsetting his comfortable way of thinking. *How dare he come here and tell me I need to change . . . where does he get off? Who does he think he's kidding telling me that he wants to help me? That's bull! What, does he think I'm stupid? Nobody does something for nothing, so what does the guy want from me?*

But another force, a gentler one, was also placing thoughts in Durk's head. *But what if Jim is right? What if there really is a chance to change? What if I could have the kind of life that these people have? What if God does believe in giving people a second chance?*

Chaldeth fought for control by taking over Durk's thoughts, *Yeah, but what if Jim is wrong? What if he has an ulterior motive? What if they learn how bad I've really been and dump me? What if I lose my strength and determination because of them. Then what? Why even bother to try—I'll only fail. Is there ever any real chance for people like me? Why would I expect anything from people like them?*

Just as Satan had planted doubt in Eve's mind, one of Satan's fallen angels had now planted the same doubt in Durk's mind. Doubt was an incredibly powerful force. It was more powerful than any of earth's mortals realized. It was so powerful, in fact, that God admonished His children over and over again to believe, to have faith, and not to doubt. God addressed the power of faith specifically and succinctly when He said in Matthew 17:20, "And Jesus said unto them, because of your unbelief: for verily I say unto you, if ye have faith as a grain of mustard seed, ye shall say unto this mountain. Remove hence to yonder place; and it shall remove; and nothing shall be impossible to you."

Chaldeth and his cohorts knew the power of doubt, and they used it well. They brought it unceasingly to all of mankind, whispering such little phrases as *Does that really help? Are they really sincere? Does God really mean . . . ? If you did that, would it really accomplish anything? Why would God care about you? Why would anyone care about you?*

Durk was tortured by his thoughts. He felt as if he was being pulled in two different directions, and he simply could not decide which thoughts were the best thoughts. He was confused, and he felt that whatever choice he made now would ruin his chance to ever move in the other direction. He didn't like to see any of his possibilities closed off, any of his choices denied to him.

But Jim was praying for Durk, and he'd put a special offering into the offertory at church just for Durk. Jim knew God wanted to help Durk as He did all of mankind. God did, after all, want all mankind to be saved, and He was willing to forgive anyone who was truly repentant and would follow His ways as best they could. Jim thought that he would show Durk the words written in 1 Timothy 1:4 which read, "For this is good and acceptable in the sight of God our savior, who will have all men saved, and come unto the knowledge of the truth."

But ultimately it would be Durk who would have to choose. He could *not* live in both worlds. He might slip once in a while back toward the world without God, but ultimately he would have to denounce that world and actively seek God's world. Satan might strike to prevent this, but once the commitment was made, God would step in and help. While Durk did not understand these spiritual truths just yet, he did finally find himself looking forward to Jim's next visit. He'd decided that he'd at least hear him out and maybe just try Jim's way for a short time. It probably couldn't hurt, and maybe—well, just maybe—it would help. That is if Jim was really going to visit him again.

When Jim arrived, he carried a bag of goodies for Durk which contained an inspirational novel, a few candy bars, some mints, and a small bottle of men's cologne. He had also brought, for each of them, a nice cold bottle of Stevia-sweetened mango-flavored green tea and a huge blueberry muffin. That had been a real treat for Durk and had paved the way for them to slip back into the camaraderie they'd established before Chaldeth had stirred Durk's inner fear and caused his fear to manifest itself as anger.

Jim talked about his mother's struggle against the harm that her neighbor brought her and told him of his personal struggles to rid himself of the anger he'd had toward God for allowing his mother to be hurt. Jim told Durk that he'd often felt isolated, felt a kind of disconnect when he was with other people, and when that changed it had been as if he had glimpsed happiness for the first time in his life. He told Durk that he'd always been personable, was well liked, conversed easily, yet hadn't felt really connected to anyone, and it caused him to experience a constant sense of loneliness.

Durk, having felt all the things that Jim was mentioning, was amazed that someone like Jim would ever have felt the same things that had plagued him all his life. Durk had always questioned why his father was allowed to hurt his mother, and then later, why he was allowed to hurt him. So Durk asked Jim, "What made that disconnect, that loneliness, go away?"

"Well, it didn't happen overnight. Just as I am talking with you now, a friend—who is now my wife—spoke with me. She told me that without God in my life, I'd always feel empty. Of course I didn't believe her, but in time, having a family around me who loved God so much that they actually practiced what they preached, I began to know love. Love isn't just a physical love—it's deeper. It can exist between friends, between family members, and even between strangers. It's something that comes from God and is so pure that it can, in time, fill you and when it does, it emanates out of you to others. It's a true miracle, a true gift. It's free too. All you have to do is to give your commitment to God that you will try your best and will not give up. Just keep trying to live as God asks us to live. Even when we fail God loves us, and He will continue to help us as long as we keep on trying, especially when we feel badly that we failed and really mean it when we start trying again."

"That doesn't seem too hard to do, Jim."

"Yeah, except for one thing. Satan, evil, whatever you want to call it, will do everything in its power to stop you. The goal of evil is to prevent God from obtaining the number of souls He wants for the new heaven and earth he has prepared. So sometimes it's a battle. In fact it's a battle every day. Let me tell you a cute little story. My wife Barbara has a sister-in-law named Sarah. Sarah and her husband Matt have become sort of the glue that holds the family together because Sarah's grandmother passed the gauntlet of faith to Sarah. And that's another long story I'll tell you one day. But what Grandma did with Sarah was kinda like in the old days when the father gave his blessing to the oldest son. Anyway, Grandma, as we all call her—she died a few years back—told Sarah that Satan attacks day in and day out even if you are just 'somewhat' faithful to God. In fact, he attacks the strong in faith even more. Grandma told Sarah that whenever Satan knocked on her door and wanted to fill her with doubt or with angry thoughts toward someone or with lingering hurt over a situation, it was like a bird making a nest on your head and pecking their way into your brain. She said that everyone has birds flying overhead, meaning that everyone has thoughts that run through our minds. That's okay. But if thoughts that are not right with God land and try to make a nest on your head, you must shoo them away. If you allow them to land and to make a nest, then the thoughts become your responsibility and your fate. But if they just circle and you chase them, then you are not held responsible for them. Her remedy to stop the birds from landing, even if they constantly flew over, was to simply yell aloud, '*No!*' She said that whenever she did this those thoughts would disappear. It was as if the spirits who were trying to plant those thoughts ran away in fear. She said that she'd started this when she read how Christ had yelled, 'Get thee behind me, Satan,' and Satan fled. So now we all do it!"

"That's neat. I've been getting those thoughts, and I hate them, so maybe I'll try that."

"That would be great, Durk, because Satan will not want to let you go. But you know, you can also surround yourself with God's word, His children, a minister, a church, and accept what He offers, and that too will help to make it all okay. If you want, Durk, I'll stand by your side."

To his embarrassment, Durk began to cry. It had touched Durk's heart that someone could be this kind—to him of all people—and especially after what had happened with Rebecca. When he composed himself, Durk stood, moved toward Jim, extended his hand, and with tears in his eyes said, "Thanks . . . thanks . . . thanks . . . thanks. I would like to try, and I hope that I don't disappoint you, Jim."

"You won't. I know you won't, but remember, God knows whether we are sincere or not, and he warns us not to lie about committing ourselves to Him. But if we mean what we say, if we are sincere, He promises to totally cleanse us of our sins and to stand by us." Jim opened the Bible he'd brought for Durk saying, "Let me read you something. 1 John 1:6-9 warns, 'If we say that we have fellowship with him, and walk in darkness, we lie, and do not the truth: But if we walk in the light, as he is in the light, we have fellowship with one another, and the blood of Jesus Christ his Son cleanseth us from all sin. If we say we have no sin, we deceive ourselves, and the truth is not in us. If we confess our sins, he is faithful and just to forgive our sins, and to cleanse us from all unrighteousness.'

"Durk, it's not going to be easy, but God will help you, and so will we. We must overcome our past, leave behind the things we know are wrong, and though we may sin again, maybe backslide, we should love God so much that we are devastated by our slip up, really feel and express our remorse, and go on intending not to slip again. We may then slip up somewhere else, but hopefully not into the same thing that had entrapped us in the first place.

"I'll leave my Bible with you, and I'll come again. When we get you out of here, we'll talk some more. The more you learn, the more you'll be able to spot those spirits of evil and the easier it will get. In the meanwhile, I'm gonna talk to your guidance counselor and see what we can do to let you make up the classes you've missed and find out what you can study so you can take the exams and finish this semester. They kicked Jayden out—he couldn't take classes—but they have allowed him to get his class information from the professors so he could study on his own and then maybe they will let him take the exams. Let's see if we can do this for you too!"

"Geez, Jim, thanks again . . . I never thought . . . I mean . . . I'd given up hope . . . I mean . . . gee, thanks. I'll work hard, you'll see."

"I know you will, Durk. Now how about we pray before I leave? We'll ask for God's blessing on you and we'll ask for His protection and His guidance, and we'll also ask Him to keep any of those pesky, rotten spirits outta here and away from you too. If you ever feel them comin' at you, pray and they will have to leave. Say 'no' loud and clear! I'll explain more about that once you're outta here. Okay?"

And so they prayed, and as Jim spoke, tears of thanksgiving flowed down Durk's face. *I have finally found something worthwhile,* he thought. *I finally know what path I am supposed to take. Finally, maybe I can get out from under my past and do what's right for a change.*

Chaldeth continued to plague Durk's thoughts day and night filling him with doubt and fear. Durk faithfully walked his cell yelling aloud, "*No!*" and the thoughts did not come as often and they did leave when he yelled "No!" They came again and again, and he yelled again and again, but it was working and they lessened.

Chaldeth began inciting other inmates to attack Durk. He needed Durk to believe that there was no other life for him and certainly no help for him. Durk struggled every day to stay out of trouble despite the goading of some of the men he'd meet in the cafeteria or in other areas of the detention center. They tried to pick a fight with him, but Durk used all his willpower to walk away from it . . . for the first time in his life. He could see that the ones who wanted to fight him were like his father and also realized that he no longer wanted that way of life for himself. And so Durk struggled and held on to the hope that Jim would be back and that Jim was doing everything he could to get him released.

And with that, Durk's healing had also begun. But what Durk did not know was that Chaldeth was making new plans to pull Durk back. Chaldeth was not about to let Durk go.

Chapter 11

The Power of Evil

When Kara learned that Jayden and Ken had made peace with one another, she was delighted. Always thoughtful and caring, Kara planned a special evening for them in her little sitting room. She purchased Italian-style submarine sandwiches stuffed with all kinds of deli meats and cheeses topped with shredded lettuce, tomatoes, pickles, and jalapeno peppers. And of course, the bread was slathered with the mayonnaise she knew they liked. She also purchased a large bag of potato chips and prepared a pitcher of ice tea. For a special treat, she also purchased a tiny cheesecake topped with strawberries. To remind them of how important their friendship was, she created two large banners by stapling eight sheets of computer paper together upon which she'd written, "Friends Forever!" Underneath those words she'd written, in smaller letters, "Jayden, Rebecca, Kara, and Ken." She hung one banner over the entry door of the suite and the other on the wall above the little loveseat. After they had eaten, they began to chat and found their conversation moving to the subjects of education, morality, their future, and the unseen loving hand that seemed to guide them through this difficult month. They also spoke of evil and how surprised they were by its power and the ease with which it had surrounded them. They felt as if they'd had a wake-up call that had come almost too late.

"I knew all about evil," said Jayden, "but I guess I never thought that it could touch me personally. I've watched it operate, even in a family member—my dad, for instance, was owned lock, stock, and barrel through his drinking and gambling, and he lost everything of true value. My aunt Sarah was attacked when she and my uncle Matt published a manuscript that Sarah's grandmother wrote explaining God's plan of salvation. Rebecca's birth mother Mary was attacked at the age of fourteen, and the trauma caused her to succumb to another more subtle attack until Aunt Sarah and Uncle Matt helped her. I've seen the attacks firsthand, and I still failed to recognize it when we were attacked. I should have alerted my family right away. I really feel badly that I didn't. If I had, perhaps Rebecca wouldn't be in the coma."

"Jayden," Kara replied, "I think that God may have planned the timing, because if your family had come sooner, you and Rebecca would have been transferred to another school. Now, however, so much has been discovered that, by the time this is over, I'll bet that every student on campus will be safer."

"Both you and Jayden sure recognized it before I did," Ken added. "I'd never before in my whole life realized . . . well, what I mean is I thought that evil was simply . . . you know, doing something wrong . . . either one person or a whole lot of people collectively. But I never in a million years connected it to . . . well, that all or any of us could have an individual . . . uhhh . . . entity . . . personally directing its attention toward us. That's creepy. Let's face it, if we tried to say something like this . . . you know . . . about an evil spirit . . . to the general student population, they'd lock us in the funny farm or figure we'd fried our brains on dope."

"You're right, Ken, that's why it's so hard to talk about it, warn anyone, even get your own head straight about it. How could anyone get their own head straight if they had no one to talk to about it . . . someone who also understands the power and actions of what's behind all the bad stuff? I think that being able to talk about things helps you understand them so much better. Do you know what I'm trying to say?"

"I sure do, Jayden, I do. I can't think of anyone I could talk to about this stuff other than you and Ken. But I sure am going to try to teach my family about this when I go home for Christmas," Kara added. "I wouldn't be surprised however if they try to shut me up and think that I've been under the wrong influence here at school instead of the right one. In fact, I'd like to copy this stuff from the Bible, put those verses in my computer, maybe even along with some explanations, so when I get home, I can talk about it and back up what I say by the corresponding scripture. Perhaps I could even print it out so my family members could study it. I didn't believe it at first, so they probably won't either."

"It is mind-boggling though. People in general know about Satan, know that he's also called the devil, maybe they even know that he was thrown out of heaven with a bunch of other angels. Perhaps they even know that he tries to keep people away from God and is in a battle with God—the battle between good and evil. But that's *it*. There is no association with an actual hands-on thing . . . an actual entity . . . that can make us . . . cause us . . . to do or think what is wrong."

"I think Ken's right, Jayden. So how do we go about explaining this without sounding like we've lost our marbles, or that we've become religious zealots, fanatics?"

"That's a tough one . . . but you know, maybe we should tackle that job even if we are considered weird. Perhaps we could help someone someday. Even if someone can't believe it today, maybe someday in the future they will find themselves in a difficult situation and remember what we said and then look it up and maybe even develop a closer relationship with God because of what we told them. I think this information has changed me, helped me recognize the danger and taught me what to look for. We really should make a list of all the things that the Bible says about this subject. You know what? We could bring our stuff, like our laptops, after we load them with the Bible and concordance, and work in Rebecca's room for a few hours each day whether we are alone or together. We can tell her what we are doing. We are supposed to keep talking to her anyway to bring her out of the coma. And to tell you the truth, sometimes I'm stumbling with my words because I run out of things to talk about. I guess that's why some of the family read to her. But this . . . this subject is fascinating, and we could talk about it in her room. She would be interested in this too!"

"I love that idea, Jayden. But since we already have the list you gave us, maybe we should divide our new research into two 'hows.' How does evil attack, and how can we protect ourselves? You know, KISS: keep it simple, stupid!"

"Yeah, Kara has a point. Let's not get bogged down in it. I mean, no one will listen to a long spiel. They want it quick and to the point and backed up with some proof. You'll have to lead us, Jayden, because we sure don't know how to locate all this information."

"Okay, I'll make a list of every single verse in the Bible that uses the words evil or spirit or any of the names applied to Satan. When I get that together—and it will be a lot—we'll go through them together and eliminate the ones that don't tell us what we want to know and keep those that do. After that, we'll tackle the question of how to be protected. Does that sound like a plan?"

"Terrific!"

The three friends were happy. They were together again. They were committed to their friendship, and they had a great project to work on that could include Rebecca. Despite the information they had about evil, they had no idea that Chaldeth was with them, listening, plotting. They understood quite a bit, but they were not aware of the close proximity, the day in and day out constancy, nor the personalized interest that one evil spirit in particular had in mind for them.

Chaldeth, as had happened too often this past month, had to regroup. Everything that could have gone wrong had gone wrong, and he had to put a stop to it. He had to come up with a new plan that would slowly and subtly begin to lead these infuriating *nerds* back to where he needed them without them realizing what he was doing. But how? He needed to pit the three friends against one another again. To separate is to conquer. Somehow he needed to insert a disruptive influence into their plans. He needed to calm down and start over. His power was still intact, so he had to use it; he just had to use it more effectively.

Surprisingly Chaldeth was comforted by some of the words in scripture. His favorite was the story of Eve and how easily she had been seduced. He loved the verse from Genesis 3:13 that said, "The serpent beguiled me, and I did eat." Chaldeth needed something that would tempt them, beguile them, and which they would unsuspectingly ingest. Another of his favorite verses was a tribute to his natural ability. It was from Genesis 3:1 and read, "The serpent was more subtil than any beast . . ." Chaldeth had learned long ago to be subtle and patient and to start small, and them *bam*! . . . hit them with everything he had. He smiled to himself and thought, *Just lay the trap, Chaldeth, and listen to it snap closed! But enough gloating. Now for a plan . . .*

Chaldeth was not the only one who was making plans. It seemed that many were. Jim was planning to help Durk; John had plans he wanted to discuss with Elizabeth; Jayden, Kara, and Ken were planning how to get Rebecca to respond to their conversation, Sarah was planning for Christmas, and their American history professor Doog was making plans to resign his position and seek one at Liberty University where he would be encouraged to teach an accurate history of the country he loved so well.

When news of what had happened to Rebecca reached the classrooms and Professor Doog learned of it, he began to think of the courageous young woman who'd spoken in his classroom in support of the accurate history of this country. She'd stood bravely in front of the entire class in support of teaching those things that current history books had either omitted or perverted. Her courage was admirable, and her love for her country evident. He'd been impressed with this young and lovely woman, and he began to wonder about her family, those who had taught her so well. He was sure that if he ever met them he would admire them as well. But he was now questioning his own courage and decided that it was time for him to stand up and be counted as well.

When he learned of Rebecca's coma, he began to inquire about her; and when he learned where she was, he decided to visit her to pay his respects. He also hoped to initiate a plan that would allow her to make up the work she had missed in his class and possibly arrange for her other instructors to help as well. If so, perhaps she could complete the semester. Her grades had been excellent and in fact were straight As, so he surmised that they might be equally impressive in her other classes.

Lunching with a few other professors who were, as he was, forbidden the "privilege" of lunching with those who were considered the elite professors of the campus, he was surprised to hear a professor who happened to be a good friend, speak about two students whom she wanted to help complete the semester's work. When he realized that one of those two students was Rebecca, he excitedly told her that he too wanted to provide that opportunity to Rebecca. They put their heads together to see what they could do and decided to make their visit to Rebecca's bedside together. Surely there would be someone there who was a member of Rebecca's family with whom they could discuss the matter of her schoolwork.

Professor Doog and Professor S. Sendnik had always been lunchroom friends but had never spoken of anything other than their busy schedules or simple things such as the weather or their plans for a vacation. But as they talked about the help they could offer Jayden and Rebecca, and then exchanged world views as they traveled to the hospital, they tentatively addressed the detrimental influences that had beset the college just over the past few years. They ventured into the recent intrigue concerning Professor T. Nagorra. Neither had been surprised by his arrest because they had heard hair-raising tales of his activities and complaints that many female students had lodged against him, all of which had been swept under the rug. They both hoped that this time, justice would be done, the truth would be made public, and the campus could be healed.

When Professor Doog mentioned that he had been terribly disappointed with the new textbooks he was required to use for his classes, and Rebecca's courage in speaking out against them, Professor Sendnik asked him why the textbooks had been changed. He explained that for years the newer textbooks had been slowly but surely changing history; important facts were either omitted or changed, and many perverted just enough to give the wrong impression. "How?" she asked.

"Well, the truth about the strong faith in God that the founding fathers had has been both changed and perverted, and the important contributions of African Americans who worked side by side with the founding fathers have been entirely omitted."

"That's an outrage. How is this possible?" she asked.

"Well, it started years ago and was done little by little with the purpose of causing the faith of all Americans to be lost in terms of its application to the founding and governing of this country. By erroneously claiming that the founding fathers were racists, those behind this movement to change our textbooks hoped that African Americans would at some point decry the Constitution and support their goal of changing the Constitution. The goal of the Progressive movement is to turn the country toward socialism and then to Marxism and possibly to a world leader who could stay in power without term limits. Now, today, almost all our textbooks deny the faith and God-fear that was the foundation of this country and claim that racism dictated the Constitution, and that is simply not true. There are many other areas of history that have been changed. Some changes portray liberal or communist leaders as heroes, even aggrandize those who were mass murderers, and others portray conservative leaders as criminals."

"Can you give me an example of some of these false heroes?"

"Mao and Che Guevara, for starters. Rather than demonstrate the extent of their cruelty and mass murders, some books extol them as having made great strides in providing social justice to the people. Our Constitution supports equal justice, not social justice. And there are strong differences between those two concepts. One creates a dependent malleable welfare state, and the other gives everyone the right to work to become independent. One quells or quenches personal liberty, and the other supports personal liberty."

"But how can that happen? Isn't there any watchdog group to protect our textbooks, thus our history, and prevent such a thing from happening?"

""Well, yes . . . but even these groups were slowly and insidiously infiltrated to the point where the Progressive party—that's the group that came up with this plan—had enough votes on school boards across the country to get their agenda passed. I can give you some printed info I have about Woodrow Wilson, about communism and Marxism, about Saul Alinsky, and about a couple named Richard Cloward and Frances Fox Piven. Read those and it will make your hair stand on edge."

"I'm glad that I teach a subject that really cannot be changed. Your leg bone is your leg bone, and no one can say that it's your arm bone. Although, I have to admit that I will be shutting down my dissection lab by the end of this school year. We will only be allowed to dissect via a computer, kind of like operating a mechanical hand and have it move around a computer-generated cadaver. It's called progress . . . and animal rights. But I find that the real thing provides the students with a better experience and certainly gives them more empathy. They don't like working on a cat. They have empathy for the cat, and that's a good thing. When faced with caring for a real person and thinking of the lessons learned through their cat dissection, that empathy is recalled, and they are more prone to a humane approach with the patient. The computers teach a cold and dispassionate application of medicine."

"I think I agree with you. Empathy and compassion are probably what makes a really good, a really caring, and thus more competent physician. But can I ask you another question? And please don't answer if you'd rather not. Are you comfortable on campus? I mean . . . I feel that we are ostracized because we are not activists for certain agendas on campus. We don't support a far-left liberalism, but on the other hand we respect the arguments of a centrist liberalism, and we certainly respect their right to choose where they stand on various issues. While we are expected to embrace their point of view, they won't even *tolerate* our point of view and vehemently and sometimes quite cruelly attack conservatives. I don't understand that.

"I am uncomfortable with and devastated by what's been going on at this campus. We have a responsibility to these kids. We should not be indoctrinating them but opening their horizons and getting them to think and explore and see the beauty in our God-given gifts. We should teach them how to openly and calmly discuss various issues and then, given all the facts—not just a biased look at some of the facts, but all the facts—we should let them make their own decisions . . . without rancor! I can no longer do that. I am being attacked, my family is being attacked, and I feel that I have to leave this campus. Further, this drug business and the jeopardy that the students are in sickens me."

"It would be an outrage for you to be forced out. You are one of the most loved professors, and amongst your true peers you are one of the most respected. It would not be right for you to be forced out. What should be forced out are the unscrupulous people who support such practices!" Professor Sendnik replied.

The professors pulled into a parking space. Grabbing their attaché cases, they entered the hospital and requested directions to Rebecca's room. When they arrived, they were surprised by the number of people in attendance. Jayden, Ken, and Kara were at Rebecca's bedside and had papers all over her bedside table and some on her bed, and their conversation seemingly included Rebecca.

Matt and Sarah were also in Rebecca's room but were planning to leave that night to go back home. They were sitting with Jim and Barbara who had just arrived. A few minutes before the arrival of the two professors, the two couples had insisted that Elizabeth and John and Mary and Kevin take a short break and go to a nice restaurant for dinner instead of eating the usual hospital fare. Mary and Kevin planned to leave the next morning and be back again in four or five days.

The two professors introduced themselves to the two couples and apologized for arriving unannounced. Kara was thrilled to see Professor Doog and explained that she and Rebecca were students in his early American history class. Jayden was delighted to see that his A and P professor had also come. Both he and Kara babbled about how grateful they were to have classes with these professors.

When the two professors explained that they wanted to make it possible for Rebecca to receive her class credits for this semester, everyone was overjoyed. Professor Doog then asked if anyone knew when Rebecca would be well enough to study.

"We can't answer that, unfortunately. You see, Rebecca is still in a coma, and no one knows when she will awaken. We are praying for her day and night, so we believe that she will awaken and that it's just a matter of time. Thank you so much for your thoughtfulness," Sarah said.

"We want to help. Will you let us know if there is anything we can do?"

"Professor Sendnik," Jayden asked, "the doctors and nurses tell us that Rebecca can hear what we say but she cannot respond. Kinda like falling asleep in front of the TV, and you can still hear the TV but can't follow the story. Maybe Rebecca will remember what we say to her though, or at least some of it. So what if we . . . I . . .

kinda read the material to her over and over a couple of times, and sort of quiz her . . . then when she wakes up maybe it won't take much more work for her to pass the final exam. Can I do that?"

No one had the heart to deny Jayden his request, and everyone would be thrilled if his idea worked. "Sure, Jayden, why not. I'll be glad to prepare the materials you will need for such a project."

"Thanks, Professor Sendnik."

"I can do the same for Rebecca's work in American history if that's okay with you, Professor Doog," Kara added.

Professor Doog smiled and nodded his assent, and Professor Sendnik went on to say, "We'll give you the texts to read and some sample questions from last year so you can see how the exams are set up. This year's exam will be different, but if you nail the questions we give you from last year, you will get an idea of how the tests are formulated and the type of questions we'll be asking this semester."

A hearty thank you fell from the lips of Rebecca's friends and family, chairs were offered, and lemonade and cookies magically appeared in everyone's hands. The two professors spoke for a few minutes directly to Rebecca each holding one of her hands. "Hey, Rebecca! We just wanted to say hello and let you know how much we miss you in class. We are waiting for you to return and brighten up our classroom again. Jayden and Kara will be teaching you everything that you have missed, so when you come back you'll be up and running!"

Kara felt a lump in her throat from the gratitude she felt for what these loving instructors were providing for Rebecca. As the conversation continued, and everyone began to feel comfortable, Kara could no longer curb her enthusiasm and blurted, "Aren't our professors wonderful people? They are true teachers—the real thing. Professors who really care, really want to teach—so different than what Rebecca had to deal with in Professor Emils's class where he threatened to fail her because she spoke against his . . . his . . . single-sided ideology . . . then later he wanted to see her . . . in private . . . late at night! Wow. Thank goodness that he's in jail now! And thank goodness for Rebecca's family and all their prayers . . . and that Jayden's dad was able to learn about Professor Emils's evil deeds."

Matt and Jim were shocked that Kara had said anything about Professor Emils in front of the other professors and had also mentioned the clandestine activities of the family to get at the truth. But since they couldn't stop Kara, as she continued to speak they watched the faces of the two professors seated across from them. They saw a look of approval pass between the two professors. What they'd all thought was a terrible faux pas on Kara's part they now felt might be an opening for them to gather some additional information.

When Kara finished speaking, Matt added, "We agree with what Kara said, especially the part where she spoke about both of you. You are to be commended for what you do and for caring so much about your students. It is a wonderful gesture for you to come all this distance to see Rebecca and to make this incredible offer to help them with their school work. We really do appreciate it. I do have to mention however,"—Matt hesitated before continuing—"what you just heard about our involvement regarding Professor Emils is not for public knowledge, but now that it's out . . . well . . . perhaps you can help us. Let me explain why we need your help.

"Jayden has been charged with drug possession, intent to sell, and with being responsible for Rebecca's coma. We know beyond the shadow of a doubt that these charges are not accurate. I would venture to guess that you feel that way too. But to clear Jayden's name we are working hard to uncover the truth about what really happened. Some of the students have been willing to provide us with information, and from some of the small bits of information we gathered in talking with them, we paid a little . . . uhh . . . visit to Professor Emils and he . . . decided . . . to confess to some incredibly horrific deeds and to blame other horrific deeds on others.

"There is still a lot that we don't know . . . that we will have to learn so we can clear Jayden of the charges lodged against him. What we have learned so far . . . or at least think we learned—and we are trusting you not to let this information leak—is that Professor T. Nagorra and Professor Emils were . . . uhhhh . . . allegedly associates in purchasing and selling drugs to students. There is also some information which leads us to believe that there are tapes . . . movies . . . of . . . of these professors with some of the female students. We think that the police have these tapes and also have confiscated a large cache of drugs.

"We want to get leads, any leads that may help us clear Jayden's name. Perhaps information about other professors who might be involved, or from whom they might buy their drugs, or perhaps which students might shed more light on what these guys were doing. We sure would like to know if these professors were extorting money or favors from the students. We also believe, from what one of the police officers let slip, that there is a great deal of money involved, possibly offshore accounts. The money had to come from something. Maybe it just came from the drugs, and maybe from something more. But if it came from the drugs alone, then there is a pretty big operation going on here that has to be stopped—from the bottom, the students, all the way to the top, the big man who only comes to campus to deliver a shipment and pick up his cash."

Both professors interjected their approval of what Matt wanted and needed to do, and while they knew that something ugly had been going on, they hadn't realized that it was so deeply imbedded or so large. "You know, I always tell my students something that Thomas Jefferson once said," Professor Doog added, "and I will paraphrase it to keep it simple: 'Tyranny can only exist when good men remain silent.' I have despoiled my own admonition by remaining silent when I suspected a problem. I am ashamed of myself."

"Please don't feel that way. Without more information, it isn't possible for any of us to make accusations or to ask someone to fix something that they might be a part of themselves. And that's why we need information, facts, right now. We have a huge family—seven men and seven women who are, as they say on TV, 'on the case' right now. We are taking turns blending in with the students, listening, following leads, and we will, with the grace of God, get to the bottom of this.

"The police appear to be understaffed . . . or they are simply satisfied with the information they already have and don't appear to be digging any deeper. But we would like to see—in addition to Jayden's name cleared, that is—we would like to see the campus completely free of this . . . these . . . drug pushing . . . dirtbags . . . and free of these kinds of . . . of biased . . . teachers . . . if one can call them that. We believe that God will help us in this endeavor. Can you, would you, be willing to give us some leads—anything that could even remotely be linked to these things—and pay closer attention to the comments and conversations of the other professors?"

Almost imperceptibly, both professors nodded to one another, and both Matt and Jim had picked up on it. Professor Doog began to speak, "We will tell you all we know and what we suspect. However, it is only that—suspicions. We have no facts . . . but at least what we say may give you the leads you need. I must reiterate, however, we are not pointing the finger at anyone because we really don't know anything for sure . . . but we too wish that the . . . uhhhh . . . deterioration that we've seen occur on this campus could be stopped. We will also gladly listen, and we might even have the opportunity to ask some questions about what others know. If we learn anything, we will let you know right away. Maybe we can exchange our cell phone numbers. But if it is all right with you, may we speak in private?"

"Absolutely! Good thinking. I am sorry that I didn't recognize the importance of that. What would you suggest? Perhaps the two of you and just two of us could talk?"

"That would be perfect. Where can we talk?"

"There is a small waiting room across the hall that is usually empty" Matt replied. "Jim and I will walk over with you, and Barbara and Sarah will stay with Rebecca if that is okay with you."

When they were seated, Professor Doog explained that about two years ago the curriculum began to change, the unity felt amongst the professors began to deteriorate, and more students seemed to be smoking pot. "These changes," he said, "appeared to occur when the College of History and Political Science hired a new dean. His name is Dean Peerca. He seemed to fall in with Professor T. Nagorra almost from his first day on campus. Dean Peerca allowed Professor T, as he prefers being called, to break the rules in many areas of school protocol. He would intervene when a student from those disciplines found himself in trouble with the local police or a complaint was filed against those students by another student, or against the professor. These complaints would somehow be 'lost'.

"Within a relatively short period of time, the campus was buzzing about Dean Peerca and how he treated those who were his 'favorites.' Shortly thereafter the campus began buzzing with talk about him hiring a famous New York designer to redecorate and remodel his home. Evidently, he also bought himself and his wife new and expensive sports cars and bragged about hiring a fashion consultant to provide them with a new wardrobe of impressive clothing. At first some of the professors joked with him about winning the lottery, but the anger this provoked made them immediately bite their tongue.

"And it might be important to know that a series of arguments broke out between the dean and a professor on his staff which resulted in the professor leaving his position here to join the staff at a college about an hour's drive from this one. The gossip grapevine said that the professor who left did so under the ultimatum to resign or be fired. He had accused the dean of ruining the lives of many students by encouraging them to use drugs and providing them with free drugs until they were . . . hooked. It was an incredibly ambitious accusation, and nothing ever came of it . . . sadly. So you might consider talking with this professor and with others who know Dean Peerca . . . maybe even talk with him directly. But for sure you might want to visit Professor Nari, the one who was forced to leave the campus."

Matt and Jim were thrilled with these important new leads and profusely thanked both professors. Professor Sendnik suggested that Matt and Jim be very careful in approaching the local police because it was rumored that there had been a payoff to someone on the police force for 'losing' documents that would have incriminated Professor T. Nagorra for something nefarious. "It may be only one police officer or many, I don't know, but you need to move very carefully."

Matt and Jim told the two professors that Jayden's stepfather Wade had been warned away from helping in the case against Professor T and Professor Emils. They wondered if the two stories were related. This would mean that they had to work fast and obtain good information themselves—info that the police, or one rogue cop, could not later suppress. They were all thinking, *There's something very wrong here.* And they all hoped that soon the campus could be free of the terrible influences they now realized had been running rampant.

The two professors also gave them the names of three students who might be able to tell them who sold the drugs on campus. They had been impressed when Matt explained that they'd decided to protect the students who would open up to them as best they could. Assuring the two professors that what they told them would never be repeated, and thanking them for what they were willing to do to clear Jayden's name and help Rebecca and Jayden complete the work and exams for this semester, they went back into Rebecca's room. The professors said their good-byes.

As soon as they left, Jim phoned Wade. When Wade heard what the professors had said, he told Jim that he'd opened his Bible before Jim called, and had just finished reading from Psalm 18:28 which said, "For thou wilt light my candle; the Lord my God will enlighten my darkness." "This is exactly what God has done for us. He has opened another avenue for us to explore."

The next day, Jim and Elizabeth went to see Dean Peerca with the excuse that they wanted to talk with him about Rebecca's options for passing the two classes that she had taken in this dean's area of supervision: more specifically Rebecca's political science class. Jim and Matt had not yet told Elizabeth what the other professors told them. They did not want to worry her or cause her to appear nervous in front of the dean. The more natural she appeared the better. Jim wanted Dean Peerca to believe that Elizabeth was just a mother, concerned about her daughter, who wanted to make everything right despite the terrible circumstances that occurred on this dean's watch.

Dean Peerca was extremely solicitous and wanted this incident to simply go away, and as for these people who he'd heard were snooping, he wanted them to go away too. *Maybe they are snooping just to get the kid passed for the semester,* he thought. *It's probably in my best interest to give them what they want to shut them up.* Dean Peerca assured them that, while he commiserated with them over Rebecca's injury, this incident was relatively harmless and that the charges against Professor T. Nagorra would surely be dropped. Then he said, "After all, he hasn't done anything that isn't done all over the country, nor has your daughter." Jim was furious. *What a sleezeball. How dare he slough this off. How dare he be so cavalier about Rebecca. This guy is as guilty as sin!* Jim thought.

The words that the dean had spoken and his demeanor gave Jim the certainty that this man was not only involved, but also had no compunction about harming the students, and was definitely covering for Professor T. His words made Jim determined to stop him in his tracks. Thinking he had pulled off the interview successfully, the dean concluded their visit by assuring Jim and Elizabeth that Rebecca would pass her political science class with flying colors. Elizabeth thanked Dean Peerca profusely, but because of what Jim knew beforehand and from what he felt about him after their conversation, Jim could not spit out even a fake "thank you."

Later, when Jim told Matt what he'd learned, they called Wade again. Wade informed the other men. They all concluded that they had found their next target.

Six of the men—Matt, Jim, Caleb, Josh, Kevin, and Wade, along with three of the women, Sarah, Barbara, and Mary—participated in a conference call to discuss what they had learned from Professor Doog, Professor Sendnik, and of course from Dean Peerca's conversation and attitude. They also discussed who would visit the professor who'd left the college for another job. His name was Professor Nari.

When Jim told them to which college and town this professor had relocated, Kevin offered to call on him because he was scheduled for a meeting the following week in a city nearby. They discussed some of the questions that Kevin might ask and made lists of what they knew and what blanks they needed to fill in. They were pleased because they felt that the information they were gathering was pointing in a similar direction.

"We need to find out who the mastermind is, which professors are involved, and what exactly they were dabbling in that brought them such big money. It would be a bonus to find out which cops, if any, may have helped them or been involved themselves and who on the force we can rely on. I wish I'd have thought to ask Emils that question when I had him running scared. Can anyone think of anything else?" Wade asked.

"How about the names of any of the students involved and to what extent they may have been involved?"

"That would be helpful too, Mary. It would be especially helpful if they have information about who sells and who the big guy is or even know something about the tapes."

"We want to keep the students out of this as much as possible—I mean, not in terms of talking to us or giving out information, but in terms of getting them in trouble—don't we?"

"Yes, definitely, because they are the real victims here . . . and maybe we should let them know how we feel about keeping their names out of it," Caleb added. "Kevin, are you getting all this down?"

"Yeah, I've got my recorder on, and I'll copy what I need when we hang up and go over it until I know it well so I'll be prepared to question Nari. I am sick to my stomach by what has been going on around this campus. It's bad enough when kids get into trouble, but it's downright disgusting if their professors are the cause."

"Sadly, I'll bet that this campus isn't the only one where this stuff occurs, but maybe it's the worst as far as the professors go . . . especially that part about the tapes. Boy, I hope we can do something about it," Josh interjected. "You know, pot was on my campus too, but usually from the outside. The students knew what was up, but they also knew that the professors would turn them in if they found out . . . and believe it or not, that kept a lot of students away from the stuff. If the school has a zero-tolerance policy but the professors don't adhere to it, then why should the students? So it's a good thing if the kids feel their professors are on the up and up."

"Okay, guys and gals," Sarah added, "while I have you on the phone, what do you think about Matt and I packing up some of Grandma's Christmas things and using them to decorate Rebecca's hospital room and we all spend Christmas eve and Christmas day there together? Let's hope Rebecca will be home by then, so this is just a contingency plan—and we can wait to actually put it into effect until a few days before Christmas—but I need to know ahead of time so we can prepare. Whatta ya think?"

"That's a great idea, Sarah. We'll all be together, and Rebecca's room will feel like home. We'll all help, and we can all make a special dish to bring from home. The rooms we usually take have that mini-kitchen and a pretty good-sized refrigerator and freezer, and every patient floor of the hospital has two microwaves in the little juice room, so we could swing it."

"Okay, plans set. Kevin, phone us as soon after speaking with Professor Nari as you can. We'll be sitting on pins and needles to learn whether or not you obtained any leads. Love you all. So long."

Kevin had phoned Professor Nari to make an appointment with him. He seemed hesitant to meet with Kevin at first, but when Kevin explained that Professor Doog and Professor Sendnik recommended that they meet, he was more obliging. When Kevin arrived, the professor remained quiet, not committing himself until Kevin finished his first few sentences. Kevin had quickly explained that he was the stepfather of the girl, a freshman at the college, who lay in a coma; that Jayden, also a freshman and a friend of Rebecca's, had been falsely accused of selling drugs; and that Professor T. Nagorra and Professor Emils had been arrested and appeared to be the source of the problem. Still not sure that Professor Nari would open up to him, Kevin added that he brought a message from Professor Doog. "Professor Doog sends you a personal message that he said you would understand and said that if he used his normal paraphrase you would know that it came directly from him. He wanted me to tell you, 'Tyranny exists only when good men refuse to act.'"

It worked. Professor Nari stood and walked from behind his desk and began to circle the room with his hands behind his back and his head down. He hesitated, swallowed hard, hesitated again, but then he began to speak. "It started about two years ago. I wanted to speak with Dean Peerca about teaching one of the summer classes, but when I arrived at his outer office, I saw that the door to his inner office was closed. I could hear voices through the open transom over the door so I knew he was there and decided to wait. I recognized Peerca's voice, and soon thereafter I also recognized Professor T. Nagorra's voice. As I sat in the outer office, I realized that the transom over the closed door carried their voices quite clearly so I concentrated and could easily understand what they said.

"Nagorra was yelling, telling Peerca that he was taking too much profit and that Nagorra was the one who took all the risks and did all the dirty work. He told Peerca that he was the one who had to meet 'the kingpin' to pick up the drugs, and he was the one who had to phone for a new supply, and he was the one who had to travel there with the money and back to the campus with the drugs, and he was the one who had to store their supply of drugs.

"Peerca asked him where he'd be today if he hadn't funded him and put him in contact with the kingpin in the first place. Then Nagorra told him that Emils was also asking for more money—a better split—because he was the one recruiting the students who would sell. Nagorra demanded that Peerca raise both their takes by 5 percent saying that would only diminish Peerca's take by 10 percent. He also said that Peerca shouldn't forget that Nagorra had the tapes. Peerca was angry but said that he would think about it.

"Then Nagorra stormed out of the inner office and stopped short when he saw me. He stared at me for a moment, then called out to Peerca telling him that he had a snoop in his outer office. Peerca came out of his office and also stared at me. He looked around, and when he saw the open transom, he threatened me, threatened my job, even threatened my family saying that, if I ever repeated anything that I might have heard, I'd be hurt . . . and maybe my family would disappear. I was shocked . . . and so intimidated by his threats that I pretended that I hadn't heard anything. I adamantly insisted that I'd come to the dean to ask if I could teach one of the summer classes and asked why they were upset with me. Then I followed through on my request for the summer work so he wouldn't suspect me. He calmed down and said something to the effect of being embarrassed that I could have heard him speak harshly to one of his professors, and he didn't want anyone to know that he'd lost his temper. I nodded, said that I could understand that, and reiterated that I did notice that a voice was raised but hadn't heard any argument.

"I kept quiet. I was afraid to speak up, thinking that, without proof, no one would believe me. The dean and the professor were tenured, I wasn't, so I'd lose either way . . . you understand how the tenure system works. Surprisingly, a few months later, 'proof' just fell into my hands. It was a total surprise. I was walking along the pathway between two of the campus buildings on my way to the parking lot intending to go home when Nagorra ran right into me. I'm so much taller and broader than he is that when he bumped into me with such force, he fell. I was fine. He was okay too but embarrassed. He'd been carrying a couple of large rectangular boxes.

"To this day I remember that I could smell the pot when the force of the box hitting the pavement released some of the odor of its contents. Nagorra was indignant . . . angry with me and probably mortified by his fall . . . and began yelling at me, telling me to watch where I was walking, blaming me for bumping into him. He got himself up, then picked up his boxes and left. But lying on the walkway was a navy blue vinyl folder with a zippered top. I picked it up and called to him. But he was too far away to hear me, and I was tired and angry with him, so I just took it with me and went home planning to return it to him the next day. Curious because I had smelled the pot, when I arrived home, I went through the papers in the folder and found a list of his drug purchases, the date of each purchase, and how much he'd paid for each of them. The papers were labeled 'Merchandise'.

"Within perhaps ten or fifteen minutes, my doorbell rang. I quickly stuffed the papers back in the folder and zipped it shut. I placed the folder under my briefcase as if it had never been opened and went to the door. Both Nagorra and Peerca stood on my doorstep. Accompanying them was a police officer. I never got his name, but I'd recognize him if I saw him again. They gave me a cock-and-bull story about a sting operation that I'd interfered with and demanded that I hand over the envelope that Nagorra had dropped when I 'knocked him down.'

"I pretended that I was just about to call him. I told them that as I gathered myself together to resume my walk to the parking lot I saw that he'd dropped a folder. I told them that I'd called to Nagorra, but he hadn't heard my call and was already entering the door to his office building. I explained that I decided to take the folder home, call him and tell him I would bring it to him the next day. If he needed it right way, he could come and get it or I would bring it over after dinner.

"I told them that I'd just walked in the door and had dropped my briefcase and the folder in my home office and then I turned to lead them to the folder. They followed me, saw the position of the briefcase and the folder, grabbed the folder from underneath the briefcase, and turned to warn me that I'd better keep quiet about what had just occurred. I did. They seemed satisfied that the folder hadn't been opened. They believed my story. But as time went on, my guilt soared.

"Then a few months later a student died from an overdose, and I wondered if it had been from something that these . . . these . . . pigs had sold them. And then I wondered if I could have prevented that student's death if I had just said something. I agonized over it. Finally I went to the police and told an officer what I had seen and experienced. He took my statement, and a few days later that same cop who had accompanied Nagorra and Peerca when they came to my home rang my doorbell. When I opened the door, the police officer stepped into my foyer, stared at me for a long moment, and then arrogantly pulled my statement from his pocket and looking at me, slowly and deliberately ripped it into pieces and dropped the pieces one by one on my rug. He said that if I pulled anything like that again, my kids would disappear. I changed jobs. I was a coward. But when I moved, I vowed that I would never be a coward again."

Kevin slumped in his seat, horrified by Professor Nari's tale. The professor walked back to his desk and sank, exhausted, into the chair with his head in his hands and elbows on his desk. "I'll help you. I'll tell what I know. But you can't go to the local police station unless you can be sure that you are talking with a good cop, a courageous cop, one willing to turn a bad cop in for being on the take, a fellow officer."

"We'll go higher up when we are ready. Hang in there for now. We are going to nail them, and we are getting close to having enough evidence to do so. We now have three well-respected professors willing to tell what they saw, heard, or suspected. We also have two professors who are under arrest and have already admitted to some pretty heavy wrongdoing. Even if they get out on bail, which we doubt they will, they will have to appear in court. They will talk if they believe that they will get a lighter sentence or can blame their deeds on someone else. But we really want to get the so-called kingpin, and with him we'll also get enough on Peerca so he won't be able to claim that he didn't know what the others were doing. When we do get them, they will be off campus forever. Do you have any shred of information about who this kingpin is?"

"No, but I do know of a student who was once involved but has really turned his life around. I wouldn't want him implicated by name . . . but he accompanied Nagorra on a pickup and knows the car and maybe even the license plate of the person who handed the merchandise over to Nagorra that one time. I can call him and ask him if he'll help. But only if I have your word that his name stays out of this."

"That's a deal! We hope to keep all student names out of this. Thanks, Professor, you won't be sorry that you helped us. We will try to keep your name out of this too . . . we'll try."

"You don't have to worry about that. I want to vindicate myself and make up for all this time when I should have spoken up and I didn't. This is something I need to do, and if my name stays out of it, great, but if my testimony is needed, you can count on me."

The two men shook hands, and Kevin told the professor that he was a good man. The professor wished Kevin good luck and great speed in getting the job done, and Kevin went back to his hotel room to call Wade. Wade was ecstatic and quickly phoned the others and told them the good news. They expected to hear from Professor Nari as soon as he could speak with the student who may have additional information—possibly by tomorrow—and then they could make further headway.

Chaldeth, of course, was again beside himself with fury. He couldn't seem to stop this parade of horrible failures, terrible setbacks, to his plan. He was so angry that he resorted to petty little attacks to spend his fury. He caused a huge nail to flatten Professor Nari's tire so he'd be late to work the next day. He'd caused Jim to drop his favorite cup and watch it break into a million pieces. He'd gotten Sarah to burn her finger on the oven, and he'd made Matt's watch stop and cause him to miss a meeting. He'd given Kevin a debilitating head cold. *But what can these things do to stop these snooping little wimps from ruining my plans?* It was time, again, for Chaldeth to regroup.

Meanwhile, Dean Peerca had been feeling uneasy about Nagorra's arrest and decided to visit him to assure himself that Nagorra would remain quiet until his release on bail. He dressed in his usual ostentatious manner. He dangled the cane from his wrist that he didn't need but felt made him stand out from the crowd, and with the hairdo that had given him the nickname of the "Silver Fox," he paraded into Nagorra's cell acting the part of his concerned employer. When the guard had distanced himself from them, he began to address to Nagorra.

"Are you keeping your mouth shut? Do you realize that we can get you off if you do? I have everything prepared for you to simply disappear to your favorite destination—you know, where all your money is hidden, where wine, women, and a beautiful beach and sunny days prevail?"

"You better get me outta here or I am gonna sing like a canary, you understand? What took you so long to get here? I want outta here. If I have to stay here much longer, you are gonna join me. You should be in here more than me. When am I gonna be out?"

"You will be out within the week. You just keep your mouth closed. Is there anyone else who knows anything? Anyone else I should visit to shut them up?"

"Maybe you should go see Durk. He is an easy mark: stupid, does what I say, worships me. He'll be quiet, you can count on him. But we'll have to do something for him—get him out too, or just graduate him, give him some money or something."

"I didn't ask you what to do about anyone. I asked you if anyone knows anything. So tell me, what does he know?"

"Well . . . not too much. He knows I buy the stuff . . . you know, go through town to the abandoned shop outside of town to meet some bigwig. But he doesn't know who I meet. Durk sells some pot to the guys he knows, but he doesn't sell the hard stuff or the date rape stuff. He's clean himself except for the occasional smoke. He does know where I stash the stuff though, and he knows . . . well . . . ."

"What? What does he know? Tell me . . . it's important"

"Well, he knows about Rebecca. You know, that student who, uhmmm . . . uhhh . . . you know . . . was found outside my office?"

"You mean the one in a coma? You mean you had something to do with that? I thought the other kid did that because he got jealous of Durk?"

"No, Jayden wasn't even around. It was just Durk and me . . . and I didn't mean for it to happen . . . for it . . . ."

"For what to happen? What? You better level with me or I can't help you."

"Geez, stop yelling. It was just that I, well, I . . . I hit her . . . I mean . . . you know, it was just an accident. I had to shut her up . . . I didn't mean for her to fall and hit her head."

"My God, what have you done? If she dies, we'll all be in trouble. You have to get out of here. You have to make a run for the islands. I'll make sure you have plenty of money . . . a regular supply, in fact, but you have to get out of the country."

"You have to get me outta here first."

"What does Durk know about this, about Rebecca?"

"I'm not sure, but he kind of yelled at her because she was telling him to get out of the drug business and . . . then he was all solicitous and . . . and when she started to leave she was mad at him, so he tried to hold her back because she said she was going to tell someone about the drug selling unless he promised to stop . . . so I . . . I . . . I came into the office and . . . well . . ."

"What? Well what? Where were you that you could hear what they said, or could see them, and then decide to come in? Where?"

"Well, you know, I like to tape them . . . you know . . . just hoping for a little excitement . . . so I was at the camera in the outer office and heard them and decided I should come in when she threatened to tell . . . and then I . . . I just . . . well, I hit her . . . hard I think . . . because she had started yelling! She fell, hit her head . . . twice, I think."

"If she fell in your office, why was she found two offices down from yours?"

"I . . . I . . . I was afraid that . . . she . . . I just needed her outta there in case . . . you know . . . in case, that's all. So I dragged her out into the hall, tidied the office and went home, took Durk with me for an alibi. Durk thought . . . thought . . . well . . . maybe that he hit her or shoved her off balance or that she tripped . . . and I . . . well, I let him think that."

"Good, then if she dies, Durk will take the rap, or that other kid, Jayden, but you gotta get out. If you don't, the big boys will silence you. You have to go, you understand?"

"Yeah, okay, but only as long as you give me the money."

"Don't worry, you'll get it and your plane tickets and a fake passport too. You'll also have the personal stash you've been putting into your offshore account, so don't cry poor to me."

"How did you know about that?"

"You bragged about it to me, stupid. Now call the guard. I've got to go and make arrangements for you to be released. Remember, as soon as you are released, grab the stuff I'll have ready for you and run. They will be coming back for you, so run. Understand? I'll go talk to Durk."

With those instructions, Dean Peerca left and Professor T. Nagorra buried himself in thoughts of his favorite island and all the money he'd been saving all these years for this very day in case something ever went wrong.

Professor Peerca was close to hysteria when he left Professor T. Nagorra. He hadn't known how deeply Nagorra and Durk were involved in what had happened to that girl. His thoughts ran rampant with possible scenarios of what could happen next. If she died and the drug charges became murder charges, Nagorra and Durk would never get out of prison and then they would sing like birds. He had to think.

Peercas went to his favorite restaurant for a good meal and some relaxation so he could calm down and take time to think. He had to be careful. Again he considered his options. *Nagorra knows too much, and he is so stupid that he could easily say the wrong thing and implicate me. I need to do something about him. But what? I can probably pull a few strings and get him released on bail, even put up the bail money myself . . . No no no, that won't do because I'll lose it when he runs. Or I can take my chances and just deny anything either of them might say . . . No, no, too much of a risk. Or I can tell the kingpin that he has to shut them up or they will sing and implicate him. Yeah, that's it. I'll let the kingpin do the dirty work: either get them released or . . . silence them. Actually, it would be best for me . . . if they were silenced forever . . . and let that other kid . . . Jayden . . . take the rap for everything else.*

Chaldeth saw an opportunity. If Nagorra could get away or was even silenced forever, then perhaps Chaldeth could keep the charges that had been lodged against Jayden in full force; and if Rebecca died, maybe Chaldeth could have Jayden blamed for her death. Then he'd have his revenge after all. *Maybe I should help Nagorra get away, or better yet, help Peerca silence Nagorra. Maybe I can bring that family down after all . . . despite their meddling.*

Meanwhile, Chaldeth kept the pressure on the family by causing a thousand and one little inconveniences while he planned the greater destruction for them. He knew that Sarah wanted to turn Rebecca's room into a "Grandma Christmas" for the family to enjoy. To satisfy his cruel temperament and need for immediate gratification, Chaldeth caused Sarah to drop one of her precious boxes as she descended the attic stairs carrying too many items at one time. As she looked down in horror at the crushed boxes below her, Chaldeth wrenched her hand off the rail and she fell too.

Sarah fell on top of one of the boxes, having bounced off the remaining steps, and she landed on her right hip with her right leg up in the air hooked around the last spindle of the railing along the stairs. Chaldeth hoped that something was broken. At first Sarah couldn't move because the pain was so great. Within a few minutes some of the pain ebbed along with the shock she'd sustained from the fall. She gingerly extricated her foot from between the spindles, and while it hurt, she didn't think it was broken. She realized that since she could move her leg without excruciating pain, most likely her hip wasn't broken either. She waited another few minutes and then took her cell phone from her pocket and called Mary who she knew was at home just across the street. Mary came running, opening the front door with the key she kept in her own house. "Are you okay? Should I call an ambulance?"

"No, Mary, I'm pretty sure that I'm okay. Would you help me to the chair? Then I can see how much I might be hurt, maybe check for swelling, make sure that I have the ability to move all parts—everything, you know . . ."

"Okay, but if you really hurt anywhere, please let me call for an ambulance. Should I phone Matt? Where's Jason?"

"No, actually, I'm okay. I'll probably just have lots of bruises in the morning and maybe a sprained ankle. Jason is sleeping soundly. Nap time. I see that you didn't bring Teddy, so is Kevin at home? Can you stay a minute . . . . can we have a cup of tea together?"

"Yes, Kevin is at home. Do you want me to pick up these boxes and move them away from the stairway? Gosh, some of these boxes are crushed. Anything precious in them?"

"Yes, I fell on them and they broke my fall. They are Grandma's Christmas decorations, but I'm hoping that it's just the boxes that are damaged and not the contents. Just push them to the side so the hallway is clear if you don't mind. Matt and I can go through the boxes tonight, and maybe he can repair anything that is damaged."

"Okay, then when I get that done, I'll go get our tea."

When they sat together to sip the warm liquid and nibble on the cookies that Mary had also brought from Sarah's kitchen, Mary said, "Sarah, I think that all of us are being attacked—every one of us. I think that it's a good sign—a sign of anger on the part of the attackers. I think that it means that Rebecca will be okay and Jayden will be exonerated! I never thought I'd celebrate an attack, but here I am. I guess, though, that we'd all better pray even harder for protection. I don't want to make light of this, you know. I realize the danger. But somehow it reminds me of a spoiled child having a tantrum and we're the target of that tantrum."

"I think that you are right on all fronts, Mary. But we mustn't make light of it . . . this is a dangerous and powerful force. However, you know what, we're gonna just carry on with our plans and keep asking for God's blessing on what we are trying to do, and He will protect us."

"That's true. Oh, Sarah, I am so thankful for the day that God brought us together and you helped me learn what was really important in life. I've been thinking of trying to put a melody to the words of that poem you gave me when I was so despondent. You know, the one your grandmother wrote that put into poetry the story of the footprints in the sand? Remember?"

"Yes, I do, and I know it by heart:

Where Were You?

Lord, I saw some footprints
impressed upon the ground
and recognized one pair was mine,
the others, Yours I found.

I saw then that You walked so close,
and shared my joyous days.
I felt assured of kinship,
and of all Your loving ways.

But then, there came another day,
one filled with great despair,
and I asked, 'Oh God, Where are You?'
for the footprints were one pair.

'Do I really walk this path alone?
Where are You in my pain?
What did I do to make You leave?
How can my soul make gain?'

And gently then, the Lord said,
'I never left you child,

I carried you safely in My arms;
those are My prints through the wild.'"

"Beautiful, Sarah! You should recite it again to the others. It's exactly what we need to hang on to: that even if we struggle to solve the problems we have encountered, God is carrying us through them."

"Yes, let's do that because I too am always strengthened to remember that even when we think we're alone we are not. There's also a scripture that speaks about God helping us and also speaks about punishing the evil that has harmed us. Let me find it." And Sarah reached for the Bible on the table next to the chair she sat in, and using her concordance to locate where the verse could be found, she opened the Bible. "Here it is in Revelation 21:7, 8, 'He that overcometh shall inherit all things; and I will be his God, and he shall be my son. But the fearful, and unbelieving, and the abominable, and murderers, and whoremongers, and sorcerers, and idolaters, and all liars, shall have their part in the lake which burneth with fire and brimstone; which is the second death.'"

Chapter 12

And Then They Asked God

When Mary left, Sarah began thinking about the strange multitude of inconveniences that each one of them had been experiencing. Her thoughts ran primarily to how naïve they had been. None of them had realized the scope of danger that Jayden and Rebecca might face when they left for college. *Certainly there are circumstances, or perhaps it is better described as "coincidences of life," where things happen in threes or happen often and then all is well again, but this is different. Jayden and Rebecca obviously walked into a nest of vipers when they went off to college. And we'd had absolutely no clue. We saw the campus as a quiet, sleepy little college town and assumed—yes, assumed—that there were, well . . . watchdogs who would look after the welfare of the young people under their care. We'd also been so sure that we had prepared Rebecca and Jayden for what they would face. We hadn't thought about a personal attack from the spirits of this world . . . and we should have.*

Sarah had been horrified by Kara's story about how Professor Emils had personally attacked Rebecca in front of the whole class. *It wasn't right for him to do such a thing or to threaten to fail her for her remarks. What kind of a person would do such a thing? Weren't those with so-called higher learning supposed to exercise self control, care about their students, and be a role model to them? Weren't they supposed to know better? And how creepy that he wanted to meet with her alone at night to discuss what she could do to alleviate her failing grade after she'd had straight As in his class!*

What are parents supposed to do? How can we protect our children? We can't put them under lock and key forever—we have to let them go. Maybe we are to teach them with a far greater emphasis that the world they will enter is filled with evil. How sad. If I'd gone to college with such a strong warning, I'd have been jumping in fear at every turn. Is this what we can expect for all our children? But what else can we do? We have to warn them.

Jason was still sleeping, but as Sarah looked at him, at his perfect beautiful little face, it hurt to think that he would have to stop trusting as he did now. *He'll have to suspect everything someday. He'll never be able to act spontaneously, impulsively. He will have to be cautious, careful, always on guard. What a terrible way to live.* And Sarah felt the tears slipping down her cheeks for the losses that she now knew her son would have to endure . . . and all because the morality of the world was falling apart.

When Matt came home early because of Sarah's fall, she asked him if they could talk for a while. She explained how heavy her heart felt. "Matt, evil is blatantly thriving all around our children. Our children are walking into a viper's nest every time they leave the confines of the family, and I don't know what we can do to protect them. I'm frightened for Jason, for Jayden and Rebecca, for every child."

"Sadly, I have to say that it is a good thing that you are frightened, Sarah. We should all be frightened! But what's even worse is that not every parent *is* as concerned as they should be because they have no clue about the danger and activity of evil. Few parents warn their kids, prepare them for what the world offers. Sarah, sometimes I want to grab the people I meet by the shoulders and shake them. So many simply have no idea about how evil works and don't want to know! They've never read the Bible, so they think you're el nutso if you talk about evil as a . . . a . . . an entity . . . out there stalking your kids. They are clueless, and that makes their kids clueless too. I mean, it's like never teaching your kids that if you stand in the middle of the train track when a train is bearing down on you, you will be killed. Or that if you touch a hot stove, you'll be burned . . . and it will *hurt*, maybe even scar you for life! If you don't know something, you can't act accordingly! It really frustrates me."

"You're right, Matt. I always felt that even if there was a remote chance that something could harm someone, they should be taught about it. So even if I wasn't *sure* about something, like the devil, I'd at least warn my kids."

"Yeah, but, Sarah, the parents don't even know. They never even heard of the devil or evil except as some made-up fantasy or from some movie. They are clueless, so they can't, even if they wanted to, they can't warn their kids! And then they too have to suffer the consequences of what befalls their kids. They wring their hands in despair when bad stuff happens. I mean, gee, Sarah, they can't even get help, because they don't know what happened or who to turn to. God wants to help, but they don't ask because they again have no clue about God and what He can do or how to tap into His help! Gosh, that's sad. And you know what's even worse? Those who try to turn to God are the ones most often attacked. Those who are godless can be left alone unless those spirits want to use them to harm someone who does turn to God. That's why this political correctness is harming us too!"

"Matt, what should all of us do? We all feel that we are in the midst of something very evil, and maybe we should use this opportunity to talk about this with everyone, even with our little ones. Maybe we can't help people in general, but we surely can help our family and our friends."

"That's a good idea, Sarah. Let's bring it up when we all meet again. The Bible tells us that we are living in the end times and that evil will become even more powerful. We will talk about this and see what we might need to do to prepare our kids, and maybe even talk about how we can help others. By the way, are the plans for Christmas still on? Are we all going to spend Christmas with Rebecca and Elizabeth at the hospital?"

"Yes. Actually, I think that everyone is planning to take a few days vacation before Christmas so we can decorate together, and while we are doing that we hope to talk about each item that had belonged to Grandma, you know . . . . how she used that item in her home, maybe when or why she bought it . . . . and we will try to engage Rebecca. We were thinking that the way she's always loved Christmas and loved the ethereal way we all decorated for Christmas, if she thought she could open her eyes and see her surroundings being transformed, she might awaken. If we will all be there a few days before Christmas, we are going to order a Christmas dinner for all of us from a private caterer who is the sister of one of the nurses rather than try to cook ahead of time and bring everything from home as we originally planned."

"That's a good idea. I was worried about how we'd store and reheat and wash up, so that will be a lot easier and give us more time for one another. I like the idea of engaging Rebecca in the decorating process. We have to figure out how we can do more of that. She just *has* to snap out of the coma. She just has to. We'll be going to the hospital again on Saturday so we can talk with the others when we get there."

Josh and Deb also left Saturday morning to drive to the hospital, and as they traveled, they too talked about how naïve they'd been not to think that the enemy who'd stalked Grandma all those years would not jump at the chance to stalk this new generation. When they arrived at the hospital and walked into Rebecca's room to greet Elizabeth, they were pleasantly surprised to find Ken, Kara, and Jayden engaged in a lively discussion of the power of evil and how to overcome it. The teenagers had gathered around Rebecca's bed and were incredibly innovative as they laughed and teased to make their points. It was obvious that each had carefully prepared what they would say and had wanted to make their presentation a time of fun for everyone. It was also obvious that they had searched their concordances because they had so much information to impart.

Elizabeth and John felt that they were watching a delightful little play as they watched these youngsters and had pulled their chairs into a position that gave them the best view of the production. After opening the play with Ken, Kara, and Jayden reciting some of the scriptures describing Satan's work and abilities, Ken began acting the part of evil. Jayden played a good angel, and Kara played the innocent damsel being pulled in two directions. Having an audience made them ham it up a bit, but they were right on target with their information. Deb and Josh also pulled chairs next to Elizabeth and John so they could watch the teens perform.

Kara, Jayden, and Ken created little signs to give their "audience" an idea of what to expect in their three-part play. The first part was to be the seduction of Kara by the evil Ken, the second part was to be the warning Kara received from the good angel Jayden, and the third part was to enact the jeopardy and rescue of Kara. First each of them, in costume, paraded around the room holding their computer-generated signs which read:

PART ONE:

THE SEDUCTION

PART TWO:

THE WARNING

PART THREE:

THE RESCUE

A few minutes after the little play began, Matt, Sarah, and Jason also arrived, and they too turned their chairs to watch. Halfway through part one, two nurses who were just ending their shift, and a physician making his rounds also lingered near the entrance door. Mary and Kevin arrived with Teddie, and soon the room was filled and everyone settled down to watch the creative little production.

Ken's costume was comprised of a fake mustache and a black cowboy hat, and he wore a cape fashioned from a sheet with which he occasionally hid part of his face. Kara wore an old-fashioned white bonnet with a huge bow at her neck, bright red lipstick that formed her mouth into a perfect heart, and tied a sheet around her waist to fashion a long skirt. She batted her eyelashes trying to look innocent and unaware of Ken's malevolence. "Good evening, young lady," Ken began. "You look lovely, so fresh and young and innocent." And then Ken turned aside and whispered to the audience, including Rebecca, "Kara is a perfect target for me. I will capture her and fill her with my evil. Hee hee hee hee." Then he turned to Kara and said, "My dear sweet innocent girl, come with me and I will give you riches and fame and keep your beauty alive forever."

Kara batted her eyelashes, obviously flattered by Ken's attention, and replied, "Do you really think I am beautiful?" Then she turned to Rebecca whispering as loud as she could, "Oh, Rebecca, I've been *so* protected all my life, and I've *never* had anyone pay attention to me like this. Shall I follow this handsome man? Will I be okay? I've never been taught to recognize evil, but he doesn't look evil!"

Jayden, in a white Fedora hat and a set of wings they had fashioned from cardboard which they had strapped to his back, walked up behind Kara and in a loud whisper over her shoulder and into her ear, said "Watch out, Kara. Beware! Ken is evil. He is out to *get* you. You are vulnerable . . . beware!" And Jayden then turned to Rebecca saying, "Rebecca, help me. We have to warn Kara about the spirits of this world. She doesn't understand!"

The play continued with Ken acting out the various powers of evil which they had previously read to the audience, and Kara succumbing to Ken's malevolent charm despite Jayden's attempts to warn her. Then Ken recited the words from Isaiah 14:13-14 saying, "I will ascend into heaven, I will exalt my throne above the stars of God; I will sit also upon the mount of the congregation, in the sides of the north; I will ascend above the heights of the clouds, I will be like the most High."

Jayden confronted Ken and pushed Kara behind him in an effort to protect her and spoke to Ken in a loud voice saying, "God has said in Isaiah 14:15, "Yet thou shalt be brought down to hell, to the sides of the pit." Then Jayden turned to Kara and said, "Remember, innocent Kara, God warns you in Revelation 12:9, 'The Devil, and Satan, which deceiveth the whole world . . . ' so you must do as it says in Isaiah 55:6, 'Seek ye the Lord while he may be found, call ye upon him while he is near.'"

Kara obediently folded her hands in prayer, and as she stood in that position, Ken tried to grab her hands to prevent her from praying, but the angel Jayden knocked his hand aside each time he reached for her. Ken turned to the audience saying, "I cannot touch her while she prays. I lose my power when she prays. She wears the armor of God! Oh, I am doomed to failure."

Jayden pushed Ken aside and said, "Yes, the armor of God is prayer, love, learning God's words, repenting your sins, availing yourself of all the sacraments God offers. With these, evil is thwarted!" And with those words, Ken fell to the floor defeated and the play ended. Then the three stood shoulder to shoulder to bow to their audience. "Come on, Rebecca, take your bow with us," Jayden added.

When the applause subsided, Jayden asked everyone to stand to pray. He prayed mainly for Rebecca, but also for all of them and the circumstances that they were living through asking God to bind the forces of evil that were attacking them. Jayden then thanked his family for their support and for working so hard to find the real culprits. They were all grateful that they had come together to help one another and that they had God on their side. They had begun to make inroads toward solving the problems that Jayden faced. They knew that it was because God was directing their steps toward those who could help them.

One day before the play, Jayden's stepdad Wade and his Uncle Jim had visited the president of the university. They wanted to see if there was a chance that this man could be trusted. He would be a great asset to them if he turned out to be one of the good guys. They wanted to ask him if he was familiar with what had happened to Rebecca and Jayden, describe their perfect grades, proclaim Jayden's innocence, and simply tell him that the family wanted to clear Jayden's name. Then they would sit and listen to how he would respond.

Both Wade and Jim had greeted him warmly when they met, hoping for the best. They shook hands firmly and were glad to receive a firm handshake in return. They came on strong, spoke their piece about their desire to exonerate Jayden and asked, "Can you help?" and then sat back to listen. They could see that President Legna was sizing them up just as they were him. He spoke hesitantly at first, telling them that he was aware of what happened and was in fact in the process of composing a letter to Elizabeth. To prove his point, he lifted a single piece of paper from his desk and handed it to Wade. They were impressed.

He went on to say that he was sorry about what had happened to Rebecca and that when he had phoned the hospital, he'd learned that there was a good chance that she would emerge from her coma. He told them that he was going to conduct a full investigation and that he too, given Jayden's performance at the college, his high school record, and his impressive list of extracurricular activities, was sure that Jayden was innocent. He told them that he'd reviewed their records and noted that Jayden and Rebecca had been very active in their church, in religious youth activities, and in various outreach programs. He'd also been contacted by two professors who vociferously supported Jayden's innocence and wanted both Jayden and Rebecca to receive full credit for the semester.

"I believe that neither Rebecca nor Jayden have done any of the things that some suggest, and that they are completely innocent of any wrongdoing. I too want them to get full credit for this semester. I believe that nefarious activities have been conducted by some of the professors at this university, and I will see them punished. I have some irons in the fire, but I cannot disclose these at this time." Then President Legna hesitated and looked carefully at Jim and Wade. After what seemed a long time, he appeared to make up his mind about something and then began to speak again.

"I can only tell you that God will be with you and that I pray that He will help me get to the bottom of this. I will ask you to remember God's words in Isaiah 54:7, 'For a small moment have I forsaken thee; but with great mercies will I gather thee.' I believe that with God, with faith, with our prayers, we can clean up this campus, and I promise you that I will watch more carefully, and I will pray and tithe more for this university in the future."

Jim and Wade looked at one another and nodded to one another. This was their signal that they should tell this man all they knew and try to engage him in their efforts. Wade began, "Thanks for those words. It has given us a reason to trust you even though we have learned that there is a faction here on campus which we cannot trust, and sadly, we have also learned that there may be some on the police force who cannot be trusted. We've been busy. We've talked to professors, to students, and extensively to Jayden as well as Jayden and Rebecca's roommates. We've been able to uncover an incredible amount of information."

"If you will share what you know with me, it will help me move forward. Please do trust me. I need to know what you have learned so I can rid this campus of the evil influence that I now realize exists here. I can really use your help."

"We too believe that God will bring us through this, and we believe that He has guided us to the information we have been able to garner. We'd rather not have the local police in on this just yet because we are very close to having so much information that there is not much chance that these creeps can get away with what they've done. But we do need help. Do you have a source, outside of the local police, who has the authority to watch, follow, tape anyone if we can show you what evidence we have that warrants such attention?"

"Yes, I do. I have had some of the same suspicions that you mention, and I have already contacted a friend of mine who has a high position in the government. He put me in touch with another gentleman and told that gentleman to listen carefully to what I'd learned and to follow through. He is with the Drug Enforcement Agency. Actually, I am meeting with him here in about an hour. If you can tell me what you know and then stay, I'd like you to join that discussion."

Again, Wade and Jim nodded to one another and Wade replied, "Absolutely, thanks. Well, here's what we know." And Wade and Jim filled him in and watched his face change with intermittent frowns and grimaces and saw the shock in his eyes. But as their story wound down, his eyes lit up with the prospect of believing that they had enough information to end the horror that had come to his beloved university. He thanked Wade and Jim profusely and marveled aloud at their prowess and determination. His face beamed to know that he had such fine and caring professors in Professors Doog and Sendnik and felt badly for the good professor they'd lost to another school over these troubles. Then he stood and asked the two men if they could all pray. He said that he wanted to humbly ask God for His intercession during the upcoming meeting and ask Him to help them bring this situation to a conclusion. He asked Wade to pray first, then Jim. When it was President Legna's turn to pray, he added a request that God would heal Rebecca before Christmas. Wade and Jim were so thankful that God had placed this man in this position at a time when they needed someone like him—a godly man!

Wade and Jim told Jayden about their visit with the president. Jayden was thrilled to learn that they had another ally. They decided that they would not mention anything about the investigation to anyone outside of the family and say only that the president would be helping Jayden and Rebecca obtain what they needed to complete the semester. Now they could all lay aside their anxieties knowing that something was being done, and they could try to enjoy Christmas at the hospital.

They knew that great plans had been made to decorate the hospital room with Grandma's Christmas items.

Before Mary, Kevin and Teddie, and Matt, Sarah, and Jason left for the hospital that weekend, Mary and Kevin helped carry a slew of boxes to Matt's truck. The boxes contained many of Grandma's Christmas decorations. They'd painstakingly gone through all the items and chose those that would best fit the dimensions of the hospital room. Nothing had been broken that could not easily be repaired when some of the boxes had fallen, and Sarah had fallen on top of them. Sarah was relieved. Her ankle was fine too.

They had all agreed to help to make Rebecca's hospital room look like home and to fill it with the beautiful items that always brought the family so much joy, especially since they were a reminder of the wonderful Christmases they had spent with Grandma. They would decorate with Grandma's Divine Proportion and Monkey Swing concept.

They decided to create a village of miniature houses and trees and people and to bring a bookcase to display the village in the same manner that Grandma had displayed her creation. If they did this, Rebecca could see it from her bed. They brought a train set to place under the tree along with its different style and much smaller houses. Matt built a heavy-duty stand to which he could attach a huge wall mirror without damaging the walls of the hospital room. This would be outlined with garlands and lights and hold from its two top corners the two foot tall gold angels with billowing sleeves. It would also reflect all the Christmas lights in the room.

As they unpacked the items they wanted to use, Sarah spoke about their Christmases with Grandma. "On two forty-eight-inch shelves of her bookcases she would create a village of ceramic houses and shops, which had sidewalks of miniature bricks filled with people and gates and fences. There was a miniature park with a skating pond and skaters, and pine trees and snow-covered streets with old-fashioned automobiles and a horse and carriage. There were chestnut vendors, puppies, old men on benches under ornate lanterns, and yet every year it was arranged a little bit differently."

"Let's put Grandma's sled and reindeer on Rebecca's window sill, and I think we can also fit the Santa playing a fiddle and the Christmas elves with the tiny gifts. We'll place it on a garland and use the miniature lights under and around it and then add the tiny packages, teddy bears, sleds, rocking horses, and snowman. But where shall we place the huge Nativity scene? The papier-mache figures are two feet tall!"

"We brought one of our long folding tables so we could place the Nativity along the back of the table and use the front for our buffet."

"Perfect, and we can place pine garlands around the Nativity and place the Nativity on the large beautiful tablecloth that will completely cover the table! And we can put the table on the wall opposite the window so Rebecca will have something special to see no matter which way her heads turns!"

"Oh, wouldn't it be wonderful to have Rebecca awaken to so many beautiful expressions of Christmas surrounding her?"

"Definitely. And we'll pray that, before the end of Christmas day, we'll have Rebecca back. I just read this morning, in Isaiah 42:6, 'I the Lord have called thee in righteousness, and will hold thine hand, and will keep thee . . .'"

They looked forward to placing all the decorations around Rebecca's room. They would spend the weekend with her and then travel back home for a few days, and then two days before Christmas they would return to the hospital once again. Elizabeth and John would stay with Rebecca. As they thought about Rebecca and prayed for her, Rebecca too was thinking, and fighting to rise above the dark clouds that kept her from responding to those she loved.

Rebecca struggled with the guilt that plagued her. Even deep in the abyss of her coma, she remembered how she had hurt Jayden, hurt Kara and Ken, and kept so much from her mother. She had partied and had spent so much time with Durk and she had forgotten and forsaken her friends. She began to think that even if they forgave her they could never trust her again and would always remember what she had done. They would know that she'd thrown everything that her mother had ever taught her right out the window. She was horribly embarrassed to admit her callousness and what she had done. The guilt she felt tired her and made her lose hope.

Chaldeth wanted Rebecca to feel guilty. If he could destroy her hope, she could die or she could be trapped forever in her abyss by the subconscious mind that sought to protect her from further trauma. Chaldeth knew the power of guilt and he laughed. He also knew that guilt was the folly of so many humans. It was their own self importance, their own inability to admit that they could be found lacking; it was their own exaggerated ego which demanded no one ever view them as less than perfect. These produced the kind of guilt that Chaldeth had caused to plague Rebecca's mind. Feeling guilty over a sin was a good thing if it drove these silly humans to ask for forgiveness and to try not to fall into the same trap again, but to moan and groan and feel embarrassed was pride. Plain unadulterated pride! And God hated pride, yet these wimps rolled in their pride, hid their embarrassing moments out of pride, hid their mistakes and wallowed in the false guilt that told them that failure of any kind must remain a secret. Their pride caused their guilt and then, if Chaldeth was really lucky, their inability to seek forgiveness and seek to overcome their faults would keep them bogged down by that guilt.

But to Chaldeth's horror, when Rebecca would feel remorse, she would ask God to help her. She would struggle to stay awake and to try her best to open her eyes and speak to her family. She wanted to apologize to them. But as she came close to surfacing, Chaldeth caused her thoughts of the past to rear its ugly head, and with them came the fear. The fear of rejection, the fear of not being forgiven, the fear of admitting her mistakes became too great for her to bear, and she would slip back into the abyss to try again another time.

But Elizabeth had seen the tears slide from the corners of Rebecca's eyes and roll toward her ear from the gravity caused by lying down. She'd wiped them away and began to talk to Rebecca. She suddenly understood that Rebecca was unhappy and that she had to take that unhappiness away for Rebecca to come back to them.

Elizabeth suddenly felt the need to remind Rebecca about something they'd once discussed. She felt that God was inspiring her to speak to Rebecca about why they had to struggle. She remembered an e-mail she received that addressed the reasons why people had to experience difficulty and how those difficulties could result in an awareness of the wonder of God's love for His children. Elizabeth began to recite the points made in the e-mail after first telling Rebecca that she should remember and think about what she was about to hear.

"Rebecca, you must come back to us. You can do it if you remember that God loves you and we love you and will do so for all eternity. Do you remember when we spoke about how God teaches us . . . about why we must go through difficulties and make mistakes? He said that if we never felt pain, we would not know that He is our healer. He also said that if we never had to pray, we would not know that He is our deliverer. He said that if we never felt sadness, we would never learn that He is our comforter. Please Rebecca, remember that God works miracles through what we go through and that He can even use us to help others by what we have experienced."

Elizabeth began to brush Rebecca's hair as she continued to speak. "Rebecca, God wants you to know that if we never had a trial to go through, we could never call ourselves overcomers. If we were never in trouble, how would we know that God always comes to our rescue? If we never suffered, how could we possibly comprehend what Christ suffered on the cross? And if we were never broken, how can we watch God make us whole again?"

Rebecca heard her mother's gentle words and marveled at them, and she began to believe that perhaps she could be forgiven after all, could resume her life once again. Perhaps she could even help others because of what she'd learned from her experiences. She recited to herself another sentence she remembered from that e-mail, "If your life was perfect, what would you need Me for?" and she was comforted. She could feel her shoulders relax and her jaws unclench and through those changes realized how tense she had been. Elizabeth detected a change in

Rebecca's breathing and sensed that she'd heard and that she'd been comforted by Elizabeth's words.

Elizabeth was grateful for God's inspiration. She too needed to hear those words for they also strengthened her. She was grateful for all the love and hard work that Mary and Kevin and their friends were providing to help these children and to rid the campus of its scourge. She was aware that Jim was working with Durk, and she struggled with her feelings of anger toward Durk for what had happened to Rebecca. She hoped that Jim was not making a mistake to help him and that Durk really did want to change his ways. But as Elizabeth spoke those words to Rebecca, she also knew that God might be working on Durk's heart too.

Jim had been successful, with the help of President Legna, in getting Durk's bail posted and was anxious to see Durk and tell him the good news.

When Jim walked into the cell, Durk had already been told to get ready to leave, and he was ecstatic. He thanked Jim for his help and excitedly told him what he'd been reading from the Bible that Jim had left with him. Jim had also given him a pocket concordance. Jim was delighted when he heard Durk's enthusiastic words.

"Jim, Jim. You know what? Listen to this . . . just listen.

"In Matthew 10:9-14, I found that Christ told His apostles that they need not worry about money or clothing, lodging or food. 'Provide neither gold, nor silver, nor brass in your purses, Nor script for your journey . . . ' Maybe that also applies to me?

"And in Deuteronomy 30:19, God says, 'I call heaven and earth to record this day against you, that I have set before you life and death, blessing and cursing; therefore choose life, that both thou and thy seed may live.' And now I have chosen God, so that's good, right?

"And . . . and in Luke 24:45 I read, 'Then opened he their understanding, that they might understand the scriptures.' So God is helping me understand, right, because I understand all this, right?"

Jim laughed, so pleased by Durk's enthusiasm and his obvious joy, and most of all, for the hope and determination he detected in Durk's voice. "Absolutely, Durk, you sure are being task oriented and helped with your study. Keep up the good work! Jim saw all the post-it notes that Durk had placed in the Bible so he could find the passages he wanted to recite to Jim and he was so pleased and sent a quick 'Thank you" to God.

"And I also got a warning about staying away from, you know, Nagorra and all that stuff. I mean, it said in Judges 2:3, 'They shall be as thorns in your side . . . their gods will snare you.'

"Well, that's true, Durk, but it's also a warning that Satan will come again and you have to be ready for him. You have to hold fast during an attack and not give in. See, being stubborn and determined can be a good thing, right?"

"Yeah, yeah. That's true. Boy, I sure wanna do this. I wanna get all that old stuff out of my life, and maybe I can be okay and maybe even obtain the kind of blessings and the future that you have."

They prayed before leaving the jail and thanked God for what he had done for them. Jim prayed that Durk's efforts would be rewarded and that he would find what he was looking for. And with that Durk and Jim walked out of the cell into the light. Jim smiled at Durk when Durk quoted, "Out of the darkness and into the light!"

A few days after Jim and Wade had visited with him, President Legna learned about the plans that the drug enforcement agency had put into place. He did not tell Wade and Jim because he did not want them to have false hopes. He also did not want to jeopardize the operation by saying too much and had decided to keep it secret until they'd obtained the information they required. For a long while, President Legna had been concerned about rumors that hinted at a lack of integrity on the part of some of his professors. But he could never obtain enough information to act on these rumors. He was a religious man, conservative in his views and lifestyle. He was someone who loved his country and loved the Constitution that the founding fathers wrote to ensure that everyone would have equal opportunity and government would work by the people and for the people. He longed to provide not only a safe campus for his students but an excellent education as well. To him this meant providing instructors who were role models and whose honor and integrity were of great importance to them. He wanted his professors to teach their students how to think and why it was important to listen to both sides of a debate and and learn the facts before committing to a point of view. He wanted to see courage rewarded because this is what made men stand up and be counted, fight for freedom, honor, integrity, and faith. He wanted professors who would not allow harm to come to the fresh-faced doctors, lawyers, businessmen, politicians, and parents of tomorrow who were temporarily under their care.

The information that Wade and Jim had brought him had given him hope that perhaps he could achieve his goals after all. He'd shared these thoughts with them and with his friend from the drug enforcement agency, and each of them had vowed to see this to the end and rid the campus of what had slowly been destroying it. They had all prayed and asked God to help them, and for the first time in a long time, all was well in his heart. Now, perhaps today or tomorrow, Dean Peerca would be arrested and would probably give evidence when he learned that he and his activities had finally been compromised.

God had heard the prayers of all these good people. He knew that most of the officers in the local police department were honorable, that only two were complicit with the drug sales on campus. Most of the officers took pride in their integrity and in upholding the law. Of those, one had suggested that a man be put into the cell next to Professor T. Nagorra in case he said something that would help them in their investigation. Therefore they heard the entire exchange between Dean Peerca, who they previously had not known was involved, and Nagorra, and now had their words on tape. The detectives decided to sit on this new information for a while so they could tap the dean's phone line and put a tail on him. They wanted the big guy, the supplier, badly.

When the detectives on the local police force learned that the drug enforcement agency would be taking over the case, they gave them the information that they had obtained. Unaware that his phone lines were tapped, Dean Peerca placed a call to the kingpin, and through that phone call the number was traced and his location pinpointed. The words that were spoken were caught on tape. Two days before Christmas, Dean Peerca was arrested at his home. It had been a difficult decision for President Legna not to tell Jim what was about to happen, but now the outcome would make up for holding back that information for a few days. The president had wanted to be sure that the evidence against the dean and his cronies would be so solid that they'd never see the light of day.

They'd taped Dean Peerca's telephone conversation with the kingpin. During that conversation, Dean Peerca had described the part Nagorra had played in Rebecca's injury, how he'd framed Jayden, how his drugs had been confiscated, and he had asked the kingpin to see that Nagorra "disappeared" as soon as he left the jail. This was to help their case immensely and put Dean Peerca in jail for most of his life. When the dean finished his description of events, the Kingpin said, "Shut up, you idiot. Never tell me that crap over the phone. Meet me at the usual place tomorrow at 7:00 p.m. and bring me the information about when Nagorra will get out. We'll talk about how we get rid of him tomorrow." Dean Peerca met him, the undercover agents who'd followed the dean, then followed the kingpin, and with a warrant to search his house, confiscated an incredible amount of illegal drugs and other contraband and arrested him. They moved that same evening to arrest Dean Peerca.

When his friend at the drug enforcement agency phoned him to tell them that the deed had been done and both had been arrested, President Legna sighed with relief and phoned Wade. When he told Wade that Jayden was completely exonerated, and that both the dean and the ring leader had been arrested, Wade was delighted and could not stop the happy tears that rolled down his face. Wade phoned Ruth right away. And Jayden's mom suggested a conference call to Jayden so they could tell him the good news together. Afterward, Wade phoned Jim, and soon the entire family knew that God had answered their prayers not only for Jayden but for the entire college campus as well.

Dean Peerca, once he understood that his conversations had been taped, had given his statement to the police and had agreed to testify. He had also named the two police officers who they had been bribing and providing with drugs. When Professor T. Nagorra and Professor Emils were told that both Dean Peerca and the kingpin had been arrested and had talked, they each sang like a bird. Jayden was exonerated from all the charges against him.

Jim spoke with Durk's lawyer and with President Legna, and together they convinced the judge that Durk should be given a second chance and asked that his record be purged after a hundred hours of community service and six months of drug-free testing.

With Peerca, Emils, Nagorra, and the kingpin and many of their pals locked up and the key thrown away, President Legna phoned Wade again to thank him for their help and to tell him that, because of their courage and what they had done, the campus now had the chance to become all that he'd hoped. Then President Legna phoned Professor Doog and Professor Sendnik and asked them to come to his office. When they arrived, he walked from behind his desk and greeted them warmly. He could barely suppress his excitement as he led them to their chairs, and the professors looked at one another in bewilderment. They discussed the usual things—the weather, the upcoming holidays, their families—but then President Legna asked them if they had a wish list for the university which they would like to see fulfilled, and if so, what would it be? The professors hesitated a moment, then plunged in with complete honesty.

Professor Doog began, "I'd initiate a class . . . a mandatory class . . . that taught the students about bias and how important it was for them to look at both sides of every question. I'd tell them that the act of questioning, not the answers, was the most informative process and to be bold in their questioning. I'd warn them about spin, about the danger of empty rhetoric, and about the need to carefully vet any and all candidates who seek to represent them in any way . . . and fight for term limits, allow no career politicians or lobbyists. I'd teach them about the importance of the liberties that our Constitution affords them. I'd tell them about honor, integrity, about becoming a better person. I'd try to plant the fires of patriotism in them so that they would be armed to the teeth to go out into a world that will not teach these things, and in fact may try to destroy those great qualities."

President Legna was surprised by the enthusiasm and ready words the professor spoke and was delighted by them. He beamed and said, "Good, Professor Doog, good . . . very, very good . . . and said with such passion! Wonderful . . . great ideas. Okay now, let's do it."

Then Professor Sendnik spoke up. "I agree with Professor Doog completely. Someone has to teach our young people honesty and honestly. It used to be their parents who taught these principles, but nowadays many parents have taken these qualities for granted because they were raised with these values. In today's world, parents are bogged down by the need for both parents to work, or perhaps by a one-parent household, or by financial pressures, by a lack of time and energy, and cannot or do not instill these values in their children. I think that our learning institutions should pick up this gauntlet and run with it because it is so very important.

"I'd also like to see some kind of a system in place that would make the students proud of this campus. So proud, in fact, that they felt the importance of stepping up themselves to quench those things that could tear the university down. I'm not saying that we should install a tattletale system but rather the desire—and they might gain this after taking the class that Professor Doog just mentioned—to fight for the dignity and honor and reputation of what an institution of higher learning *should* be all about. When they understand their duty to this, they will apply it to other areas of life and be willing to fight for these values in other areas as well. Our country has been dying because of our own complacency in teaching and extolling these values!"

"Another group of excellent ideas. Wonderful! Terrific. Thank you. Anything else?"

"Well," Professor Doog added, "it sure would be great if we could instill the goals just mentioned by Professor Sendnik into every one of our professors and, in fact, the entire staff on this campus. Maybe we should take our own advice and vet more carefully, eh? And there should be some way to get around the tenure process where professors often think they can get away with bad behavior. Maybe set some standards for them and enforce them. Maybe a system of merit. We'd sure have a force for good then!"

"I am amazed. I hadn't even thought of many of the goals you have just mentioned, and I've wanted to change this campus for years now. Thank you so much. You both have a good head on your shoulders and a great eye . . . and heart . . . for what is good. Tenure was implemented to assure professors their freedom of speech and not have them forced to teach only the ideology of the school's board of directors or its administrator, but you are right, tenure has gone too far and allowed teachers to force their own ideology on students. I like the idea of adding some provisions to the process of tenure and perhaps benchmarks that demonstrate that those provisions are being met. Would both of you be willing to help me get your ideas in place?"

"Absolutely!"

"Yes!"

"Well then, Dean Doog—nice ring to that—you are hereby invested with the authority to do so. You will head up your school of education, and both of you will administer a new branch of education that we will call . . . uhhh . . . how about 'American Ethics' or 'Ethics for Patriots' or 'Behaviors and Ethics'?"

"Dean? Dean? You mean . . . you mean . . . I'm to be . . . promoted?"

"Yes, that's exactly what I mean. But there will be a price to pay," he said laughing. "You'll have to sit on my advisory committee too. So since you will be awfully busy, I will appoint someone to help you, perhaps in the capacity of an assistant dean. We will have to vet very carefully because we have a new agenda that demands a certain dedication to the goals we have set forth. Do you know of any such person? Congratulations, Dean Doog!"

And before Dean Doog could answer the question put to him, President Legna turned to Professor Sendnik and said, "As for you, young lady, your title is now assistant dean to Dean Doog. You too will sit on my advisory committee, and you will hire an assistant—approved by Dean Doog of course—who will be named your director and help you put our goals into place! Congratulations, Assistant Dean Sendnik. Any questions?"

The three new friends beamed at one another and their hearts soared by what they each envisioned for the university and for the students that would come forth from what they were about to institute.

When the two new deans left President Legna's office, they were so thrilled that they held arms and skipped in glee from the door of the building to their vehicle, laughing like teenagers. They were also thrilled to think that now their wonderful university would become an asset to every student who walked its corridors and that now they could send students into this world filled with honesty and integrity who understood what this country stands for, what the Constitution protects and what patriotism means, and how these represent God's earthly gifts.

The family was thrilled to learn of the promotions of their two favorite professors and sent them their heartfelt congratulations. Wade invited the new Dean Doog and Assistant Dean Sendnik and President Legna to join them at Rebecca's bedside anytime they might be free over the days celebrating Christmas Eve, Christmas Day, and Christmas evening. He also invited them to join them for Christmas dinner and told them to bring whomever they wanted along with them.

When Wade phoned each of them, he described the incredible decorations that the family had placed around the hospital room for Rebecca. To his delight, each agreed to come and to be there for dinner. Dean Doog usually traveled to his children's homes during the summer, and they visited him for Thanksgiving and Easter so he was free for Christmas. Dean Sendnik was single and had no family, so she was delighted by the invitation. President Legna said that he and his wife would have a house full of children and grandchildren, but since they would be there for a week, he and his wife could certainly take a few hours to visit with Rebecca and her family. "After all," he said, "you are responsible for the incredible turnaround on campus, and I am thrilled and privileged to know each one of you!"

Wade reiterated that they should bring any family or friends they'd like to bring. "We have a large circle of family and friends, so please bring your entire family. Our kids will be there, so your kids are welcome too!" Wade told Jim to be sure to invite Durk.

Durk couldn't believe the good news that he would have the opportunity to have his record purged. It gave him another chance to make good. Jim had obtained a student loan and a part-time job for him that would carry him through his next two and one half years in college. Durk easily acknowledged that he'd been given an incredible gift and told Jim that he promised God and would now promise Jim that he would not break the trust they had extended to him.

Durk picked up the Bible Jim had given him. It was filled with little scraps of paper and post-it notes marking various passages that Durk wanted to revisit. Jim could hardly recognize it. He told Jim that, as he'd been studying the Bible, he'd been astounded at the complexity of it, but as he read and as Jim began to provide in-depth explanations and instruction, he was further astounded, conversely, by the simplicity of it. "Jim, in essence, it tells of the plan that God placed into the physics of the world. And through His Son's sacrifice, and because of His perfect love, all mankind—and that includes me—have been given the opportunity through this plan to become a child of God and partake of an incredible future with God."

Jim could hardly keep himself from grinning as he witnessed Durk's enthusiasm and listened to his breathless description of the new discoveries he'd made. Jim's heart swelled in thankfulness as Durk spoke. "Jim, Jim, listen to this. In Micah 4:2, God actually tells me, 'Come, and let us go up to the mountains of the Lord . . . he will teach us of his ways, and we will walk in his paths.' And he even explains in Romans 11:25, 'For I would not brethren, that ye should be ignorant of this mystery . . . '"

"It is wonderful, Durk, isn't it? It's so simple and so incredibly *loving* how God tells us and teaches us everything."

"Yeah, yeah, He does! And he even warns us about stuff! In Revelation 3:15, 16, I read, 'I know thy works, that thou art neither cold nor hot. I would thou wert cold or hot. So then, because thou art lukewarm, and neither cold nor hot, I will spue thee out of my mouth.'"

"There are a lot of warnings throughout scripture, Durk. They're needed because we get lazy, we get complacent, and we are subject to the 'blinding' that Satan brings to us. God doesn't want us to fail and will support us in every way so we can make it to the goal of our faith, the First Resurrection."

"I read about that too . . . in Isaiah 30:19, it says, 'He will be very gracious unto thee at the voice of thy cry; when he shall hear it he will answer hence.' And in Isaiah

39:26 it even tells me something that I actually experienced myself. Listen! 'The Lord . . . healeth the stroke of their wound.'"

"You know, Durk, it's time for you to come to the hospital to see Rebecca and let her know what wonderful things God has done for you. She will be so happy for you, and so will Jayden and Kara and Ken."

"I guess I have to face them sometime. I hope they will forgive me. I hate to face them, but I know that I will have to at some point. This will be tough."

"You will be amazed at how easy it will be. Remember, they are children of God, and they know about the power of Satan and the minions who follow him, so they will be a lot more understanding than you think. They will look only for the sincerity of your new commitment."

And so Durk made his first trip to the hospital, with Jim at his side, to face his fears. He was more afraid than he'd thought he'd be; his heart pounded, his hands began to sweat, and his mouth went dry, but he knew that this was something he had to do. Despite his fears, he managed to greet everyone warmly and was pleasantly surprised by how cordial they were. He went to Rebecca's bed and took her hand telling her that he was sorry for his part in what happened to her. Then something inside him made him realize, as he gazed at Rebecca, that he'd been drawn to her because he'd seen the good in her. He understood that he hadn't really wanted Rebecca the way he'd thought he did; he wanted what she was, what she had inside her heart. And he suddenly realized that God had arranged their meeting.

When he moved away from Rebecca's bedside, Jayden offered Durk a seat next to him. Because Jim had told them about Durk's tremendous effort to learn about God and to change the direction of his life, Jayden had decided to put the past behind them and extend his friendship to Durk. Again Durk felt a wave of tears threatening to overflow his eyes and embarrass him. It came out of the thankfulness he felt that Jayden could do what Durk didn't think he could have done in Jayden's circumstances. *These are truly God's children,* Durk thought, recalling yet another verse he'd read that fit this circumstance perfectly. He remembered reading Jeremiah 33:3, "Call unto me, and I will answer thee, and shew thee great and mighty things . . ." and this helped not only to allay his fears but also to believe that what he was aspiring to do would be successful.

Rebecca had heard much of what was said. She was floating in a room that seemed to be enveloped in a swirling gray mist. On one wall was a huge window through which bright sunshine made a concerted effort to break through the gray mist. She had floated to this position many times, but then the light would begin to fade and she'd fall again and drift back down away from the light and into the sleep that held her prisoner and wouldn't allow her to move or speak. But when she did glimpse the light through her gray mist, she'd listen to the conversations around her and she'd struggle to respond. It grieved her to see how worried they were, all these people who still seemed to love her. But no matter how hard she tried, she couldn't break out of her prison.

She knew that Elizabeth was always at her side and that Mary too was there more often than not. She wanted to let them know that she was okay, but somehow the mist kept them separated and kept her from speaking to them. She was aware of Elizabeth telling her that she had to experience many things in life . . . good and bad . . . so God could teach her. She also remembered Mary sitting by her side, stroking her hair and telling her softly how much they all loved her and reminding her of the miracle God had brought Mary by solving a problem that she never thought could be solved. Mary had said, "When I had to give you away, Rebecca, I thought I'd never see you again, and it broke my heart. But now I can understand that if I'd never had such a difficult problem, how could God have shown me that He could solve all problems?"

It seemed to Rebecca that she was recalling more of their conversations than before and that she floated up from the abyss and into the mist a little more frequently. Anticipating this slight emancipation, she strained to listen and to tell them that she was okay. Sometimes she heard her sweet gentle mother crying, and it broke her heart. She knew that her mother was remembering when her husband died and was worried that Rebecca would leave her too. Mary cried as well, and when she did she kept telling Rebecca that she had to come back to them. Rebecca was always aware of their constancy and their ministrations. She was glad someone else was always there when Elizabeth or Mary was there so they would have someone to look after them. Sometimes she tried to look for Teddie, but she was unable to turn her head.

Rebecca loved Mary. She was, after all, her birth mother. But Elizabeth had raised her, and she had felt an allegiance to her that had caused her to pull away from Mary. But now, seeing Mary support Elizabeth in this, care for her, never try to take her place, stay at Rebecca's side yet not usurp Elizabeth's position, and so tenderly speak to her, Rebecca came to appreciate Mary. She also began to understand that it was through Mary that she and Elizabeth had gained such a wonderful extended family, and through that, Rebecca had gained such a special friend in Jayden.

There were the others, too, who seemed to come and go and express such heartfelt love and concern. She wondered if where she lay was close to home. She knew that Jayden was by her side too. His voice soothed her, and she wished she could touch him, let him know that she appreciated what he did for her. She'd begin to sink back into her sleep whenever she thought of how she must have hurt him, how she'd distanced herself from him. She wondered how she could ever have done such a thing after all he'd been to her. She'd heard him say, "Rebecca, remember that if we never had to go through fire, we would never become purified." And his words had been important to her.

Over time she learned that remorse or sorrow seemed to drive her back into the chains that bound her and held her, refusing to allow her to surface and to listen to what was said. She also realized that though now she could see the room and the people, her eyes were not open. She began to understand this when Kara pleaded with her to open her eyes. As she tried to determine how she could see them yet not have her eyes open, she realized that she was looking through just a sliver of space and seeing through her thick black eyelashes. She exerted every ounce of her strength to force her eyes open, but she could not. It was then that she used her energy to absorb what was said. She'd noticed that every time someone prayed, when they finished, God would help her climb a little bit closer to the surface. She began to wonder if some evil force had bound her; maybe she needed to pray that she would be freed.

As Rebecca moved closer to awakening, Chaldeth became more irritable. "They will *not* beat me, they will *not*!" he roared. "I will not *let* them!" And he called in every ugly spirit that he could to help him. He realized that he could no longer make his plan work by himself. He remembered the words in the Bible that told of Christ teaching his disciples about the power to cast Chaldeth and his cohorts aside. He'd read in Matthew 10:1, "And when he had called unto him his twelve disciples, he gave them power against unclean spirits, to cast them out, and to heal all manner of sickness and all manner of disease."

Chaldeth was suddenly afraid. He also remembered the story of Job. One of Chaldeth's friends had worked diligently to harm Job and to cause him to lose everything. But then, as Job 42:10 related, it all changed, and his friend lost his power over Job. "And the Lord turned the captivity of Job . . ."

"That cannot happen to me! It cannot!" Chaldeth screamed. His friends gathered around him, willing to help, waiting for instructions. But they all knew that Isaiah 14:25 said of them and their boss, "I will . . . tread him underfoot, then shall his yoke depart from off them, and his burden depart from their shoulders."

The entire family had squeezed into Rebecca's room for Christmas and didn't mind the tight quarters at all. Ken and Kara phoned their parents and explained Rebecca's condition to them and told them that Rebecca's family would be spending Christmas at the hospital with Rebecca. They asked if they could come home on Christmas evening and spend the remainder of their break with them, but for Christmas Day they wanted to support their friend. Their parents graciously acquiesced and sent their best wishes to Rebecca and her family.

Thus, Jayden, Kara, and Ken spent Christmas together and delighted in all the children. Whenever the children would get restless, they would take them for a walk or take them across the hall to the tiny waiting room and play board games with them, read to them, or help them color. The children seemed to understand the family's desire to support Rebecca and willingly prayed along with the family; and when a prayer was finished, all of them, even the youngest, added their loud and clear "Amen."

The room looked absolutely exquisite and made everyone think of Grandma. They remembered how she loved her clocks and their different kinds of ticking sounds and their wonderful chimes. They exclaimed over Sarah's idea to bring one of the chiming clocks to the hospital room so Rebecca could hear it. They admired once again the lovely Nativity set, each figure almost two feet tall with exquisite robes in green and burgundy, gold and blue. They, like the angels, had deep sleeves and full skirts. The three wise men wore shapely crown hats with gold trim and carried shining gifts—one a chest filled with precious pearls and gold chains which spilled over its edges and cascaded to the feet of the Christ child. A manger held the Christ child as he lay in a bed of greens ringed with pinecones that were intertwined with delicate gold ribbons and tiny silk rosebuds. His arms were lifted toward His mother, His beautiful crocheted wide-sleeved gown slipping down one of His outstretched arms. Matt lit the scene with a small spotlight which made the Nativity the focal point in the room.

They talked about Grandma, about Christmas, about family matters, and then they began to talk about how God had formed and blessed this country. Matt said, "The words 'The Year of Our Lord' was actually written in our Constitution, and Sundays were acknowledged as a day that precluded government activity. The Declaration of Independence contains the words 'endowed by their Creator' and 'a firm reliance on the protection of divine Providence.'"

Caleb added, "John Adams said that our Constitution was made only for a moral and religious people. Daniel Webster acknowledged the Constitution as 'Divine interposition in our behalf.'"

Sarah reminded them, "Even on our currency, and carved into stone on our memorials and state buildings, was mention of God. We had prayer in our schools. We sent food and water, medicines and doctors, teachers and ministers to other countries, and we have been blessed as a country for doing so. We have been further blessed because our forebears had such a strong faith that they placed God into everything they planned for this country."

"You're right, Sarah," John agreed. "That blessing has continued from one generation to the next. I hope that we can be a generation that reinstates those values, or we may lose our country as we have known it, and lose God's blessing too."

"I'll second that," said President Legna as he walked through the door. They all laughed and jumped up to greet him and to introduce themselves to his wife and his granddaughter, and he boomed, "If any of you want a job devising how we can put those values back into our country, our government, our politicians, our schools, and our children, I have that job for you! And you young whippersnappers—Jayden, Ken, Durk,

Kara, and Rebecca—I want you to man my student advisory board for the university's mandatory *Everyday American Ethics* program. How do you like them apples?"

As Mrs. Legna looked around the room, she said, "I am so taken by the beauty of this room. I would never know it was a hospital room because of the lighting you've added and the incredible, exquisite Christmas items you've decorated it with. It is absolutely beautiful. It takes my breath away!"

The women gathered on one side of the room to talk about Christmas, and the men gathered on the other side to discuss the goals that President Legna had mentioned. Soon thereafter, Dean Doog and Assistant Dean Sendnik arrived and joined the conversations. As chairs were rounded up and moved into position, all the adults were handed a clear glass mug filled with the wonderfully warm aromatic glogg that made their Christmas so festive. Jayden, Kara, Ken, and Durk received permission to join them in the glogg after Sarah added more orange juice to their mixture. They stood around Rebecca's bed and toasted her while pretending to order her to get up and have some glogg with them. Rebecca heard them, and though she could not speak, she felt as if she had smiled.

Rebecca heard Sarah talking about her grandmother. "Grandma always wanted to create lasting memories for us, memories that were so family-oriented and loving that they could carry us through the hard times. Sometimes those memories came from her talent for decorating. The ticking of her clocks and the sweet sounds of their chimes were soothing to her, and she wanted us to appreciate the serenity it provided, so we all learned to listen for the tick-tocking and the chimes when we entered her house. She said that it would teach us to listen for the silence so we could hear God speak. Now we all do that in our own homes."

Sarah continued saying, "Grandma's house always looked beautiful. Sometimes she'd make exquisite centerpieces for the dinner table that took your breath away, or fashion napkin rings from something that suggested the theme of her gathering. She knew what everyone's favorite dish was and would draw everyone into the kitchen delegating little jobs that brought us together so we would all share the experience. Through these activities she created a day where we would, as she liked to say, make family memories. She would always make this glogg, and the aroma would waft through the house as it warmed on her stove . . . and we associated the smells of Christmas with the spices in her glogg. Unfortunately, today we could only fill thermoses with the glogg because, here in the hospital, we are unable to have it in a big pot heating on a stove to have it send its magic aroma into the room."

It's amazing," Mrs. Legna said. "It tastes wonderful, but it's the aroma that really grabs you. Can we have the recipe, or is it a family secret?"

"Of course," Sarah replied. "It's probably on one of our computers, so we can get it to you before you go home and you can use it for New Year's if you want."

"That would be wonderful. Thanks!"

Rebecca was fully aware of what was going on in the room, and she wanted to be a part of the festivities. She was looking at Jayden and felt as if she was seeing a part of him that she'd never seen before. His jaw seemed stronger, firmer, his body tall and lithe, and she saw a kind of strength and kindness emanate from him as she watched him talk to Durk. *Durk,* she thought. And for the first time, she compared them, and she suddenly realized that it wasn't Durk who she was in love with—it was Jayden. Jayden had been her friend, her confidant, her protector all those years. He'd brought her to a greater understanding of God and he'd . . . he'd . . . why he'd . . . loved her too!

She was horrified by the thought that perhaps he no longer loved her. She had to find out if he could love her after all that had happened! She prayed that he did. And then she asked God. She promised God that things would be so much different, so much better, if she could have this second chance to make things right with Jayden.

Suddenly Kara let out a yelp. "Everyone, come quick. I think that Rebecca just moved!" But as they watched Rebecca, and as Mary and Elizabeth each held one of her hands, there was no movement, and soon they drifted back into their conversations. But Jayden had also asked God for help and when he did he felt as if Rebecca wanted to tell him something. Then he thought about all the things he'd never told Rebecca and should have.

Jayden walked over to Rebecca's side and pulled a chair close to her bed and took her hand. As he looked around the room, he saw that everyone was involved with other conversations and so he leaned down close to Rebecca's face and whispered, "Rebecca, I should have said something a long time ago about how I feel about you. I should have told you that I love you. I should have told you that I want to get an education, become a physician, and settle down someday with you. I want us to have kids, to buy a house, and to be a family just like our family. I want us to go to church together and pray together and teach our children about God together. Please come back to us, Rebecca . . . please come back to me."

Rebecca heard Jayden's words and wanted, more than she had ever wanted anything before in her life, to surface from her captivity and tell Jayden that she loved him too. She strained to surface, to move, but felt as if she was pushing against a stone wall . . . yet she was sure it would eventually move if she did not give up. Suddenly there was no mist, and she knew that all she had to do was open her eyes, but again it was as if something held her eyes closed. She strained even harder and felt as if she could do no more when, finally, just as Jayden was about to turn away, she opened her eyes and smiled at him.

Jayden smiled back at Rebecca and mouthed the words 'thank you'. He savored those few seconds alone with Rebecca and told her once again that he loved her and she whispered as she looked into his eyes that she loved him too. Then he called Elizabeth and Mary to Rebecca's side. The whole family positioned themselves around her bed. Elizabeth took Rebecca's hand and said, "Rebecca, Rebecca, can you hear me? Can you squeeze my hand?" Rebecca squeezed her hand, and Elizabeth, with tears running down her face, exclaimed, "She did it, she did it! Oh, Rebecca, you have just given us the perfect Christmas present!"

To everyone's surprise, Rebecca rasped with great humor, "Where's *my* glogg?"

Everyone had tears in their eyes; everyone sent thanks to their Heavenly Father for her recovery. Only Wade had the presence of mind to run down the hall and ask the nurse to have the doctor come immediately. He did not know whether or not Rebecca needed some special attention as she awakened.

The doctor came running and saw that Rebecca's strength seemed to return. She'd come alive again. He told them that she should remain in bed now, but tomorrow she would be allowed, with help, to try to walk. He said that she needed to gain back the strength that may be somewhat diminished despite the physical therapy they had provided every day. "If she takes it slow, she'll be home in a week!"

They all rejoiced, and Kevin asked if he could pray aloud to thank God for what He'd done for them. After the prayer, which truly touched everyone's heart—especially Rebecca's—she teased them by telling them that she'd heard every word they said while they stood vigil and they would have to pay the price for what they'd said! She'd been shocked to learn that three weeks had elapsed since she'd last been awake. She'd had no concept of time. "I am going to call each of you on all the things you said about me," she quipped. And then she said, "Durk, I am going to rename you Jonah. Can you guess why? Jonah means *ran from God.*" Durk beamed, knowing that in those few words Rebecca too had forgiven him, and he replied. "Yeah, but eventually Jonah, like me, did do what God asked him to do." And they all laughed, so pleased that Durk had known that fact and pleased that Rebecca had obviously forgiven Durk and was so alert.

A little bit later, propped up by extra pillows, Rebecca signaled Jayden to come to her and took his hand. She said, "Jayden, I want you to know that I love you, that you are the most wonderful gift that God has given me, and that I am so sorry for all the mistakes I made. If I could have a wish just for us, it would be that when we finish school, you let me drag you down the aisle and force you to marry me and we would be just like our own wonderful families."

Jayden smiled and said, "Force me? Never! I love you too, Rebecca, I think I've loved you from the first day we met when we were only fourteen years old and I rode my bike to your house almost every day. God has been so good to us, and if I could have a wish about us, it would be the same one that you have!"

Chaldeth's power had been severely impaired by the prayers and faith, the love and forgiving hearts of these stubborn soldiers of God. He'd been doing so well with his plan until they asked God for help. But Chaldeth was never going to give up. He may have lost this battle, but he'd be back to fight another day. Their power had come from God and from their knowledge of His word. They had known from John 16:33, "These things I have spoken unto you, that in me ye might have peace. In the world ye shall have tribulation: but be of good cheer; I have overcome the world." And from 2 Peter 3:9 where Peter reminded the congregations, "The Lord is not slack concerning his promise, as some men count slackness; but is longsuffering to us-ward, not willing that any should perish, but that all should come into repentance."

But Chaldeth still had time before his end would come, and he was determined to wreak as much havoc as possible on every soul God loved. Chaldeth would be back!

Excerpt from

What Every Christian Needs to Know: Addressing 50 Tough and Timely Issues

By Helen Gumienny Glowacki

Confusion reigns in today's world not by chance but by design. We are led to believe that our confusion is the result of our busy and harried lives, but in reality it has been carefully planned and executed by the architect of Christian complacency. That architect is sly and subtle and knows that confusion leads to doubt, doubt leads to complacency, and complacency leads to inaction. His name is Satan and his goal is to confuse us and twist our natural desire to love and support others into conflict with God's admonition to teach right and wrong.

Sadly, many Christians have fallen into the clever trap of political correctness that has nudged us away from developing and supporting a strong conviction about important issues. Thus, we don't act upon the loss of Biblical prinicples or question that loss and we no longer know what we should do or what stance we should take when they are gone. Instead, we choose the easy route of leaving everything up to God and allowing, even supporting behaviors that the Bible tells us are wrong. We no longer explore the Bible and discuss what God tells us to do about our troubled times. It's time for us to do as Isaiah 1:18 tells us: "Come now, and let us reason together . . ."

Prior to writing this book, I wrote seven novels using the principles God provides for guiding us through our trials and tribulations. But I have written this non-fiction book in order to provide a concise and topic-specific guide to gaining immediate insight into what stance Christians must take in today's world to avoid the subtle trap that is destroying our moral fiber and our country. That stance may be unpopular, but is based upon what the Bible tells us we should do.

While an author writes to develop a reading experience that informs, comforts, or entertains, this book is directed toward informing quickly and concisely. It is designed to explain what Christians must consider as we face our many dilemmas and as we see our Christian way of life attacked and biblical principles eroded. If we don't respond to this loss with conviction and with a united stance, the moral fiber and Christian principles of our country could be badly damaged and lost to future generations. We no longer take the time to read the Bible and discuss how God's words apply to today's situations, nor do we seek to know how we should react to these situations. I attempt to address this problem by listing the verses that describe many of the issues we face in today's world and have added a scriptural index at the end of each discussion to assist the reader in further examination of the directives put forth on each topic.

This is a book of Christian principles directed toward many specific contemporary issues. It is different than my novels where I use characters plagued by heartbreaking circumstances to explain why God allows so much pain and confusion to exist. In this book, each chapter focuses on one timely issue and provides concise direction for how a Christian should address that issue. The advice is hard-hitting and to the point. Those familiar with scripture are aware that scripture can provide answers to any issue, but we all understand that today's world saps our strength, our energy, and our time, which can leave us bereft of the ability to seek these answers.

My challenge is to create a thorough but concise understanding of the complex contemporary issues Christians face and what God says about them. Exploring these concerns is a daunting challenge for the Christian who wears many hats and feels crushed by their weight. With no time and energy to pursue God's words, guilt, depression and lethargy add to the mix of confusion and anxiety that stalks us every day, and political correctness touting our need for tolerance leaves us wondering if we dare to disagree.

Thus, this book addresses the questions we face and researches scripture as a guide to the answer to those questions. Nevertheless, while adhering to the standards God has set for us, the Christian must also never judge, must teach by example, and must offer help when possible. While writing requires only a simple succession of words, to be effective those words must touch the mind with common sense and move the heart with the desire to act. Those words must also touch the soul with the importance of taking a stand and recognizing that we are engaged in a spiritual warfare so malevolent and desperate that we are in jeopardy of losing those things we have always cherished.

God wants to help us. He wants to bring us through our difficult situations. And He wants to bless us. But if we don't know what He tells us, we are lost. God's love is so great that He provides us with every possible tool. If we do not read scripture, He has given us ministers who do, books that provide this information, and role models who act as He directs, and He does all this to bring His word to us. But whether we listen or not, whether we accept His direction or not, is solely up to us. Sadly, if we do not, we will lose God's blessing and in time will lose the goodness upon which this country was built and our family values were established.

I hope that this book will help answer the questions stirred by our current world crisis and show us how to bring forth the courage we need to stand firm in our faith and be willing to fight for our principles. We cannot continue in our complacency and simply allow our Christian values and liberties to be attacked. We have to define what we believe; we must clearly understand what God says about our values, and find the courage to act on them. Courage comes from the conviction of our position.

We have a powerful enemy who fights God to prevent his own demise, and we are the targets of his effort. He uses us and encourages the complacency we have long been exhibiting to prevent God from completing His plan of salvation. He needs to destroy our faith, and by reducing our values and our freedoms, he can also steal our hope and increase our complacency. But we can thwart this enemy if we tap into the power of love, the power of prayer, and the power of the perfect plan God placed into the physics of our world to help us. To do this, we need to know what to believe and what to do to defend our beliefs.

I hope that through this book those who hunger for more information about what scripture tells us will understand that they are not alone, that others are also searching, and that there is a godly answer to the complex situations we face today. Our Heavenly Father knows that we can become exhausted from the constant battles we face. He knows that there seems no end to our job list and no time to study His word. He also knows that, as we learn and gain an understanding of what He wants us to do, we will gladly take up the banner and fight to protect what He has given us.

What I hope to impart . . . through this book, and through my novels . . . is an understanding about the enemy we have, why he does what he does, how we can thwart his efforts, and most of all, exactly how we are to do battle. When we understand the battle in which we are engaged, our fear is reduced and we can become a formidable Christian warrior. We will also fight wiser. But when we do not understand, when we wonder why our world has been reduced to what we are witnessing today, when we are not sure how to address the difficult questions, we are uneasy, we become complacent, and we lose our hope and our strength. When we learn of God, His enemy and of God's plan, we learn that He is always with us to uplift us, protect us, and provide us with the energy and determination we need to see this battle through to the end. But if we do not act, we can lose everything. It is important that when we do act, we act with compassion, understanding, and forgiveness while maintaining our stance about right and wrong.

Our struggles and our difficulties have increased as we move closer to the ultimate goal of our faith, the First Resurrection, because Satan works harder than ever. He knows that his end will come when the number God longs for is fulfilled, and therefore He works to prevent God from fulfilling that number. We need to do our part and stand up and be counted so those numbers can increase, not decrease. But to do this, we need to know what we stand for.

We can't effectively fight an enemy when we don't know our own position or the position God wants us to take. Sadly, few do know this, and if *we* do not understand, we cannot teach others. This is why I have written this book. God wants us to win this battle and will help us. It is through God's words that we learn how to fight, what to believe, and how to gain the courage to make a stand. It is through our united understanding of God's direction that we can become a formidable force against the loss of morality in our country.

God gifted us with a country built on Christian principles, and He has gifted us with the freedom to practice those principles. Let's develop a new appreciation of God's gifts and join the populous eager to learn and determined to protect these gifts. Let's demand more from our school systems, textbooks, politicians, and government. Let's fight for the honesty, integrity, morality, faith, and loyalty our faith teaches us.

Many stand back, afraid to become involved, afraid of the few who want to turn aside our biblical principles in the name of social justice. It is shocking to know that the few who want to take these principles from our schools, our government, our churches, our press, and want to indoctrinate our children to oppose and negate our faith are far outnumbered. But their power comes from Satan, and it goes forth easily only because we have been complacent.

We need to fight back. We can accomplish this noble goal if we know what God says, and why we must live our faith every day, not just on Sundays, and live our faith as Christ asked us to live it. But we also need the courage to *fight* for our faith and our values, and can only be effective when we think about what these values are and where we stand on them. Malachi 2:8 warns, "But ye are departed out of the way; ye have caused many to stumble at the law; ye have corrupted the covenant of Levi, saith the Lord of Hosts." If we don't protect our values, we will cause our children to stumble.

God not only shows us what dangers we should watch for, but He also shows us how to live together, how to set the right example, how to instruct our children, and clearly and unequivocally promises wonderful rewards for doing so. He promises us His protection. He gives the ultimate guarantees about our life and our home. This doesn't say we won't have problems, but it does say we will be brought through those problems, will be refined in the process, and that we need not fear the outcome when we fight for right. But the Bible also tells us what God hates, what is a sin, what is an abomination and what is causing mankind to succumb to these actions.

As biblical values are lost, so is mankind's ability to recognize the same lies offered today that Satan used to trap Eve. In today's world we are not only fighting for our morality, but also against political corruption and terrorists who plot the death of our faith, our way of life, and our country. If we are complacent in the face of the destruction of our individual right to pray, the destruction of unbiased education and a free and honest press, and of a corruption-free government, we give Satan a huge platform from which to work.

God's word is our most potent protection and the most potent protection our country can have against its current onslaught. Instituting God's words into our minds and hearts and thus our lives can help us immensely, not only because we now live in a world of uncertainty, but also because we long to attain the goal of our faith: an eternity with God. I hope that this book will show you what stance the Bible tells us to take as a Christian and inspire you to cherish our faith and our values, and cling to them even if they are lost to the world.

If you, the reader, will share what you know and what you learn about God's plan with others so they too can understand, you will touch the heart of God. May God bless you and keep you always, and may He grant you the wisdom to understand His ways, His words, and the future He so freely offers us all. And may He open your understanding to the wonder of His word and to His all-encompassing love for you.

Helen Gumienny Glowacki

Preach the word; be instant in season;
reprove, rebuke, exhort with all longsuffering and doctrine.
For the time will come when they will not endure sound doctrine;
but after their own lusts shall they heap to themselves teachers, having itching ears.
And they shall turn away their ears from the truth, and shall be turned unto fables.
But watch thou in all things, endure afflictions, do the work of an evangelist,
make full proof of thy ministry

2 Timothy 4:2-5

Bibliography

The Holy Bible, King James Version, published by The New Apostolic Church, Canada, Thomas Nelson, Inc., Camden, NJ, 1972

James Strong, LLD, STD, *Strong's Exhaustive Concordance of the Bible*, Abington, Nashville, thirty fourth printing 1996, copyright 1890

Henry H. Halley, *Halley's Bible Handbook*, Zondervan Publishing House, Grand Rapids, Michigan, 24th edition, Copyright 1965

Henry M. Morris, *Many Infallible Proofs*, Moody Press, Chicago, 3rd printing 1977

Henry M. Morris, *The Bible and Modern Science*, Moody Press, Chicago, 1951, 1968

Donald Grey Barnhouse, *The Invisible War*, Zondervan Publishing House, Grand Rapids, Michigan, 12th printing 1976 copyright 1965

Robert Boyd, *Boyd's Bible Handbook*, Eugene, Oregon: Harvest House, 1983, pgs 122-124

Helen Gumienny Glowacki, *Grandma's Little Book of Poetry:—The Story of God's Plan of Salvation*, 2009.

Helen Gumienny Glowacki, *The Granddaughter and the Monkey Swing*, 2009

Internet Sources:
http://en.wikipedia.org/wiki/Hex_sign

Scriptural Index

The following scriptural index is assembled in a slightly different manner than usually expected. This index places each scripture into a category with others that address a similar topic. This allows the reader to locate all verses applicable to a specific concern or a specific subject. The categories are listed alphabetically. Each scripture within a category is listed in the order it is found in the book. The scriptures are divided into ten categories:

The Commitment God Asks of Us

The Devil, Satan: His Power and Influence

The Forgiveness We Need to Obtain

The Generational Sin We Can Inherit

The Instruction God Gives to Help Us

The Power that Is God's Alone

The Mystery of God and the Bible

The Protection God Freely Offers

The Refining Process We Must Endure

The Warnings God Issues to Help Us

Scriptural Index

HELEN GUMIENNY GLOWACKI

The Refining Process We Must Endure

The Warnings God Issues to Help Us

About the Author

Helen Glowacki is an interior designer, writer, teacher, and motivational speaker. As the host, writer, and producer of the television series *The Contemporary Woman*, broadcast by UA Columbia Cablevision, Helen addressed interior design and the health, relationship, parenting, spiritual and life issues of interest to women. She co-hosted a number of twenty-four-hour telethons featuring celebrity guests to support various charities and has donated her books to *The Henwood Foundation* in Zambia, Africa which welcomes Christian books to use as teaching tools. She also donates her books to cancer centers, substance abuse centers and prisons. A graduate of William Paterson University, Helen received her Bachelor of Arts degree in Communications, magna cum laude. Additionally, she has earned an Associate of Science degree, with honors, and is a registered nurse. She has served on the boards of directors for two associations and was listed in "Who's Who of American Women" and "Who's Who of Women Executives". Helen is a popular speaker, at ease with an audience, and has received a number of community service awards. Her beautiful novels are touted as spiritually uplifting and biblically correct. Helen is married and has two children and four grandchildren.

For additional copies of this book or to view a description of each of the seventeen books Helen has thus far published, please visit her website at: www.HelenGlowacki.com. To become a distributor or to purchase for fund raisers please email the author through her website at helen@helenglowacki.com.